RUTHLESS BETRAYAL

SYDNEY LEE

"In the end, we will remember not the words of our enemies, but the silence of our friends."
    -Martin Luther King Jr.

AUTHOR NOTE

Thank you so much for picking up Ruthless Betrayal. Before you dive in, please be mindful of the triggers.

This book is intended for audiences that are 18+. It contains themes such as anxiety, drinking and driving, violence, gun violence, drug use, some bullying, and sexual content.

Happy reading, I hope you enjoy it as much as I do.

Chapter One

JOSIE

"Do you think he'll be there?" I hesitantly ask my best friend, trying to steady my nervous hand as I swoop the mascara wand over my lashes.

"Oh, he's definitely going to be there. He and Chance are inseparable. I swear, if I weren't dating Chance, Jake would swoop in and take him for himself." She pauses, and I can practically see her brain working as she pictures it. A devious smile curls her lips. "Actually, that would be kind of hot." She winks when I scoff at her sex crazed ideas that her mind always seems to conjure up. "Besides, when has he ever missed a party?" She asks rhetorically from my side, putting the finishing touches on her lip gloss.

I'm so nervous, I have to force my hand to stop shaking so I don't smudge mascara on my eye. How I let her talk me into asking Jake to Chances' end-of-the-year party next week, I'll never know. She could convince the pope that God doesn't exist, only to have him praying to him seconds later when she corrupts the poor man. So, I'm not surprised she was able to talk me into going to this party, let alone talking to the boy I've been crushing on and asking him to go to Chance's famous end-of-year bash. But what if he says no? It's not as if he's not already going, I mean, like Kiera said, he and Chance are connected at the hip. And he's one of the hottest guys in our grade. I'm sure somebody has already asked him, and I honestly don't think I could handle his rejection. Why would he commit to a date with me when he has countless options?

He wouldn't say no...would he? He is the nicest guy I've ever met, and he's never once made me feel like he was only friends with me just so he could get closer to my sister, like the rest of the dickwads at this school.

If I had a nickel for every time some asshole tried to get close to me just so he could "bag my hot sister", their words, not mine, I could probably just buy a date for the party.

"Josie, if you think any harder, your head is going to explode, and I don't need your brain matter all over my new dress," Kiera says with a playful smile, smoothing her hand down the front of her tightly fitted dress.

"Sorry. I'm just so nervous. You know my experience with boys isn't exactly stellar, and it never ends well." I remind her.

"I get it, your sister is a class A bitch, and a beautiful one at that," she says as I roll my eyes, attempting to hide my insecurities when it comes to my older sister. "That doesn't mean you have to sit on the sidelines and watch. You need to go after what you want. Besides, she might be beautiful, but you've got beauty and brains. Most importantly, you're the funniest damn person I've ever met." She finishes and tosses a grin in my direction.

Easy for her to say. Kiera is just as beautiful. Her waist-length chocolate brown hair, coupled with hazel eyes that have an amber sunburst in the middle, outlined by a sage green, will bring any man to his knees. Don't even get me started on her hourglass figure. I would understand if boys befriended me to get to her. She's much more beautiful than my sister, but she would never allow anyone to treat me that way, or her, for that matter. She knows how beautiful she is, but doesn't crawl into bed with every man who breathes in her direction. Chance should be counting his lucky stars that he snatched up such a beauty before anyone else could.

"I can't talk to you when you're being all reasonable," I say with all the sarcasm in the world. "But thank you. I don't know what I would do without you."

After I've finished my makeup and squeezed my size eighteen ass into a pair of shorts that feel like they're cutting off blood flow, I slip on my black silk camisole. I finish my ensemble with black gladiator sandals as Kiera slips on her black Louboutin heels, which Chance bought her BTW, when there's a knock at the door.

"Are you bitches ready yet? If you're not in my car in five minutes, I'm leaving without you." My notorious sister yells through my bedroom door.

"We'll be down in two minutes!" I yell back. Reaching for the doorknob, I hear her huff and stomp down the hallway as if the floor has offended her in some way.

I turn to Kiera, "Ready for this shit show?"

"Stop. You look hot. He would be an idiot to say no."

God, I hope she's right.

Apparently, everyone and their whole damn ancestry line knew about this party because finding somewhere to park was next to impossible. We could have gotten Kiera's usual spot in the driveway, but of course, Ashley had to stop and buy cigarettes, then proceeded to flirt with the cashier for twenty minutes. By the time we got here, the driveway was full. My feet are already screaming from the three blocks we had to walk from where we parked, and we haven't even made it to the party yet.

"Don't embarrass me tonight. It's bad enough I have to show up with you." My sister chastises me like I'm some kind of feral person who's never been out in public before.

"What crawled up your twat and died?" Kiera loyally rebukes, knowing how much Ashley's rude words sting. As always, I force it down, so she can't see how they affect me. You would think I would have gotten used to them by now, but I've learned it's easier to stay quiet.

"Just make sure you stay out of my way. The guys I like are going to be here, and I don't need you getting in the way." She says, flipping her long blonde hair over her shoulder.

"Look, Ashley, I know you're about to graduate and bless us all with your absence when you leave for college, but just because you have a big cunt doesn't mean you have to act like one. I think you forgot I'm dating Chance, and I could make it so you don't even step foot into that house, let alone go to his end-of-the-year party next week. So do us all a favor, and kindly fuck off."

I could kiss my best friend right now. I've never seen Ashley so mad before, let alone speechless. I have, however, seen that look in her eyes before. It's devious and calculating, and it puts me on edge. Just as she turns to stomp away, I catch the tiniest bit of a smile ghosting the corners of her mouth. So small, I wouldn't have noticed it if I weren't paying attention. I get this gut-churning feeling that this night isn't going to end well.

Oh, how I wish I had listened to my instincts and called an Uber, or at the very least walked home. If I had known what was about to happen in that house, I would have happily walked through fire to get away from this God-forsaken place.

Walking in the front door, you would think the pristine

Italian marble floors that greet us would be distracting enough, if it weren't for the two staircases that run up each side of the foyer that look like they were made for royalty. Wrought iron railings run up each staircase, while the stairs themselves are also made of the same white Italian marble. A giant crystal chandelier hangs between them, and the light reflects off the tiny glass pieces, making it sparkle like expensive diamonds.

Celebratory balloons line the archway under the stairs that lead to the massive living room, and when we walk under it, the giant room is a whirlwind of bodies and noise. I don't think I've ever seen his house packed full with so many partygoers. I mean, his house is huge, don't get me wrong. With both of his parents being lawyers, I wouldn't expect anything less, but I've never seen this many people at one of his parties. Some of the people I recognize from other schools, obviously, word got out. I can't even imagine what his end-of-year party is going to look like if this is just his birthday party.

As we wade through the sea of people and head toward the kitchen to get a drink, I scan the room to see if I can spot Jake anywhere. All I can concentrate on is the loud music vibrating through my body, when a strange feeling stirs the air around me.

A prickly sensation that makes the hair on the back of my neck stand on end, and goosebumps erupt all over my body. My heart picks up speed at the unexpected feeling, and excitement flutters in my belly. Like when you're sitting in the very front seat of a roller coaster, and you plummet down a steep drop. Your brain tells you that you should be scared, but the adrenaline coursing through you overrides the fear, and its thrilling high makes you feel like you're floating.

Just as I'm about to brush off the strange sensation and continue to the kitchen, I see them. Three sets of eyes are staring at me like I'm their prey. Three sets of eyes I've never seen before. Three sets of eyes that have so much emotion behind them, I'm not sure which ones to focus on. I've never seen these boys before, or should I say men. They don't look like any high school boys I have ever seen.

Are they from a different school? They have to be. I would definitely remember seeing them.

The one in the middle has the iciest light blue eyes I've ever seen, which is ironic because he's looking at me with so much heat I'm about to start sweating. With his dark eyebrows scrunched together, he looks to be deep in thought, like he's... worried? His jet-black hair is shorter on the sides and longer on top. His wavy length hangs perfectly over his forehead, and a slight stubble covers his jaw.

The man on the left also has blue eyes, but not as piercing, more the opposite in fact. Like the navy blue of the bottom of the ocean or a midnight sky. He has a look of such adoration in his eyes, and a warm sensation stirs my stomach. Tattoos cover his whole left arm and down to his fingers, making his muscled form even more drool-worthy than it already is. His honey-blonde hair is pulled back into a bun on the back of his head, while his short, trimmed beard hangs down neatly.

A gasp lodges in my throat when I swing my eyes to the man on the right. One, because he's looking at me with such carnal lust, I don't know whether to run to him or away from him. Two, because the warm beige of his skin is in such stark contrast to his jade green eyes. Opposite to the other two men, his hair is buzzed, and he has no facial hair. His pink lips look so pillowy soft. I want to sink my teeth into them.

What the hell? Where did that come from? Get your shit together, Josie, just because the hot creatures are showing you attention doesn't mean you need to fall in love with them.

I'm not sure why they're staring at me. They're looking at me as if they know a secret about me, and the messed-up part is I want to uncover it. If I wasn't on edge when we walked in, I am now.

I start to squirm because I don't know how to handle this kind of attention. I don't think I've ever held anyone's attention this long. Besides, I couldn't look away if I wanted to. My eyes are glued to them, appraising them like art in a museum. From the way they're appraising me, it seems the feeling is mutual.

The one on the right catches my fidgeting, and a wild grin spreads across his face, knowing their attention is overwhelming me. Just as he looks like he's about to pounce, Kiera steps up next to me, keeping him in place. "What the hell are they doing here?" She says curiously.

My head snaps in her direction. "You know them?"

"Well, yeah." She says it as if it should be obvious who they are. I stare at her with confusion, waiting for her to explain. " The one in the middle is Jake's half-brother."

Huh? I didn't know he had a half-brother.

"I seriously forgot how hot they all are. They go to Southview High on the other side of town," She states, and I'm still trying to catch up with the fact that Jake has a brother I didn't know about. A hot brother. "There are usually five of them, though. I bet the other two are around here somewhere."

Still trying to process this information, I turn my head to get another look at them, but they're gone just as mysteriously as they appeared. Before I can absorb what Kiera divulged, she's dragging me toward the kitchen again.

Just as we step into the kitchen, my eyes lock onto Jake. Now I'm a whole different kind of nervous. It's suddenly too hot in here, and I feel like I'm about to vomit. Sweat slicks my palms, and my mouth suddenly feels dry.

We wander to the counter that's packed full of beer and liquor. Kiera offers me a shot of whiskey as she begins filling multiple shot glasses. There's seriously no other way I'm going to be able to make it through this night without a little liquid courage. Or a lot of liquid courage.

"Atta girl! I love drunk Josie," Kiera says and grins. She's seen me drunk many times. She knows my guard comes down, and fun Josie comes out.

Fun Josie isn't reserved and insecure.

Fun Josie doesn't have a care in the world.

Fun Josie would march right up to Jake and demand a date.

"Cheers!" Kiera clinks our shot glasses together. A shiver works its way through my upper body when the burning liquid settles in my stomach.

After about three shots of the sweet, sweet alcohol that is my backbone right now, I fill a cup with keg beer. Kiera links her arm through mine as we head toward the beer pong table in the corner, where Chance and Jake are playing against my sister and her friend Shantel.

"BABE!" Chance shouts at Kiera just as we reach the table and tugs her into his chest to give her the sweetest kiss.

Jealousy pokes at me when I see how happy they are together. I try not to be envious of my friend, but for once, I just wish I could have that with someone. I hate being the stepping stone guys use to get to someone better. I'm tired of being the in-between person who only gets friendship. I want more.

Before I can spiral, I feel a nudge in my side and look over to see Kiera, who nods her chin in Jake's direction with a look on her face that says, "What are you waiting for?" I roll my eyes playfully at her and turn towards Chance, "Happy Birthday, Chance. This party is huge. I didn't think this many people even liked you." I joke sarcastically, and he throws his head back and laughs.

Chance leans in with a shit-eating grin on his face,

completely ignoring my little jab. "Go for it. He's good and liquored up. He'll say yes to anything right now." He whispers, flicking his eyes toward Jake. I don't know if I want to die of embarrassment or be humiliated, that's he's implying he'll only say yes because he's drunk.

I'm second-guessing myself when I feel a small shove on my back, and I'm not sure if it was Chance or Kiera, but I can hear them both giggling like two children causing mischief.

Thanks a lot, assholes. I'm glad my embarrassment is entertaining to you, I grumble internally as I approach Jake with the confidence of a deflated balloon.

"Hi," I squeak out as Jake turns to look at me, and holy shit if that smile doesn't melt my panties.

Get it together, Josie. You talk to him every day at school. Well, if you can count a shy "Hello" as talking. This is no different, I scold myself, but who am I kidding? This is a lot different; I actually have to speak full sentences and carry on a whole conversation with him.

"Hey, Jojo girl!" He says and throws his arm over my shoulder, and I get a whiff of his musky cologne. If his smile hadn't melted my panties, then the smell of his cologne would have.

"Beat it, Josie. We're playing a game," Ashley says with all the venom she can muster. I turn to look at her and see nothing but anger and jealousy in her eyes. A look that says, "I told you to stay out of my way tonight."

I roll my eyes at her because she thinks she can intimidate me. Which she usually does, but I'm busy trying not to faint from nervousness. That or the whiskey is kicking in.

"Can we go outside for a minute? I kinda need to talk to you." I turn and blurt out to Jake before I lose my courage.

"Of course, Jojo. Kiera, fill in for me 'til we get back?" He asks Kiera, and she steps up to take his place. She gives my elbow a reassuring squeeze before we walk off in the direction of the back door.

Thank god for my buzz because there's no way I could do this sober. My heart feels like it's about to beat out of my chest, and my palms are drenched. If I'm this anxious after a few drinks, I can only imagine how bad it would be without alcohol in my system.

As we step onto the back patio and make our way past the pool, we weave our way to a quieter place so we can talk without having to shout over the loud music. I'm very aware of all the stares we're getting. Well, that he's getting. All the girls are looking at him with stars in their eyes, and the guys are staring at him with a mix of envy and respect. Suddenly, I'm feeling unsure of this and realizing this is a mistake. I can barely take the attention of one person, let alone a hundred. He's always the center of attention, no matter where he goes, and I want to go to a party with him?

Nope. No way. I can't do this.

Just as I'm about to chicken out and tell him we should head back inside, we reach a gazebo in the far corner of the yard. He drops his arm from my shoulder and plops down on the bench there. He pats the seat next to him, gesturing for me to sit. Luckily, it's just dark enough he won't see the blush staining my cheeks.

"What's on your mind, Jojo?" I set my drink on the ledge of the gazebo and sit next to him. I set my hands in my lap and start twiddling my thumbs, as my leg starts to bounce. Both are sure signs that my anxiety is rising.

I feel his hand settle gently on my thigh, trying to reassure me that I don't need to be nervous. My eyes dart from his hand to his face, and I see nothing but kindness there. I'm reminded of why I like him so much. He's always been kind to me, and he's always patient when he knows I struggle to speak what's on my mind.

"Will you go to the end-of-the-year party with me?" I rush out in one jumbled sentence before I can give it a second thought.

That megawatt smile is back on his face, practically lighting up this dark gazebo. " Of course I will. Is that what's got you all frazzled?" He softly teases.

I nod my head and look down at my hands, convincing myself he can't see how awkward I am if I don't look at him. His finger gives a gentle tap on my chin, encouraging me to look up at him.

"Don't be nervous, cute girl. Of course, I will go with you. I've been wondering when you were going to ask. Chance told me you were going to like, two weeks ago." He chuckles, pulling me into his side when I groan out of embarrassment.

When he drapes his arm over my shoulders, I rest my head on his, sighing out a relieved breath, "I know. Every time I would get up the courage to ask you, I would psych myself out. Besides, you know my dating history isn't great."

"I know Jojo, but you don't have to worry about that. In a couple of months, your sister will be off to college and out of your hair." He smiles down at me, and the mention of my sister makes my gut tighten. Doubt starts to creep in, and I start to wonder what she'll do to take Jake away from me. Then I remember that he's different and isn't the type to risk his friendships for cheap thrills. "Plus, we're going to be seniors. It's the perfect way to end our junior year. Maybe I'll finally get to see you in a bikini." He wags his eyebrows at me, and the action has the doubt vanishing.

I let out a giggle. "Yeah, I don't think that's going to happen. I don't want to scare you off."

His eyebrows scrunch together."Don't put yourself down like that. You're beautiful, Jojo." He says as he tucks a piece of hair behind my ear. I bite back a smile as my cheeks flush.

I shrug my shoulders. "Sorry. Just a habit, I guess."

He gives me a soft, sympathetic smile and squeezes my shoulder. "Text me sometime next week and we can work out the details, yeah?"

Nodding my head, he stands, and I tell him, "I'm going to stay out here for a bit. Get some fresh air." I jerk my chin in the direction of the house. "Tell Kiera I'll be in shortly?"

"Ok, Josie. Can't wait for next weekend." He winks and walks off.

I can't help the damn grin that takes over my face and the butterflies that erupt in my stomach. I squeal excitedly when he's out of sight and do a little happy dance in my seat. I cannot contain my happiness as I jump to my feet, wiggling my hips and doing a giddy little shuffle. I'm lost in my elation when an unexpected voice turns my happy squealing into terrified screams.

"You should leave."

Chapter Two

JOSIE

I scream so loud I'm surprised no one hears it over the music. I turn to see who the jackass was who dared to rain on my parade. I was not prepared for the Adonis standing there looking like anything but a jackass, more like a stallion. Piercing blue eyes glare back at me, and all I can think about is how they still look so icy bright blue out here in the dark.

I press a hand to my chest, willing my heart rate to settle. Once I calm down, I process what he said, "Excuse me?" I say, matching his glare with my own.

"I said, you should leave." He says through clenched teeth, sounding inconvenienced, that he had to repeat himself. His voice comes out gravelly and annoyed, like my being here is such a bother.

His anger throws me off, and his whole demeanor is so opposite of Jake's that I can't help but get distracted by their differences. When I saw him earlier, I could see his jet black hair and tall frame resemble Jake's, but out here in the dark, it's harder to make out the smaller similarities. From what I can see, Jake's eyes are a dark coffee brown, and this guy has such a cool blue that they could freeze anyone to the spot.

Jake is tall with more of a toned muscular body; his brother is tall and lean, with a jawline so sharp it rivals that of a knife's edge. Even with the sliver of moonlight glinting off the slight scruff on his face, his jawline is still prominent, and I feel the urge to run my fingers along it. His black t-shirt hugs his torso in all the right places. If he were to flex his muscles, his shirt would rip right off his body.

God, I bet his abs have abs. Is there a subtle way to ask someone to take their shirt off, so you can drool over them, without sounding like a sex crazed pervert? Who am I kidding? he doesn't need to take his shirt off for me to drool over him.

I hear a throat clearing, and my eyes snap back up to his. I'm instantly mortified by the amusement in his eyes and the twitching of his lips as he tries to hold back a smile. My sense of shame is renewed when I finally process the fact that I'm sure he heard me asking his brother out, and now I'm standing here like a dog in freaking heat salivating over him. I can feel how red my face is from blushing so hard, and bless his heart, he doesn't point it out, or it's just too dark to notice. I give my head a slight shake as if to rid it of his hypnotizing features and remember the annoyance on his assholeish glare seconds prior.

He notices the moment I open my mouth because all the amusement slips from his face and is replaced by a blank expression I can't decipher. " Why should I leave? I was here first." I say a little more petulantly than I intended.

"I meant you should leave this party. Nothing good is going to come from you staying, trust me," he grits out.

I've never seen this person before in my life, and he expects me to trust him? Something is telling me to listen to him and get as far away from here as possible, but my buzzed brain is more focused on the mysterious man himself. I don't know where he came from, or where Jake has been hiding him and his gang of hot friends. Two of which I've yet to lay eyes on, and the two I have seen I want to lay more than my eyes on them.

Ok, what the hell is happening to me? There's got to be something in this alcohol, making me think like a horny teenage boy who just found his dad's porn stash. That's the only explanation. That or Kiera put something in those shots, I mean, I wouldn't put it passed her.

I dump the remaining alcohol out of my cup because Lord knows I don't need any more. "Why would I trust you? I don't even know you, or your name for that matter." I finally answered.

"You're right. You shouldn't trust me." he pauses and hesitates to say his next words. "You shouldn't trust anyone here. ANYONE. Even the ones you think you can trust the most," he says cryptically.

For the first time, his cold, intense stare scares me. I slowly take a step back, never taking my eyes off him. A myriad of emotions flash across his face, and I can see that he is holding something back. He purses his lips like all of his secrets are going to come spilling out, so he's trying to tell me with his eyes. I see uncertainty and anger that is replaced with hunger and desire. That quickly morphs into sadness and longing, but for what?

"Please," he croaks like he's in pain. For a second, just for a second, he lets his emotions bleed out, looking like heartbreak and grief. The sorrow is palpable as distress pours off of him in waves. I want to wrap him in my arms, to squeeze the pain from his body and tell him that everything will be ok. Just as I go to step toward him, that intense mask is pulled back over his eyes, his face turning into a blank canvas. " Please, just promise me you won't stay." He demands, clenching his fists.

I give him a small nod of my head because, for some

reason, I feel like my life just changed, and he's the only one who knows why. I don't know if that's a good thing or a bad thing, but I know, deep down into my soul, that if I ask him why, I'm not going to like the answer.

He flicks his eyes up and down my body as if he's committing it to memory. As if he's committing this *moment* to memory, and then he disappears back into the dark. I feel a little pang of disappointment in my chest, not knowing if I'll ever see him again.

Walking back toward the house, his words replay on a loop in my head.

"Nothing good is going to come from you staying."

"You shouldn't trust anyone here".

"Even the ones you think you can trust the most."

I'm not sure what to make of it. He told me not to trust him, so why should I even listen to what he said? More importantly, why shouldn't I trust him? He doesn't seem like a bad person. A bad person wouldn't warn me to leave and ask for promises from me. Would they?

Then I remember that stricken look on his face, and it's like a punch to the gut. I get the urge to strangle whoever made him feel that way in the first place. No one should be filled with that much pain.

A cackle of laughter from a group of partygoers brings me back to the present as I make my way by the pool. Choosing to ignore the hot stranger's words since he told me not to trust him, I decide I'm here to have fun, and this is something I can obsess about tomorrow. Besides, my buzz is starting to wear off, and that's just not acceptable.

Before I can take another step, I feel a hand wrap around my elbow and spin me around so fast I almost lose my footing. Two giant hands are placed on my shoulders to steady me, lifting my eyes, relief instantly fills me when I see the familiar person standing in front of me.

"Hey Josie," Zeke says with a broad smile on his face. I screech, unable to contain my excitement, and throw my arms around his neck. "I've been looking for you. Where have you been?"

I unravel myself from his neck so I can look at his face when I tell him, because I know he's not going to like the answer. "Well, you know how I told you I was going to ask Jake to the end-of-year party?" The smile slips from his face, and I hurry to finish before he tells me how disappointed he is. " Well, I asked him, and he said yes."

Zeke doesn't trust Jake. He thinks he's just like every other guy at our school who only has one thing on their mind, and it's not me. Zeke knows all of my insecurities front, back, and center. So whenever I do anything involving boys, he can be a little overprotective.

He's been one of my best friends for as long as I can remember. He has seen all of my struggles and is one of the only people I truly feel I can be myself around. I can talk to him about anything, and I know he won't judge me.

So when I see that annoyed expression wash over his face, I know it's because he's concerned. "Come on, Josie. He's the fakest one of them all." He huffs and crosses his arms over his chest. "He smiles too much." He grouses.

I snort out a laugh. "So what, he's just happy all the time. How's that a bad thing?"

"Exactly! No one is that happy ALL the time. It's like he's using his smile to cover up what an asshole he really is."

"We're just going to a party together. It's not that big of a deal. The whole school will be there." I say to try and pacify him, because I know he won't let it drop. So I try to change the subject instead. "We're here to have fun, so let's go get our drink on and talk about this tomorrow."

He looks like he's warring with himself. Trying to decide if he wants to continue this conversation or drop it. Then I bat my eyelashes at him, and that grin invades his mouth again. "You know it isn't fair to bat those beautiful lashes at me."

"I know, but it works every time." I bat them exaggeratedly and give him a peck on the cheek. Chuckling and shaking his head at my antics, he guides me inside.

Making our way through the door, we step past the living room filled with a sea of people swaying to the music coming from the loud speakers that are positioned on each side of the DJ booth that's set up in the corner. Somehow, it looks like there are more people now than when we first arrived.

Shoving our way through the crowd, we finally make it into the kitchen, which seems to have just as many people. I find Kiera over by the beer pong table where I left her with Chance. Now they're playing against Jake and some guy I've never seen before. I haven't seen my sister, and honestly, I would be happy if I didn't see her for the rest of the night.

Jake throws me a wink as I catch his eye, and I give him a shy smile. Then his eyes flick to Zeke, who is standing behind me, and that playful look that was just on his face drops like a sack of marbles.

Okayyyyyy. Don't know what to make of that, and I'm desperate for a drink, so that's going to have to be a future Josie problem.

I turn to Kiera. "Let's do shots!" I practically yell because of how loud it is in here. She starts clapping and jumping up and down like a child who was just told they're going to Disneyland.

She pulls me into a hug and whispers. "I told you he would say yes." And God, I want to die. Obviously, they talked about it. She sees me blush and reaches down to give my hand a supportive squeeze.

We mosey over to the counter holding all the liquor, and Zeke pours three shots of whiskey. We hold our glasses up. "To hell: May the stay there be as fun as the way there!" Zeke shouts as we all clink our little shot glasses together, and a wave of hoots and hollers goes over the surrounding crowd.

We each take two more shots and guzzle down some ice-cold beer from the keg. I finally have the world's best buzz going, and I feel the urge to dance. Ok, scratch that, I'm not buzzed, I'm drunk. I never dance. Sober me is way too self-conscious to dance and too damn insecure.

Drunk me? Drunk me doesn't care who is watching and will happily flip two birds to anyone who cares.

Apparently, Kiera is feeling the need to move her body as well. She tugs on my arm and pulls me along to the middle of the dance floor, which is so crowded there's barely enough room to dance. It's just bodies grinding on bodies. You can't tell where some people begin and others end. It's intimate. I almost feel the urge to flee because of how suffocating the crowd is. Almost.

You Can Do It by Ice Cube is playing over the speakers when Kiera starts grinding behind me, and I follow what she's doing, because I really have no idea what I'm doing. She's been dancing since she was four, and I'm sure I look like a newborn giraffe next to her.

Letting the music take over my body, I start swaying and gyrating my hips to mimic that of my best friend. She places her hands on my hips to help get me in the flow with the song. "That's it, you got it!" she cheers, and I can't help the proud smile that spreads across my face. I dance about as often as I let loose, which is just about never. A sense of accomplishment fills me for stepping out of my comfort zone.

Before I know it, we've danced through two more songs, and when Pretty Ricky's song Grind on Me comes over the speakers, the crowd loses their minds with excitement. I spin around and wrap my arms around Kiera's neck and roll my body with hers in time with the music. I can feel sweat running down my neck, and it feels like the heat in the room has been turned up ten degrees.

Lost in the music, I startle when I feel a heavy hand land on my side. "Relax, it's just me," Zeke murmurs in my ear. I smile at him over my shoulder as I settle against him. He lowers his hands to my hips as I'm sandwiched between him and Kiera. I rest my head back on his shoulder while keeping my arms wrapped around Kiera's neck.

I close my eyes and just feel the music wash over me. I feel Zeke's hot breath on my neck as sweat trickles down it. I feel the heat from Kiera's body at my front as she continues to rotate her hips. I feel content in my drunken state; here, in this spot, with the two people I trust most in the world. Who are always there for me, no matter what. I let out a relaxed sigh as I settle further into Zeke, letting myself get lost in the writhing mass of bodies.

I don't know how many songs have passed, maybe three? When I start to feel that needling sensation at the back of my neck again and my skin starts to tingle. I don't have to open my eyes to know it's one of them. I'm not sure which one of them it is, but there is no doubt in my mind that it's one of the strangers from earlier.

So when I lift my head from Zeke's shoulder and open my eyes, I'm not surprised to see those intense eyes again. The desire shining bright in them is quickly replaced with the same anger he revealed when we were outside. The muscles in his jaw are working overtime, and if he clenches his fists any harder, his knuckles are going to tear through his skin.

The sight of his rage is sobering. So much so that I snap out of my drunken dancing haze and notice Kiera is no longer in front of me.

Once I peel myself away from Zeke, I realize I'm covered in sweat, and I'm hit with a wave of dizziness. I feel like I'm overheating, and my mouth feels like cotton. I turn to let him know I need to cool off.

He stays on the dance floor as I make my way to the bathroom on shaky legs. We had been dancing long enough for my legs to feel like Jell-O and lose all sense of reality. I have no idea how long we had been dancing for, or what time it is, for that matter. I hadn't even noticed that Kiera had left.

I stumble my way up the never-ending staircase to the bathroom at the top. After I get inside and close the door, I instantly head for the sink. Leaning over the cool porcelain on my forearms, I cup my hands together and splash my face with cold water a few times. Once I feel I've sufficiently doused my face, I sip some of the water from my hands and feel the heat start to subside.

I sway on my feet just a bit as I stand and grab the hand towel to pat my face dry. I cringe as I catch a glimpse of myself in the mirror. My wavy red hair looks like I just rolled out of bed, as I try to run my fingers through it to tame the mess. My emerald green eyes usually look more alive, but they just look unfocused and glossy. To top it off, my skin looks dull and lifeless.

Bleh! I look terrible.

Wiping away some of the makeup smudged around my eyes, I try to make myself look at least presentable before I go back downstairs. But when I turn around, I see another door behind me. How the hell did I miss that? It looks like it leads to a bedroom. It's cracked ope-"Oh God." I hear someone moan out, cutting off my thought.

Chapter Three

JOSIE

"Oh my god," the same breathy voice moans again.

I slap my hand over my mouth to try and smother my immature drunken giggle. It's a miracle whoever is in there didn't hear me. Then again, based on the hot and heavy noises coming from the other side of the door, they're a little preoccupied. If I were hooking up with someone at a party, I would definitely be paranoid of people walking in, or at the very least, hearing me. But someone would want to have sex with me for that to even happen. They're probably just super drunk and not paying atten-"Oh baby." I hear another moan as I try to stifle another giggle.

Call it drunken bravery, or curiosity got the cat, or whatever you want, but my curiosity has officially been piqued. Besides, I have to look, because if I go back down and tell Kiera what I heard, she'll be furious if I didn't get all the juicy details. So, I have to look to save myself from her rage. At least that's the best excuse my alcohol hazed brain can come up with. I curl my fingers around the edge of the door. *Close the door, Josie. You wouldn't want someone to invade your privacy.* My annoying instincts try to warn me.

Oh, how I wish I had listened.

When I pull the door open, I immediately regret it. My stomach bottoms out, and I can feel bile inching its way up my throat. My vision tunnels, and all I can focus on is the three, yes *three*, bodies in front of me. Tears prick the corners of my eyes as I'm overwhelmed with anger and utter agony.

I feel the urge to flee, but my feet feel like they're cemented in place. My arms are heavy, and my chest burns with the urge to scream and lash out at myself. At myself because this is what I get for getting my hopes up, this is what I get for believing someone wanted to go out with me, this is what I get for thinking that it is impossible that she would do this to me again!

How could I be so stupid!

How could Chance do this to Kiera?

A renewed sense of rage takes over me as I watch as my sister is completely naked on all fours, while Chance is at her front, on his knees, pumping his dick in and out of her mouth at a leisurely pace. With his head thrown back, making a grunting noise that I will never be able to unhear. Right now, he looks as though he doesn't have a care in the world. Little does he know, his world is about to be shattered, because they haven't even noticed me yet, and I'll be damned if he thinks I won't tell my best friend what I'm seeing.

The lump that is working overtime in my throat and trying to hold back my tears is becoming painful. My eyes work their way to the back of her and settle on the disgusting human being thrusting in and out of her. Why would I think he would ever want to go out with me? Clearly, he's just another asshole using me as a stepping stone so he could get to the vile person sandwiched between him and his best friend.

Then her words from earlier tonight come back to me.

"The guys I like are going to be here."

Guys! plural! As in two. How did I not put that together?

Even when they were playing beer pong, she had told me to beat it. She had been planning this all night, and she knew I was going to ask him out. She knew! Yet, here she is being fucked five ways to Sunday.

Stabbing me in the chest would feel less painful than this excruciating torment. I press a palm to my chest to try and ease the pain of my heart being shredded into ribbons as I'm once again proved that I'm not good enough.

A loud bang goes off in the distance, but it sounds like everything is gurgled and drowned out when Jake's eyes swing in my direction and lock onto mine. He freezes in place, and the shocked look that comes across his face will be burned into my brain as I let the dam break that was holding back my tears.

"Jake, don't sto-" Ashley doesn't finish her sentence as she and Chance finally realize I'm in the room. A wicked grin spreads across her face as I hear a muffled curse from Chance.

Both guys separate from her, and I take a step back. Chance looks at me with pleading eyes, begging me not to tell Kiera because he knows he'll lose her once I do. Jake's wide-eyed expression flits between regret and guilt. Realizing he's no better than all the other assholes that have used me, he hangs his head out of shame.

Agony and anger war inside me as I look away to scan the rest of the room. There are clothes and blankets strewn about everywhere, and it dawns on me that we're in Chance's room. Condom wrappers lay next to the bed haphazardly, and I hold back a snort. At least they had the sense to use protection, because once we all exit this room, everything is going to be fucked. Before I can even process what to say to them, another gunshot- wait, gunshot!

That was a fucking gunshot!

My vision comes back into focus as I hear screaming

coming from downstairs. I quickly skim the room again for my sister's pants and find them flung over a chair. I snatch her car keys from the front pocket, then dash out the door, leaving them to fend for themselves.

"Josie, wait!"

"You can't go down there."

"Where the fuck do you think you're going?"

I hear them all yelling at me. No way am I sticking around with any of them. They can all rot in hell for all I care.

More gunshots are going off as I scramble my way to the stairs. When I reach the bottom, it's pure chaos. People are frantic and screaming, all trying to rush in different directions to hide or make their way out of the house.

I step foot into the madness and almost fall to the ground when someone runs into my side, making a mad dash for the front door. I right myself and scan the sea of people for Zeke and Kiera, but I can't see them anywhere. I push my way towards the kitchen only to find it empty. Red plastic cups and liquor bottles litter the room, looking like a tornado came through here.

My heart rate lurches, and my ears begin ringing as another boom goes off. I cover my ears, and the anguished tears that were falling are now falling out of terror. My breathing turns rapid when I step out of the kitchen to head through the living room. Trying to suck in a deep breath is difficult as I take in the scene before me.

Puddles of blood stain the hardwood floor that everyone had just been carelessly dancing on only minutes ago. The windows that line the far wall are all shattered, and broken glass lies scattered on the floor, mixing with the blood and empty plastic cups. Three figures block the doorway that leads out to the backyard, but my frazzled state doesn't stop me from seeing who they are.

"ZEKE! KIERA!" The frightful scream tears out of my

throat, but it's no use. Between the music still playing, the riotous crowd, and gunshots, there's no way they're going to hear me. I pull my phone from my pocket with shaky hands as I bring up Zeke's name. Before I can hit call, someone slams into the back of me as a bullet goes whizzing by my head, and we crash to the floor.

"You need to get out of here, Gem. Go back through the kitchen and out of the garage." The mystery man quickly whispers in my ear. I don't have time to question who just saved my life, because they're gone in the blink of an eye, running back into the mayhem.

My head is spinning, whether that's from the alcohol or the chaos, I don't know. I push myself up on wobbly legs, phone still clutched in my hand. Turning to head for the kitchen, I notice the bullet embedded in the wall behind me, and panic starts to claw at my chest. A little sob escapes my throat. If it weren't for that stranger, I would be dead.

Fuck! I need to get the hell away from this nightmare.

Bolting through the kitchen, I find a door tucked into the back corner. It looks like someone had the same idea as my mystery man, because the garage door is already open when I step inside. Sprinting to the end of the driveway, my phone starts to vibrate in my hands. The name on the caller ID looks fuzzy, but I answer it already knowing who it is.

"Zeke." I sob out his name.

"Please tell me you got out." I hear his worried voice rush out.

"Yes, I got the keys to Ashley's car. I'm heading there now. Do you know where Kiera is?" before he can answer, I hear wailing in the background, "Take me back! I have to find Chance!" A sense of relief washes over me because they're both safe, but then I remember what I just saw up in that bedroom before mayhem ensued.

"Josie!" Zeke snaps before I can spiral. Now is not the time." You shouldn't drive, you've been drinking."

"I'm fine." I grit out. I know he's right and I should listen to him, but I have so many emotions and so much alcohol buzzing through me right now, I couldn't think straight even if I wanted to. I just need to get away from this hellhole.

"You're not fin-"

"I'm fine, Zeke. I promise I will call you when I make it home, so you know I'm safe." I hang up before he can argue with me. Shoving my phone into my pocket, I run towards Ashley's car.

Her red Volkswagen Jetta comes into view, and I sprint the last few steps. I hit the unlock button on the key fob and jam the key into the ignition to start it. I flick the lights on and speed away from the curb.

Chapter Four
JOSIE

Once I'm a safe distance from Chance's house and I can no longer see the street crowded with cars out of my rear-view mirror, a loud sob bursts from my throat. The events of the whole night are finally settling into my brain now that it's quiet. Tears are blurring my vision as I try to keep my eyes on the road.

The time on the dash says two fifteen, it's late, but I still stick to the back roads to avoid what little traffic there is this time of the night. I know I've been drinking, and I shouldn't be driving but I just had to get the fuck out of there.

Trying to wipe the tears from my face is useless as they pour from me like a faucet has been turned on.

My frantic sobbing makes my breathing shallow as I try to get the image of Jake thrusting into my sister out of my head, and the memory of Chance grunting makes my stomach coil with disgust. I place one hand on my stomach as if that will make the feeling go away. That fucking smile that lit up her face when she noticed I was in the room plays on a loop and it infuriates me.

A scream tears from my throat as I bang my hand against

the steering wheel, letting out some of my rage. "Fuck, fuck, FUCK!" I scream and scream until my voice becomes hoarse.

I shake my head, trying to get rid of the gory details, but it just makes me dizzy, and the car zigzags all over the road. *When will I learn? When will I ever learn? I'm so freaking stupid, I should have seen this coming. With her track record, I should have expected this.* I chastise myself as I attempt to drive the vehicle in a straight line.

Then those gunshots. I don't know how many people got hurt, but with how much blood there was, it had to be a lot. I could've died. I almost died.

"I almost died," I repeat out loud, realizing the gravity of the situation. "Shit!."

Terror settles in my stomach like a bowling ball. I cry out and clench my hands around the steering wheel so tight my knuckles turn white. My chest begins to heave up and down as I try to force in breath after breath.

My rising panic causes my throat to tighten, as I try to suck in air. My lips start to tingle with the lack of oxygen, and I roll down my window, hoping the cool air will soothe me. A shallow breath can pass my closing throat, but it's not enough.

Black dots start to dance in my vision as headlights from behind reflect into the rearview mirror, blinding me. The cool breeze whips my hair around as I continue to try and gulp down air, but I'm still met with resistance.

I don't know how long the vehicle has been behind me, but I'm sure it's been long enough to see me swerving all over the road. When I start to claw at my throat, I feel, whoever it is, ram into the back bumper, making me jerk the steering wheel.

I feel my face go white and hear the whoosh of blood in my ears as they ram the car again. I let out a scream as the car weaves all over the road, and I try to gain control of it once again. Dread takes over my body as it distracts me from the fact that I can't breathe. The mystery vehicle is on me again, blinding me with its lights, but before I can think twice, they slam into me for a third time, delivering the blow that will change my life.

Screaming loud enough to rip a hole in my esophagus, the car starts to spin in a circle from the hit. I yank on the steering wheel to try and correct the car, but it's spinning so fast I overcorrect it, and the car starts to roll. The last thought that registers before it flips is, I didn't put my seat belt on.

Before that thought has time to settle, I'm inundated with the sound of crunching metal as the car slams onto the asphalt, glass shattering from the pressure. I'm flung around the car like a limp noodle. The adrenaline that's pumping through my body blocks my brain from any pain that the damage wreaks.

My head slams into the roof of the car as I'm tossed around. I attempt to put my arms out to try and brace myself, and am met with a snapping noise that I'm not entirely sure where it came from. As I'm thrown back down, the gear shift jams into my side, and then I'm hurled against the roof, battering my head once more.

I don't know how many times the car rolls, but it seems like it goes on for a lifetime. Everything becomes a blur; giving in to the chaos, I close my eyes and relax my body. Accepting my fate that I may not live through this. It's not like I can control anything at this point. I should have listened to Zeke. Hell, I should have listened to the beautiful stranger who tried to get me to leave, but it's too late now, and thankfully, darkness overtakes me.

The screeching of tires is the first thing that registers. I couldn't tell you when the car finally stopped rolling, or how long I've been lying here.

Trying to peel my eyes open to see where the noise is

coming from is futile. They're so heavy it feels like they're made of lead. The sensation of a boulder resting lazily on my back makes my battered body feel like it's being squished like a bug, jamming whatever I'm lying on into my stomach. Attempting to move, I instantly freeze when a sharp pain shoots from my head down to my fingertips, and I shriek out as dizzying pain lances through me.

Everything hurts. The world spins behind my closed eyelids as I try to focus and figure out where the pain is coming from. Gravel scratches against my cheek when I register that I'm lying flat on my stomach with my face pressed into asphalt. The car must have landed on its roof, because the lower half of my body is hanging out of the driver's side window, and the other half is plastered to the road. I decide the pain in my stomach must be from the car's frame, maybe?

Warm liquid trickles down my face, and when I finally can force my eyes open, I cry out from the bright light emanating from the streetlamp that sends a stabbing pain through my head. I flinch when I hear a car door shut, and the thudding of approaching footsteps. I expect panic to rise, but it never comes, I'm just met with overwhelming pain, making me wish someone would put me out of my misery.

That's what I'm expecting from the approaching strangers, but I'm surprised to hear panicked voices. They sound distraught, like they're the ones who were just run off the road and were thrown around like a rag doll.

I can't make out their faces. Everything is fuzzy, and it's too painful to hold my eyes open for longer than a few seconds. Taking in a deep breath, I'm once again met with an excruciating pain that radiates through my side. It's so painful it knocks the wind out of me, and I let out a choking, gurgling cough. The metallic taste of blood fills my mouth as it spills over my lips.

A large, warm palm gently comes to rest on my cheek that's so comforting, I would nuzzle into it if I weren't in so much pain. " Fuck!" I hear a panicked voice shout in the distance.

"You weren't supposed to be in the car, my sweet *Roja*. I'm so sorry." I hear him sniffle. He rubs his thumb across my cheek, wiping away a tear, or blood, of which I'm not sure.

I attempt to lift my heavy lids to try and get a look at him, but everything is so blurred I can only see the outline of him. I hear footsteps again as another outline appears from over his shoulder, and I only have a few seconds to take in before I have to close my eyes again. I hear the other man crouch down beside me, and feel as another hand comes to rest on my head.

I want to savor their warmth and bathe in their affection. Affection I've never felt before, I think, as I move to lift my hand, but a whimper of pain comes out instead.

"Shhh, it's okay. Try not to move, sweetheart." One of them murmurs.

"We have to get out of here." The same voice says.

"We can't just leave her." The other snaps

"I called 9-1-1. The cops are on their way. There is nothing else we can do."

Before they can argue further, a shrill siren blares out, causing the pain in my head to intensify.

A soft kiss is placed on the crown of my head, followed by retreating footsteps.

Another kiss is placed on my forehead. If I weren't crying from pain, then I would cry at how tender his warm lips feel against my skin, and the affection that he pours into it.

The sirens sound like they're getting closer, and I feel his palm lift from my cheek. "Don't go," I mumble. Suddenly, his warmth is gone, and I feel a coldness settle into my bones.

"*Lo siento hermosa, por favor perdoname.*" He says, and I

have no idea what any of it means. All I can focus on is his retreating footsteps and the start of an engine.

"Don't go." I cry out weakly. "Please don't go." Tears stream down my face as I beg them not to go, even after I've heard them drive off. At this point, I don't know who I'm begging to stay, them, or me.

The pain becomes unbearable, and my breathing turns ragged. My body starts to tremble from shock. Growing lightheaded, I try to hold on to the comfort the two strangers provided, but before the darkness succumbs, his words slam back into me. *"You weren't supposed to be in the car."* And then it hits me... someone tried to kill me, or rather, my sister.

Chapter Five

JOSIE

"......broken ribs"

"......brain is bleeding"

"...... broken arm."

I hear muffled voices speaking, only making out bits and pieces of their conversation, because they're standing too far away. That, and how can anyone hear anything over that god awful beeping noise?

I try to open my mouth to speak, to tell whoever it is to shut off that damn beeping but my mouth won't move. Whatever is pressing down on my tongue snakes down my throat, stopping any words from escaping my mouth as alarm takes hold.

Attempting to lift my hand and yanking out the offending object in my mouth, I'm immediately met with a searing pain in my left arm. My heart rate soars, and the incessant beeping becomes louder and faster. A stabbing pain shoots through my head and burrows into my brain.

A warm hand comes to lay on top of mine in a comforting manner. "Shhh, try to relax." An unfamiliar voice coos.

Before I can process who that voice could belong to,

excruciating pain darts through my chest and throughout my ribs as I try to lash out in frustration. It's as if my brain is awake, but my body isn't. I can hear and feel things, but my body's frozen in place. I feel the bed dip on my other side as a gentle hand rests on my leg, and another on my foot, kneading lightly to soothe me.

"It's ok, sweet Gem." That same voice says, the gentleness of his voice is surprisingly soothing.

I hear some shuffling above my head, followed by some clicking. Shortly after, I feel liquid fill my veins, and almost instantly feel the pain lessen to more of a dull throb.

"How the fuck did this happen!" the voice snarls viciously. I would flinch at the venom in his voice if I weren't desperate for that answer as well.

"Later. This is not the time or place." Another admonishes. The hand resting on my leg grips it slightly to acknowledge that he knows I'm listening, and whatever they have to say will cause more pain. Which is laughable because Lord knows, I've experienced enough pain to last a lifetime.

As if the drugs flowing through my body can read my mind, they start to tug at my consciousness. The beeping sound starts to fade, but the warm touches never leave.

"Don't worry, sweet girl, we've got you." Is the last thing I hear before darkness envelops me.

The cold chill that forces a shudder through my body is what wakes me. The harsh light of the room makes me wince when I open my eyes, only to squeeze them shut again. Squinting them open so they can slowly adjust and take in my surroundings, another chill passes over me. "Why is it so cold?" I mumble, as the thin sheet that's being passed off as a blanket does nothing to warm me.

Reaching down to pull the "blanket" over my chest, I feel a jab in my right arm. I look down and notice the I.V. along with the pulse oximeter that's clamped over my pointer finger. Which brings my attention to the cords hanging out of the top of my gown that are connected to the stickers on my chest to monitor my heart. My throat feels scratchy, and my tongue is so dry it's sticking to the roof of my mouth. Pain drums in my chest as I try to reach for the cup of water on the tray table next to my bed.

After taking slow, steady breaths to quell the pain, I slowly lift my head to scan the room. There are at least a dozen vases of different flowers scattered throughout. One vase holding my favorite flowers, roses, and sunflowers, draws my attention, and a warm, cherished feeling nullifies the dull pain in my chest.

Movement in the far corner catches my eye, and I take in the rumpled form that's curled up on the small couch. Tears flood my eyes as an unexpected swarm of emotions takes over at seeing the sleeping body.

"Zeke." I croak out, my throat feeling just as dry as my mouth. Clearing my throat, attempting to get his attention again, "Zeke." His raspy name burns through my dry throat.

Tears wet my cheeks as I attempt to wake him again. "Zeke." I force out a little louder. My hand flies to my chest when the dull pain returns with the repetitive force of a jackhammer. Just as I open my mouth again, his eyes snap open, and he's sitting next to me before I can even blink.

Holding my hand out to him, he links his fingers through mine, raising his other hand to cup my cheek softly. His eyes hold so much sympathy, it only makes more tears spill over. "Are you in pain?" He asks when his thumb swipes away the wetness.

"Not much." I shake my head and wince at the feeling of

someone stabbing an ice pick through my head. "Well, not as much as I was in yesterday."

His brows dip in confusion. "Yesterday? What do you mean?"

"I woke up in a lot of pain yesterday. I couldn't move or talk. I could hear others, though, but then I fell back asleep."

"Babe," he says with sadness in his eyes. He tilts his head down to look at our linked hands and rubs his thumb across my knuckles. I get a sinking feeling in my stomach when he looks back up at me with anguish in his eyes. "You've been in a coma for three months."

Chapter Six

JOSIE

Three months!

I know I hit my head, but did he say three months? No. Surely, he didn't. Staring at Zeke with my mouth gaping open, and what I'm sure is a stunned look on my face, he nods his head, knowing what I'm thinking.

How the hell has it been three months? That means I missed the whole freaking summer, and Chance's end of the year part-before I can even finish that thought, it's drowned out by the memories of how I ended up here in the first place.

All the worrying about being in a coma for three months is suddenly shoved to the side and overshadowed by new worries. Did they find out who was responsible for the shooting? How many people got hurt? Do they know who caused me to crash? Oh god! Does Kiera know that Chance is cheating on her? Somehow, the idea of Kiera not knowing seems like the worst of all, because if she doesn't know I have this huge secret I've literally been sleeping on for three months, and I have to be the one to deliver the bad news.

She must have known I was thinking about her because the next thing I know, the door swings open, and Kiera makes a beeline straight for me. Zeke places a chaste kiss on my forehead and steps to the side just as Kiera throws her arms around my neck. I grimace as she hugs my body, and I jerk back like I've been burned.

"Sorry, I didn't mean to hurt you. I'm just so happy you're awake." She sniffles, pulling back and wiping tears from her eyes. "I was so worried about you. *We* were so worried about you." She flings her hand around, gesturing between her and Zeke.

Wiping away a few stray tears of my own, I give her a sympathetic smile. "I can't imagine how worried you both were. If anything happened to either one of you, I would be beside myself."

"How do you feel?" Zeke asks, coming to perch on the other side of the bed, resting a consoling hand on my shin.

"Like I've been in a car wreck," I say sarcastically, trying to rub the tension from my temples, only to notice the brace on my left arm. The sight of it prompts me to take in the rest of my injuries. Lifting my good arm, I reach for my head and let out a surprised gasp when I feel a thick bandage wrapped around it. A dull ache pounds through my chest and sides at the startled breath. "How bad is it?"

I ask no one in particular, but it's Kiera who answers. "It's not great. You hit your head pretty hard, and they put you in a medically induced coma so your brain could rest. You were in bad shape, babe." Her chin wobbles, and guilt lands heavy on my shoulders.

"Josie," Zeke says my name so softly, and when I flick my eyes over to him, he's staring down at the bed, fidgeting nervously with the blanket draped over my legs. "What happened?" He asks, but as he looks up at me, I'm surprised to see the sorrow that's staring back at me. The emotion is so raw that it seems like there's more to it.

I reach out for his hand to comfort him, but before our

hands connect, the door whooshes open again. In walks the doctor with my mom trailing behind him. "Later." I mouth the words to him, and he dips his head in understanding.

He and Kiera step away from the bed as my mom and the doctor step up. My mom drops down, placing a kiss on my head and sits in the spot Zeke had just vacated. She puts her hand in mine. "You gave us all a good scare." She states with motherly love filling her eyes. I'm not sure how to respond to that, so I give her a watery smile.

"That you did, young lady." The doctor says in a condescending tone that has me putting my guard up. "I'm Doctor Craig. I'm your primary doctor, and you, young lady, are lucky to be alive. Driving under the influence is a very serious crime."

If I weren't so distracted by the fact that he just said, "Driving under the influence is a very serious crime," I probably would have cowered at his reprimanding tone and the way he keeps calling me young lady. Instead, I sat there staring at him with a blank look on my face, trying to process the words that just came out of his mouth. I guess that answers my earlier question of who caused me to crash. I just wasn't expecting the answer to be me.

It's my fault that I crashed, at least that's what they think. I guess it does look bad. I had alcohol in my system, and okay, I was a little tipsy, but it was not my fault. Someone ran me off the road; there's no way I could have prevented that. Then I remember Zeke telling me I shouldn't drive, and shame sits heavily on my chest. The sorrowful look he had on his face suddenly made sense.

At the heavy feeling of disappointment, I lowered my head out of embarrassment. "It wasn't my fault," I say gingerly, knowing no one will believe me, because why would they? I had alcohol in my system, and that's that. I knew I shouldn't have been driving, but I did it anyway.

"Well, that's not for me to determine." Dr.Craig rebukes. "You can tell that to the cops. They'll want to talk to you anyway." After he has sufficiently scolded me with the vigor of a disappointed father, he finally looks up from the tablet in his hands to tell me about my injuries.

The worst one is my brain. I hit my head hard enough to cause my brain to bleed and swell. The doctor explained that they put me in a coma to give my brain a rest so the swelling and bleeding could heal on their own. "What's the bandage for then?" I asked, confused, pointing to said bandage that's wrapped around my head.

"You had a nasty cut on your hairline." He traces the bandage to indicate where the cut is underneath. "There were a few pieces of glass we pulled out. Stitched you up for a couple of weeks, then took them out to let the wound heal on its own. It's mostly healed, the bandage is just to keep it clean."

Nodding in understanding as the doctor continues, his voice becomes muffled as anxiety niggles at the back of my mind. For some reason, the doctor listing all my injuries is worse than seeing them. I attribute that to the fact that not all of them are visible, making it seem as though there aren't that many. But with the doctor here, in front of me, bringing my attention to every single one makes my chest tighten

The severity of my situation makes it feel like an iron weight is crushing my tender ribs. I pull my hand from my mom's and start to pick at the skin on the side of my thumb out of nervous habit. She stands to rest her hand on my shoulder to soothe me when she notices my growing anxiety.

After telling me my arm and wrist are broken, he moves on to tell me about my broken ribs. Two on my left, and one on my right. They're mostly healed, but there is still some tenderness that is to be expected. The severe bruising on my sternum has mostly healed. The yellow-green bruising on my chest would be proof enough, but the aching with each breath makes me think otherwise.

"Other than that, you're recovering great for someone who was in the state that you were in." He says nonchalantly.

Pinching the bridge of my nose, like that will get rid of the headache I feel coming on, I let out a shaky breath. "I don't mean to sound cold, Josie, I just want you to understand the seriousness of the situation." Dr. Craig utters and gives me a weak smile to show that he's not the complete asshole he was coming across as.

"I can't thank you enough for everything you've done for my Josie." I refrain from rolling my eyes as my mom thanks the doctor in a voice so sweet it's going to give me a cavity. I know she's single, but hello! I'm literally lying in a hospital bed, and just woke up from a three-month nap.

I huff out a breath as I rest my head back against the pillow and squeeze my eyes shut.

Before the doctor leaves, he tells me he'll be back in a couple of hours to check on me, and my nurse should be coming by shortly to bring me some lunch. "Wait!" I shout before he can walk out the door. "When do I get to go home?"

A new level of disappointment hits me as I stand out in front of the hospital, waiting for my ride. I am ecstatic to finally be going home, but when my mom came into my hospital room early this morning to sign my discharge papers and drop off a change of clothes, I thought she would be taking me home.

"Oh no, baby, I'm just here to sign your discharge papers. I have to be at work in twenty minutes." She had said in a rush, leaving some money for me to take the bus. With a kiss to my forehead, she darted out the door, leaving me feeling dejected by my own mother. Tears gathered in the corners of my eyes, but I refused to let them fall, not wanting to be the girl who cries all the time.

Living with a single parent, money is already tight, so for her to miss just a couple of hours of work can sometimes mean we have to choose whether we want power or hot water for the week. Suddenly, I felt selfish for wanting even just a little attentiveness.

School started last week, so I would feel too guilty to ask Kiera or Zeke to come pick me up, but when Kiera called me on her lunch break and I told her I was walking to the bus stop, she wouldn't have it. I wasn't about to argue. I didn't want to take the bus, besides, I still needed to talk to her about Chance. It's been two weeks since I woke up. I've either been busy doing some kind of physical therapy or resting, and with school starting, I still hadn't found the time to talk to her, so this would be the perfect time.

Sitting on a bench waiting for Kiera, with the vase of my favorite flowers I decided to take home, I noticed a large idling black SUV across the parking lot. They're too far away to see who's in the driver's seat. They've been sitting there since I sat down, and I haven't seen anyone get in or out of the vehicle. I decide to pay it no mind, figuring they must be waiting for someone.

Fifteen minutes later, Kiera pulls up in her white Honda Accord. Reaching for the passenger side door handle, I startle when the door swings open and out steps the blue-eyed, blonde-haired asshole I want to junk punch. Also known as Chance.

"Hey Josie, long time no see." I'm dwarfed by his height as he stands in front of me, staring down at me with a toothy smile that doesn't quite reach his eyes. I crane my neck up to scowl at him. Neither of us brings up the reason for the tension in the air, using only our eyes to communicate. His saying *Keep your mouth shut,* and mine saying *You tell her, or I will.*

"Are you ready to go, Josie?" Kiera asks as she walks around her car, snapping us out of our staring contest.

"Let's get the hell out of here," I say, tearing my eyes from Chances. Carefully settling my sore body in the front, Chance slides in the back. "Thanks for picking me up. I was dreading taking the bus."

"Anytime, chick. You should have called sooner."

I shrug, "I didn't want you to miss school because of me." There's an awkward silence. "How is school, by the way?" I'm not so naïve to think that there wouldn't be rumors about my "accident", but I'd rather not be blindsided when I walk in tomorrow.

Picking up on what I was so vaguely asking, Kiera reaches over and pats my leg. "It's not as bad as you think. Most of the gossip is about what happened at Chance's party," she looks at me out of the side of her eye. "But some of it is about you."

I nod my head, having already expected that, though my palms are slick with sweat at the thought of being the center of attention. Unfortunately, I have to go back sometime. The doctor recommended another week to rest, but I'm sick of resting. I need to get back to my normal life before I go stir crazy. Might as well use the rip-it-off like a band-aid approach, and jump back into it.

"Don't worry, Josie, we've got your back." Chance voices from the back seat, patting my shoulder.

My traitorous heart warms at his show of friendship. I'm furious that he not only cheated on Kiera, but I feel betrayed because I thought we were friends. Friends don't do what he did. I try to keep that in the back of my mind, at his supportive words, not wanting to get my hopes up.

Before I can respond, a dog darts out in front of Kiera's

car. She slams on the brakes, and I jerk forward in my seat. A cry escapes my mouth as the seatbelt squeezes my chest and ribs. My grip tightens on the vase as panic consumes my entire body, remembering how I almost died in a steel trap similar to this one.

"Jesus Christ, babe! We just picked her up from the hospital. Are you trying to kill her before we get her home?" I hear Chance say before my hearing becomes fuzzy.

My chest starts to rise and fall at a rapid pace, and my heart feels like it's beating a million miles a minute. My knuckles turn white as my grip tightens on the vase to stop them from trembling. The sound of crunching metal embeds itself into my brain, causing me to hyperventilate. Reaching down to unbuckle my seat belt, I reach for the door handle so I can jump out before the car starts rolling.

"Let me out!" I shout frantically, tugging on the door handle that won't open. "I need to get out. Let me out!" I continue jerking on the handle, but it won't budge. Tears start streaming down my face. "Please, I need to get out. I can't breathe." I yell and start pounding on the window, trying to hold on to the vase with one hand, each breath becoming shorter and shorter.

The door swings open, and I scramble out as fast as I can, dropping the vase in the process, slamming into whoever released me from this coffin of a car. Two warm palms cup my face, and I'm met with those glacial blue eyes, "Breathe."

Chapter Seven

MILO

Sucking in a deep breath smoke fills my lungs, and the taste of woodsy tobacco sits on my tongue. Closing my eyes and tilting my head up to embrace the warmth from the sun, I puff out the smoke with annoyance. I run a hand through my hair to keep from strangling the yapping brunette and her posse that took it upon themselves to track me down in the parking lot. I couldn't tell you what she's droning on about because I only have one thing on my mind.

I tuned her out one and a half cigarettes ago, and if these pricks take any longer, they'll be forking over money for my next pack. At the rate she's talking, I'm bound to make some kind of record for speed smoking through a whole carton.

"...you should come over tonight, we can get in my hot tub." She babbles in the sweetest voice that I'm sure would hook any other guy. Little does she know I have my eyes set on someone far more beautiful and a lot less full of herself. "Come on." She purrs, "We can go skinny dipping." Winking, she steps into me pressing her over inflated tits to my chest.

Christ, this girl doesn't quit, I think as she runs her hands up my chest, testing my patience. Just as she reaches my neck, I snatch her wrists and drop them back down by her sides. "If my lack of a response isn't a big enough hint for you, then let me spell it out for you." I lean down so we're eye level. Anger pinches her eyebrows, but her eyes shoot to my mouth as I wrap my lips around my cigarette and take a deep inhale, then speak. "I would rather go skinny dipping with a toaster than do anything with you." On the last word, I exhale the smoke into her face, and can't help but feel delighted as I watch her cough and splutter around it. Screeching and huffing like the spoiled brat I assume she is, she finally gets the hint and stomps away. Faithful posse in tow.

A smirk takes over my face knowing I pissed her off, and I give a sarcastic finger wave to their retreating backs. My smile gets bigger when I finally see the merry band of assholes making their way toward me. Taking a final puff from my cigarette, I drop it to the ground and grind it into the pavement.

"It's about fucking time. Sophie was about to mount me right here in the parking lot." I let out a small chuckle at the audacity of that girl. Since we stepped foot in Northview High, she's persistently made a pass at every single one of us.

"Sorry," Kyler shrugs, "I was letting Liam know we were leaving for lunch." Climbing into the front seat of my black Range Rover, he jerks his thumb over his shoulder. "Blame it on this asshole. He can barely make it out the door without a dozen chicks throwing themselves at him. "

"Don't be jealous, bro. You just have to learn to roll your R's like I do." Javi says with a shit eating grin on his face, earning an eye roll from Kyler. "Now let's go check on our *Roja*." He puts extra emphasis on the R, as Adrian and Carter laugh from either side of him in the back seat.

At the mention of her, my chest warms with an unfamiliar emotion. I pluck the cigarette from behind my ear and shove it between my lips when that warm feeling turns to a sharp sting. "Yes, let's go check on our Little Fox."

I almost forgot how beautiful she is. Not being able to see her for two weeks has been hard on all of us, but now that she's finally leaving this place, we'll be able to keep a better eye on her.

When I first saw her at that god damn party, I wanted to throw her over my shoulder and take her far away from all the awful things I knew would happen that night. The worst part is she doesn't know half of what went on was because of her. The other half, because of that nasty excuse for a sister.

The only thing that wasn't supposed to happen that night, that wasn't planned, was the car wreck. She was never supposed to be in that fucking car. Guilt digs its ugly claws into us each day, getting deeper and deeper, making us crazy. Carter and Adrian distract themselves with football, while Kyler focuses on Liam and his car. I've been smoking more than a wildfire, and Javi hides behind humor and his playful personality.

All of our hearts belong to our red-headed beauty, and she doesn't even know it yet. I have a bullet with my name on it, because if she ever finds out what happened that night, she'll never forgive us. Not having her in my life is more painful than a bullet to the brain.

At that thought, I reach for the cigarette tucked behind my ear. The car is dead silent as I flick open my favorite Zippo and light up. Everyone's eyes are glued to said beauty sitting on the bench in front of the hospital. The forlorn look on her face makes my palms twitch, wanting to go to her and scoop her up to erase the sad look in her eyes and bring immense pain to whoever put it there.

"Do you think she remembers?" Carter croaks out. I'm sure they're all feeling the same guilt and the urge to go to her as I am.

No one dares to acknowledge Carter's question. Letting it hang heavy in the air, I take another puff of my cigarette, the crackle of the burning paper the only thing that can be heard in the quiet SUV.

A few moments later, when I see her friend Kiera pull up, I pull my phone from my pocket to check the time. "What the fuck is he doing here?" Kyler snarls from next to me. I snap my eyes up to see Josie standing toe to toe with Chance.

"Do you think he would tell her?" Adrian questions with worry in his voice.

"I don't know, but if the stare she's giving him is anything to go by, I'd say she's not his biggest fan." I point out, uneasy with how close he's standing to her.

"He better back the fuck up." The threatening tone in Javi's voice is much less playful than it was minutes ago as we all grunt our agreement.

Seeing the fiery look in her eyes, that only seems to be there when she's standing up for someone she cares about, I can't decide if I'm more turned on by her rare show of fierceness or pissed off that this asshole is putting her on the defensive.

Watching as she gets in the front seat, we follow as they leave the parking lot and drive in the direction of Josie's house. Staying at least two cars behind them so they don't notice we're following them, just to make sure she gets home safe.

Right as that thought leaves my mind, I see her friend's white car jerk to a stop, prompting me to hit the brakes to keep our distance. "What the hell just happened?" I snap out. "They just left the hospital, she doesn't need to end up there five god damn minutes after she just left."

Nobody answers my rhetorical question as we all keep our eyes focused on the passenger seat. That's when I see her fist pounding against the window and the panic-stricken look on her face. My foot is already on the gas when everyone in the vehicle yells "Go!"

I screech to a stop next to her door and jump out, ripping her door open so fast I'm surprised it doesn't detach from the car. She's in such a hurry, I don't think she even noticed anyone opened her door. She crashes into my chest, and the flowers she was holding fall to the ground and the vase shatters into tiny pieces.

Instinctively, my hands reach to cup her face, watching as her big green eyes volley between mine. "Breathe," I say calmly when I see pure terror staring back at me. Rubbing my thumbs softly across her cheeks to wipe away the tears, she brings her hands up and wraps them around my wrists. Squeezing her eyes shut, she takes in a deep breath, blowing it out slowly. "That's it, just like that. Nice and slow." After taking a few more breaths, she opens her eyes, and the terror is replaced with gratitude.

I take a deep breath to steady my own heart at seeing her in such distress. Still rubbing my thumbs on her soft cheeks to keep her calm, I get trapped in her emerald eyes. If the way her eyes hold me captive isn't fortelling, then the way she makes my heart pound should be. Finally able to see her face up close, I take in the smattering of freckles on each cheek that meet in the middle of her button nose. Her plump lips call to my own, and I'm tempted to bury my teeth into her bottom one to see what she tastes like.

Her grip tightens on my wrists, reminding me where we are. Not wanting to lose the feel of her in my hands, I can't bring myself to let go. Who knows when I'll get to touch her again?

"My flowers." She says barely above a whisper. Keeping

her eyes locked on mine, it feels like we're having two different conversations. One with our eyes, and one with our mouths.

"Don't worry," I say just as softly, scared that if I speak too loudly, it will snap us out of this bubble we've found ourselves in. "We can buy you new flowers."

"We?" She asks. She peers over my shoulder to see my car, and a blush crawls over her cheeks. The pink color awakens my desperate dick, and the way she's biting her lip has him begging me to pin her against this car. I hear a groan come from behind me, not entirely sure who it was. I would bet my left testicle I know exactly what they're thinking.

A small grin tugs at my lips, but it drops just as fast when we're interrupted.

"What the hell are you guys doing here?" Kiera asks in an amused tone, with a grin wider than the Grand Canyon.

Ignoring her, I hesitantly drop my hands from my Little Fox's face. "Are you okay?"

Nodding her head, she rests her hand on her chest. "Yeah, I'm just a little sore still." She starts rubbing her chest as a look of humiliation occupies her face. Looking at her feet, she shrugs her shoulders. "And, I guess I was just startled when that dog ran out in front of us."

Reality washes over me like ice-cold water when I realize the reason she had such a visceral reaction to something so small. We're the ones responsible for her fear. Her physical wounds will heal, but her emotional and mental wounds will always be there. We're no better than her sister, or my brother, or anyone else who has ever done her wrong.

Always gets the short end of the stick and never gets the attention she deserves. Paying for other people's actions or being on the receiving end of deceit. We're no better than the people who have made her feel like she's just an afterthought.

Her gorgeous green eyes are my first thought every

morning. Her painfully sweet smile invades my thoughts hourly. Her infectious laughter consumes my thoughts when I lie in bed at night. She is my every waking thought from sunup to sundown.

Nausea burns my stomach like acid. Needing to get the hell out of here, I rush out, "I'm glad you're okay, Josie. We'll see you at school tomorrow." Flashing her a weak smile and jumping in my car, I drive off like the fucking coward I am. I know we don't deserve but like hell am I going to let her slip away when we're this close.

Chapter Eight

JOSIE

After being coaxed back into Kiera's car and driving the few blocks to my house, I barely have time to go over what just happened. There was a reason I was drawn to that black SUV in the parking lot of the hospital, and I don't think it's a coincidence that the men I was drawn to at the party are the same men it belongs to. I could barely speak to the man with those piercing blue eyes, whose name I still don't know, and he was staring at me with heart-fluttering fondness. I'm sure if I weren't in the middle of a freak-out, his intense stare alone would have made me spiral.

Insisting that I'm ok, I finally wave off Kiera and Chance so they can get back to school. Stepping in the front door, I could cry all over again, but happy tears this time. There's nothing like the comfort of your own home, it's like a warm hug after being gone so long. I close my eyes, take in a slow, steady breath, and let the cozy feeling wrap around me.

Shutting the door behind me, I head straight for my room. Kicking off my shoes, pants, and bra, I climb into my bed. Resting my head on my comfy pillow, that seems like a cloud compared to the paper-thin one at the hospital, I let my eyes fall closed. The lack of beeping machines makes it easy to drift off.

Peeling my eyes open after the best sleep I've had in two weeks, I'm shocked to see the dark sky outside. Standing, I stretch my arms above my head and wince at the pull on my sore body. Reaching for my pants, I dig my phone from my front pocket, still amazed that it didn't get damaged in the crash, because seriously, how the hell does this look brand new, and I look like I've been thrown into oncoming traffic?

Sifting through the new messages, I find one from my mom saying she's going to be working late because she picked up another shift. A few from Kiera checking in to make sure I'm ok, but the last one is the one that makes my blood boil. Deciding not to even open the message from Jake, I opt to block his number instead. "Fuck him," I grumble into the quiet of my room, angrily curling my fingers around my phone at the balls on this guy.

Shaking off the anger, I toss my phone on my bed and head for the bathroom. Turning on the shower, I strip down, no longer startled by the bruising and healing scrapes that cover my body when I glance in the mirror. It's what's underneath all that damage that catches my eye. The pasty skin and stretch marks. The lack of muscle and abundance of skin. Thighs big enough to strangle someone, and an ass big enough to crush them. My body has always been my biggest insecurity, and though I did lose a little bit of weight while I was in the hospital, it wasn't enough to stop the loathing I feel for myself. I avert my disappointed eyes, and I step into the warm spray of the shower.

Once I have sufficiently scrubbed the hospital smell from

my body and have washed my hair at least twice, I let the hot water sluice down my body. My pale skin turns pink, feeling the warm liquid cascade over me, lulls me into a sense of tranquility.

A pair of familiar blue eyes pops into my brain suddenly, making the water feel hotter. Dark blue eyes come to mind as I rub the muscle between my neck and shoulder. A tingly presence makes itself known as my hand moves down my neck and between the valley of my breasts, when intense green eyes stare back at me. Light fingers tickle down my stomach when two sets of brown eyes come to mind. One set a chocolate brown, and the other a golden honey brown, both equally piercing and panty-melting.

My heart rate kicks up when soft fingertips dance over my mound, but before I can reach that sweet spot, I jerk my hand back suddenly. Feeling dirty for fantasizing about five gorgeous strangers I barely know or have even talked to, even though I'm sure I'm not the first female to ever fantasize about them. That thought makes irrational jealousy rear its ugly head.

Ugh! Something must have gotten knocked loose when I hit my head. It's the only explanation I can come up with for acting like a jealous Jezebel. Huffing out a heavy sigh, I turn off the shower and step out, wrapping a towel around myself. I saunter back to my room. Slipping on a pair of panties and putting on a tank top, I slide back into bed.

Forcing my mind to stay away from my drool-worthy shower thoughts, I instead wonder the reason why they showed up out of nowhere. I don't think it was serendipity that brought them to Chance's party, and the most traumatic night of my life. Not to mention, I almost died. Twice. I don't know why they've suddenly decided to show their faces, but I can't help but feel like something more sinister is going on.

Before a million theories can run amok in my head, my bedroom window slides open.

As I'm about to let out an embarrassing scream, I recognize the tall frame of the person stepping through. "Zeke, holy balls! You scared the shit out of me."

The night he moved in next door was the first night he came to my open window. His parents had just gotten divorced, and he couldn't sleep because his mom's sad cries were keeping him awake. I'll never forget his red-rimmed, desperate eyes. Wanting to take away his pain, I invited him in, and we stayed up all night talking. He told me how his parents were in the middle of a nasty divorce. How his dad cheated on his mom. He told me about his best friends he had to leave behind, as tears welled in his eyes. Making it apparent that his leaving his friends was the reason for his bloodshot eyes.

From that moment on, he's been the best friend I've ever had. There isn't a night that goes by that I don't leave my window unlocked for him. Even though he doesn't come by every night, I still want him to know I'm always here for him.

He lets out a little chuckle, closing the window. "Sorry. I was trying to be quiet. I figured you would be sleeping." Reflexively scooting over so he can lie in his usual spot next to me, he kisses me on the tip of my nose. The comfortable routine comes so naturally, as if it hasn't been almost four months since the last time we were here.

"I'm glad you came by. I've been wanting to talk to you." I snuggle further into my bed." And I wanted to have this conversation before school started." I start to chew on my lip, feeling unnecessarily nervous. "I know you've been busy with football and school. I've been a little preoccupied as well. I wanted to talk to you in person, in private." Okay, I'm just rambling now, and Zeke notices my nervous habit.

"It's okay, babe." He consoles, taking my hand and

holding it in his against his chest." I know it's been hard finding the right time. You just woke up from a three-month coma. Give yourself a break." Nodding my head, deciding on where to start. I decide to deflect instead. A little deflecting never hurt anyone. Right?

"How's football going?" I chew on the inside of my cheek, waiting for him to call me out on my "distraction".

"It's good. Coach has us practicing twice a day, although I don't mind. We have two new players this year, and I spend most of practice drooling over them. Do you know how hard it is to play football with a boner?" He jokes. At least I think he's joking.

I shriek out a surprised giggle at his admission, then give him an admission of my own. "Do you know how hard it is to go almost four months without any release?" At that, I wiggle my eyebrows at him playfully.

"Alright, you win." Chuckling, he pulls me closer to tuck my head against his chest. "I'm so glad you're back, JoJo." I sigh into his chest contentedly, but that's short-lived with the words that come out of his mouth next. "Now, quit deflecting and tell me what happened."

"Okay." I huff. I know I'm not going to get out of this, and it's been put off for too long. So, I tell him what happened. From when I got off the phone with him that night to the strangers who stopped to see if I was ok. I told him how terrified I was, that I thought I was going to die, that I just gave up at one point because I didn't know what else to do.

After I've finished, the heavy silence is deafening. He's so quiet, I don't know how to take it. The rise and fall of his chest is the only indicator that he's even alive. His arms feel tense around me, but he isn't squeezing me. I don't know how he's feeling, but the silence becomes too much, and I feel obligated to fill it. "I'm sorry, Zeke. I should never have gotten into that car. I should have listened to you."

Still nothing. I slowly crane my head to look up at him, and almost flinch when I see the thunderous look on his face. He's not looking at me like I expect, he's just staring straight ahead. I've never seen him so mad; if he clenches his teeth any harder, they'll shatter. "Zeke?" I whisper, scared to make any sudden movements or loud noises.

Finally, finally, he looks down at me. The look of rage mixed with pain that I see swirling in his hazel eyes has me taken aback. I don't know whether to hug him or back away slowly. There's so much emotion in his eyes it's overwhelming, so I lower my chin instead, resting it back on his chest.

He places a finger under my chin and tilts my head so I can meet his eyes once again. "Did you say you gave up?" Not knowing how to answer that I keep my mouth shut. It's hard to explain what kind of mindset you're in in a situation like that.

"Zeke, I-"

"No, Josie. I know you were in a shitty situation, but you don't give up." He growls as remorse fills my veins. I stare at him blankly, not knowing what to say to him. Something passes over his eyes, and his face softens. "I don't know what I would do without you. You don't ever give up. Do you hear me?" Bringing a hand to cup my cheek, he rests his forehead on mine.

"I just……I wasn't……I felt so……" Defeated at trying to find the right words, I place my hand over his. "I'm sorry. You're my best friend, I don't know what I would do without you either." With that, a hush settles over the room, as we both soak up the support of the others' words.

"Do you know who it could've been?" His shaky voice breaks the quiet.

"No. I couldn't see the vehicle, but I remember their

headlights reflecting off my rear-view mirror. I'm assuming it was a bigger vehicle, like a truck or something."

Breathing out a hulking sigh, air puffs up his cheeks. He scoots closer to me, and I roll onto my side, so his chest is pressed to my back. "We'll figure it out, but promise me you'll never do that again?"

"I'll do you one better; I'm never touching alcohol again. I've more than learned my lesson." I hold up my pinky to him, and he wraps his around mine as I give him the sacred pinky promise.

Yawning as I close my eyes, I slide my hand under my pillow to feel the coolness underneath, a tired hmm leaves my lips. "I missed this, but if you start snoring, I will kick your ass off my bed," I say, attempting to lighten the mood.

"There she is." He laughs, and the comfortable sound makes me snuggle in closer to his chest. "Get some sleep. You have a big day tomorrow." He kisses my hair and drapes his arm over my side, careful of my sore ribs.

Unfortunately, he's right. A sense of foreboding plants itself in my chest, but I know that having my best friend at my back, it doesn't seem so bad.

"Love you, Z."

"Love you too, JoJo." I hear him mumble something else under his breath, but can't quite make it out as sleep gets its hold on me.

Chapter Nine

JOSIE

One thing I did not miss is the fury-inducing sound of an alarm clock. Hitting snooze for the fifth time, I decide it's time to get out of bed. Rubbing the sleep from my eyes, I heave myself from the luxurious comfort that has nothing on that slab of concrete I was sleeping on at the hospital. With a groan that could rival that of a zombie, I stretch until the ache in my torso causes me to flinch. Throwing on my pink fluffy robe, I snuggle into the soft material as I swing my bedroom door open.

Just as I open my door, I'm met with the back of a stranger quietly closing the door across from mine as if he's trying not to wake anyone else in the house and alert them to his walk of shame. As the stranger turns around, my eyes widen when they connect with the familiar face, and I realize he's not a stranger at all. In fact, he's also a senior this year at Northview High and a jerk to the highest degree.

He runs his eyes up my body as a hungry look takes over his face. "Josie." He smiles smugly. "Where have you been hiding that body?" I look down and notice that I forgot to close my robe. My face flushed at Cody getting a look at me in my panties and tank top. Embarrassment flushes through me as I tie my robe closed, cinching it a little too aggressively when I think about how disgusted he must be of all my flaws. My thick thighs still peek out from under my robe, and my stomach is far from flat. His comment is a little confusing, and I don't know if he's mocking me or trying to make me uncomfortable.

Either way, this suddenly feels like my walk of shame.

"What are you doing here, Cody? I mean, other than contracting syphilis." I ask, folding my arms across my chest, annoyed that he saw me in such a vulnerable state."You may want to go get a shot of penicillin, you know, just to be safe." I add picking at the skin on my thumbs, humiliation making me snap defensively.

A sinister expression takes over his face, but as he goes to speak, the door behind him swings open and the blonde-haired devil steps out. "What are you still doing here?" She asks Cody with a sweetness I know is false.

Ignoring her question, he peruses my body once more. "See you at school, Josie." He winks smugly, and I want to gag.

My body unclenches when I hear the front door close, and I continue my trek to the kitchen. "I hope you're going to do something with your hair." Ashley scolds to my retreating back, all sweetness wiped from her tone as I leave her to stand in her doorway.

Deflecting her words with my own so she doesn't see how they affect me, my mouth runs away from me, wanting to get my own dig in. "You know, I'm pretty sure this makes you a pedophile. He's still in high school, and you're eighteen. You're technically an adult now."

"It was consensual." She screeches.

"Yeah, I don't think that would hold up in court, but hey, maybe you could sleep with the judge." I snark as an unwanted image of Jake driving into her creeps into my mind. I brace myself for her usual vitriol, but it never comes.

She slams her door hard enough to rattle the wall, and my steps slightly falter from surprise at her lack of hostility. I hiss when I press my finger to the hot coffee pot, expecting to wake up from this dream any minute now. Confusion swamps me when I don't bolt up right in bed, gasping for air. Shaking it off, I pour myself a cup of coffee before I'm late for my first day of school, and head back to my room.

Pulling on an old Ramones band t-shirt and a pair of black skinny jeans, I pair with my red Converse. Thankfully, my red hair is naturally wavy, and all I have to do is run a brush through it. Most days. I swipe some mascara over my lashes, some soft pink lip gloss on my lips, and fasten my favorite black velvet choker around my neck. Ready to go, I snatch my backpack off the chair at my desk and shove my phone into my front pocket.

Topping off my coffee with enough creamer to give me a sugar high to go with my caffeine high, I'm out the door. Normally, I would catch a ride with Zeke, but his coach has them practicing twice a day, plus I'm not comfortable being in a car right now. Luckily, the school is only up the street from my house, so walking the few blocks isn't much of a hindrance.

The closer I get, the slower my steps get. When the school comes into view, I have to stop and take a couple of deep breaths to calm my nerves. "You can do this. You can do this. You can do this." I chant over and over in my head. The backbone I seemed to develop during my interaction with Ashley is nowhere to be found, and my feet have turned leaden. Breathing in one last deep breath, I force myself to move.

Reaching the parking lot, the chanting in my head quickly turns to "Turn around. Turn around. Turn around." I grip the strap of my backpack with the hand that isn't trying to strangle the life from my coffee. My knuckles are turning white, and it feels like there's a hundred-pound weight strapped around my ankles, making me drag my feet.

Doing my best to ignore all the watchful eyes, I weave my way through the parking lot. I keep my head down when the whispers and mumbles from the vultures that are my peers start, propelling my anxiety up a few notches. My hands start to tingle, I resist the urge to try and shake the feeling away, not wanting to look like a crazy person.

Unable to find Kiera as I scan the sea of students standing around the front of the building, socializing before the bell rings, I decide fuck it, I'll find her later. Climbing the stairs to the front doors, I hear a loud rumbling behind me. Uninvited butterflies flutter to life in my stomach at the sight that greets me when I glance back at the parking lot.

The chatter amongst everyone dies down when the hottest car I've ever seen pulls into the parking lot. Everyone stops to stare as it's followed by a black SUV I'd now recognize anywhere. The tingling that was in my hands has moved pleasantly throughout my body, as my foolish heart pitter-patters to the visceral reactions their mere presence pulls from me. When he said, "We'll see you at school tomorrow." I didn't know what to think, but I wouldn't have thought that meant they were enrolled here. To be fair, I was in a bit of an emotional state when he said that.

The old ruby red muscle car pulls into an empty spot right up front, the black SUV doing the same. They certainly didn't waste any time making themselves comfortable.

Pinching the bridge of my nose out of annoyance that the little interactions with them have turned me into a blushing idiot, I turn to make my way inside the school. Regrettably, when I turn around, I'm met with that same stupid smiling face I saw this morning. Only now he's flanked by his equally jerkish friends. I tilt my head up to the sky and let out an exasperated sigh. Luck is not on my side this morning.

"We have to quit meeting like this," Cody says, and his friends laugh like funnier words have never been spoken. I roll my eyes and go to walk around him, and he steps in front of me so abruptly that I crash into him. He reaches out to steady me, causing me to drop my coffee, the brown liquid splashing onto my shoes. His hand grips my bad arm, and a wince escapes my lips.

"You're hurting me." I whimper. "Let go." I try using a stern voice, but it comes out weak. All I can focus on is the throbbing that's forming in my arm under the pressure of his grip.

"I see your pain tolerance isn't as high as your sisters." I want to punch the triumphant look off his face, but the threatening step he takes toward me has my heart dropping to the ground, and the insecurity I felt this morning rears its ugly head. "But we can change that." He leans to whisper in my ear, pressing his chest into mine. If I had eaten anything for breakfast, I would've thrown it up all over his shirt at his vile comment.

"If you don't back up, I'll snap your arm like a twig, and then we'll see who has a high pain tolerance." The breath I had been holding rushes out at the growly voice behind me. Cody's eyes flick up to the person standing there, vexation clouding his eyes. Reluctantly, he lets go of my arm, never looking away from whoever the threat came from. He straightens his spine and puffs out his chest in a laughable show of dominance.

I cradle my arm against my chest and take a step back, never taking my eyes from the asshole in front of me. The warm presence at my back has me sagging with relief. His warmth wraps around me, as I fight the urge to plant myself against him like a lizard on its favorite rock, soaking up the sun.

"This isn't over," Cody growls with a menacing scowl on his face when he looks at me. The deadly look he's giving me causes goosebumps to rise on my arms. His fearsome words sound more like a promise than a statement, and a shiver works its way up my spine. Cody's always been a bully, but I have no idea what I have done to be on the receiving end of it. Other than this morning, I've only ever seen him at school, and even then, I tried to steer clear of him. Thankfully, he walks away and I feel like I can take a full breath.

Realizing the audience that has gathered, my face glows bright red. Fortunately, people begin milling about once they realize the show's over. Turning ever so slowly to the faces I know I'll be greeted with once I turn around, I'm surprised to see the tattooed giant standing behind me.

A concerned look pinches his eyes when he sees me cradling my arm against my chest. "Are you hurt?" His deep voice rumbles.

Mother Mary! His question is drowned out as I take my fill of this gorgeous man. His crossed arms make his biceps look even bigger, if that's even possible, and his form-fitting t-shirt makes it easy to see the lines of his abs. His left arm is decorated in black ink that no high school student has any business having. He towers over me, making me have to tilt my head to look up at him. He has a hoop pierced through the right side of his nose, and the look in his eyes has gone from concerned to amused. No doubt it's from my ogling. It's not my fault he's a freaking dreamboat covered in ink.

Clearing my throat, "My arm is a little sore, but it's nothing a little Tylenol won't fix." The amusement is replaced by so much rage, I'm surprised smoke isn't coming out of his ears.

A small hand comes to land on his shoulder, and for the

first time, I notice a similarly blonde-haired boy with almost the same eye color as the gentle giant. He is significantly shorter, but he has the happiest smile on his face that goes from ear to ear. His infectious grin causes my smile to make itself present. "Is this the girl you guys are always talking about?" I hear a groan from his other side and take in the other two familiar faces. I'm not sure which one of them groaned, but are they blushing? I would laugh if I weren't blushing myself.

"Liam, dude, come on. We've talked about this. Think before you speak." The big guy huffs out.

"Whatever, bro, she has pretty hair. I can see why you guys like her." He turns his grin on me, and his cheeks pinken as if he only just realized what he said. He ducks his head and takes off. Not entirely sure of what the hell just happened, I laugh and shake my head at this whole situation.

"Sorry about him. He's harmless." The big guy says, watching after the boy with a sympathetic look on his face.

"No problem. It's just...that was unexpected." I reply, feeling my mood lift at his sweet compliment.

"Meeting someone with Down Syndrome?" he questions curiously.

"No. However, he is sweet. There's just been a lot of surprises this morning, and I'm not sure what to make of them." I answer honestly, looking at three of those surprises. I'm not sure how I expected my first day to go, but I didn't expect them to be my white knights, yet again.

All three men look stoic at my words. Not knowing what to say. The air around us grows awkward with silence, and I start to shift on my feet. "Well, I'd better get going. I still need to get my schedule and find my locker." I give them a small smile and an awkward little wave as I spin around to walk inside.

I hear a "We'll see you later, Little Fox." And I'm not sure what to make of that, so I decide to just tuck it to the back of my mind as I head for the office. If how my morning started is any indicator for the rest of the day, it's going to be interesting.

M aking my way out of the office, schedule in hand, I set out to find my locker. Turning down the senior hallway, time basically stands still when just about every head turns to stare in my direction. No longer caring if I hear them gossiping or not when they speak to each other.

"I heard she stole one of Chance's cars." Someone states

"I thought she got shot?" Another questions

"I heard she was one of the shooters." Someone replies.

Each piece of gossip is like a slap to the face. Doing my best to tune them out is becoming impossible with each outlandish rumor. Keeping my head down, I fight the urge to run and hole up in a bathroom stall until class starts. A warm liquid touches my fingertips, and when I look down, the raw skin on the sides of my thumbs is bleeding. I hadn't even noticed that I started picking at them; the nervous habit comes so naturally.

"What happened?" Kiera asks, and I couldn't be happier to see a friendly face in this sea of gossipers. Not wanting any more attention than is already on me, I quickly change the subject as she falls in line to walk next to me.

"I was looking for you this morning," I state as I pluck a tissue from my backpack and wrap my thumbs.

"Sorry, I was running late. I had to pick up Chance." At his name, I'm reminded I still haven't talked to her, but school is not the place to have that conversation.

"Do you want to hang out after school? I need to talk to you." Wiping fingers on the tissue. I finally find my locker and spin the lock, avoiding the curious look I'm sure is on her face.

After shoving some of my binders into my locker to lessen the weight of my backpack, I'm proven right when I turn to see Kiera looking at me with a raised brow. "Is this about Jake? He's been asking about you." Hearing that fuck boy's name, I have to force back a snarl, because unfortunately, it is partly about him.

"Partly, but it's not what you think. Just meet me at my house after school?"

"Sure, babe." She answers, plucking my schedule from my hands. "Oh girl, we have second and fifth period together." She links her arm through mine. "Our teachers are going to hate us. It'll be so much fun." She's bouncing on her toes with excitement.

"Maybe they'll hate you. You talk enough for both of us." I tease her, her shoulder nudges mine playfully. "You could just inch your skirt up a few more inches, and you could probably get away with whatever you want." I sarcastically point out her already short skirt. She gets a wicked gleam in her eye, telling me she was already planning on it.

"You know me so well." She says, sarcastically giving me a quick peck on the cheek and sauntering away. I shake my head at her, wishing I had her confidence.

The bell rings right as I walk through the door of my first period, photography. I make my way to the back of the class, taking the only empty seat left. The side eye glances and snickering aren't lost on me. Photography has been my savior, inside and outside of school, and I refuse to let these people perturb me from it.

When I was thirteen, I took my first photography class, and quickly realized how much I love capturing people's emotions. What started as just taking pictures of friends and family morphed into birthdays and celebrations of all kinds.

The sense of fulfillment I get from capturing raw emotion on film is rewarding, as I get to see the looks of adoration on clients' faces when they see the pictures.

Not being able to be behind my camera for almost four months makes my skin itch.

After Mrs. Whipple takes roll and class begins, everything else is drowned out. All my attention is on the lesson, and before I know it, the bell rings signaling that class is over. "Josie." Mrs. Whipple calls. "See me after school so I can give you the assignments you missed last week."

Nodding my head in acknowledgment, I stroll on to my next class. Second-period math and third-period history, thankfully, are uneventful. Fortunately, having Kiera in my math class made it seem to go quicker. Unfortunately, I was on my own in history, making it seem like the class was never going to end. Sadly, fourth-period science is just as lonely. Sophie and her bitch brigade made sure of it. Trying to ignore them is impossible; their gossiping is so loud I would be able to hear them if I were still in a coma.

Their giggling and gossiping start to grate on my nerves. The teacher pays them no mind as he carries on with his lecture, surprising me that he in no way reprimands them. Of course, when he hands out the assignment, their chatter only gets louder as I will the time to go faster so I can flee from this torment.

"How did her ass get bigger? She was asleep for three months." Sophie states so loudly that the whole class hears. Some chuckle while others look at me with pity, and insecurity paralyzes my tongue.

My chin starts to tremble when tears threaten to fall. Rather than scolding them for their hurtful comments, I berate my pathetic self for not taking a stand. It's different when I chastise myself for my appearance, but when I hear that people see and think the same thing? I want to shrivel up and die.

Startling when I feel a stinging in my hands, the bell rings before I think anything of it. Ignoring the loud cackling that sounds out behind me, I dart out the door. Shoving past students on a mission to get to fuck out of here.

Rushing outside, I power walk to a side of the school that people rarely go to. Leaning up against the brick wall, I wrap my arms around myself to quell some of the shame I feel coursing through my veins. A small sob escapes my throat, finally letting the tears fall with no one around to see them.

What the hell is wrong with me? I just fucking sat there and let them say those things about me. How can I think so little of myself that I let other people treat me that way? *Because you know they're right, and how can you argue with someone when you have no argument?*

Shaking my head at my cowardice, I squeeze myself tighter. Hoping the squeezing will distract me from my thoughts long enough to stop the flow of tears. To my surprise, it's not the squeezing that distracts me, but the smooth, sultry voice I hear coming from my left.

"Who did this to you?" The sound of his voice doesn't match the set of hostility on his face.

Focusing on the six studs in front of m- wait! Six? My brows pinch in confusion. I thought Kiera said there were only five?

Chapter Ten

JOSIE

Have you ever looked at someone you've known for most of your life and seen them in a different light? Like a friend, for example, you've only ever seen them as a friend. Someone who makes you laugh and knows how to make you feel better when you cry. Someone who is always there for you in good times and in bad times. Someone who isn't afraid to tell you when you're wrong or when you're making a mistake.

Then one day, there's a moment when you're looking at them. It's like a veil has been lifted from your eyes, and you *see* them. You couldn't see who they were the whole time because you only had your "friend" goggles on. Everything comes into focus, and you not only realize how smart, loyal, and dependable they are, but you realize how their mere presence consoles you. How their hugs feel homey, and how their words make you feel better.

That's how I feel looking at the sixth figure in this little group, but then my eyes come back into focus as Zeke steps forward, and I force the "friend" goggles back over my eyes. Too scared and confused with all the feelings I'm feeling in this moment of clarity.

"Josie, what happened?" Zeke says softly, taking a step toward me, pulling me against his chest.

Shaking my head before I even get the words out, because I know how he'll react when I tell him. "It's nothing." I sniffle. "I'm just having a bad day." He knows Sophie is one of my biggest tormentors, and he's not exactly one to stand by and do nothing.

I hear feet shuffling behind him and notice the other five have stepped closer. Crowding behind Zeke, six sets of eyes are focused on me. Normally, the attention would make me squirm, but this feels shockingly comfortable.

"Was it Sophie?" The gentle giant asks. "I saw her come out of the same classroom you ran out of, cackling like a deranged hyena."

I snort out a small laugh at the image. Coyly tucking a strand of hair behind my ear, my attention snaps to the blood that's trickling down my thumb.

"What the hell is that?" Mister ice blue eyes practically snarls.

"It's just a nervous habit I do when I get anxious," I mumble as my cheeks turn red out of humiliation. Pulling the tissue from my pocket that I used this morning, everyone frowns at it, noticing the already dried blood on it, realizing that this isn't the first time I've had this little issue today. Not wanting to talk about it, I quickly changed the subject.

"Are you guys all, like, friends now, or something?" I question looking at Zeke because I had no idea he started hanging out with them.

"I'm on the football team with Carter and Adrian." He points them out, and I have to bite the inside of my cheek to stop from smiling. There's no doubt in my mind they're the two new players he told me about. If I were a guy, I would probably have a boner right now. He gives me a small wink, knowing where my train of thought has gone. "Milo, Kyler, and Javi saw you run out of class. I was walking out of class with Adrian and Carter when we saw them walking after you, so we followed."

Glad that I can finally put names to faces brightens my mood, but then I hear a familiar voice that has me wanting to rip my skin off, rather than just picking at it.

"Leave her alone." I see everyone's posture stiffen at the voice, and the tension in the air becomes suffocating. All six of them slowly turn around to look at the idiot who dares to tell them what to do, blocking me from view. Zeke pulls me into his side to show support, draping an arm around my shoulder.

"Jake." Milo snaps. "Why are you here? This doesn't concern you." I watch as he pulls a cigarette out from behind his ear, a silver lighter from his pocket, and lights it. "Besides, shouldn't you be off fucking her sister?"

Great. So everybody knows. Mortification washes over me. One, because Zeke tried to tell me what an asshole he is, and two, because who hasn't slept with my sister, and three, because I'm the idiot who had a crush on him.

"What the fuck!" my best friend yells out next to me, squeezing my shoulder. I can hear his teeth grinding from how hard his jaw is clenched. Okay, so obviously not everybody knew.

Jake has the decency to look embarrassed. A red tint heats his cheeks, but I can't tell if it's from anger or embarrassment. "That's none of your business." Jake hisses out.

Milo chuckles like he can't believe what a dumbass his half-brother is. "Well then, brother," He says sardonically, and I can hear the smile in his voice. "Maybe the next time you're talking on the phone about your sexcapades, you should make sure no one is around."

Instead of acknowledging his comment, Jake's eyes lock

on mine. "Can I talk to you? Please." He sounds so ashamed, I almost want to hear him out.

I feel a warm hand wrap around mine, intertwining our fingers. Looking next to me, I see a sympathetic look in Carter's golden brown eyes, framed by the thick black frames of his glasses. A small smile tips his mouth up when he raises our linked hands between us. I see the raw, angry skin on my thumb and the understanding look in his eyes. Realizing he linked our hands together to prevent me from terrorizing the skin further. He places a soft kiss on my hand before he lowers it back down. I give him an appreciative smile before I turn back to Jake.

"I don't care to hear what you have to say, Jake," I say sternly

"Come on, Josie. At least let me apologize." He whines.

"Fine." I wait expectantly for him to utter those two simple words, but he just stands there awkwardly with all of us staring at him. "Well?"

"Can we talk in private?" He asks, rubbing at the back of his neck.

"No." I rush out, getting impatient. "You can tell me here. In front of all of them." Not one of them says a word or moves, for that matter. They all stand like statues, giving me their silent support, and dammit if that doesn't make me feel giddy.

"You shouldn't be hanging out with them. They're bad ne-"

"You do not get to tell me what I should and shouldn't be doing. You made it abundantly clear that you don't care about me when you slept with my sister." I grit out, annoyed that he thinks he has the right to tell me who I shouldn't be talking to. The reminder of him with my sister lights a fire in my veins, and I don't think I could stop my mouth now, even if I wanted to. "If you want to talk about bad news, we can talk about the cesspool that is Ashley. Did you have fun? Was it everything you hoped it would be?" My voice is shaky, attempting to hold back my angry tears. "I certainly hope so, because it killed our friendship. Now you're just one more pitiful jerk who got to bury himself in her dick graveyard, proving once again that no one gets out alive."

My heavy breathing is the only thing that can be heard; no one even bothers to fill the silence, letting my words fester. Carter gives a slight squeeze to my hand, bringing my attention to the death grip I have on his. Loosening my grip so I don't break his knuckles, I look up to see pride in his eyes. Giddiness makes me tingle all over again.

"Josie, I," Jake goes to take a step, but is swiftly cut off by Javi.

"You need to leave." He growls, and the others grunt in agreement.

Ignoring them, Jake keeps his eyes on mine. He looks so shameful and sorrowful, I start to feel bad for my harsh words. I find myself wanting to apologize to him for my hurtful words. I bite down on my lip to stop myself from speaking and turn to hide my face in Zeke's shoulder.

He finally gets the hint, and I hear his feet dragging as he walks away. Just as I lift my head from Zeke's shoulder, I see a small purplish pink hickey peeking out from beneath the collar of his shirt. Curiosity has me raising my eyebrow as a guilty look mars his face. I know he knows that I saw it because he won't look me in the eye. Which has me even more curious.

Before I can question him, Adrian speaks for the first time, and I find myself wanting to bathe myself in his deep voice, and I feel the need to run my hands over his cocoa skin.

"God, I can't stand him." He spits, looking at his phone. "We have to get out of here." Something niggles at the back of my mind at hearing those familiar words, but I can't quite put my finger on it. "We're going to be late."

Carter gives my hand one last squeeze, Zeke kissing my temple before he steps away, leaving me feeling cold. I want to reach out and pull them back, but I don't want to look needy.

"We have to go, Little Fox," Milo says, coming to stand in front of me. His hand cups the side of my neck, rubbing his thumb across my jaw. "Are you going to be okay?"

Bobbing my head up and down, speechless, looking at his emotion-filled eyes. "Call us if you need anything," he states.

"I don't have your number," I say in almost a whisper.

"You have mine." Zeke points out and successfully pulls me away from Milo's eyes.

"Wait! You're leaving too?" I ask with a slight frown on my face.

"Yes. We have to go talk to coach." He gestures between himself, Carter, and Adrian.

"We have to go meet someone for lunch," Kyler speaks up, coming next to me and placing a kiss on my forehead, then stepping back.

"Promise you'll call Zeke if you need anything?" Javi asks, and I nod my head, unsure of what to make of all this affection. Too caught off guard to question it. "Good. We'll see you later, Red." He cups my cheek tenderly, then steps away.

"I'm proud of you, Little Fox," Milo says, placing a kiss on my cheek. They all begin walking away, just before they're out of sight, Adrian turns to lock eyes with me, the intense look he's giving me has me holding my breath. He looks like he's warring with himself. The look in his eyes is a mixture of anguish and annoyance. He's holding himself back, but I have no idea why.

Not sure how to take that, I head for the doors to go inside for lunch, completely disoriented by everything that just happened. My gut is telling me I shouldn't trust five random strangers whom I barely even know. My gut is also telling me there is more to them than meets the eye. The night they mysteriously showed up, all hell broke loose, and I don't think it was a coincidence.

My stupid, contradicting heart is telling me I can trust them. I hardly know these men, yet already they've shown me more affection and care than anyone in my family has, at least lately. I know my heart is going to win, and I should listen to my brain, but the way my body reacts to them when they're around is addictive. I should be more intimidated that I'm attracted to five men, but for some reason, it just feels normal, it feels right. Which just goes to show I need to listen to my brain because with five men there's only one way this can end, and it's not with a happily ever after.

***

"Girl, if you don't jump on at least one of them, some other desperate girls here will." Kiera so helpfully points out after I tell her what happened only moments ago. She says it so loud that a few guys at the next table over look at us with interest.

"Could you say that a little louder? I don't think they heard you over on the other side of the cafeteria." I say jokingly, trying to cover my embarrassment with humor.

"Nope, we heard you, but who are you talking about?" Chance says, plopping down next to Kiera. Unfortunately, his best friend followed him over and sits on his opposite side.

"No one," I say quickly before my best friend can answer. I give her a look that says If you say anything, I will murder you where you sit. She giggles and shakes her head. Promptly changing the subject, I ask her, "You're still coming over after school, right?"

Chance's shoulders stiffen just slightly at my question. "We're supposed to have dinner with my parents." He reminds Kiera. She looks at him with uncertainty on her face, like this is news to her.

"It's okay." I throw out. "You can come over after. My mom will be at work all night, and I'm sure Ashley will be gone." The mention of her name has both Jake and Chance's eyes flicking in my direction. Jake is giving me the biggest puppy dog eyes, and Chance's are filled with desperation. "Just text me when you're done with dinner."

Giving Chance a look of determination to let him know I will be telling her whether he likes it or not.

After lunch, we split from the boys and head to our fifth-period English class. It turns out English is just as boring as the rest of my other classes. Well, except for photography, of course, but having Kiera there to distract me makes the time go much quicker. Constantly giggling and whispering at the back of the class, we got more than a few reprimanding looks from Mrs. Porter.

I mean, who can sit in a class with their best friend and not get into a few shenanigans? I'm pretty sure that it's in the best friend handbook to annoy at least one person. If you don't, are you really even best friends?

When the bell rings, ending fifth period, I head for my last class of the day. The one I've been dreading the most because I'm about as athletic as a newborn giraffe. Stepping into the locker room to change for my dreaded gym class, I find an empty locker to put my backpack in and head for a bathroom stall so I can change into my gym clothes. I've never been one comfortable enough to change in front of other people. More power to those who are; I just don't have the confidence to do so.

I know I've made the right choice in doing so when I hear a voice that's like nails on a chalkboard, Sophie. Great. I wait in the stall until the locker room clears out, not having the energy to deal with her right now. I know once I walk back into the gym, I won't have a choice.

Once I've made it out into the gym to find out that we're playing dodgeball, I want to pull the. "I just got into a car accident, and I'm still sore in some spots." card, but I know that will only give more ammo to the she-devil glaring daggers at me from the other side of the court.

The game starts, and balls are tossed from both sides of the court. I'm doing surprisingly well until some of my teammates are eliminated, and there are fewer people to hide behind. One of Sophie's followers zero in on me and hurls a ball in my direction. Luckily, I'm able to dodge it, but unfortunately, it distracts me from Sophie just as she launches a ball at me, hitting me on my still tender chest. A dull pain radiates throughout my chest, and I try to breathe through it, placing a palm on the area, trying to rub out the ache.

Shuffling off the court to sit on the bench with my fellow teammates, who are also out, another ball comes flying in my direction and slams into my ribs. Hissing out as pain strangles me, I wrap my arms around myself to ease some of the discomfort.

"Alright, Sophie, you're out. If you can't play fairly, you'll be sitting out for the rest of class." The teacher rebukes.

"But it slipped. I didn't mean to." She whines in that obnoxiously spoiled tone that says she turns into a toddler when she doesn't get her way. Stomping over to the bench, she plops down and glares at me like it's my fault.

Mr. Suttlemeyer takes pity on me and lets me sit out for the rest of the class. I dash to the locker room when class ends. Changing as fast as possible in the bathroom stall, I snatch my bag from my locker, toss in my gym clothes, and haul ass out just as the bell rings. The cackling at my back doesn't go unnoticed, but I pay no mind to it.

I just want to go home, crawl into bed, and sleep for the rest of the year.

Wincing, as I try to carry my backpack on my back, a light throb emits through my chest and side. Deciding to carry my bag by its strap, I make the rounds to each class for make-up work.

Walking outside feeling the warm sun heat my skin, has me sigh in relief that the day is finally over. Strolling down the sidewalk to make my way home, I send a text to Kiera to let her know she can head over whenever she's done with Chance.

I know he's trying to keep her away from me, but I need to tell her. I've been sitting on this information for too long, and I'm starting to feel guilty. I wonder if the guys know that it wasn't just Jake who slept with my sister, or if they know that it was Chance, too. That makes me feel even worse. All these people know what an asshole he is, yet she's making heart eyes at him every day, not suspecting a thing.

Before I can finish that thought, a loud, familiar rumbling comes from behind me. I freeze to the spot as a gorgeous, dark ruby red car pulls up next to me. If the hot muscle car didn't get me going, then the hot-as-sin specimen behind the wheel does.

Chapter Eleven

KYLER

The acrid smell of blood permeates the air as Javi continues his assault on the unfortunate victim tied to the wooden chair in the middle of this dingy warehouse. This is not the first time we've been here, nor is it the last. You would think the asshole tied to the chair would learn his lesson, but just like us, this is not the first or last time he will be here. This is the third time this month alone that we've had to collect from him. Then again, you would also think that Matteo would stop allowing him to sleep with his girls. Sometimes I can't help but think that he does it on purpose, just so he can keep us in his back pocket.

Since we were freshmen, Javi's uncle Mateo has been trying to get us to join his gang. We've all seen how that lifestyle can destroy a person's life. If you grew up in the poorest neighborhood on the southside like Javi did, it's inevitable, and given that his uncle is the leader of the most notorious gang, he never really had a chance at a normal life.

We've all been connected at the hip since we were kids, and we refused to let Javi succumb to that lifestyle alone. We made a deal with Mateo that in exchange for Javi becoming a part of the family business, we would be his muscle and do his dirty work until we graduate. Of course, we know it's not going to be that easy. He's not just going to let us leave, which is why we have a plan to get the hell out of dodge the second we graduate. At least we did, until we laid our eyes on the most beautiful woman to ever exist.

About eight months ago, we received an assignment from Mateo to collect a debt. Normally, we collect money, rough people up a bit, or pick up shipments. So when he told us the debt was a seventeen-year-old girl we about said fuck it and fled the state then, but I couldn't do that to Liam.

A hushed silence fell over Milos Land Rover the second we saw her at that park, you could've heard the drop of a cotton ball. None of us uttered a single word upon laying our eyes on her. I still remember the way my heart palpitated with adoration at her striking appearance. Her natural beauty could start wars, and her curvy figure could make a priest sin. The genuine smile that played across her face and her tinkling laughter had me reaching down to readjust myself. She doesn't even notice all these perverted old men, with their kids, staring at her like she'll cure their loveless marriages. Fuck, if that doesn't make her all the more gorgeous.

My heart thundered with resentment at the piece of shit who sold her off like cattle when Adrian voices what everyone else is thinking "What are we going to tell Mateo?" Not once did he take his eyes from her. The tension in the car became stifling as we came up with a plan. Knowing that he would use her as one of his "escorts", we convinced him to wait to collect her until she turns eighteen, and with the help of others, we would keep watch over her until then.

There's no way we were going to let her set foot in that house where Matteo's "escorts" work. We know what sick depraved shit goes on in there, and the scumbags who frequent the place. Much like this piece of trash, Javi is pummeling.

"Easy, Javi," Milo says from next to me. "We don't want to kill him just yet." He shoots a smile at the poor bastard tied to the chair, as a promise of violence flashes through his eyes. I know that look. I've seen it many times in similar situations. It puts people on edge, making them uncomfortable in such a serious situation. Half the time, they don't know how to take it, so they end up spilling their guts.

"Please, tell Mateo I'll have his money by the end of the week." The man mumbles hoarsely, barely able to hold his head up.

Javi steps up to my other side, uncharacteristically vibrating with anticipation to put his hands back on the man. "You ok, brother?" I question when he tightens his fists at his sides, and he nods his head.

We have all been struggling with the events that took place that night, but Adrian and Javi seem to be taking it the hardest. Where Adrian has been quieter and more standoffish, Javi is the opposite, using his humor as a defense mechanism. So when I see this side of Javi, the Javi that's thrumming with quiet rage, I know he's about to reach his breaking point. Josie seems to be the only one who can soothe his demons and bring the light back into his eyes.

"Tommy, Tommy, Tommy," Milo tsks. "We've been in this situation before. You know Mateo doesn't take payment in the form of empty promises." Pulling a cigarette from behind his ear, he lights it and blows the smoke in Tommy's face. Bending down so he's eye level with him, he says, "Perhaps you would like us to swing by your house, and show your poor wife what you've been up to, hmm?"

"Show?" This shit for brains asks, and I can't help but roll my eyes at his naivety.

"If you think Mateo doesn't keep cameras all over that

house, you're dumber than I thought you were. Maybe it was the blindfold that kept you from noticing." I pointed out as my two friends chuckled at the idiocy of this man.

Realization sets in and his eyes widen, damn near popping out of his head. "Please, I'll do anything," he begs, frantically shaking his head.

"Money, Tommy. We need the money you owe." I chastise. Being in this position on almost a weekly basis, he knows full well what we need.

"I don't have the mon-" Before he can finish his sentence, I step up and punch him in the jaw. My patience is wearing thin. I told Liam's teacher I had an appointment during lunch and that I would be back before the end of school, which was about two hours ago. School lets out soon, and I don't want him waiting around for me.

"We need the money, Tommy. Kylers growing restless, and you know how he gets when he's restless." Milo reminds him.

With his head lolling to the side, Tommy mumbles something I can't quite hear. I grab a fistful of his hair and pull his head upright. "Speak up Tommy, I can't hear you," I say to his face.

"My phone." He mumbles again. "My phone is in my left pocket. I can transfer the money."

"Good choice," I say, patting him on the cheek and stepping away as Milo digs into his pocket.

Coming to stand in front of a concerningly quiet Javi, I see the anguish and turmoil in his eyes. Knowing how he feels but not knowing how to comfort him, I grab him by the back of his neck and rest my forehead against his. "Soon. We'll be out of here in no time, and you'll be able to see her."

Letting out a heavy sigh, as sadness rolls off of him and threatens to choke me, he nods his head. "I know," he says, stepping back so we're face to face. "We have to come up with something, Kyler. She can't work for Mateo. If I have to just bite the bullet and join *Los Caminantes Nocturnos*, I will. She's already been through enough." He doesn't need to say it. I know "enough," meaning the fucking coma she just woke up from and the part we played in everything.

"We'll come up with something. We can meet up at my house after school, and come up with a plan." I reply, and instantly, some of the pain in his eyes recedes. There's no way in hell any of us are getting left behind.

After Milo gets the funds transferred over to his account, he cuts Tommy free from the chair, and he pathetically topples to the concrete floor. "We'll see you next week." He says with a sardonic smile on his face, he turns to us, "Let's get the fuck out of here. I need a cigarette."

"You're going to smoke yourself into an early grave." I joke. He's been using smoking as his coping mechanism, and at this rate, he's on his way to a pack a day.

"It's either smoking or fucking. The only person I want to fuck isn't ready for that yet, so smoking it is. When we finally do fuck, though," he pauses and that damn smile of his appears again, "something tells me I'll be needing more than one cigarette after." Javi and I grunt our agreement, knowing exactly what he's talking about.

M aking it back to school just as the bell rings, I rush through the crowded halls to Liam's classroom. I barely have my foot through the door when I see his blond head whip in my direction, and a grin a mile wide spreads across his face. Seeing his happy little face makes my smile appear.

"I thought you forgot about me." He teases as he stands up to gather his things into his backpack.

"What?" I press a hand to my chest, feigning insult. "I'm offended that you think I would ever forget you." Our playful banter is one of my favorite things with him. Except I've been trying to teach him boundaries so he doesn't blurt out embarrassing information like he did this morning.

He runs up and throws his arms around me, and gives me the biggest hug. "I know, Ky, I just like to give you shit." Okay, so add teaching him not to swear to the list. Although that one will be more difficult when he's around me and the guys.

"He was a little worried you would forget him today." His special education teacher, Mrs. Knudson, says, walking toward us. "Liam, don't forget your lunchbox." She tells him.

When he walks over to his cubby to retrieve said lunch box, she steps closer, lowering her voice, "He's doing well. He fits in great and gets along with everyone. He seems to really like it."

One of the reasons we decided to transfer schools was that Liam was getting bullied at school, and it was starting to affect his mental health. Assholes would tease him because he wasn't "normal" and because he looks different. Trying to explain to him that there is nothing wrong with him, that it's the bullies who have issues, was becoming more and more challenging the more he got bullied. It got to a point where he would have nervous breakdowns at school, and he wouldn't leave my side all day. Given my association with Mateo and our line of "work", I couldn't put him in danger. So, we transferred, and the fact that Josie attends here is just the cherry on top. It may also be the other reason we transferred.

"I'm glad he's fitting in. You'll let me know if anything changes?" I ask.

"Of course." Ms. Knudson says, giving me a small smile. Something flashes in her eyes before I can get a read on it, but she continues, "You're a good brother. I think he just got a little worried because you're usually here a few minutes before the bell rings." She stares at me expectantly like she's waiting for an explanation.

"I had an appointment that went longer than I thought it would." That's all she's going to get out of me. I don't know why she suddenly seems so interested in what I'm doing when she should be focused on Liam. "You ready to go, bud?"

"I hate it when you call me that." He says, glaring at me. "I'm not a kid. Why can't you give me a nickname like you have for your friends?"

Tilting my head in confusion, "Nicknames? What nicknames? I don't know what you're talking about."

"Yeah, huh. Like, sometimes I hear you call them dingleberry, shit for brains, chode blossom, douchebag, fu-"

"Okay!" I shout, cutting him off, attempting to hold back a chuckle. "We'll come up with a new nickname for you, but maybe don't repeat the nicknames the guys and I have for each other." Ms. Knudson's face is as red as a tomato from Liam's colorful language. "Sorry, Ms. Knudson. I'll be working with him on his vocabulary

"Please do." She says before she spins on her heel, walking away dramatically like her delicate ears are offended. If she were wearing pearls, she'd probably be clutching them.

Walking out of the classroom, I swing my arm over Liam's shoulders. "Dude, you can't say that stuff in front of your teacher," I tell him, finally letting out a laugh before I explode. I know I shouldn't be laughing, but the look on her face was priceless.

"Why? You and the guys say it all the time." He argues.

Pushing our way through the front doors and down the steps, "We do, but they're bad words, and we shouldn't be saying them." Not sure how to explain this to him without me sounding like a hypocrite or making him feel like I'm treating him like a five-year-old, so I offer, "How about you just don't repeat anything we say, and it will keep you out of trouble?"

"Deal." He agrees and holds his hand out for me to shake like we just made some sort of business deal. Reaching my car, he tosses his backpack in the back seat and plops himself down in the front. "Can we still come up with a different nickname?"

"Of course," I answer, ruffling his hair after I get comfortable behind the wheel, and pull out of the parking lot. The rumble of my old '69 Camaro relaxes me, and the stress I was feeling before I picked up Liam melts away. "What do you want your nickname to be?" I ask.

"Let me think about it." He hums, rubbing his hand along his jaw deep in thought. My phone dings with a text, when I reach down to grab it, I hear Liam say, "Josie."

I swivel my head in his direction, not sure that I heard him right. "You want your nickname to be Josie?" I cock an eyebrow, curious where he's going with this.

"No. Dingleberry." So apparently that's my new nickname. "Josie," he says, pointing out the window. I follow his finger to where he's pointing and see Josie walking down the sidewalk.

My first thought is, Why the fuck is she walking home by herself? It's not safe. She doesn't know just how unsafe, but seeing her alone makes my heart rate kick up at our negligence, and any dissipating stress ramps back up. My second thought is, she's never allowed to wear those skinny jeans again. I can only imagine all the unnoticed looks she was getting at school today, and it makes my blood boil with irrational jealousy.

Pulling closer to the sidewalk, I tell Liam, "Hop in back."

I've never seen him move so fast, and I can't help but smile knowing he's just as excited to see her as I am.

I roll down the passenger side window and call her name. "Josie!" Her head spins to the side so fast I'm surprised her neck didn't snap. "Sorry, I didn't mean to startle you. Do you want a ride?" I offer, hoping like hell she'll take it.

She stops walking, and her face turns the most adorable shade of pink. I can't help but wonder how other parts of her body would look with such a shade.

I catch her terrorizing her thumb again as she begins shifting from foot to foot. "I, um," she starts fumbling over her words, and her gorgeous green eyes fill with panic, and my chest pinches painfully. "I-It's okay." She stutters out. "I just live down the street. It's not far." I know where she lives, and it's not far, but the possessive asshole in me doesn't want her walking home by herself, but i also don't want to force her into my car. She's clearly scared to get in, though I don't know if she's still traumatized from the accident or because I'm a stranger.

Putting the car in park, I get out and walk around to the sidewalk to stand in front of her. I grab her hand and clasp it in mine."I promise I'll go slow." I say gently, hoping she hears the sincerity and hidden apology underneath. I slowly reach for her backpack in her other hand, giving her time to object if she wants to, not wanting to spook her.

Recalling the look of utter panic when she jumped out of Kiera's car makes my hands twitch with the need to pull her into my arms and squeeze her until every ounce of anxiety leaks from her body into mine. I am part of the reason, after all, that it's there.

Indecisiveness flickers through her eyes, and she bites her bottom lip. A groan gets lodged in my throat at the move. This girl is completely unaware of the effect she has on me, on us, and any male in her vicinity.

"If you can't handle it, I'll pull over and we can walk you home." I try coaxing her.

"We?" She questions, leaning to the side to see around me. When a heartwarming smile takes over her face, I know it's because she's seeing the same smile on Liam's face. She looks back at me and says, "Promise you'll pull over if I need?"

"Cross my heart." I do a criss-cross motion over my heart, giving her a reassuring smile.

Opening the passenger door for her, she slides in. After handing her her backpack, I get back into the driver's seat. Putting the car in drive and slowly beginning the drive to her house. Only this time, my anxiety doesn't immediately vibrate away, and it has everything to do with the beauty sitting next to me. "It's just a few blocks down. It's a little red-brick house on the right." She says, but she doesn't know that I already know where she lives, so I just nod my head in understanding.

"Hello. I'm Liam." My brother says, poking his head between us.

"Hello, Liam. I'm Josie." She introduces herself and shoots him a small smile.

"Do you want to help me pick out a nickname?" He asks her. Thankfully, he's here to distract her. I can't help but smile back at him through the rearview mirror. This kid could make friends with Mr. Scrooge, and I'm once again baffled how the assholes at Southview High could bully such a kind person.

"Sure," she answers, "What have you come up with so far?"

"Well, nothing yet. Maybe you can help us?" He questions.

"Hmmm, what about Lee? Short for Liam." She suggests, as I notice her leg bouncing anxiously.

He seems to think it over for a bit before he says, "I like it, but it's not cool enough. I want something that will get the ladies." He says, waggling his eyebrows. I let out a chuckle as Josie giggles next to me, making my heart warm at the happy sound.

"Do you have anything in mind?" I asked, pulling up next to the curb in front of her house. Noticing that we've parked and made it to her house already, I see her shoulders visibly relax and her leg stops bouncing.

"I can't think of anything. How did you come up with the nicknames for your friends?" Liam asks me. I let out an exasperated sigh when Josie looks at me with curiosity shining in her eyes. This kid is going to be the freaking death of me.

Before I can answer him, I see two people walking out of Josie's house, one who I think is her mom, and the other is someone I've seen one too many times. The fact that he's here, at Josie's house, makes anger ripple under my skin. I feel the urge to drive off before she can get out and take her far away from here. What the fuck is he even doing here?

"Who is that?" I ask forcing back my anger, knowing full well who the fuck that is.

She turns her head to see the two people leaving her house. "Oh. That's my mom and my cousin." She replies with a bit of hesitation. Does she know who her cousin is? What line of "work" he's in?

She opens her door to climb out when I snatch her bag from the middle of the seat before she can. Throwing my door open, I rush out and come to her side of the car to walk her to the door.

"Are you leaving?" She asks her mom when we reach the porch, with a hint of sadness in her voice.

"Sorry, honey, I picked up another shift. I have to be at work in twenty minutes." Her mom answers. I notice the disappointment settle on Josie's face. Annoyance settles next to the rage I'm feeling, that she's once again going to be left by herself.

"O-okay." She stutters out. Looking like Josie has zoned out, an uncomfortable silence fills the air. Elizabeth clears her throat, getting her daughter's attention. "This is Kyler. He gave me a ride home."

"Nice to meet you, ma'am." I nod at her

"Kyler, this is my mom, Elizabeth, and my cousin Sylus." She introduces us, and when I lock eyes with her cousin, I see amusement in his eyes when a mocking smile stretches across his face.

"Nice to meet you, Kyler. I didn't know Josie had a boyfriend." He says tauntingly.

"He's not m-" she starts.

"She's a gorgeous girl. I had to make a move before anyone else could get to her." I interrupt her. Not exactly confirming or denying that we're officially together. Judging by the displeased look that has now settled on his face, I know that he picked up that hidden meaning under my words.

Josie's wide eyes are glued to my face, trying to process what I just said. Giving her a soft smile, to show her that I meant what I said, I put my arm around her waist and pull her into my side. If this asshole thinks he has any claim over her, he has another thing coming. I would give my soul to the devil before I let him lay a finger on her.

Chapter Twelve

JOSIE

If my eyes grow any wider, they're going to pop out of my head. Heat rises up my chest and flushes over my cheeks at Kyler's words. Surely he was just joking, right? Other than the party, today is the most I've ever talked to him.

He didn't actually say yes, he's my boyfriend, but he didn't say no either. My brain can't seem to get past that word he used to describe me. Mostly because, well, no one has ever described me as gorgeous, and I'm not sure how to process that compliment. Of course, Z and Kiera have told me before that I'm gorgeous, but they have to say that because they're my friends.

Growing more and more uncomfortable as his words resonate, I realize I still haven't said anything when he flashes me a giant smile and gives my side a little squeeze. I jump when a tremor of pain shoots through my side at his kind gesture.

Wincing, I bring my hand to my side after he immediately drops his from my waist. The smile he had is now replaced with concern. "I'm so sorry. I didn't mean to hurt you. Are you okay?" He asks.

"Yeah, I'm fine. We played dodgeball in gym class today, and I got hit pretty hard." Trying to change the subject, because I can't take the look of worry he's giving me. "Really, I'm fine." Flashing him a smile, I turn to Mom. "Are you going to be gone all night?"

"Yes. I'm working a twelve-hour shift, so I will be home late." Trying not to pout, because I know how hard she works to keep a roof over our heads, I nod instead. "Don't forget you have court tomorrow. Ashley will be at your school in the morning to pick you up and take you."

Shit! How could I forget about that? The cops had come to talk to me a few days after I had woken up. They needed to get a statement about what had happened. So I told them. Everything. How someone had run into the back of me, more than once, and caused me to crash. How two people had stopped to see if I was ok, and called 9-1-1. Surprise, surprise, just as I thought, they didn't believe me because I had been drinking. They said it didn't look like there was any evidence of foul play. So they kindly gave me a citation, and now I have to go to court.

I have never been in trouble before, so of course, I was nervous and wanted my mom to take me.

"What?" I almost yell because I don't want to be stuck with Ashley tomorrow morning. It's bad enough that I wrecked her car, but having her drive me to court for wrecking her car is going to be torture. I can already hear her snide comments now. "I don't want her to take me. Can't you take me?" I'm actually pouting now.

"Sorry, honey, but I'm going to be home late tonight, and I have another twelve-hour shift tomorrow. If I take you, I'll barely get any sleep." She says, planting a kiss on my head as she and Sylus go to walk off the porch. "If Kyler is staying, please just make sure you clean up after yourselves."

"Josie, good to see you," Sylus says with a strange gleam

in his eye. "Kyler, take care of my cousin." Just as he says that, I see tension take root in Kyler's shoulders. " I'll be seeing you around." He finishes and steps off the porch. He and Mom both get in their cars and drive away, and for the hundredth time today, nerves get the best of me and I feel the urge to claw at my thumbs.

Before I can even begin to try and decipher what Sylus meant by "I'll be seeing you around," Kyler speaks up. "Do you want some company?" Of all the things he could have said, I did not expect him to say that.

"Please don't feel like you're obligated to stay because my mom brought it up," I say, blushing, as always. If I keep blushing around him, *them*, every time one of them speaks to me, my skin is going to permanently turn pink.

"I would never feel obligated to stay with you, little Gingersnap." I bite my bottom lip to keep the happy squeal from escaping my mouth at his pet name for me. He takes a step closer toward me, and my heart flutters in my chest. "I meant what I said, Josie." He says, quietly pulling my lip free from my teeth with the pad of his thumb. "You are gorgeous, we want nothing more than to make you our-"

"Hey, dingleberry! Are you just going to leave me in the car all day? I'm not a dog, ya know!" Liam shouts, sticking his head out of the car window.

A laugh erupts free from my mouth, and Kyler tilts his head back, sighing at the sky. "Dingleberry, huh? Is that the nickname he came up with for you?" I say, trying and failing to contain my laughter.

He shakes his head, ignoring my question, "If you want me to stay, I can run Liam home real quick."

"No, I don't mind if he stays too. Kiera's coming over later, too, we can all hang out." I answer, shrugging my shoulders, not minding at all. They have a sweet relationship, and their silly banter makes me laugh. "Unless he needs to be home?"

"No, but I would like to spend more time with you. Just the two of us, to get to know you better." He replies, and I have to force myself not to do a happy dance.

Instead, I decide to make a fool of myself. "I would love it if you got to know me better." I slap a hand over my mouth before another sexual innuendo can slip free. Where the hell did that come from? Is it because he called me gorgeous? Oh god, this man is going to ruin me, isn't he?

He lets out a chuckle and pulls my hand from my mouth. Leaning in, just inches from my face, he whispers. "If words make you blush that hard, my little Gingersnap, then I can't wait to see how we can make you blush with," he pauses and his eyes slowly roam down my body and back up, "other things." He kisses me on the corner of my mouth and walks toward his car to retrieve Liam.

I'm rooted to the spot, sorting through everything he just said. I can't get my feet to move. All I can think about are the "other things" he's referring to. Images of his hands on me float through my mind. How warm they would feel exploring my body, or how demanding his mouth would be on mine. How even the lightest touch from any of them would send me over the edge.

Just as that thought passes through my brain, it finally registers that he had said we. We? As in all five of them? I don't even know them, and they don't know me, but he made it sound as if they're all interested in me. I've only just met them. I'm pretty sure Adrian hates me if the look he gave me earlier is anything to go off. Carter is quiet, but he did hold my hand earlier to comfort me. I have barely said anything to Javi, though he did stick up for me with Jake. I have talked to Milo and Kyler the most now.

My heart starts pounding against my chest, and I don't

know if it's because of Kyler's words or if it's because I'm thinking about how it would work to have five boyfriends when I've never even had one. Wouldn't that cause jealousy and competition? What if one of them changes their mind? Would they go their separate ways? I could never handle the guilt if I destroyed their friendship. Especially with how close they seem to be. I'm not worth them losing each other.

I hear footsteps coming back up the driveway and force those thoughts away for another time. I start rubbing at my temples to relieve the headache I feel coming on. Kyler steps up with a wicked grin on his face, like he knew where my thoughts were. For the second time, I think this man, these men, are going to destroy me.

"**W**hat about L.J.?" I throw out, still trying to come up with a nickname for Liam.

"I like that better than Lee." He states, "But I'm still not feeling it."

After we made it inside, I gave them a tour of the little cracker box I call home. It might be smaller than most people's houses, but its homey feel is one of the only things that settles my anxious mind. The stress from the day and the shit show on the porch was almost instantly washed away when we stepped inside, feeling like a warm blanket wrapped itself around my nervous system, calming it as if it knew I was having a bad day.

I showed them my bedroom and saw Kyler linger, wanting to peek around like my room held all my secrets, and he was going to find every single one of them. I quickly ushered them out and showed them the living room and then the connecting kitchen. I grabbed us a couple of sodas from the fridge and sauntered out the back door, taking a seat on the mismatched patio furniture we have.

For the last hour, we've been so patiently trying to help Liam come up with a nickname.

"Dude, just pick one. We've been at this forever." Kyler groans. Okay, so I was the only one who was being patient. Rubbing his hand down his face out of frustration, I can see his patience deteriorating.

I jump in. "Do you have any favorite video games? Or any favorite movies? Or just any interests we can try to get something from?"

"Yeah, Liam, why don't you tell Josie what your favorite movie is?" Kyler teases him, and for once, I'm not the blushing, embarrassed one. But seeing him uncomfortable makes me come to his rescue so he doesn't feel so bad.

"I'll tell you my favorite movie if you tell me yours." I try negotiating with him.

He swiftly shakes his head, "No way." Muttering and looking down at the table, he continues, "It's too embarrassing. The chicks definitely aren't into it."

"Well, I think my favorite movie is super embarrassing as well. So how about we say them at the same time, so it's not as embarrassing." I try to make a deal with him to put a smile back on his face.

Hesitantly, he nods his head in agreement. "Okay," I agree. "On the count of three. Ready?" Once again nodding his head as his face gets even pinker. "Kyler, will you count us down?" I question, and when I look over at him, I'm surprised at the look of affection I see staring back at me. I feel the urge to pounce on him like a horned-up crazy person.

"Alright, ready? One...two...three!" he shouts.

"The Lord of the Rings"

"The Lord of the Rings"

Surprise filters through Liam's face, and his wide smile mimics mine. He's practically bouncing in his chair with excitement. "Which one is your favorite?" He rushes out, giddy as can be.

Giggling at how ecstatic he is, I answer. "Obviously, Return of the King."

"Mine too!" He practically shouts, unable to keep a lid on his excitement any longer.

Glad that ashamed look is gone from his face, and he was comfortable enough to tell me. I can't help but wonder if he was just embarrassed because his brother was teasing him, or if he was just scared he would be judged for it.

Kyler moans next to me, and I hear him mumble something along the lines of being surrounded by nerds under his breath. Shaking off his comment, I focus on Liam. "What if your nickname was Legolas? Oh, or Aragorn? The ladies love them."

"Are you one of those ladies?" Kyler asks. Waggling his eyebrows at me, trying to poke fun.

"Uh, yeah," I say, like it should be common sense. "Who wouldn't want an elf who knows how to use a bow? Or a king who is loyal to a fault?"

"Wow. You are a nerd." He retorts, throwing me a wink to show he's being playful.

"What about Lord? Or Lord Liam?" I give him more options to try and encourage him now that we have something to work with.

His face lights up at that, and I know he's finally settled on a nickname. "Yes! Lord, or Lord Liam. I will accept any of those." He says it like he's royalty, and if anyone calls him anything else, he will have their head. I can't help but chuckle at his sense of humor.

"Thank the fucking lord." Kyler huffs.

"You're welcome," Liam says sarcastically, snickering to himself.

My phone vibrates in my pocket, and when I pull it out to see a text message from Kiera, I already know what her text is going to say before I read it.

> Kiera: Hey, girl, Chance's parents are running late for dinner. Let's hang out tomorrow instead?

Noticing the time on my phone, it's later than I thought it was. I guess time does fly when you're having fun, that or I'm just used to being alone.

Letting out a sigh at the text message. It's like she knows what I have to tell her, and she's avoiding me, or her boyfriend just keeps guilt-tripping her into things so she doesn't find out what a two-timing dirtbag he is. My money is on the latter.

"Everything okay?" Kyler inquires.

"Yeah, Kiera just ditched out on me," I say disappointedly, as I respond to her text.

> Me: No problem, but I really need to talk to you.

> Kiera: I promise tomorrow we can hang out all day after school.

> Me: Okay, chick, see you tomorrow.

Just as I go to put my phone back in my pocket, my stomach lets out an embarrassing rumble. Wrapping an arm around my middle as if that will take back the noise.

"Someone's hungry," Liam says, giggling.

"I was going to order pizza if you guys want to stay?" I

try bribing. I don't want to be alone, and I have company for once, but I don't want them to feel like they HAVE to stay. "If you guys have to get going, I understand, too, but if you're not in a rush, I don't mind the company."

Kyler sets his warm hand on top of mine, and the kind gesture subdues my nervous rambling. Caressing my knuckles with his thumb, he says, "We can stay for pizza, Josie."

"Yes!" I hear Liam say, and I look over at him to see him pumping his fist in the air excitedly. He abruptly stops and gets a serious look on his face. "Wait. What kind of pizza do you like?" He asks, and I feel like this is a test of some kind.

"Ham and pineapple?" I answer as more of a question, not sure if I have said the right thing or not.

Liam's head whips over to Kyler with a serious look and states, "Brother, if you don't nail her down, I will."

Kyler spits soda out at his brother's words, which I'm not entirely sure he knows the meaning of. "Christ, Liam. You can't just say shit like that." He scolds, then, turning to look at me, he says, "I'm sorry. He doesn't know what half the shit that comes out of his mouth means. We're working on it."

His words prove me right, and I wouldn't be surprised if half the stuff he says is just words he's heard from his brother. Liam has an air of innocence about him, and I get the feeling he just says the stuff he does because he wants his brother to like him.

After ordering our ham and pineapple pizza, Kyler tried to argue that pineapple doesn't belong on pizza, but of course, he was wrong. Liam begged Kyler to stay longer because he was having fun.

He agreed, which I honestly don't think he could ever say no to him; I know I couldn't. Liam has such a pure, kind heart. Just like any other teenager, he just wants his peers' approval and for them to like him. I don't know how anyone couldn't like him, and the better I get to know him, the more I find we have in common.

I found out we're both Lord of the Rings super fans, but we both also love superhero movies. My favorite superhero is Thor, because, well, Chris Hemsworth, his favorite is Iron Man. The more we talked, the more he opened up to me. He told me he used to get bullied at his old school. He said kids used to call him mean names and pick on him. "It made me feel sad." He had said, sounding so pained.

Tears had welled in my eyes, and I had made the excuse that I was changing into more comfortable clothes, so I could get it together. How anyone could torment such an innocent person had my heart splitting in two.

I dried my eyes and quickly changed into a pair of leggings and a black tank top. Stepping back into the living room, I could feel Kyler's heated stare. I don't know if it was the tank top or the form-fitting black leggings that caught his attention, but for once, I didn't mind the staring.

Plopping down on the couch next to Kyler, while Liam sat in the recliner, we decided to watch a movie. Unsurprisingly, Liam picked Iron Man. Folding my legs underneath me and leaning my head back against the couch to get comfortable, the day had caught up with me, and my eyelids felt like they were made of cement.

Fighting to keep my eyes open was proving to be futile, and the last thing I remember is being pulled against a hard chest.

The sensation of floating startled me awake, only to find Kyler's arms wrapped around me. "It's okay." He soothed, "It's just me". I squirmed at the thought of him carrying me, as humiliation took over at the thought of him feeling how heavy I am.

Before I could tell him to put me down, he was lowering me to my bed and pulling the covers over my legs. He kneeled next to my bed so we were eye level. "I'm sorry I fell asleep. I didn't realize how tired I was." I sleepily tell him.

He lifted a hand and brushed my hair off my forehead. "It's okay. I didn't want to wake you. You looked so peaceful." He said, and I couldn't blame him for that.

"Thank you for staying." I all but whisper, feeling as if I talk any louder, he'll come to his senses and sprint out of here. "I don't like being alone when it gets dark out." I don't like being home alone, period, especially when it's dark out. But he doesn't need to know that I'm scared of the dark, so we'll just leave it at that.

"Anytime, baby." He says as he rests his hand on my cheek. If I wasn't paying attention, I wouldn't have noticed the look of irritation that had flashed across his face, but it's gone just as quickly. "Do you want me to stay?" He offers.

Nuzzling my cheek into his hand, knowing I'll miss the tenderness when it's gone. "No, I'm sure you need to get Liam home. I'll be fine, I promise." I respond.

"I don't want to leave you if you don't feel comfortable being by yourself." He says, and I see a conflict of whether he should stay or go playing over his face.

Resting my hand on top of his, that's still resting on my cheek. "Really, I'll be fine," I reassure him, but he still looks conflicted. "How about I text you if I need you to come back?" That seems to settle him.

"Promise?" He asks

Nodding my head, "I promise."

My breath stalls out when I see him slowly inching forward, and I couldn't brace myself for the sensation my body feels, even if I saw the kiss coming from a mile away.

My lips tingle at the feel of his mouth on mine, and I feel a flutter erupt in my belly. A rush of affection washes over me as his lips gently caress mine with such fondness. He lowers his hand from my cheek to the nape of my neck, pulling me closer so our mouths are now pressed together. His tongue peeks out, encouraging me to open up to him. My lips part, and his tongue dominates my mouth as it tangles with mine.

The fluttering I felt in my belly travels further south and has me clenching my thighs as it nestles into my core. The kiss turns hungry as he sucks my tongue into his mouth, and his grip on the back of my neck tightens as if he's scared I'm going to pull away from him. He nips my bottom lip, and the pulsing between my legs grows stronger, causing a whimper to escape my throat.

He pulls his mouth from mine as if he's been burned, and dread settles in my stomach. Am I not a good kisser? Was this a mistake? Before my mind spirals, I ask, "Did I do something wrong?"

He gives me a look like I've grown another head. I see the moment understanding takes over when he says, "No, Gingersnap." Resting his forehead on mine, he continues, "But if you keep making those noises, I won't be able to control myself."

With how fast this man is worming his way under my skin, it should be a red flag. I have no doubt it's going to be the same with the others. I should question it or at least slow down. But feeling such adoration from someone has my body thrumming with exhilaration. "What if I don't want you to control yourself?" I can't help but taunt him.

The intense look in his eyes almost makes me wish I could take the question back, but curiosity has me standing my ground. "Our time will come, my little Gingersnap." He brings his hand up to cup my jaw. "And when it does, you'll be running to repent for all the sinful things I'm going to do to you."

With that final thought, he puts his phone number in my phone, gives me one last peck on the lips, and walks out.

Still stunned, speechless long after he's left, I finally fall back to sleep, dreaming of more than one pair of lips.

A *heavy arm is draped over my side, and I feel a warm presence at my back that has me scooting back, snuggling closer. Hot breath wafts over my neck as the arm over my side pulls me closer. An "mmm" sound floats from my lips at the intimate contact, just as I hear shuffling at the foot of my bed.*

Opening my eyes, I slowly lift my head to see what's causing the commotion. To my surprise, I see five men that I'm becoming more and more familiar with every day, but I didn't think we were close enough that they would just let themselves in.

Don't get me wrong, I'm not mad, just surprised that they felt comfortable enough to just walk into my house. I didn't even know they were coming over. Looking at my alarm clock next to my bed, it says it's two in the freaking morning. What the hell are they doing here?

Oh god! This is it, isn't it? They've come to kill me, or kidnap me and sell me off into some sex trafficking ring for a large sum of money. I knew it was too good to be true. Damn it, Josie, always listen to your gut.

My heart accelerates as Milo takes a step closer. Like the naïve organ in my chest knows who's approaching, it settles at his soothing presence. All thoughts of killing and kidnapping are out the window when he reaches my side of the bed.

"Milo?" I say his name as more of a question. None of them has said anything since I woke, and now that he's standing so close, I realize he's not wearing a shirt. Looking at the others, I notice none

of them is wearing a shirt, just a pair of jeans. The sight of their bare, muscled chests makes my mouth water and has me clenching my thighs.

Milo's ice blue eyes practically glow in the dark as he stares down at me with such warmth. "I'm sorry, beautiful, please forgive me." He whispers. Slowly, he lowers his lips to mine, kissing me so tenderly, it bleeds adoration and absorbs into my skin like a sponge. The overwhelming feeling forces me to blink my eyes closed to hold back tears, but when I open them again, it's Kyler who is standing in front of me now with his lips locked to mine.

Pulling back, he says, "I'm sorry, beautiful, please forgive me." Scrunching my eyebrows together in confusion, trying to figure out what the fuck is going on, when Carter steps up.

Resting his warm hand on my cheek, he utters the same confusing words, "I'm sorry, beautiful, please forgive me." Then gives me the same tender kiss.

Just as Carter steps back, Adrian steps up. Replacing Carter's hand on my cheek, except Adrian's eyes are haunted, and he looks like he is in physical pain. A lone tear streaks down his face. "Adrian." I choke out as if I can feel the pain portrayed in his eyes.

I lift my hand to rest over his, nuzzling my cheek into it when he says, "I'm sorry, beautiful, please forgive me. I don't know what I'd do without you." Placing a soft kiss on my lips, I let out a small cry as his palm leaves my cheek.

When Javi steps up, he has the same forlorn look on his face that has me wanting to reach out and comfort him. Also, the need to kill whoever put that look there in the first place burns in my chest. Tucking a stray strand of hair behind my ear, he gives me a watery smile and leans in close to my ear, whispering, "Lo siento hermosa, por favor perdoname." His hot breath on my ear causes a shiver to work its way down my spine.

The same niggling feeling pokes at the back of my mind when he says those words. The same feeling I had gotten at school when

Adrian spoke. Before I can analyze it further, I hear, "Josie," come from a familiar, sensuous voice.

Looking over my shoulder with a shy smile, "Zeke," I say. Thank the lord that the moonlight streaming in isn't light enough for them to see my cheeks turn rosy. A surprised gasp leaves my mouth as I feel something poking into my back. His arm still draped over my side, he squeezes me and drops a kiss to my shoulder.

I have never had such an intimate moment with Zeke, so the gesture catches me off guard. Sure, he calls me babe and gorgeous because we're friends. But this is different. It feels different, and it has me pushing my ass back against him. Grinding into him, I hear a groan leave his lips, and the others, as they went to stand at the foot of the bed again.

"Josie," Zeke says. Still looking at him over my shoulder, eyes locked on each other, he quietly says, "I'm sorry, beautiful, please forgive me." Running his nose up my neck and to my ear, he nibbles on my earlobe as he pushes against me to get more friction.

"Zeke," I moan.

"Josie."

Letting go of my earlobe, he traces his silky lips back down my neck, leaving a trail of kisses that has me reaching my hand beneath the covers. "Zeke," I moan out again.

"Josie."

Just as I reach the pulsing bundle of nerves between my legs, his lips skate over my shoulder. I expect him to keep moving down my back, but instead, he puts a hand on my shoulder and starts shaking me.

"Josie. Wake up." An amused voice commands.

I startle awake to Zeke shaking my shoulders, practically yelling at me. Looking around for the others, only to be disappointed to realize it was just a dream. Flopping onto my back, I look over to see Zeke, who has a damn grin on his face that could rival the Cheshire cat.

Groaning, I cover my eyes with my arm, so he can't see

my shame. "What?" I ask, already knowing he knows what I was dreaming about, but just needing him to verbally acknowledge it. God, please tell me I was not moaning his name out loud.

When he doesn't answer me, I slowly lower my arm from my face, only to see him still smiling at me like he just dug up my deepest secrets. The next words out of his mouth prove that I have now woken up into a nightmare.

"Have a good dream?" He asks, words dripping with sarcasm, "I almost didn't want to wake you just to see how it ended."

"Oh my god!" I practically shout, bringing my hands up to cover my face, shielding my embarrassment. "Can we please not talk about it?" I ask, secretly wishing he didn't wake me up either. Then I wouldn't have to look at his sexy face and eyes that are sparkling with curiosity.

Wait... Sexy? Did I just think that? We've been friends forever, and not once has that thought crossed my mind. Well, there was that moment at school when they all followed me outside. I thought Zeke had looked like he was just another one of them, standing there looking all tough with concern on his gorgeous face.

Shit! What is happening to me? This just has to be residual feelings from the dream. Groaning at the questionable feelings I seem to have grown towards my best friend, he grabs my wrists and gently pulls my hands from my face.

"Come on, don't hold out on me." He teases. "I heard more than one name come out of your mouth."

Waggling his eyebrows at me, I remembered he had some explaining to do himself. "Who gave you that hickey on your neck?" I quickly changed the subject. He hasn't shown interest in anyone since he moved here. He has dated, or should I say hooked up with other people, but nothing ever comes of it. "I'll tell you about my dream if you tell me who gave you that hickey."

I can see him contemplating if it's worth answering, which has now more than piqued my interest. Zeke never keeps anything from me. If anything, we're unhealthily open with each other. He knows everything about me, and I know everything about him. At least I thought I did.

"Z?" I question when he doesn't answer. The smile is long gone from his face, and his brows are scrunched together in worry. "It's ok, Z, you don't have to tell me," I say, reaching for his hand, intertwining our fingers.

He gives a slight shake of his head like he was lost in thought, and he leans on his elbow, looking down at me. "Sorry, Jo. I'm just not ready to tell who it is yet." He finally answers. Bringing his hand up, he tucks loose strands of hair behind my ear. "It's still new. I like him, and I don't want to jinx it, and I don't know-"

"Zeke." I cut off his nervous rambling. "It's okay." I lie. I'm not going to force him to talk about it, but I'm also a little jealous that someone is getting his attention. I know it's ridiculous, but he's the first boy who saw me for me, and I don't want to lose our friendship, but I want him to be happy. "Just don't forget I'm your best friend, I had you first."

I roll on my side so I don't have to see pity on his face at my words. Snuggling up to him, I bury my face in his chest, soaking up all of the Zeke I can get. His arms wrap around me. "You know I would never forget about you, babe." He says, burying his nose in my hair. "You're my favorite person in the whole wide world." He pauses, then "You know that, right?"

Squeezing me in his arms, I nod, acknowledging that I heard him. Not trusting myself to voice it, knowing that if I open my mouth, I'll just start crying at his sincere words.

"I would tell you not to forget about me, too," he starts,

"but now that I know you dream about me, I know you would never." I pinch his nipple, and he flinches back, chuckling, "Unless you leave me for one of those other sex gods you were dreaming about."

"Well, Kyler was over here earlier," I say with an in-your-face-you 're-not-the-only-one-hanging-out-with-new-people, tone. His body tenses, but he relaxes just as quickly. I pull back to look him in the eyes to try and read what that was all about, but when I look at him, he has that same worried pinch to his eyebrows he had earlier.

"Just promise you'll be careful around them?"

His serious tone now has my eyebrows scrunching with worry. "They're always nice to me," I say for some reason, feeling like I need to defend them. "I like them, and I think they like me."

Feeling a little irritated that I have to defend my relationship, if you even call it that, with them when he won't even tell me who he's been sneaking around with. I try to pull away from Zeke, but his arms tighten around me. "I'm just looking out for you, babe. I know how accepting you are, and some people take advantage of that. I just don't want to see you hurt." I relax in his arms, understanding where he's coming from.

"I know, and I love you for it," I say, settling back into his chest.

"After hearing you moan my name and theirs, I don't know if I'm more jealous or turned on." He says, laughing, and I reach up to pinch his nipple again, only twisting this time. "OW! Okay, truce!"

Placing a soft kiss on my forehead, he burrows his nose against my hair again. "I love you, too, babe." He whispers, "More than you'll ever know." My heart pitter-patters at his words and at the fluttery feeling. I realize somewhere down the line, my feelings for Zeke have turned into more than friendly. Too scared to read into them further, because I know he doesn't feel the same way. I know he's bi, but he's never dated a girl before, and I'm not about to be the first one he has to reject.

Stuffing my feelings deep down, I decide that's a future Josie problem. Closing my eyes at that thought, one by one, the six faces that invade my thoughts when I'm awake are now overtaking my thoughts when I'm asleep.

Chapter Thirteen

JOSIE

One year. That's how long my license has been suspended. One god damn year, and can't forget the hundred hours of community service.

"I hope you learned a lesson from this, missy. Drinking and driving is a serious crime, and you could have killed not only yourself but also innocent people." The judge scolded, lecturing me like a disappointed father.

"Yes, sir." I agree respectfully, knowing he's right. I had a feeling my license would be suspended; I just didn't prepare for the self-loathing that came when I had disappointed yet another person. Of course, Ashley's snickering from behind me didn't help either.

Keeping my head down and nodding at his words, I booked it out of there the second he dismissed me, leaving Ashley behind. Late summer heat warms my skin as I step into the fresh air, sucking in as much as my lungs will allow. My white sun dress blows in the small breeze, and I finally feel like I can take in a full breath, the tightness in my chest easing up.

"You could have waited for me." Ashley huffs when she catches up to me.

Rolling my eyes, not having the energy to deal with her right now, I answer with a bored, "Will you just take me back to school, please?" I'd much rather be at school than have to spend another second around her. Also, I may be in a hurry to see a certain someone, or should I say someones.

Just as I climb into the passenger seat of Ashley's car, my phone buzzes. Pulling it out, my stomach flutters when I see multiple texts from the guys. I assume Kyler must have given them my number, and I'm not even mad about it.

> Kyler: Good luck, Gingersnap. Oh, and Liam says he expects another movie night since you fell asleep.

I snort at that because, of course, he does. I sorta can't wait since I have someone to nerd out with me now.

> Milo: When are you coming back?

> Carter: Everything will be okay.

> Javi: Text us when you get back, gorgeous.

> Adrian: Good luck.

My eyebrows raise in surprise at the last text. Adrian is hard to read, and after the way he was looking at me yesterday, i assumed he didn't like me very much. Scrolling down a little farther, I see one from Zeke as well.

> Zeke: I'm here if you need me, Jo. Don't be too hard on yourself.

Rather than texting them back individually, I create a group text. Including Zeke.

> Me: Headed back now.

I scroll down to see a message from Kiera and can't help the laugh that escapes. I wouldn't expect anything less from her.

> Kiera: Good luck in court, chick. If the judge is a hardass just flash him your tits. Nothing says sorry, I've learned my lesson like a good flash.

When I go to shove my phone back in my pocket, I look up to notice we're driving past the school, and toward the part of town that I purposely avoid.

"Uh...where are we going?" I ask skeptically

"We just have to stop by Sylus's first. I need to pick up my pay for last night." I know she likes sex, but I never thought she would start working for him.

My stomach churns at her words, and the fluttering in my stomach has been smashed by an anvil. The distraction the texts provided is now taken over by the innate need to flee this metal death trap, and an alarm starts to blare in my head to stay away from the cesspool that is Sylus's.

Before pocketing my phone, I shakily send another text through the newly created group chat.

> Me: Change of plans. We had to make a detour to Sylus's. I'll be there soon.

Every family has a black sheep. You know, that one person who no one talks to or talks about, who is always involved in some shady shit. So the family just uses the don't ask, don't tell policy. But then, when they need something or want to have a good time, they go to said black sheep. They always have the hookup, or they can find what you're looking for. Yeah, my cousin, Sylus, is the black sheep.

I guess being the leader of the Northside Sovereign will get you that reputation. Not to mention the whore house he runs on this side of town, among other things. He tries to church it up by calling his girls "escorts" to keep things legal. I don't know who he's trying to fool, but everyone knows they do more than "escorting", and everyone goes to him if they need anything.

ANYTHING.

Seeing him yesterday for that brief moment was enough for me, but going to the house I actively avoid because I know what goes on there? I have to force myself not to rip this door open and throw myself out of this car.

"Can't you just take me to school first?" I all but beg. "I don't want to go to Sylus's. When did you start working for him anyway?" I can't help but ask a little too critically, as my nerves run away with my tongue.

"Relax." She chastises. "You think college is cheap? And how do you think I bought this car? You know, after you wrecked the last one, I had to find a way to get to school."

Guilt settles on my shoulders, making me sink into my seat, wishing I could disappear. "I'm sorry," I say quietly, internally kicking myself because she always makes me feel this way, and I always just fold like a cheap lawn chair. This time it's actually my fault, and she has every right to be mad at me, and I don't blame her.

"Yeah, well, sorry doesn't pay the bills." She scoffs, shaking her head, but then her face lights up like she just received the award for the best "escort" in the whore house. "You know," she starts, and flashes me a wicked smile, "You could work for him too."

"Are you freaking crazy!" I shout, looking over at her and arching an eyebrow suspiciously at her lack of response. "I am NOT working for him. You might be okay with selling your body, but I'm not and never will be." The words grind out of my mouth as an uneasy feeling settles in my bones.

Just as we pull up, she states, "Don't be such a judgmental bitch Josie. Besides, one day you might not have a choice." With that, she gets out of the car, and minutes later, I'm still gaping at the space where she used to be sitting.

I'm glued to my seat as I obsessively replay her puzzling words, digging my nail in the side of my thumb, not knowing if she was joking to torment me or threatening me. Don't get me wrong, I have nothing against sex workers. I wish I had their confidence, but Sylus doesn't do anything above board. With all of his illegal activity and the seedy people he associates with, I would not feel the slightest bit safe.

A ruckus has me snapping my head to look up at the old Victorian-style house. Three older-looking men stumble out the front door and down the rickety steps. With their disheveled hair and grey skin, I can't tell if they came here for a fuck or a fix. Probably both. The third man, slowly trailing behind them notices me and I suck in a gasp at the predatory smile that he throws my way. His glossy eyes have an unsettling glimmer, and just when I think he's going to take a step toward the car, his friends holler at him, diverting his attention.

Feeling like a sitting duck here alone in the car, I decide it would be a good idea to go inside to find Ashley. Better to be inside where there are more people than to sit out here alone and wait for something bad to happen. Right?

Once the men have walked down the sidewalk and are out of sight, I fling the car door open and quickly make my way through the front door. Perplexed at what I'm looking at when I step through the door, I turn around to inspect the doorway to make sure I walked into the right house. The dilapidated exterior masks the almost pristine interior, and I'm still trying to decide if I stepped through some sort of portal.

I'm greeted by shiny, dark hardwood floors that look like no one has ever walked on them. The wrought iron chandelier hanging above the foyer matches the iron sconces that line the hallway in front of me. To my left is a wooden staircase with intricate details that look hand-carved, and to my right is an open room that looks like it used to be a library. Instead of books, some shelves hold liquor, and some shelves hold little jewelry, like boxes. There's a mirrored coffee table in the middle of the room that's surrounded by four wing-backed leather chairs.

Having a pretty good idea of what goes on in there, I take a step to walk down the hallway. The deep emerald green walls are decorated with a velvety fleur de Lis pattern that has me running my fingers over the soft texture. Taking slow, cautious steps as if I'm walking through a haunted house, preparing myself in case someone jumps out at me. Low moaning noises filter through the house from upstairs. Realizing that's where all the magic happens, I make a note to never go up there.

Inching my way down the dimly lit hall, floorboards creaking beneath my feet with each step, I finally reach the end of the hall. Swiveling my head to each side, to my right, it looks like it leads to a kitchen, and the my left, all I see are closed doors. But there is one door that catches my attention, that sits at the very end of the hall.

It's large and daunting, almost daring me to see what secrets it's hiding on the other side. It's the only door whose emerald green matches the walls, while the others are black. It's also the only door decorated with a golden metal crown the size of a doorknocker placed in the center of it. The jewel tone is almost inviting, but the size of the door says to stay away. Fidgeting on the spot, unsure of what to do, I feel a tap on my shoulder that just about has me shooting through the roof.

Sucking in a gasp, I whirl around to see who the hell is sneaking up on me when I'm met by the most beautiful set of eyes I've ever seen.

"Sorry." She rushes out, putting her hands up in front of her. "I didn't mean to startle you; you just look a little lost."

Apparently, my brain doesn't know how to act around attractive people because all I can do is stare at this gorgeous girl whose beauty is far too great to be wasted in a place like this. She should be in magazines, or a runway in Paris, or being lavished with gifts from a handsome billionaire.

Her eyes are mismatched with one deep green similar to my own, and another that's a golden honey color. They're framed by thick, long lashes and perfectly shaped eyebrows that make mine look like untrimmed hedges. Her olive skin makes mine seem pastier than it is, and her long, wavy brown hair hangs to her ribs.

I notice a small smile tug across her lips, trying to hold back a laugh. I slap a hand to my forehead for my creepy staring. "Sorry, I didn't mean to stare." I apologize. "I've just never been here before, and I didn't know what to expect when I walked in."

Shaking her head, she chuckles and crosses her arms over her chest. The movement causes her tank top to lift the littlest bit, and my eyes are drawn to her skin that's now visible just above the lining of her skirt. The red, angry scar that's peeking out of the top looks blistered and raw. "Don't worry about it, doll," she says, but she pauses before she asks her next question, "Are you here for work?"

That has my eyes snapping back up to hers, and she must see the look of panic that crosses my face." You look a little out of place, is all." She quickly states, followed by "You're much too gorgeous to work here."

Not sure if I'm more confused or flattered by her statement, because does she not realize how beautiful she is?

"Thank you. I um…I'm looking for my sister or cousin. She works here. My sister, not my cousin. I was waiting for her in the car and came in to look for her. She said she had to come to pick up her pay from last night." I start chewing on my bottom lip to stop the freight train that is my nervous rambling from her compliment.

"What's your name?" She asks, tilting her head to the side with a peculiar look in her eye.

"Josie," I answer. "What's your name?" I repeat her question to avoid asking the questions I really want to know. Like, how did you get that scar? Or, are you here of your own free will?

"My name is Esmeralda." She says, giving me a soft smile, then asks, "Who's your sister doll?"

"Ashley," I say, and then stupidly continue with "Sylus is my cousin."

Her eyes go wide in terror, like she just witnessed someone chop my head off. She lunges toward me and wraps her hands around my upper arms. "What are you doing here?" She asks frantically, making my heart drop to my stomach. "You shouldn't be here."

"What? Why? What are you talking ab-"

"You need to leave," she cuts me off, trying to pull me towards the door. I can feel my phone start to vibrate in my pocket, but before I can question her or answer my phone, a throat-clearing sound comes from behind us. The alarm in my head starts blaring, screaming at me to sprint back to school. Just do anything to get away from this place.

We both abruptly freeze in our spot. As we turn around, I can see pity blanket the terror in her eyes that was there only seconds ago. We're met with Sylus and Ashley standing at the end of the hall. Ashley has a suspiciously blank expression on her face, and Sylus looks like he's just captured his prey.

"Esmeralda, I believe you have some work that needs attending," Sylus says, glaring at her like she just ruined his party, and she'll pay for it later. She hesitates before she turns to walk to the opposite end of the hall, up the stairs, and a door slams shut.

"Josie. What are you doing here?" He asks with a curious tone, slightly tilting his head to one side.

My phone starts vibrating in my pocket again, and I rest my shaking hand over it. Sylus tracks the motion. "I was looking for Ashley. I need to get back to school." I say, trying to sound confident.

"Well, now that you're here, I need to talk to you." He says, walking past me and down to the used-to-be library room. He flings his arm out, gesturing for me to follow him into the room ahead of him.

Trepidation creeps up my spine as I slowly lower myself into one of the wingback chairs, and Sylus takes up the one next to me. Looking at Ashley, he nods his head to grab one of the little boxes off the shelf, nodding back in understanding. She retrieves it and settles into the chair across from him.

After she hands him the box, he sets it down on the table in front of us and lifts the lid, revealing a mountain of loose white powder. A gasp gets lodged in my throat at the pile of drugs I'm staring at in the little box. I've never been around hard drugs before, so staring at the pile in the box and all the boxes that line the shelves makes apprehension pull at my limbs, urging me to get the fuck out of here.

Stupid. Stupid. I knew I should have just stayed in the car. Stupid Josie.

"Your eighteenth birthday is coming up." He announces

as he makes neat little lines of the white powder on the glass table. He pulls a metal straw out of his pocket, oblivious to my discomfort.

"Yes, it is." I acknowledge with a slight tremble in my voice, unsure where he's going with this.

He leans forward and snorts up one of the neat lines, then hands the straw over to Ashley. She bends down and sniffs up one of the lines with a comfort that shows she's done this a time or two. She rolls her eyes at my incredulous look and hands the straw back to Sylus.

"If you need a job, I know at least a dozen men who would be willing to pay generously for you." Fear creeps further up my spine and threatens to choke me at his disturbing words. "But you couldn't start until you turned eighteen." He quickly finishes, as if my lack of an answer is because of my age.

Acid burns my esophagus, and my knuckles turn white as I grip the armrest of the chair. "I'm just focusing on school and my photography right now, but thanks for the offer." He looks at me with amusement, and the ghost of a smile haunts his mouth.

Before he bends down to snort another line, he murmurs something under his breath that I can't quite make out over the pulsing in my ears. Ashley has been uncharacteristically quiet, and when I look over, she has the same blank expression on her face. It makes me all the more agitated.

By some miracle, Sylus changes the subject. "Speaking of your photography, I wanted to ask if you would take some pictures of my girls?" He asks, passing the straw back to Ashley. " I'm having a catalog put together for my clients." I sit in silence, not sure how to tell him no because I don't want to be on his bad side. He must take my silence as confusion. "It will be a menu of sorts." He clarifies.

The incessant vibrating of my phone reminds me I need to

get out of here as fast as possible, so I nod my head yes in agreement. Just as I go to stand, Sylus rests his palm on my thigh, and my heart slams against my chest, trying to break free like a caged animal.

My breathing becomes shallow as his palm slides to an inappropriate spot on my leg, his pinky skimming the hem of my dress. I don't know if it's the drugs that are influencing him right now, or if he's always like this, but he's the kind of person who just takes what he wants. That thought has my chest heaving, and if I grip this armrest any tighter, my knuckles are going to burst through my skin.

I notice his pupils are the size of nickels, and he has powder around the ring of his left nostril when he leans towards me. He opens his mouth to say something, but the front door slams open, startling me.

Tears threaten to fall out of relief when I see Milo, Kyler, Javi, and Carter walk through the door. I watch their assessing eyes take in the coke on the table and the way Sylus is sitting so close to me with his palm still resting on my thigh. Their expressions are filled with rage, and Milo clenches his fists like he wants to rearrange Sylus's face.

My heart begins to thrash for a whole new reason. I know how this must look, but maybe if I explain I took no part in any of it, they'll understand. I meet Milo's eyes, trying to relay just that, without using my words, when his face softens.

I relax a hair at his comprehension, but when he sets his eyes back on Sylus, the fury is back. "Sylus." He says through clenched teeth.

I take slow, deep breaths to try and calm my racing heart, feeling safer that they're here, but still uncomfortable with his heavy hand on my thigh.

"Josie," Carter says my name softly, bringing my attention to him. He's looking at me expectantly, but I'm too scared to move. Flicking my eyes down to my leg and back up to Carter. The moment understanding dawns on him, he walks over to me and holds out his hand. "Come on, Josie, it's okay. Take my hand." I let go of the armrest I had a death grip on and slowly slide my trembling hand into his.

"If you don't take your filthy fucking hand off of her, I'll gladly do it myself," Javi says. I would be surprised at his barely restrained anger if it weren't for the silent panic attack that was eating me alive.

The second he drops his hand, Carter pulls me up on wobbly legs and tucks me into his side, wrapping an arm around my waist.

"She must have a golden pussy if you're all fucking her." Sylus snarls, and Ashley screeches, "You're dating all of them?"

"That's your cousin, you fucking pervert," Kyler growls, ignoring Ashley.

Disregarding Kyler's comment, a wicked grin takes up Sylus' face. "Shoot up any parties lately?" My back stiffens at the mocking question that was meant to throw them off.

My dissipating panicked state is renewed at Sylus' question. As usual, they all keep their calm, meanwhile, my brain is working overtime trying to decipher what he meant.

When I gave my statement to the cops in the hospital, I asked them if they had found the shooters. All they could tell me was that it was still an ongoing investigation and that they hadn't caught the shooters yet. They couldn't give me any more information than that. Were they responsible for the shooting? Why were they shooting in the first place? They don't seem like the type to just shoot up a place for fun.

Guilt drowns me for not being more concerned about the other tragic event that happened that night. Surely, I wasn't the only one who was traumatized.

"I could ask you the same thing." Milo retorts, then turns to me. "Little Fox, will you go wait in the car with Carter?"

Bobbing my head, I let Carter lead me out to the car. I hear shouting when we step on the front porch, and glass shatters, tempting me to go back inside to make sure the guys are okay. I look up to Carter, but he just continues guiding me as if he doesn't hear the altercation happening back in the house. I shake it off at his lack of concern. If he's not worried about it, I'm not worried about it.

At least that's what I tell myself.

Resting his hand on my lower back, Carter guides me over to Milo's sleek black Range Rover. Opening the door for me, I climb into the back seat and notice Adrian sitting in the front passenger seat.

I go to slide over to sit next to the door on the other side, but Carter pulls me back over to the middle, sidled up next to him. He grabs my chin and gently turns my head, scanning my eyes. "I didn't take any of the cocaine," I say, more relaxed now that I'm out of that house.

Adrian whips his body around. "What the fuck?!" he shouts, brows furrowed in anger and worry.

Ignoring Adrian, Carter is still staring at me with a stern expression, and the muscle in his jaw is clenching. "Did he hurt you?" Flicking my eyes down, unable to look at him any longer. Embarrassment washes over me while I simultaneously hold back vomit at the way my cousin was touching me.

"Did he touch you?" Carter says just above a whisper, and I hear Adrian curse under his breath.

Shaking my head no. "Nothing more than what you saw," I murmur.

"If you would have just answered your goddamn phone, this could have been prevented." Adrian huffs. I know he's right, but the irritation in his voice still stings.

"Adrian." Carter scolds, and he turns back around in his seat. He begins texting on his phone so aggressively, I'm surprised the screen on his phone doesn't crack.

God, I'm so pathetic. Why couldn't I just answer my phone? Why couldn't I just stand up and walk out of there? Why did I let him touch me like that? I know I can stand up for myself; I literally did it the day before with Jake. Ugh, what the fuck is wrong with me? Do I think so little of myself that I just allow bad things to happen to me?

I bite the inside of my cheek to hold back a sob as all the emotions from this whole afternoon bubble to the surface. Carter nudges my chin, forcing me to look back at him. "Don't listen to him, he's been in a bad mood all day." He says.

Not sure how to answer that because Adrian always seems to be in a bad mood when I'm around. Carter must see the skepticism on my face. Instead of trying to convince me, he just pulls me closer to him, and I rest my head on his shoulder. He kisses the top of my head and takes hold of my hand, resting it in his lap.

My adrenaline finally begins to subside, and I can feel tiredness start to take over my body. I close my eyes, soaking up Carter's soothing affection.

Just as I'm on the precipice of slumber, the door on my other side swings open. My head bolts from Carter's shoulder as Kyler climbs into the seats in the back, and Javi slides into the space next to me.

I look back at Kyler to see a concerned look on his face. "What happened?" I rush out. "Are you guys okay?" Flicking my eyes between him and Javi, checking them for any injuries.

Kyler leans forward, the tip of his nose touching mine. "We're okay, Gingersnap," he says quietly. "You scared the shit out of us when you didn't answer your phone." He leans forward and places the lightest kiss on my lips as if he needs to reassure himself that I am sitting in front of him and not still back in that house.

I blush at the intimate gesture, very aware that everyone is staring at us. Holding my breath, waiting for any indication that any of them are upset that Kyler kissed me.

I'm not ashamed he kissed me, the opposite, actually. It felt...right. It's not lost on me that these strange five men, whom I hardly know, have once again come to my rescue. But from the way they look at me and care for me, it feels different. It feels genuine. And it tugs at that part inside of me that is desperate for someone to see me. Maybe that does make me desperate, but for the first time in my life, I can't seem to care. I've felt a pull towards all of them, well, most of them. There is something about Adrian that piques my interest, but his bad mood makes me apprehensive. Even so, I don't want to cause any problems between them, and he doesn't seem to be the best at controlling his emotions.

So suffice it to say I'm shocked when none of them says a word, least of all him. Instead, when I turn to face them, I see nothing but the same concern Kyler had had on his face and a little bit of relief.

"I'm sorry," I whisper, but as the words leave my mouth, I realize something. "Wait, how did you know where Sylus' place is?" I question.

I know everyone knows who he is, but they were talking to each other like they already knew each other. Yesterday, when we ran into him at my house, Kyler seemed off then, too.

Is it just because of Sylus's reputation?

The silence thickens, but before it can become awkward, Milo finally speaks up. "Everyone who's anyone knows who he is and what he does." Letting out a frustrated sigh, he resumes with "I don't want you coming back here. It's not safe." The words are gentle but firm.

Normally, I would protest because he's telling me what to do, and also I'm stubborn like that, but I agree with him on this. "I agree. I didn't want to be here in the first place." I tell him truthfully.

That seems to placate him. He dips his head and turns to start the car, satisfied with my answer.

"You scared me half to death, Red," Javi says throwing his arm around my shoulders, burying his nose in my hair. "If he ever touches you again, I'll cut his hands off, so the only pleasure he can get is from one of his whores." He whispers, causing goosebumps to erupt over my arms.

Not sure what to say to that, I relax into him, soaking up his warmth, not sure how much longer this will last. Because for the first time, I'm realizing that they know much more than they're letting on.

Finally, having my Roja in my arms calms the demon that I so rarely let loose. Though since laying eyes on her, he seems to want to come out and play more often than not. Whether it's for pain or pleasure.

Seeing the terror on her face when we stepped into that house had me on the verge of murder. I was hanging on by a thread, but the last thing we needed was to frighten her more. The second she and Carter stepped onto the front porch, my restraint slipped.

Grabbing the slime ball by the throat and slamming him into the coffee table, shattering it into a thousand pieces, white powder floating around the air like smoke, would have to do for now. All three of us buried our noses in our arms, not wanting to inhale any of the bitter powder.

Striding over to Ashley, standing in the corner like a deer caught in headlights. I fist my hand in her hair, pulling it tight, and tilting her head back to look in her eyes. "It should've been you in that fucking car," I growl, spittle hitting her face, "don't think I haven't forgotten about you."

This crazy bitch smiles at my threat, and a high-pitched

giggle releases from her mouth. "Does she know?" The snide question has my other hand wrapping around her throat. "I'm going to take that as a no." She rasps as my grip tightens around her neck.

Her question brings back the memories of that night, the moment I saw Josie lying face down on the pavement, pain erupted through my chest, and I could feel the tendons in my heart tearing as it was ripped in two.

I've never hated myself more than I did at that moment. Feeling her pain would have been a reprieve from the disgust I felt for myself that night, and continue to feel every time I see her. I thought covering up the hate for myself with humor would counteract the feeling, but it just dulls it. It turns out that the only thing that completely calms it is Josie.

And it's all thanks to this traitorous lech in front of me.

"When you're not lying on your back for the desperate men of this town, I suggest you watch it. You won't see me coming, and it won't be quick. For every ounce of pain that Josie has suffered, you'll suffer a million times worse. *Cuida tu espalda perra*." Just as her face starts to turn a reddish-purple, I let go. Satisfaction fills me, for now, when I hear her gasping for life.

"You good?" Milo asks, stepping in front of me, worry etched across his face.

Taking in a few slow, deep breaths to get my bearings, I nod my head, and the three of us head for the door. As we make it to the front door, Sylus decides to speak up, "Does she know?" He grunts out the same question but for an entirely different reason. The three of us ignored him, not knowing how or wanting to answer him.

"Will you take me home?" Josie asks, her sweet voice pulling me from my thoughts as we pull away from Sylus's, "I don't think I have the energy to deal with school right now." She adds, leaning her head on my shoulder.

I look over Josie's head to Carter and see him holding her hand in his lap, tracing circles over her palm. A little shocked at his gentle display since growing up in a household where a slap to the face was as gentle as it gets. "Is anyone home? I don't think you should be alone right now." He voices.

"We'll go back to my house," Milo says before Josie can answer, "If that's okay with everyone?"

"Fine with me," Josie answers, snuggling closer to me.

Having her warm body pressed against me stirs my cock to life, and her warm breath fanning across my neck has me holding back a groan. Just as that thought crosses my mind, she lets out a tinkling giggle that I know doesn't just affect me, if Kyler's hushed groan from the backseat is anything to go by.

"That tickles," She giggles again, and I scrunch my eyebrows in confusion at my hand that I've strained to keep at a respectable spot on her shoulder. When I look back at Carter again to see a dopey smile on his face as he continues tracing patterns on her hand, I realize he's the one making her laugh.

He may be the quietest and most reserved one of the bunch, but he can be a real beast if he's pushed too hard. If anyone is deserving of her, it's him, and I have a feeling if anyone fucks with our little Red again, his beast won't be so dormant next time.

"Why are we at Jak-" Josie's face reddens before she can finish that question, biting down on her lip.

Milo eyes her through the rearview mirror cocking an eyebrow at her, daring her to finish that sentence. "Sorry," she rushes out, "I forgot that you guys are brothers."

"Half," he grunts. "Half brothers"

"Even if you're only half, he's still your brother," she teases, chuckling.

He scoffs, pulling along the huge driveway of his dad's mansion. "It's a bit of a sore subject for him," I whisper in her ear, and a shiver works its way down her body.

Carter must have felt it too, and I can't help the predatory grin that takes over my mouth at the desire I see on his face, reflecting how I feel at the reaction of her drool-worthy body.

Keeping my eyes locked on his, I get closer to her ear. "Do you like feeling my breath on your body, Red?" I whisper again, emphasizing my Spanish accent. Hoping she picks up on how I can roll my tongue, and the many other things I can do with it.

I know she's picked up on it when her arms sprout goosebumps. "M-maybe," she stutters, and a sinful smile tugs at the corner of Carter's mouth. Knowing exactly where his mind is, I mimic his smile.

Before things can go any further, Adrian flings his door open, signaling that we've parked. I kiss Josie on the cheek. "We'll continue this later, Red," I say, flinging my door open. I hop out thinking about getting kicked in the dick to try to get rid of this boner I've had since I felt her against me.

Walking up to the mansion that has an obnoxious number of windows, I can't help but sympathize with the unlucky bastard who has to clean them. Following Milo up the stone steps and into the glass monstrosity, he leads us to the kitchen. A floor-to-ceiling window takes up the whole wall, giving us a perfect view of a backyard that's wet-dream worthy to rich assholes everywhere.

"Wow," Josie says with awe, "This is so...beautiful. Everything is so sharp and shiny."

Shrugging his shoulders, Milo replies, "I guess. I try to spend as little time here as possible."

Transfixed with the large window and the picturesque

view on the other side of it, she takes it in like she's never seen a backyard before. Ignoring Milo's comment, she says, "All this natural light would be amazing for taking pictures." Watching her face light up at the mention of her favorite hobby has an unfamiliar feeling warming my chest.

"Haven't you been here before?" Kyler asks.

"No," she answers, and sadness settles over her face. "Jake would invite me to his parties, but my sister told me he only invited me out of pity, and no one wanted me to come," shaking her head like she's trying to rid herself of a bad memory. "It's okay, though, I have Zeke and Kiera."

A low growl emits from somewhere. Not entirely sure who it came from, but I find myself holding one back at the mention of her cunt of a sister. I should've strangled the life out of her when I had the chance. No one should feel like they're not wanted, especially someone as kind and pure as Josie.

A loud chirping breaks the thickening silence, "Zeke!" Josie squeals out of excitement, and a pang of jealousy hits my chest, hoping one day she'll feel the same way about me. About us.

Adrian stomps out of the room like his mom just told him he couldn't go outside and play with his friends. The scowls I see on Carter, Kyler, and Milo's faces echo what I'm thinking. He needs to get his shit together and just talk to her. The longer he waits, the worse it's going to be.

"Z, I'm fine. Calm down," Josie says, sliding open the obnoxiously large glass door to the backyard and stepping out. Pacing around the pool, flinging her arms out in frustration.

Anticipation makes my skin itch for the day when I can have that same easy relationship with her that she has with Zeke.

"That was too fucking close today," Carter grits.

"Way too fucking close," Milo agrees. "How did we not know Sylus was her cousin?"

"I don't know," Kyler answers, "but he was at her house yesterday. He and her mom were leaving when we pulled up."

My head snaps in his direction. "Do you think her mom knows what her sister did?" An unsettling feeling wraps around my nerves as the question leaves my mouth. If her mom is in on this, we need to get her out of that damn house. "Do you think her mom works for Sylus too?" I voice my worry, suddenly feeling jittery about this whole situation.

The pensive looks on their faces tell me they're thinking exactly what I'm thinking. If her mom works for Sylus, this brings a plethora of new questions to light, and a fuck ton of problems.

"It would make sense," Milo states, " A single mom with two kids. I imagine her factory job doesn't pay well. She sleeps all day and works all night," he ponders out loud.

"Fuck!" Carter yells. Unfortunately, he and I have experience with shitty parents, but it's one thing to know you have shitty parents and another to think they love you unconditionally, all the while they're quietly deceiving you. "We need to get her out of here." He sighs heavily, running a hand down his face.

"Her birthday isn't for another couple of weeks." Kyler points out.

"One of us should stay with her," I suggest, "or we can alternate nights staying with her. Zeke isn't always around, and she shouldn't be alone until we figure out what's going on with her mom."

Looking around, everyone dips their head in agreement, "What are we going to do with the broody asshole?" I question.

"The broody asshole thinks we need to tell her what's

going on," Adrian says flatly from behind me. We all tear our eyes away from the beauty pacing along the pool to find him leaning against the countertop in the middle of the kitchen.

"It's funny that you just know that I'm talking about you." I chuckle, and he flips me off.

"We need to tell her," he reiterates, "the sooner we tell her, the better."

"That's rich coming from you," Kyler says. "Have you talked to her yet? Or is this just another way to deflect from your problem?" he chastises.

"Fuck off. I haven't found the right time." Adrian answers sternly.

"Well, you better make it quick. She already thinks you hate her." Carter states, and I don't miss the annoyance on his face.

Rolling his eyes, he crosses his arms over his chest. "We'll tell her. Soon," he replies.

"You better. We've been working at this for too long for it to be ruined out of carelessness." I say, noticing his nostrils flare out of irritation. The tension in the air grows stifling as we all let those words sink in.

We already almost lost her once out of carelessness, and I don't think we're lucky enough to bounce back from it a second time. Self-loathing burrows under my skin like a tick, reminding me how much we don't deserve her. I must be a glutton for punishment because I'd rather look at her gorgeous face every day, reminding me of what I did, than not have her at all.

Her laugh from outside is like a beacon to my miserable thoughts and smothers them with her happiness. We all turn to see her sitting on the edge of the pool with her legs dangling in the water. Her head is thrown back in laughter, and the afternoon sun highlights her thick red hair, inviting me to run my hands through it.

When she tilts her head back and notices all of us staring at her, she freezes like she's been caught with her hand in the cookie jar. Suddenly aware of how much attention is on her, she starts to fidget, not knowing what to do with it all. She brings her thumb up to her mouth and starts to nibble on her nail, while her eyes flick between all of us. When she lands on me, I give her a wink and watch as her skin flushes that adorable pink as she starts to squirm.

"Christ," Milo mutters at the way she unintentionally makes us lust after her "when she realizes the power she holds over men, I have a feeling it's going to bring us all to our knees," turning his eyes to Adrian he finishes "I hope you're there to witness it because if she finds out what you guys have been doing behind her back you're going to be doing more than bowing."

Adrian never takes his eyes off of her, drinking in every inch of her. "I'll tell her this weekend. I promise."

"Okay, babe, talk to you later." Josie finishes her phone call with Zeke as I plop down next to her, sticking my feet in the water.

"So, how long are you grounded for?" I say jokingly, poking fun at how protective Zeke can be of her.

"A whole year," she says sarcastically, "He took away my driving privileges, and I have a hundred hours of community service."

Tilting my head in uncertainty, not sure she caught onto my joke "Oh, you mean Zeke," she says feigning confusion with a mocking smile "He was just making sure I was okay," disappointment plasters to her face and her next words have guilt eating at my bones like acid "I did get my license suspended this morning when I went to court though."

This is not the conversation I intended to have when I came out here, and the look on her face is soul-crushing, so I try to make light of the situation for both of our sakes. "Well, look at the bright side, now you can ride to school with us."

"I wouldn't want to impose," she pauses, "besides, you guys have already done enough for me."

Tucking a strand of hair behind her ear, "You could never be an imposition. If anything, it would make my morning better if I got to start it with you," I tell her honestly, wanting her to realize how much she means to us.

"Okay," she says, ducking her head, looking at me through her lashes. "Is that a Spanish accent?" she asks, changing the subject.

Her body goes rigid as I lean closer to her. "*Si*," I say, making sure my breath tickles her ear as it did on the car ride here. "Do you like my accent, Red?"

She looks at me with wide eyes, the emerald green sparkling with interest and hesitation, but before she can answer, the kitchen door slides open. "Is he bothering you, Gingersnap? Just give me the word, and I'll drown him in the pool." Kyler says jokingly, though I don't doubt he would drown me in the pool if she told him to.

She chuckles, shaking her head, "No. I was just telling him how much I like his accent." She returns my wink from earlier, surprising me with her playful side.

"Oh, sweet girl, if my accent keeps that look in your eyes, then I'll talk to you until you're weak in the knees." I flirt back, while keeping my eyes locked on hers to show how serious I am. I'm not sure how she's going to react to me being so forward.

"If you talk to me for too long with that accent," she bites on her bottom lip as if to stop herself from speaking, but carries on, "You're going to do more than make my knees weak."

That's it. I'm dead. I've barely touched her, but it's her words that are going to do me in. If her playful banter is anything to go by, we're definitely going to have our hands full.

"When you're done undressing each other with your eyes, can you come inside? We need to talk." This time it's Milo who speaks, and I don't miss the hint of jealousy in his tone.

"Come on, Red," I stand up and hold my hand out for her, "let's go before I talk you into an orgasm." I tease, and she turns scarlet. Pulling her to stand and throwing my arm over her shoulders, just so I can feel her luscious curves against my body, we make our way inside.

Just as we step back into the kitchen, her stomach growls, and she wraps her arms around her middle to try to hide it. "Could we possibly make some lunch? Or order something? I was too nervous to eat breakfast, and now I'm starving."

"How did court go by the way?" Kyler asks, pulling her onto the stool between him and Carter at the counter, while Milo and Adrian start making sandwiches for everyone. I don't miss the same guilty look on Adrian's face that I felt at the mention of court.

"I…um…got my license suspended for a year, and I have to do a hundred hours of community service." She answers shamefully.

"Well, that's not so bad." Adrian chimes in, most likely trying to make himself feel better.

Her head flips in his direction out of surprise, with just a hint of a smile on her lips. "No," she agrees, "I'm just embarrassed that it happened. I should never have gotten in that car." Everyone's silence is agreement enough. "But lesson learned. I'm never touching alcohol again." She shrugs her shoulders to brush it off, but the tinge of sadness hiding under her smile shows how much it affected her.

"So..." Kyler starts, "about Sylus." Just the mention of his name causes her back to go ramrod straight.

"I'm sorry. I shouldn't have been there in the first place. I didn't even want to go. I only went inside to find Ashley because she left me in the car. Then I met this beautiful girl who tried to get me to leave, but it was too late. Next thing I know, they were doing coke and-"

Carter reaches over and squeezes her hand to calm her nervous rambling, and Kyler rubs his hand up and down her back. "Hey, hey. It's okay, you just worried us when you told us you were stopping there, then you weren't answering your phone." He says in a gentle tone, trying to calm her sudden stress.

"You don't have to apologize, Little Fox. Just answer your phone next time, yeah?" Milo asks.

"Yeah. Yeah, okay," she starts fidgeting with her other hand, picking at her thumb. Telling me this conversation is making her anxious, "I just, he's never been so forward with me, and it caught me off guard." She starts picking at her thumb like it's offended her in some way.

Adrian slams a drawer at her confession, causing her to flinch. "Sorry," he quickly apologizes, "I just hate that you were in that situation in the first place." He clenches his jaw angrily, and if he spreads mayo on that bread any harder, he's going to be spreading mayo on the palm of his hand.

"Babe," Carter says, pulling her attention from Adrian's assault on the bread, "We don't think it's safe for you to be alone. So, we think it would be best for one of us to stay with you on the nights Zeke can't."

Contemplating what Carter said, she starts digging at her thumb more aggressively while simultaneously chewing on her bottom lip. Her absence of a response puts me on edge when worry creases her eyebrows. I flick my gaze to the others and see the same uneasiness I'm feeling. I wet a dish towel and passed it to Kyler, nodding at her thumb. He slowly takes her hand and starts wiping the blood that has started to seep from it.

"Red," I say softly, getting her attention. "What are you thinking about?"

"I...just... I...isn't this weird?" she stammers out.

"What's weird?" Carter questions, wanting her to clarify.

"This," letting go of Carter's hand, flinging hers between all of us.

The five of us let out a collective sigh, not sure where she was going with that.

"Once we see something we like, we go after it." Milo states so matter-of-factly, "and I don't think it's any secret that we like you."

"But... all of you?" Her eyes quickly snap to Adrian. I would have missed it if I weren't paying attention. I clench my fist with the need to punch him for even making her question it. "I mean, I like you guys too, if it hasn't been obvious, but isn't that weird, and soon? I mean, we hardly know each other."

"Look, we get that it's not normal, but we like you. We understand that one woman being with five men is unconventional; however, we've been friends for a long time. We trust each other and care about each other. I want to see my friends happy, and if that means sharing the right woman, then so be it." I explain to her, hoping to ease some of her anxiety.

"I've never even had one boyfriend, I don't know how I would handle five," she sucks in a deep breath. "I've never even had sex before. How does that work? What if one of you gets jealous, or what if one of you wants to break up? Or another girl catches your attention?" Her breathing is becoming rapid and shallow. "I could never choose one of you, and I don't want to be the reason you guys stop being friends. I don't want to be that person. I'm not worth a lifetime of friendship," she finishes, and her chest is heaving from her anxious rambling.

"Do you always ramble this much when you get nervous?" I point out, trying to distract her and lighten the mood.

Carter takes up Kylers' previous spot and starts rubbing his hand up and down her back. "We can take it as slow as you need. We go at your pace."

"What if my relationship with one of you grows faster than others? Won't that create animosity?" she responds.

"Like Javi said, we trust each other. We know it's going to take time. If a relationship builds quicker than some, does that mean you like the others any less?" Adrian surprisingly speaks up, and Josie's face falls in relief with his input.

Remembering Carter's words from earlier, that Josie thinks Adrian hates her, comes back to me, and her anxious questioning makes sense. Adrian is the only one who hasn't made his feelings obvious. Which is fine, but if letting her know that he's on board is what's going to make her feel comfortable, then he needs to do better.

She shakes her head at his question, "No," she states assuredly.

"That's all we ask," Adrian replies, setting a sandwich down in front of her. He cups her cheek, running his thumb along her jaw. The sense of ease that washes over her is infectious, and everyone's shoulders visibly relax. "We all just have to be patient, and we'll get there," he nods as if speaking the words to himself, drops his hand, and strides out of the room.

The guys grunt in agreement, and Josie dips her head, finally relaxing enough that she can take a full, deep breath. "Won't having five boyfriends make me a whore?" she says, the last word so soft it's like she's scared of it.

"I can't speak for you, but I don't care what people think, and honestly, our relationship is no one's business," Milo tells her. "Even so, we're all in this together. If someone messes with one of us, they mess with all of us."

"This is going to take some getting used to," she says, making sure to look at all of us. "That being said, I do want to try it, but if someone starts to feel left out or something is bothering you, you have to promise me you'll talk to me about it." We all nod our heads in agreement, "and no secrets. The only way this is going to work is if we trust each other."

Adrian walks back in, grunting his agreement as he strides over and proceeds to wrap a bandage around her raw thumb.

"Good," she affirms, taking a bite of her sandwich and moaning, "this is so good. I feel like I haven't eaten in days." Of course, she's too caught up in her sandwich to notice the effect her suggestive noises have on us.

Leaning over the counter and placing both elbows on top to hide my perma- boner, I seem to have around her, "So, you've never had sex?" I tease, waggling my eyebrows at her.

Her face blanches, and I can't help but chuckle at my little Red. Excitement courses through me at her lack of experience and all the firsts we'll get to have with her. She has no idea what she's in for and just how bad we've already fallen for her.

Chapter Fifteen

JOSIE

If Jesus himself came down and told me I wasn't dreaming, I still wouldn't believe what's happening. It all happened so fast, I wouldn't be surprised if I had whiplash. I went from never having one boyfriend to five in the span of five minutes. That's got to be some kind of record, for me at least. What the hell am I supposed to do with five men anyway?

Josie, get it together. You're rambling internally now, and you're just staring at your sandwich like you want to make out with it.

"So, you've never had sex?" Javi asks, and I feel the blood draining from my face.

How in the ham sandwich could I let that slip out? Well, if my anxiety doesn't scare them away, then that definitely will. Putting my food down and groaning, I cover my face with both hands out of embarrassment. "I didn't mean to tell you that," I whine.

I hear them all snickering like my embarrassment is amusing to them as I pray for the sweet, sweet release of death. I feel a warm hand wrap around my wrist, pulling it from my face. "It's okay, babe. Your pace, remember." Carter says, with mirth shining in those golden honey eyes behind thick-framed glasses.

"Besides," Grabbing my other wrist, Kyler chuckles, "Being the first man to touch you is a huge turn-on." he places his hand on my neck, stroking his thumb along the sensitive skin. "This is going to be fun."

My breath hitches at his spine-tingling words, and if the predatory look they're giving me is anything to go by, it's obvious how I affect them. Wanting to have some fun of my own, I say, "Oh, I didn't say you're the first men to touch me," pausing to let my words sink in, " I've just never had sex." I counter, pulling both of my hands free to casually take a bite of my sandwich.

I bounce my leg nervously, waiting on pins and needles for some kind of retort. When nothing comes, I look up to find five angry faces glaring a hole through my head. I debate whether I should tell them about my embarrassing interactions when it comes to the male species. One time, a boy sneezed in my mouth mid-make-out, and it took everything I had not to throw up in his. There was the time a boy's mom walked in on us making out while he had his hand up my shirt, trying to cop a feel, only for him to burst into tears and start sobbing about how it was all my fault for distracting him. Or, the most humiliating, the countless boys who have ditched me for Ashley. Needless to say, my history with boys isn't stellar, but do they need to know that?

A rogue smile tilts my lips when I realize none of them has said anything. "You're right, this is going to be fun."

I push my bar stool back from the counter when a hand on my wrist stops me. The intense look in his eyes counteracts the soft grip on my hand. "Little Fox, I know we're still getting to know each other, but even just mentioning another man touching you turns my blood to lava." I swallow so loud I'm sure the neighbors could hear it, "and if any man touches what's ours, they will get burned." The gravelly sound of Milo's voice has my thoughts drifting to naughty places, but the look on his face portrays his seriousness.

Nodding my head in understanding, his words sink to my stomach with a weight I'm not entirely sure how to decipher. I should be more concerned about the sincerity behind his words and the little voice in the back of my head telling me they're dangerous, but the feeling of want that they make me feel by their protectiveness overrides that little voice.

These men are going to eat me alive, and I'm not sure I'll have the strength to survive.

"Shit!" Kyler mutters, breaking my stare from Milo. "I need to go pick Liam up from school."

"Carter and I need to get to football practice, too," Adrian adds.

Scrambling down from my stool, I quickly rinse my plate and put it in the dishwasher. Heading back through the foyer, I take in all the light that's streaming in from the ungodly number of windows this house seems to have. Even the banisters around the stairs are glass. The two large, thick slabs of glass that make up the front door practically invite burglars to come and rob them.

The light shining in from everywhere has my hands itching for my camera and my mind racing with all the different pictures I could capture here. "Another time," Carter says, draping his arm over my shoulder, somehow knowing where my mind was.

Sliding into the back seat again, this time between Carter and Kyler, while Javi takes up the back. "So," I begin, "Whose sleeping with me tonight?" Everyone freezes like someone just pushed pause, and my words register in my brain too late. If I keep embarrassing myself in front of them, I'm going to turn into a tomato with all this blushing.

Clearing my throat, "I meant, who is staying with me?" I

explain, "Zeke said he's busy. So he probably won't stop by tonight."

"Well, Carter and Adrian have football. Kyler and Milo both have family obligations. So, it looks like you're stuck with me, Red." Javi answers for everyone, "Though I can think of a few things other than sleeping to occupy our time." He adds, flashing me a panty-melting smile.

Not wanting him to see how his words affect me, I deflect, "You mean like homework?" I respond sarcastically, and the others chortle around me.

Flipping my palm over, Carter traces a smiley face, mirroring his silent amusement. His way of communicating in silence with the others around makes my stomach flutter as his soft fingertips dance over my hand, forcing a smile to lift the corners of my mouth.

"Are you starting tomorrow?" I ask him. I know he's the quarterback, but before they transferred, we had a decent one. They've only had one game, and I missed it since I was still in the hospital, so I've never seen him play. If the rumors are true about him being scouted already, I can't wait to see him play. Plus, I'll get to see Adrian and Zeke play.

I don't get an answer from him, so I just assume he didn't hear me. Tapping my finger on his hand that's resting on my palm, he turns to look at me. "Are you starting tomorrow?" I repeat, and his eyes light up.

"I am. Are you coming to the game?" he questions excitedly.

"Yes, I haven't missed one of Zeke's games since sophomore year," his smile falters, I don't know if it's because he thinks I'm only going for my best friend but I don't want him feeling like I won't be there for him as well, "but now that you guys are on the team, I have all the more reason to go," much to my relief his face lights up again "maybe I'll even paint your number on my face." I tease, nudging his shoulder.

He traces the number 12 on my hand and turns his head to stare back out the window. I haven't known these guys for very long, but I'm quickly realizing I have something in common with all of them.

Carter has a shy side that I can relate to, while Javi and Kyler's playful sides bring mine to the surface. Adrian's strong silence speaks to my stubbornness, and like Milo, I'm protective over the people I care about.

Judging by the reactions they had at Sylus's, I know they have a dark side they are shielding from me that will come out sooner or later.

"What about my number?" Adrian asks, turning around in the passenger seat, feigning offense that I didn't offer to put his number on my face.

"Oh, do you play football too?" I joke, soaking up all the interactions I can get with him. Out of the five, he's the most guarded. I'm determined to wear him down and get him to drop his guard, even if it's just the tiniest bit.

"Ha ha. If you didn't already know, my number is 7. I expect to see it painted on that pretty little face of yours tomorrow night." He says with finality, turning back in his seat.

"Are you guys going too?"

"Of course. We can stop and pick you up on the way." Milo answers, staring me down in the rearview mirror.

Opening my mouth to reply, I'm cut off by my vibrating phone. Seeing Kiera's name on the screen, I let out a heavy sigh, already knowing what it's going to say.

Kiera: Hey, chick! I hate to do this to you, but I need to reschedule again.

I'm starting to get a distinct feeling that she's avoiding me, but I have no idea why. The longer I hold onto this secret, the worse it's going to be when I tell her.

"You look like someone just killed your puppy," Kyler tells me.

"I was supposed to hang out with Kiera, but she rescheduled on me, again." I feel guilty for holding this secret, but if she's avoiding me, how am I supposed to tell her? "I need to talk to her, but she keeps blowing me off." I express my frustration, taking it out on my bottom lip.

"Didn't she reschedule last night, too?" Kyler asks, cocking an eyebrow, "What do you need to talk to her about that's so important?" I see the suspicion on his face, which just makes me feel more guilty that he thinks I'm keeping something from them.

Deciding I need to tell someone about it before I explode from guilt, I tell them. I tell them how I stumbled up to the bathroom to splash water on my face, and how I discovered the stomach curdling threesome. I even told them that was the reason I took Ashley's car and was driving so recklessly. I didn't, however, tell them how someone pushed me off the road, and the strangers who stopped to check on me.

I'm still getting to know them, and I'm not sure they wouldn't believe me anyway because I was drunk. I don't need their pitiful looks. I got that enough from the nurses, and doctor, and that judgy judge.

"It's not your fault she keeps blowing you off," Kyler says, "maybe you should pull her aside at school tomorrow and tell her, just so you can get it off your chest." He finishes as we pull into the school parking lot, right as the bell rings for the end of the day.

Getting out of the car, Carter kisses me on the forehead, and Adrian gives me an awkward hug that says I'm not comfortable kissing you on the forehead, but I want to give you a hug to show that I'm trying and that I don't hate you. Or I'm reading too much into it.

After they walk off to the locker rooms for football practice, I agree to meet the guys back in the parking lot after I've gotten my homework for the classes that I missed.

Walking out of my last class, I'm just about to turn the corner when I hear a familiar voice that has me stopping in my tracks and plastering my back to the wall. "….. she wasn't at school today. I saw them this morning, but I haven't seen them since."

"Sylus said she left with them. They must have ditched the rest of the day," Cody responds to Chance's statement, "Either way, he's fucking pissed. He seems to think she's with all of them."

"Being a whore must run in the family," Chance says, and they both begin to laugh like deranged frat boys. "She should get used to laying on her back, so maybe that's not a bad thing."

My earlier concern about dating five men is brought to light by his words. Much to my surprise, the shame I expected to feel never comes. No humiliation or embarrassment makes itself known; if anything, I'm angry. Angry because who the hell is he to judge what someone does with their body and who they do it with?

The hypocrisy of his words doesn't escape me either. Coming from a man who cheated on his girlfriend in a threesome with his best friend only goes to show what a self-righteous asshole he is. The building anger only renews my urgency to tell Kiera that he's cheating on her, to hell with the consequences.

Anger builds in my bones, and I chastise myself for thinking he was my friend. Though I don't know if I'm more upset at that, or the fact that they somehow know and communicate with Sylus. A nagging feeling of suspicion prods at the back of my brain as I realize, not for the first time, that something else is going on and somehow I'm a part of it.

"Hey, guys." The high-pitched feminine voice is my cue to walk away. Sophie's grating voice has me taking a few deep breaths to calm my simmering rage and making my way back out to the guys.

My mind is running rampant with questions, and I'm not even sure how to begin finding answers. How do Chance and Cody even know Sylus? Why are they keeping tabs on me? Why does it matter who I'm dating? Then a gut-curdling thought has dread blooming in my chest: was Sylus the one who tried to run me off the road?

No, that doesn't make sense. His disgusting touching and odd questions earlier made it seem more like he wanted me to work for him to make money. Could it have been Cody? He was at my house the day after I got out of the hospital, and there was the incident at school.

Shit! I need to talk to Zeke.

I make it my mission to talk to him tomorrow; if not, these thoughts will spiral and fester, causing me to be in a permanent state of panic. Well, worse than usual. But really, how much worse can it get?

The uneasy feeling I had is instantly washed away when I make it back to the parking lot. Liam bursts into a sprint faster than a Kentucky Derby horse the moment I step onto the parking lot. I tried to brace myself for the moment of impact, but there was no stopping him once he started running. The moment the guys noticed where he was running to, Kyler hollered at him to slow down, but he must not have heard him.

A moment later, he collides with me, throwing his arms around me and giving me the biggest bear hug. I wince a little at his grip around my waist, still a little sore from the accident, but there was no way I could tell him to stop and ruin his happy mood.

"I missed you guys today," Liam says, pulling back from me. "Can we have another movie night?" He's practically vibrating with joy.

"Another time, Liam. We're having dinner with Mom and Dad, remember?" Kyler spoke up before me, thank God. I couldn't be the one to crush his spirit.

"Okay," he says, sounding disappointed and looking to the ground.

"Hey," I say, trying to get his attention, "how about this weekend?" I offer, not able to take the sad look that's come over him. His eyes light up at the words, and he looks over to Kyler, silently asking for permission. Kyler nods his head as he looks at me adoringly, but quickly follows it up with "We'll have to double check with mom and dad first, though."

"Yes!" Liam shouts, pumping his fist in the air. "Thanks dingleberry!" He throws his arms around a groaning Kyler as Milo and Javi begin to laugh hysterically. I can't help the laugh that breaks free at the unfortunate nickname.

"Dingleberry, huh?" Milo finally gets out between laughs.

"Shut the fuck up." Kyler snaps. "Liam, let's go. We need to get home so we can do our homework before dinner."

Liam throws his arms around me one more time to hug goodbye before dashing over to Kyler's car.

"I'll see you tomorrow, Gingersnap. I know Javi will be with you, but text or call me if you need anything." He says before leaning down and placing a soft kiss on my lips. I give him a bashful smile, knowing that Javi and Milo saw the kiss, but not sure how they're going to react to it.

The curious stares of the few students who are still lingering in the parking lot don't go unnoticed either.

Watching as Kyler climbs into his car and leaves the parking lot, I saunter over to Javi and Milo, feeling a bit sheepish about the kiss they just witnessed. To my surprise, neither of them looks angry or jealous, which makes me feel better. If anything, they look content, like we've been doing this for longer than we have. Like, this is nothing new to them.

Here I thought they would be jealous of each other, because the thought of them sharing another girl has jealousy digging its ugly claws into my chest. My grip tightens on the binder holding today's homework as my insecurities threaten to choke me.

"What's wrong?" Milos questions, eyebrows pinching with concern.

I feel like it's too early to ask them about their dating history, so instead, I settle on "That didn't bother you? When Kyler kissed me?" I ask, and his face slackens with relief.

"No, Little Fox," he says, resting a hand on the nape of my neck, bending to my eye level. "Like Javi said earlier, we've been friends a long time and just want to see each other happy." At his reassuring words, he presses a kiss to my forehead, "Now come on, I'll give you and Javi a ride home."

"Let's go, Red." Javi swings his arm over my shoulders and guides me to the front, opening the door for me.

A few short minutes later, we're pulling up to my house, but before I climb out, Milo grabs my hand and shoots a look at Javi. "If you guys need anything, text any one of us." They appear to be having a silent conversation with their eyes as mine ping pong between them, trying to figure out what's not being said.

The earlier events of the day must have them all on edge, and the all too familiar feeling of guilt creeps up on me.

"We'll call if we need anything," I promise and squeeze his hand before I open the door to hop out of his ridiculously expensive SUV.

After spending the afternoon in Milo's luxurious house, mine feels like a shoebox in comparison. Javi follows me inside, and I begin to feel self-conscious about how little it is. I notice him looking around and taking everything in, and I have to force myself not to squirm with discomfort. I didn't feel this way when Kyler was here, but after seeing Milos' place and the expensive cars he and Kyler drive, thoughts of not being enough for them start to take root.

Watching as Javi walks over to stare at some picture frames hanging on the wall, all thoughts of not being enough are out the window, and I groan internally as he gets a good look at pictures of me as a child. I hear as he softly chuckles to himself, but he never says anything, just takes it all in.

"Do you want something to drink?" I ask, going to the fridge to give myself something to do, "We have juice or soda."

"I'll take a soda," he answers with his eyes still glued to the pictures.

Pulling two sodas out, I set them on the counter. A sharp pain shoots through my side as I reach to pull a glass from the cupboard, causing it to drop and shatter on the floor. "Shit," I hiss out, curling my arm around my side to lessen the pain.

Javi's feet slap against the wooden floor as he rushes to my side. "What happened? Are you okay?" he rushes out, worriedly.

"My side is still a little sore. We played dodgeball in gym, and Sophie nailed me in the side." I don't admit she did it on purpose. How embarrassing is it that I'm a senior in high school and still have a bully?

"Sit down. I'll clean this up." Javi says, irritatedly, as he helps me over to the table.

"You don't have to do tha-"

"I don't mind." He interrupts, his impatience taking me by surprise. "I'm sorry. Just the thought of you being injured," he trails off with a faraway look in his eyes. "Please, just let me help." He all but begs.

If this small amount of pain gets him this worked up, it's a good thing he didn't see me the day of my accident, or in the hospital for that matter.

His concern for me shows how much he cares, and that I made the right decision in giving them all a shot at this unique relationship. Pointing him in the direction of the broom, hoping that letting him take care of this small thing will make him feel better, I sit down at the kitchen table.

Once he's done sweeping up the broken glass, he grabs our drinks and sets them on the table. He leaves the room and comes back shortly with a backpack I hadn't realized he brought with him. Hanging it on the back of the chair, he pulls his books out and places them on the table. Handing me my homework before he sits down, "Do you need anything else?" He checks, and my chest warms at his attentiveness.

Shaking my head, he sits down and cracks open his history book, and doesn't move his eyes in my direction, almost like he refuses to look at me. Wanting to break the tension in the air, I reach over and place my hand on top of his. "It's okay, Javi. I'm okay." I reassure him softly.

He finally looks up at me, and the heartache I see staring back at me makes my chest pinch. I intertwine my fingers through his to try and comfort him. I don't know why he's having such a visceral reaction to this, but all I can think about now is taking away his pain.

"Are you sure?" he croaks out.

I stand up and crawl into his lap to show him that I am okay, to let him feel that I'm okay. I wrap my arms around his neck as he cradles my back and rests his hand on my thigh. "I promise, I'm okay." I rest my head on his shoulder.

He breathes out a shaky breath, and I rub my hand over his chest, hoping to soothe his worries. "I'm right here, Javi," I say to reassure him, and his grip on my hip and thigh tightens as if he doesn't believe it.

Pulling back to look at him, he gives me a watery smile, and he leans forward to press his forehead against mine. "I'm sorry. I didn't mean to react like that."

"It's okay. I know how it feels to get inside your head. Just remember I'm right here."

Silent minutes go by with me sitting in his lap with our foreheads pressed together, feeling the warm comfort of his hands resting on my body. My hand mindlessly travels from his chest to his neck, and I move my thumb back and forth across his neck as a shiver works its way down his spine.

"Red," he whispers tentatively, scared to speak any louder and bursting this comfortable bubble we've found ourselves in. "If you keep that up, I'll have you spread out on this table like the finest of desserts."

"Mmm…" The little moan slips out accidentally. Having developed a pretty good imagination to make up for my lack of experience, the image of him feasting on me is vivid. Just the thought of his hot tongue against my skin makes me squirm in his lap and causes another accidental moan to escape my lips.

Lifting my head from his, I stare into his jade green eyes. The heartache that was there is now covered by desire. I lift my hand to cup his cheek, and he turns his head to place a kiss on my palm. His soft lips feel like velvet as he trails kisses down my hand and to the sensitive skin on the inside of my wrist.

His warm lips brush the tender spot just below my wrist when a loud jingling startles us both, followed by a loud knocking on the front door that might as well be a cold bucket of water.

Javi throws his head back and groans. "Whoever that is, better start running because I'm going to murder them for interrupting us." I snicker at how dramatic he is and untangle myself from him.

Callaghan Enterprises is the name that's on the large manila envelope that is delivered every two weeks to my mother. I'm not surprised to find it sitting in front of the door when I swing it open. I pick it up and set it on the entry table next to the front door, where she'll see it. I've tried getting her to tell me what's in it, and the answer is always the same: "It's just some paperwork I've been expecting, don't worry about it, honey" is what she tells me every single time. Finally, I gave up and stopped asking and figured she would tell me if it was important.

"It was just a package for my mom," I say, plopping down in my seat at the kitchen table.

"Don't say package," Javi whines, dropping his head on his textbook that rivals the drama of eighteenth-century royalty.

We settle into a comfortable silence as we do our homework. Occasionally asking the other for help, or asking for their opinion. The quiet lulls make me feel the same sense of security I feel when Zeke is here or when Kyler was here. It's comfortable and makes me feel less alone.

There's no suffocating silence that comes with being alone when all you want is for someone to care enough to want to fill that silence. Not even with words, just their mere presence helps to fill the void of loneliness.

On nights that I'm alone, which let's face it, is just about every night, the sound of nothing was daunting, and I'm sure if it had a voice, it would mock me. I would turn on the TV or music just to fill the silence. If I didn't do that, I would be forced to listen to my thoughts, leaving me to spiral into a fit of anxiety with no one to help me crawl out.

Now, with Javi here, the sound of the silence is more than nothing. The sound of nothing has turned into the sound of Javi's breathing as it quietly soothes me, as if it's offering me a shoulder to lean on. The sound of the ticking clock in the living room doesn't sound as thunderous. It isn't reminding me that with each tick is just another second spent alone, now, it's reminding me to savor this moment of contentment. Hold on to each second with both hands because these moments are precious, no matter how significant they are.

It wasn't always like this. My mom would work while we were at school so she could be home in the afternoon to be with us. To help with homework and to make us a home-cooked meal, and to do all the mom things kids take for granted growing up.

I've never known who my dad is. Every time I ask my mom about him, she says she met him at a bar one night when she went out with some of her friends. She said he had the thickest red hair she had ever seen, with a red beard to match. What really drew her in was his Irish accent. She always jokes that just the sound of his voice is what got her pregnant, and I want to rip my eardrums out every time she says it because...gross! She never got his name, and she never saw him again. She assumes he went back to Ireland because he was just here for work.

Ashley's dad, however, is a deadbeat alcoholic and would rather get drunk and have a good time than be in his daughter's life. She has the typical daddy issues, and I often find myself feeling bad for her. I would rather not know who my dad is than to know him and to know he doesn't want me.

Which is why I've never really thought of her as just a half-sister. She's my sister whom I grew up with and shared clothes with, and we did each other's hair. Then we got to junior high school, and the attention she got from the male population became more important than our relationship, and she turned into the she devil.

Finishing my homework and flipping my binder shut, I hear Javi's stomach growl. "Are you hungry?" I ask sarcastically.

"I'm starving." He replies, looking adorably zoned in as he scribbles something down in his notebook, "I'm about done, though. I just need five more minutes."

"Take your time, I'm going to make us something to eat," I grunt, standing to stretch my stiff muscles.

At the fridge, I pull out the cheese, butter, and ham to make my favorite grilled ham and cheese sandwich. I begin slicing up the cheese and buttering the bread. I start assembling the sandwiches and popping them in the oven once it's warmed to the right temperature. I open the cupboard to reach for some plates, but think better of it when I remember the cup debacle. Before I can ask Javi to reach them for me, he's already behind me, pulling two of them down.

"Thank you," I murmur.

"You're welcome. Now that I'm finished, what can I help with?" he asks, his warm breath brushing against my hair.

"Everything is done, we just need to wait for them to warm up," I say. Thankfully, he doesn't catch the breathiness in my voice.

"What did you make?" He asks, setting the table with a rigid posture.

"Grilled ham and cheese sandwiches, though we don't have any tomato soup to go with them," I answer, chewing on my bottom lip, hoping that will be enough for him. I feel a little embarrassed that I don't have more to offer.

"Grilled ham and cheese sounds perfect," his smile

resembles the stiffness of his posture. "Do you mind if I use the bathroom?"

I slap a hand to my forehead because I forgot to give him a tour. "Sorry, I should have shown you where everything is. Just take a right down the hall, and it's the door at the end."

"It's okay, Red, don't beat yourself up over it," he chuckles and disappears down the hall.

Just as he closes the bathroom door, the timer for the food goes off. Pulling the food out of the oven, I set it on our plates and cut it in half. Setting the plates on the table, I spin around to grab napkins when I bump right into Javi's chest and look up to see a wicked grin on his face.

"Um…hi," I squeak, surprised at his sudden appearance.

Still smiling, he holds up a red lacy thong. "I wondered what kind of panties you wear," he says like he's just uncovered life's biggest mystery.

I run my hands up over his chest and pull him down towards me to whisper in his ear. "Well, keep wondering, cowboy, because those are Ashleys."

He drops them like they're diseased and immediately runs to the sink and starts scrubbing his hands with hot water and more than enough soap.

"I share a bathroom with her, so maybe don't touch any clothes that are left in there, or, you know, just don't go touching underwear in bathrooms you've never been in," I tease, laughing.

After his hands are thoroughly scrubbed clean, he finally sits down to eat, and I almost choke on my food when I notice how red his hands are from scrubbing them. "Oh my god!" I shout, "You scrubbed your hands raw. They have scratch marks!" I shriek, reaching for them to run my hands over them.

"No offense, but I don't like your sister, and knowing that I touched her panties makes me want to dip my hands in bleach." He confesses, and I feel a little stunned at his confession. Usually, the opposite sex follows her around like a starving dog waiting to get their teeth on any scraps that she'll give them.

"I'm not sure what to say to that. Usually, she has the opposite effect on men. They can't seem to stay away from her." I say, and dread fills me unexpectedly. Once she takes notice of my guys or vice versa, are they going to drop me as easily as everyone else?

"Stop it," Javi says. "Whatever is going through your head, stop. We want you, Josie, and only you."

Javi reaches over and takes hold of my hand, and all I can do is flash him a weak smile, unsure of what to say. His words make my stomach flip, but my past experiences make my heart clench with trepidation. Judging by the determined look in his eyes, I know he means what he says. I just hope that I'm enough for them.

Chapter Sixteen

JOSIE

After dinner, we moved out on the back patio to enjoy the short amount of time we had left of the warm end of summer Boston air. I had spent the majority of my favorite season in the hospital, and with fall approaching, I'm trying to soak up any remaining warmth I can get. The setting sun casts an orange and pink glow across the sky, creating a cozy atmosphere for Javi and to get to know each other better. Similar to the night before with Kyler and Liam.

So far, I've learned that Javi is an only child and that his parents got divorced when he was in first grade. His father cheated on his mother, and she kicked him to the curb. He grew up with a single mother, the same as I have. He knows what it feels like to be pushed to the back burner by a parent, but he also understands that she doesn't do it intentionally. She does it so she can keep a roof over their heads and food on the table.

I've also learned that I like the feel of his piercing jade eyes on me, which is saying something because I absolutely hate being the center of attention. At first, I wasn't sure how to handle it, but the more he looked at me with such rapt focus, the more I felt cherished and the more I felt cherished the more I felt valued. It was a warm feeling that I couldn't help relax into.

"I don't know what I would do without them." The sincerity in his tone brings my focus back from the depths of his mesmerizing, icy green eyes. The fondness he has for his friends makes me think of Zeke and Kiera, and how lucky I am to have them. "I'm lucky to have them," he continues as if he's reading my thoughts, "If it weren't for them, I would be in a bad place." His tone sharpens, and I reach my hand across the small wicker table between, offering support.

When his large palm connects with mine, he begins to tell me about the black sheep in his family, his uncle Matteo.

My hand squeezes involuntarily when he says, "He's the leader of *Los Caminantes Nocturnos.*" Also known as The Nightwalkers, the most notorious gang on the southside. It's a name I've heard more than enough times growing up on the northside, which is home to their biggest rival, The Northside Sovereign, or as I know it, Sylus's group of assholes.

"That's fucking bullshit!" I shout, jumping to my feet as he finishes telling me that Matteo expects him to join the family business. A rage I've only felt a few times in my life prickles under my skin, preparing to release on those who dare to provoke it.

The Nightwalkers and The Northside Sovereign have been enemies for as long as I can remember. I've heard rumors about how violent and ruthless both gangs are, and Matteo wanting to drag his own nephew into it just because he's family makes me want to commit murder. Then a new thought settles in at the memory of Sylus asking me to work for him. Was he asking me to join when he asked me to work for him? Or does he want me to work for him because I can make him money?

I didn't even realize I had been chewing on my bottom lip

until Javi stood to pull it from between my teeth. "It's ok, Red. The guys and I have a plan to leave after graduation," he says, running his thumb along my bottom lip to soothe the pain. I want to ask if I'm included in those plans, but it's way too early to be thinking about that. Even if that doesn't include me, I'm just happy Javi will be getting away from his uncle.

"You're really cute when you get mad. Your nose gets all scrunched up and your face turns as red as your hair," he teases, trying to lighten the mood.

I find that I have a lot in common with Javi and that he's easy to talk to. So much so that when I glance at the time on my phone, it's already ten o'clock. "Crap, I didn't realize it was this late already," I say as we make our way back inside, and I show him where my bedroom is.

"Don't worry, Red, my eyes usually have that effect-, What the hell is that?" he abruptly changes the topic when we enter my room. If I weren't contemplating changing my name and running away out of mortification, then I definitely would when I follow his line of sight and realize what has got him dumbstruck.

God, why am I such a nerd!

"It's...um...my nightlight," I answer, stumbling over my words, trying not to sound like a two-year-old who's scared of the dark.

"I know it's a nightlight, but it's a giant eyeball with spikes on it. It's creepy," he says, pretending to shiver.

"It's the eye of Sauron from The Lord of the Rings," I say, shrugging like it's no big deal, but inside, I want to crawl under my bed and disappear.

Under there, so I have no choice but to stand here as he looks at me like I'm crazy.

"First of all," he starts, walking towards me, sensing my discomfort. "It's adorable that you're scared of the dark," he bops me on the nose, "and second of all, Kyler told us that you and Liam were nerding out, but I thought he was exaggerating."

Sucking my lip back between my teeth, feeling self-conscious, and wait for him to tell me how embarrassed he is of my nerdiness. Instead, when I meet his piercing mint-colored eyes, all I see is adoration. "Hey, it's okay. Don't be scared to be yourself. There's no judgment. Plus, I think it's great that you and Liam have something in common." Once again, he thumbs my lip from beneath my teeth and rubs the spot tenderly.

A smile creeps across my face, and I nod my understanding as he winks and steps away to peruse the rest of my room. When he finds the shelf with my camera and all my photo albums, he starts flipping through them. "These are really amazing," he tells me, flipping through an album that has random shots of days at the park. Mostly flowers and nature, but also some pictures of children playing with their parents and having picnics."You're really good at capturing people's emotions."

Blushing, once again, at his compliment as he sets down one album and picks up another, then another, then another. Finally, when I think he's gone through all of them, he finds the one that I must not have put back in its hiding place after I added new pictures to it. Whereas all the other photo albums are blue and have different floral patterns on them, this one is plain black with nothing on it.

"What's this?" he asks curiously. As he goes to open it, I slam it shut and snatch it out of his hands.

Raising an eyebrow at me questioningly. "Sorry," I murmur, "this one is private. I didn't realize I left it out."

"Well, now I'm intrigued. What's in the photo album, Red?" He questions with a curious twinkle in his eye. I can tell he wants to push me to show him, but doesn't want to pressure me either.

"It...it's just private." If I'm not blushing around these men who are practically Greek gods, then I'm stuttering and looking like an illiterate idiot.

He raises his eyebrow at my nervousness, and his curiosity doesn't waver. My heart rate kicks up, and I shuffle back and forth on my feet, averting my eyes from his silent probing, but his vibrant jade eyes hold me in place. The whooshing sound of my blood pumping and his penetrating stare have me breaking.

"Ugh! Fine, I'll show you," I mutter, and a victorious smile curves his lips, "but you have to promise you won't tell anyone?"

"I promise," he agrees quickly, eager to see what the photo album holds.

I reluctantly sit down next to him with our backs against the shelf and flip it open to the first picture. A voluptuous woman is lying on her back with her head at the foot of the bed. Her back is slightly arched, accentuating her curvy breasts in the black lace corset hugging her torso. Her knees are bent, and one leg is crossed over the other. Her wavy raven black hair lies against the red satin sheets with one of her hands combing through it.

Flipping through the album, all with similar poses that are sexy and alluring, I'm not sure what to make of Javi's silent reaction. His face is expressionless, and the only sound in the room to be heard is our breathing. He obviously thinks I'm some kind of perv taking semi-nude pictures of people and keeping them.

While I love capturing people's emotions on film, whether it be happiness or sadness, or love, I also enjoy capturing pictures of people who feel good about themselves. I often feel insecure about being curvier than most girls and am very self-conscious of everything I wear. Not wanting to draw attention to my curves or my weight.

Taking pictures of confident women, especially those who have the same body type as me, makes me feel better about myself. Watching how comfortable they are with themselves and how proud they are of their bodies fuels my confidence, if only momentarily.

Then I walk out the door, and it all melts away. Keeping the photos is just a reminder that I felt secure for at least a little while and that it's okay to look different. These pictures give me hope that one day I'll get over my insecurities and find my own confidence.

Not wanting Javi to see the photo on the last page, I hurried and flipped it shut before he could see it. He doesn't say anything this time, and he sits in silence as he stews over what he just saw.

"You must think I'm a weirdo," I say softly, not able to take the silence.

His head snaps in my direction with confusion on his face. "Why would you think that?" he asks.

"Because I take pictures of half-naked women, sometimes more than half-naked," I say, like it should have been obvious

He reaches his hand up and cups my cheek. "I don't think it's weird, Red, I think they're great, amazing really. You're good at what you do, and you shouldn't be ashamed of it. No matter the photo you take."

"Thank you," I murmur. "I enjoy taking them. The women are so confident. I only wish to be that confident someday." Flicking my eyes down, feeling vulnerable at my admission, I fidget with the corner of the photo album.

He tilts my chin back up, and the anger I see staring back at me surprises me. "I don't know why or who made you feel ashamed of your body, but you are the most beautiful person I've ever met. Inside and out."

Tears spring to my eyes at his words, and I want to cry at the sincerity behind them. I rest my forehead against his, soaking up all of his affection as we sit in silence.

Breaking the intimate moment and climbing to my feet, I walk to my dresser and pull out some pajamas and toss them on the bed. Going back, I walk to my nightstand, where I keep the TV remote, to give it to Javi. If I thought he would think I'm a pervert for the photos, then he would definitely think so if he saw what I keep in this drawer.

"I'm going to jump in the shower. You can get in after me if you'd like." I tell him, handing him the remote. Not waiting for the naught retort I can practically see on the tip of his tongue, I spin on my heel and book it to the bathroom.

I can hear his chuckle as I shut the door and start the shower, turning it to the coldest as I can get it, imagining what he was about to say. Lathering myself with my peach body wash, excited anxiety creeps up at the anticipation of sleeping in the same bed with this man.

I haven't known them for very long, but when I'm in their presence, there's a sense of belonging I haven't felt in a long time. It just feels right. I've never believed in fate, but I don't think it's a coincidence that they showed up at one of the worst times of my life.

After washing my hair, shaving my legs, and making sure the redhead between my legs looks presentable, I step out of the shower and wrap a towel around myself.

"Red bushed idiot," I say, quietly scolding myself, as I realize I left my pajamas lying on the bed.

I was too distracted avoiding Javi's words that I forgot to grab them. I slap a palm to my forehead at my stupidity. I frantically search the bathroom looking for a spare pair of pajamas that might have been left in here, or at least a robe. When I find nothing, and the pair I wish for doesn't appear out of thin air, I tighten the towel around my body and reluctantly open the door to step out.

Slowly walking to my room on my tippy toes, hoping he fell asleep so I could grab them and go back to the bathroom.

My wishful thinking is futile because when I open the door, Javi is sitting at the end of the bed holding up my pajamas with a playful smirk on his face. "Forget these?" he grins sardonically.

I clench the top of the towel where it sits above my breasts as if his words alone will make it unravel from around my body, knowing that inevitably that's what is going to happen. His eyes turn hungry as they slowly travel down my body, and back up. "Well," he swallows and I watch his throat bob with the motion, "Are you going to take them?" he taunts, the playful look long gone from his face.

Frozen in the doorway, staring at the sexy specimen on my bed, choosing not to answer him to avoid drooling as I ogle his caramel-colored skin. My eyes flick to his mouth when his tongue peeks out to swipe at his bottom lip. His mouth may not be speaking words, but his full, pink lips are begging me to taste them.

"Red," he says, sounding like he swallowed gravel, "You need to stop looking at me like that."

"Sorry," I say, not entirely sure what I'm apologizing for. Focusing back on my pajamas, I step into the room and reach for them in his outstretched hand. "I'm just going-"

My sentence is cut off when he wraps his hand around my wrist and pulls me to his chest. His six-foot frame towers over me. I crane my neck to look up into his eyes, and the lust I see staring back at me has me holding back a gasp. "Don't apologize, but if you keep looking at me like that, I'm not liable for the things I do to you."

He rests his hand on my neck and traces his thumb over my pulse point, causing goosebumps to erupt over my skin.

A shiver works its way up my spine from his gentle caress, making my eyes fall shut, savoring this feeling.

"Are you cold?" He questions with a hint of concern in his tone.

Deciding quickly if I'm ready to take this relationship further because I can feel it in my gut that once the word leaves my mouth, I will be anything but cold. Slowly lifting my eyes open, meeting his so he can see the certainty in mine. "No," I say in a hushed tone.

His eyes grow darker, and I bite the inside of my cheek, worrying that I made him angry. I make a sad attempt to pull away at his silence, but before I can get too far, he wraps his arms around my waist, pajamas long-forgotten. "There's no getting away from me now, Red," he says, slowly running a knuckle down my cheek. "You've awakened the monster, and he's not leaving until he tastes you."

My response is swallowed up when his lips fuse to mine. His silky soft lips envelope mine with a controlled hunger, as they dominate mine with a gentle fervor. I rest my palms over his pecs to steady myself when his tongue nudges the seam of my lips.

I eagerly open for him, and his warm tongue invades my mouth. Whereas Kyler's kiss was sweet and gentle, Javi's is passionate and firm, both equally erotic. Javi kisses me like he's been waiting a lifetime to do so, like he could crawl inside me to make us one being, and it still wouldn't be enough.

His tongue expertly massages mine, coaxing out a small whimper. His hands travel down the sensitive skin on my neck, down my chest, and come to stop at the towel still wrapped around my upper body. He stops kissing me to look into my eyes, searching for approval.

I nod my head at his unspoken question, thanking every deity imaginable that I took the time to spruce up the other redhead in the room. His fingers hook under the towel, and for a brief moment, doubt creeps into my brain. What if he's turned off by my body? I'm certainly not as skinny as a lot of girls my age. I don't have a flat stomach, there's no trace of any gap between my thighs, and on some days, I have to do the wiggle dance to get my jeans over my ass.

You are the most beautiful person I've ever met. His words come back to me, and I trust that he meant what he said.

He unravels the towel, and I reflexively wrap my arms around my middle to hide my stomach, as it falls to the floor. I drop my chin to my chest to avoid any disappointment I might see on his face.

Though I do trust and believe his words, I've never been naked in front of a man before. I've never let a man see all of me, and I've never been as vulnerable as I am now.

A finger slides under my chin and tilts my head up. The heat I see staring back at me has my belly swirling with warmth. "Don't hide from me," he says, reaching to pull my arms away from my middle. "I want to see all of you," he finishes.

Letting my arms fall to my sides, feeling the cool air against my skin, "I'm sorry," I murmur, "It's just...I've never let anyone see...all of me." I tell him honestly and begin to anxiously nibble at my lip.

The heat in his eyes flares at my statement. "Oh, gorgeous, your body was made for me. You have no idea the things I want to do to you," he trails his finger down the valley of my breasts, "but this is at your pace, remember. You say stop, and we'll stop. You won't hear any questions or complaints from me. Got it?"

"Yes," I whisper, as his words awaken a familiar ache between my legs. My cheeks redden, and a wolfish grin spreads across his mouth, knowing how his words affect me.

His mouth slams back down to mine, kissing me with a

renewed hunger. One of his fingers brushes over a nipple, while his other hand cups the opposite breast, massaging the soft flesh. I clench my thighs together as if the massaging of my breast is relayed straight to my clit, and I moan into his mouth from the sensation.

His lips move from my mouth, peppering kisses along my jaw and down my neck. He turns me, and I feel the back of my legs bump into the frame of my bed, as he continues to glide his lips down to the hollow of my throat.

I reach for the hem of his shirt, and he doesn't hesitate to lift it from his body. I groan at the sight of his abs. How is it possible for a human being to look this good? He looks like he is training to be the next Superman.

"We all try to train with Adrian and Carter to help keep them in shape for football," he answers, and I want to shrivel up and die at having said that out loud. Thankfully, he chuckles and plants his lips back where they were and moves down to my chest.

I nearly jump out of my skin when he wraps his warm lips around my nipple and flicks his tongue over the delicate peak. I hiss out a moan and rest my hand on the nape of his neck, keeping him there, afraid he'll pull away too soon.

He moves over to my other breast, doing the same thing, and my knees begin to weaken. As if reading my mind, he pushes me further toward the bed, forcing me to plop down. Bringing me eye level with the button of his pants.

I reach my hands up and slip the button through the hole and push his pants down his thighs, letting them fall to the ground. I gulp at the sheer size of his erection, attempting to rip through his boxers. If they all look like this, then I'm in way over my head, and we may need to keep a doctor on speed dial.

Desperate to touch him and feel the weight of it in my hand, I reach out, but he intercepts my hand. I frown like a child who was just told they couldn't play with their favorite toy. Laughing and shaking his head, "This is about you," he tells me, but that doesn't seem fair.

"But I want you to enjoy this too," I say, voicing my concern.

"Trust me, Red, I'm going to enjoy this." Stepping out of his jeans, he leans over me, guiding me to lie on my back.

Settling a knee against my center, as he hovers above me, his piercing eyes are filled with fondness. I reach up to cup his cheek to reciprocate the feeling, as his eyes fall closed and he nuzzles my hand like he's desperate for human touch.

He nips at my bottom lip, shooting pleasure straight to my core, and I involuntarily lift my hips to grind against his thigh, needing the friction. I let out a moan while I continue to rub my pussy up and down the hot skin of his muscled leg. The pressure from the motion causes a fire to light under my skin. My breathing becomes heavy the more I grind, rolling my hips up and down, up and down, up and down.

My fingers dig into his boxer-clad ass, trying to pull him closer, to grind harder. "Greedy girl," he teases, lowering closer to whisper in my ear. "Take it, take what you want. It's all yours." He promises, sucking my lobe into his mouth, as I desperately mewl beneath him.

He sits up, keeping his knee firmly planted against my pussy, and I want to cry out at the loss of his warm body above me. His eyes become hooded as he watches me fuck myself against his thigh with such carnal need that I have to close my eyes from the intensity.

"Look at me," he orders, and my eyes fly open, "keep those gorgeous greens on me." His hand dips into his boxers, pulling his cock from its fabric prison. Thumbing the pearly moisture at the tip, his erection sits proudly in his hand. He starts to slowly stroke himself as I continue my assault on his thigh. "See how you affect me?"

I let out a whimper as the pressure builds on my clit and his leg becomes slick. Muscles ripple against my core when he reaches down to trail two fingers through the slickness and paints his cock with it. Marking himself with it. Showing me that he is mine and I am his. A possessiveness I've never felt before creeps to the surface at the sight of my arousal on him.

Dragging two fingers through my slickness for a second time, his eyes locked on mine, conveying so much want, it's like he's trying to make me cum with his stare alone. Lifting his hand to his mouth, sucking his fingers greedily, "Mmmm," he groans out like he's tasting his favorite dessert. The sound causes me to clench around nothing.

My grinding becomes desperate, seeing his desire overtake him as he tastes mine. Needing more but not exactly sure of what, I start to knead my breasts and pinch my nipples between my fingers, trying to push myself over the edge.

Mimicking him, I lift my finger to my mouth, wetting the tip of it and circling my nipple, making it wet and shiny. Doing the same to the other, the cool air causes them to stiffen as I teeter on the edge of eruption.

"Fuck," he laments, watching me tug on my sensitive pink buds. "You're going to have me coming before I even touch you."

His words nearly send me over the edge, but my orgasm is frustratingly out of reach. I need more, more, more.

He steps away, and I want to cry at the loss as my pussy pulses with the need to release. "Javi," I whine out, "I need-"

"I know Red," he says softly, cutting me off. He lowers to his knees and spreads me open, "I'll always take care of you."

He places soft kisses on the insides of my thighs,

alternating between the two. His velvety soft lips make goosebumps spread across my skin, and I fight the urge to yank his head to my center and bury his face in my cunt.

"Javi," I whine out again, as my pussy begins to ache. I feel his smile against my thigh, and I want to scream out of frustration.

Finally, he decides to quit torturing me, because the next thing I feel is his hot tongue licking me from entrance to clit. I let out a loud moan, and he does it again. The feeling of the flat of his tongue against my little bundle of nerves has me clenching the blanket in a tight fist.

Firmly planting his mouth around my clit he sucks it into his mouth. "Oh fuck," I moan out as my lower body begins to tingle. Keeping his promise of showing me how he rolls his Rs, he rolls his tongue over my clit as he's sucking it. The sucking and licking in tandem creates pressure, skyrocketing my pleasure to new heights.

Sucking and licking...

Sucking and licking...

Sucking and licking...

"Javi, baby," I mewl, begging and pleading for him to push me over. My thighs begin to quiver, and the tingling turns electrifying. The next movement has me exploding when the pad of his thumb starts rubbing at my entrance, and his rolling tongue is fervent, coaxing me to shatter.

Time stands still when my back arches off the bed. My eyes fall shut as a white burst of stars explodes behind them, and my hands grip the blanket beneath me. A loud moan leaves my mouth as Javi continues to suck, his hands go to my hips to keep me in place. Everything is drowned out as pleasure invades my body, causing my brain to go offline. The only sound heard is the static in my ears as my thundering heart causes blood to whoosh through my body.

He continues his abuse on my clit until every last ounce of

my orgasm is wrung from my body. Relaxing my back, the cool comforter on my heated skin brings my brain back to reality. The tingling lessens, and I loosen my grip when the pressure from Javi's tongue gets lighter.

I open my eyes when his lips leave my clit, and he places reverent kisses on my legs and hips. It's as if he's cherishing this moment, committing it to memory.

Littering kisses up my body and after placing a gentle one on my lips, his arms band around me. He buries his face in my neck as the weight of his naked form settles on top of mine. My arms wrap around his back, and a contented sigh leaves his mouth. Neither of us speaks as we lie in comfortable silence, somehow making this moment feel more intimate than the one we just shared.

After a short time, Javi's so quiet I think he's fallen asleep. "Javi?" I tentatively question.

"Hmmm?" he grunts sleepily.

"We should get washed up and go to bed."

"Just a little bit longer," he mumbles, "I like having you in my arms, plus that feels amazing." I hadn't even noticed I had started tracing my fingers up and down his back. Being in his arms feels so natural, my body's on autopilot.

I'm not sure how long I lay there with Javi's long body over mine like the world's softest, yet muscular, weighted blanket. His breathing evens, signaling that he has fallen asleep. My hands continue to roam over his body while the rest of me is still as a board, not wanting to wake him.

I close my eyes and bask in the feeling of his solid body pressing me into the mattress. The coziness of it makes everything wash away, and the same sense of security that I felt when we were doing our homework in the kitchen roams over me, much like how my hands are roaming over Javi.

The thought makes me realize that I'm as much a sense of security for Javi as he is for me. This also reminds me of how similar we are, and my heart pitter-patters with sympathy. With the urge to make him feel important, I wrap my arms around him and squeeze, hoping he feels my support even in his sleep.

Banding my arms around him with his weight pressing down on me feels as though I'm hugging myself, and I squeeze a little tighter. Rubbing a soothing palm over his back. "You're not alone and I'm here for you," I whisper, though I'm not sure if the words are for him or me.

"Javi baby," I say quietly, reluctant to wake him, but my legs are beginning to prickle with discomfort.

Apparently, that little pet name is sticking, I think, when an unintelligible mumble tumbles from his lips.

"My legs are falling asleep," I try again.

"Those words sound good coming from your mouth." His voice muffles in the crook of my neck.

Confused, "My legs are falling asleep?"

Nipping at my neck playfully, " No. The ones you said before that."

"Javi baby," I whisper teasingly, trying to sound seductive, but fail miserably when a giggle escapes me.

He groans and nuzzles into my neck, "Hearing my name on your lips is like heaven." He places a soft kiss just below my ear, "and the day you stop saying it is going to hurt like hell."

A small ache pings in my chest at that last statement, and I should have paid more attention to the foreshadowing they brought with them, but as Javi trails kisses along my neck and his arms tighten around me, all my worries are drowned out.

Chapter Seventeen

ZEKE

"We have to tell her," I say to the man sitting at the foot of my bed. Tugging on my hair out of frustration as I pace back and forth, forcing my feet to stay away from Josie's window.

When I got the call that Josie had been in a car wreck, my world stopped spinning, and sorrow weighed heavy in my veins like cement. Despair followed me around like a shadow, and the thought of never getting to tell her that I love her tortured me.

I fell in love with Josie's kind soul the first night I showed up at her window. My mother's muffled cries kept me up, and when I closed my eyes to stave off my own, a different muffled sound had me going to my window. When I saw the girl with wild red hair, she was sitting in front of her TV watching one of those Lord of the Rings movies she loves so much. Her big green eyes were glued to the screen as she was saying the lines out loud along with the movie, and I couldn't help but smile.

Before I knew it, my feet were moving me toward her open window, and I haven't looked back since. At least I hadn't until about eight months ago, when my five childhood best friends reappeared in my life and turned our lives upside down. We may have grown apart over the years, but once they told me what was going on, it was like nothing had changed.

Don't get me wrong, moving away from them had been difficult, and we still kept in touch, hanging out here and there, but the older we got, the harder it was to keep in touch. Only sending a text about once a month to let them know I hadn't forgotten about them makes me cringe just thinking about how neglectful I became towards my relationship with these degenerates I call friends.

One of which is the man I love, who is sitting at the foot of my bed, looking just as guilty as I feel. "We have to tell her," I repeat, wearing a hole in my carpet. There are so many secrets that have piled up I'm not sure where to even begin. "Keeping all these secrets from her is fucking killing me."

"How do you think I feel?" he replies, looking just as frustrated. "She thinks I hate her. The fact that I've made her feel that way breaks my heart, and I want more than anything to take away her doubt." He averts his gaze, staring down at his lap, and the next words out of his mouth cause anger to stir in my chest, "but you know we can't tell her yet. Not until we figure out what's going on between her sister, Mateo, and Sylus."

When the five of them came to me eight months ago and told me how Josie was sold off to Mateo by her cunt of a sister, the plan to hurt Ashley came pretty easily after that. Then Sylus' guys showed up and fucked everything up.

We assumed Sylus' people showed up because they heard some of Matteo's guys would be there to collect from the idiot who thought it would be a good idea to steal some product from Matteo. Still, given the incident with Sylus earlier today, I'm going to take a shot in the dark and say it has something to do with my Josie. When we received that group text from her that she was at Sylus', panic struck me the same way it had when I had found out about her accident.

"Call it a hunch, but you know once we tell her everything, she's never going to forgive us, Zeke." His voice cracks when my name leaves his mouth, and I know he's hurting because the only other time I've seen him break is the day I moved away.

"Adrian," I sigh, wishing I could turn back time. When his coffee-brown eyes meet mine, the torment in them has me in front of him in a flash. Standing between his legs as they hang off the end of my bed, I wrap my arms around him, and he buries his face in my neck. He fists the back of my shirt and hangs onto me, clutching me to him. " We need to at least tell her that we're together. She saw the hickey on my neck, so she knows I'm seeing someone." I try negotiating at least this secret to lessen the load. "If she finds out from someone else, it's going to crush her."

"Are you sure she'll be okay with us? Being together?" he says into my neck, and his hot breath makes a shiver roll up my spine. "When we brought it up at Milo's earlier, I thought she was going to pass out."

"I've known Josie a long time, and she's always been scared to get too close to anyone who shows any interest in her because of her succubus of a sister." The thought of Ashley makes my blood boil. She's a major part of the reason Josie has retreated into herself over the years, and the reason I've held myself back from telling Josie how I feel about her. I didn't want to spook her and lose her as a friend too, but with the bucket of shit that has been thrown at us, I don't have much of a choice."I know her better than anyone," I say a little too smugly to distract my rising anger, "so yes, I'm sure."

"You just love throwing that in our faces, don't you?"

Adrian grunts, dragging his teeth along the hickey he left behind.

"I've got to keep you guys on your toes somehow," I rebuttal teasingly, lifting my hand to rest on his shoulder to hold me steady when his lips attach to that sensitive spot on my neck he knows so well. "Anyways, she knows I'm bi, so I don't think it will be a problem."

"You're right," he whispers into the crook of my neck. "I've seen the way she looks at you."

I don't answer him because I've noticed the way she's been looking at me, too. When she thinks no one is looking, especially me, she stares at me with a sort of longing curiosity in her eyes that shows she thinks of me in more than a friendly way, but she doesn't know if I feel the same way.

That's the part that kills me the most, knowing that she feels the same way I do, but not being able to do anything about it. At least not yet. "This weekend," I force out, trying to focus on my next words as he nibbles on my neck. "I'll tell her to come over on Sunday, and we can tell her together."

He groans his agreement as he continues teasing kisses all over my neck. Movement catches my attention at Josie's open window, and I see Javi pulling the curtains closed with a cocky smile on his face. I know better. He can act as cockly as he wants; I already know he's wrapped around her finger. I'm just not sure she realizes it. Jealousy hits me in the chest thinking about him over there with her, because it's me who should be there. It's always been me. I guess now that she has five boyfriends, soon to be six, I need to get used to sharing her.

The idea of sharing her with Adrian conjures up a million different scenarios of her curvy body between the two of us, and a moan escapes my lips. My stiffening cock presses into Adrian's stomach, and I can feel a smile spread across his lips as if he knows what I'm thinking about. "I've thought about it at least a thousand times," he murmurs, trailing his lips over my shoulder, and I let out a groan. "You in the front taking care of her sweet little pussy, and me in the back taking care of her luscious ass."

"If you keep talking like that, I'm going to come in my pants," I breathe out. My hand goes to the back of his neck, and I dig my nails in when he bites on my collarbone. I hiss out when his warm tongue soothes the area and continues to the front of my throat.

"If you're going to fuck, can you hurry and get it over with? We have places to be."

My eyes flick to the mood killer standing in my doorway. "Jealous Ky?" I say sarcastically, noticing the twinkle in his eye. Assuming he heard our conversation, I find myself asking, "How much did you hear?"

A smile ghosts his face, and the twinkling in his eyes turns devious. "Enough," is all that he says before he walks away.

Chuckling under my breath at his quick retreat, I return my attention to Adrian, give him a quick peck on the lips, and step back before this goes any further. "Let's go get this shit over with."

"We'll pick this up later," he answers, hopping off the bed reluctantly. Following him out of my bedroom, we find Kyler waiting by the front door with a hand stuffed in his pocket, looking like he's arranging himself. I hold back a laugh, knowing how he feels. *Yeah, you and me both buddy*, I think as we make our way out to Milo's waiting car.

"You two climb in first, you can share the backseat," Kyler says like he's some sort of comedian.

I punch his arm, "Fucker! I knew you heard us." He roars with laughter as I climb into the back, followed by a chuckling Adrian.

Once Kyler climbs in and we're all situated in our seats,

Adrian asks, "What if Josie sees us?" sounding a little worried.

"Javi texted and said she's in the shower," Milo says, and the whole car falls silent, and I can practically hear what they are all thinking. Mostly because I'm thinking the same, and jealousy stirs in my chest again that Javi is the one who gets to be there with her.

Clearing his throat, Carter speaks up, "Let's get this done and over with," speaking similar words I said earlier, but I don't miss the tension in his shoulders. I don't blame him. Doing these jobs never gets easier, and if Josie knew the jobs we do for Matteo, she would probably run for the hills.

If she knew the reason behind us doing the jobs, however, I do not doubt that she would help, no questions asked. That's just the kind of person she is. Always there for the people she cares about, but no one is there for her when she needs it. Luckily, she now has the six of us at her back, and if anyone dares to do wrong to her, we'll break jaws first and ask questions later.

Unfortunately, it's the people closest to her who always seem to cause her pain, and we're no different. If she finds out all the secrets we've been keeping, that might just be her final straw, and I can't imagine a world without Josie in it.

"What's this I heard Kyler say about sharing?" Milo's grin and devious tone broke me from my dark thoughts.

My eyes connect with his in the rearview mirror, and the playful stare I see looking back at me fills me with a sense of camaraderie I hadn't realized I missed so much. " I missed you assholes."

***

"Diego," Milo greets the man standing in the center of the room at this decrepit warehouse. He turns away from the pile of human trash, bound and gagged, lying on the floor in front of him.

Los Caminantes Nocturnes are made up of a plethora of assholes, but some decent guys got stuck in this lifestyle because they have nothing else going for them, or they're just buying their time until they can find a way out.

Similar to us, he's only sticking around because the woman he's in love with is tangled up in some bullshit that, surprise, surprise, involves Sylus. So when he called Milo a few hours ago and said that we need to meet him at the warehouse regarding information about Sylus, we didn't ask questions.

"Hey guys," he says as we approach, stuffing his hands into the pockets of his jeans. "Sorry you had to drive out here so late, but I think you're going to want to hear what he has to say," nodding his head toward the pathetic figure lying on the ground.

"Was he causing problems again?" Milo questions curiously, not sure why we would want to hear what the man has to say.

Given that I only started working with them eight months ago, I have never dealt with this man, but they all seem to know who he is. Trailing my eyes over him as if I'll be able to figure out who he is, I don't see anything out of the ordinary. His brown hair looks greasy, and his cheeks are covered with pockmarks. He has a bit of a gut, but he's not fat. More like a dad bod, and he's wearing a cheap suit.

"Who is he?" I lean toward Carter on my right, but of course, he doesn't hear me. So I lean to Adrian on my other side and ask the same thing.

"He's one of Matteo's regulars," he tells me with his eyebrows scrunched together, looking just as confused as I feel.

"No, not at Matteo's, at least," Diego folds his arms across his chest, answering Milo's question.

"So why are we out here then?" Carter speaks up next to me, urging Diego to get to the point.

"I found him over at Sylus's," he says, running a hand down his face, and we all stiffen almost in unison at the mention of that prick's name.

I clench my hands at my sides, knowing that whatever he is about to tell us isn't going to be anything less than gut-ripping.

"Explain," Kyler says flatly.

"I was driving by to check on my girl," he sighs, and I turn to Adrian and raise my eyebrow out of curiosity. Adrian gives his head a slight shake, so I just file that little bit of information away for a later time.

"I parked along the curb across the street, and as soon as I put my car in park, this asshole," he points with his thumb over his shoulder to the man, "was being tossed out the front door."

"Does Matteo not like his clients going to Sylus'?" I ask, confused, still not understanding where he's going with this.

"No, Matteo doesn't care as long as his clients pay, and Frank always pays." Diego explains, then continues, "him being there isn't what caught my attention; it was what he was yelling at the men who threw him out."

My stomach curls in on itself at his words, and dread looms over me like a cold shadow. Even though it's the end of summer, the concrete floor and metal walls of the building made it feel about ten degrees cooler, and goosebumps sprouted along my arms.

"He was yelling that he pays for his membership and should be allowed to fuck whoever he wants."

"Well, that doesn't sound so bad," Adrian replies, and we all look at each other like we're missing something.

"No, but once the men went inside, Frank stumbled to his car, which was parked in front of me. Before he got in, I approached him and asked him about the membership." Diego grits out the last word, "My girl works in there, and I needed to know what he was talking about."

At the mention of his girl again, I can't help but wonder who she is and why she's working as Sylus'. I can't imagine he's happy about it. I couldn't even fathom Josie working in that line of work. Just thinking of another man putting his hands on her in any way that's more than a handshake makes me want to commit murder.

"So," Carter says, sounding annoyed that this is taking so long for him to get out.

"So, when I asked him what kind of membership it was, he told me he couldn't tell me because he signed an NDA," he huffs out and spins around to look at the man whose name is Frank.

There's an unspoken rule in whore houses where you don't talk about who you see or work with when you're there. Mostly out of courtesy or embarrassment, depending on the client or girl, but to have someone sign an NDA usually means there's some seedy shit going on.

"When I pushed him for more answers, he became belligerent, so I had to restrain him." he pauses to look at us. "And pop him in the face a few times...for good measure," He finishes. The smirk on his face tells me the beating he got wasn't necessary, but I don't blame him. I would have done the same if I knew my girl was working for Sylus.

We form a half-circle around Frank. He grunts as Kyler pulls him up to a sitting position by his hair and leans him against the cement pillar that's behind him. Kyler crouches down so he's at eye level with him, plucks the bandana from his mouth, and tosses it in his lap.

"Please," Frank begs pitifully, snot and tears running down his swollen face, "I can't tell you. I signed an NDA."

Surprisingly, it's Carter who steps forward and delivers a bone-crunching punch to his face. Frank's head lolls to the side, and blood starts to drip from his mouth.

Carter has always been the quiet one of the bunch, and the others have told me about the beast inside of him that lies dormant until he's provoked. I've never seen this side of him before, and getting to see a glimpse of it shows how much rage he's holding inside, and that thought causes a dull ache to form in my chest. Guilt at not being there for him more over the years mingles with fury, knowing what his home life is like.

"What's the NDA for?" Carter grits out.

"I can't tell you!" Frank yells.

Carter lands another crack to his face on the opposite side of the last one. The sound of flesh pounding on flesh is the only thing heard in the quiet warehouse.

"What's the NDA for Frank?" Carter repeats, sounding like he's about to reach his limit. His body is vibrating with anger, and I fear that if he doesn't calm down, he's going to give himself a heart attack.

"I can't te-" Frank doesn't even get the words out before Carter lands another blow to his face, causing him to cry out. The sound of bone cracking echoes off the metal walls of the building. The jagged line in Frank's nose makes it obvious that the cracking we heard was his nose breaking.

"I can do this all night, Frank," Carter chastises like he's a petulant child, wiping his bloody knuckles on his pants as he steps back.

"Come on, Frank, the more you hold back, the more of a beating you're going to take," Milo says, looking way too casual, puffing on a cigarette, like this is just a regular Thursday night for him.

"If I tell you Sylus will kill me," Frank stops to consider his next words, deciding on how much he can say without giving too much information. "The basement."

Nothing good ever happens in the basement, no matter where it is. It's where kidnappers keep their victims. It's always the place in horror movies where someone gets trapped because there's nowhere to go. It's the place where people bury their secrets. It's cold and dark, and no one could hear you scream for help.

Those two little words crawl up my spine and fester in my brain. My hackles immediately rise, and my feet involuntarily move towards this pathetic man.

My hand wraps around his throat of its own accord and tilts his head back so he's looking me in the eye. "What the FUCK happens in that basement?" He's already shaking his head before I get the words out. I can feel panic taking over my body as my imagination spirals with all the depraved things that could possibly take place in that basement.

I squeeze just a little bit tighter, and his eyes widen in fear. "I'm going to remove my hand from your throat, and when I do, you're going to give us some answers." He nods his head in acknowledgment. "Good, because if I have to put my hands on your throat again, I won't be able to control them, and I will kill you," I say through clenched teeth, using all the willpower I have to let go of him.

I can feel Carter standing close to my side. Whether it's because he also wants to strangle Frank or if he's just keeping close in case I take this too far, I'm not sure.

Frank coughs and desperately starts sucking in air, as we all wait expectantly for him to spill it. "I can't tell you everything," I lunge towards him, and hands land on my shoulders to hold me back.

"But, what I can tell you is that people pay a lot of money for the memberships," he rushes out, eyes so wide they're about to pop out of his head. "I can't tell you who has a membership, but there are some important people who have them. That's one of the reasons he has membership holders sign the NDA."

"That still doesn't answer my question. What happens in the goddamn basement?" I all but yell, barely restraining my anger. My heart is thumping in my chest, and the hands on my shoulders give a small squeeze, telling me I need to calm down.

"That's where he keeps all his best girls, at least that's what he calls them. Really, it's girls that are just barely legal," he hangs his head out of shame, and refuses to look at us as the next words leave his mouth. "Some of them are still in high school, but all of the girls down there are eighteen."

Bile inches its way up my throat, and I hold back the need to throw up. If the girls are legal, why does he keep them in a separate part of the house? There has to be more to it than just the girls.

"Fuck!" Milo shouts just as I open my mouth to question Frank further. All of our heads snap in his direction. "Josie turns eighteen next week." His words hang heavy in the air, and I can feel the blood draining from my face.

"Do you think that's why he's suddenly showing an interest in her?" Adrian asks, and no one says anything because we already know the answer.

"Wait, Josie Ellis? His cousin?" Frank says quietly, as if he talks any louder, it will anger us more. I nod my head in answer, and trepidation fills me when he says her full name like he knows who she is.

He shakes his head, "He already has her on the menu." Nobody says a thing, and the tension in the room grows so thick only the jaws of life could cut it. Frank takes this as his cue to continue. "There's a bar in the basement, and above it hang two TVs that list each girl like their food on a menu.

Josie is listed on it and has been there for about a week now."

Carter turns on his heel and storms out of the warehouse. Milo lights another cigarette and puffs on it, staring into space like he didn't hear the bomb that was just dropped.

My head whips in Kyler's direction when he yells out and throws a fist at the cement pillar Frank is leaning against. Blood splatters against the concrete, and he turns and follows the same path outside that Carter took with a concerning shade of red filling his face.

Adrian's grip on my shoulder is so tight it would be painful if I weren't numb with shock. I don't know how long we've sat in silence, but it's long enough that the numbness has taken over my entire body, and Josie's beautiful face is the only thing I can see.

Her deep green eyes remind me of sparkling emeralds that hold so much warmth, I can't understand how anyone could feel anything but love for her. Her adorable freckles paint a picture of our childhood when we would spend days outside playing from sunup to sundown. Her full, pink lips remind me of all the times I was tempted to kiss her but held back because I didn't want to ruin our friendship. My skin begins to itch with the desire to tell her how much I want, no, need her. My palms twitch with the need to feel her in my arms and never let her go because wherever she is, that's where home is.

The numbness is overshadowed by wrath for the unfortunate soul who thinks they can take my home, my Josie, from me. Not only will they have me to get through, but my five brothers, and if there's one thing I know about them, it's that they fight for what they love.

Diego clears his throat, and I come back to the present in this depressing warehouse. I turn to find Adrian, who has the same look of determination that I feel. I nod my head at him in understanding.

"I'll take care of him," Diego nods his head towards Frank. "You guys can head out. Go check on your girl and figure out what you're going to do." He says as sadness falls over his face, but it is gone just as quickly. No doubt he's feeling the same way since his girl works for Sylus.

Milo walks over to Diego and claps him on the shoulder, "Thanks, man," he says, looking him in the eye. "If you ever need anything, let us know," Diego dips his head, and I clap him on the shoulder as I follow Milo and Adrian out.

We all pile back into the car, where we find an eerily silent Carter in the front passenger seat and Kyler in the back seat holding his hand against his chest. Nobody says a word as we all sit in our mutual hatred for the situation, for Matteo, and for Sylus.

"No one says anything to Josie," Milos says, starting the car and pulling away.

Great, just one more secret to add to the pile.

Chapter Eighteen

JOSIE

The soft sound of birds chirping wakes me, and a warm stream of sunlight gently coaxes me to open my eyes, making me feel like a Disney princess. I stretch my sleeping muscles when a grumble comes from the warm presence behind me, and a swarm of butterflies takes flight in my chest when Javi's breath fans over my neck. Very un-Disney-princess-like images play over in my mind, and I suddenly understand why they're all looking for their prince...to get laid.

My thighs tighten thinking about the best orgasm I've ever had, as phantom tingling has me clenching around nothing, and causes me to squirm. Another tired grumble comes from the man behind me, who deserves a Nobel prize in cunnilingus. I mean, I don't have a lot to compare it to but I'm almost positive not everyone is that good at it. I'm not entirely sure how he even got his tongue to move the way it did.

"Red, gorgeous, if you don't hold still, I'm going to come all over your back," Javi groans, then suddenly I'm being flipped to my back and he settles his weight over me. Pressing his erection into my stomach, he leans down to whisper in my ear, "Which would be a shame because I'd much rather come on your front." He nips my earlobe, and a blush paints my chest and works its way up to my neck.

"What do you say? Should we give Milo a show?" He asks, sitting up to look at my face.

"Milo?" I question with scrunched brows, not sure how he would see since he isn't here. At least I didn't think he was until I startle at the sound of an amused chuckle.

My eyes snap to my bedroom door, and the blush creeping up my neck halts as all the blood drains out of my face in humiliation at being caught in bed with one of his best friends. Realizing I'm never going to have another glorious orgasm again, which is probably a good thing since it seems the after-effects cause temporary blindness, as I wait for Milo to lash out and start calling me the whore that I immediately feel like.

My heart rate speeds up, and Javi's weight over me now feels suffocating, as it dawns on me that I'm just like Ashley. Panic threatens to take over, and my chin begins to tremble because I'm the reason their friendship is going to be torn to shreds.

They both must see the panic on my face. The next thing I know, Javi settles on the side of me, and Milo rushes over to my other side, cupping my chin to turn and look at him. "Hey, hey. What is it? What's wrong?" he asks, propped up on his elbow, looking down at me. Javi is doing the same on the other side.

"I don't want to come between you, any of you," I reply. My heart aches, and his brows scrunch together, out of confusion or anger, I'm not sure, so I elaborate, "because you caught me in bed with Javi," I say, and now they both look even more confused as my eyes volley between them. "Aren't you upset that you found me in bed with your friend?" I ask, and amusement instantly takes over their faces.

"Little fox," Milo says, running a knuckle down my cheek, "as I told you yesterday, and I'll tell you every day if I need to, we just want to see each other happy, and you make us happy. We knew what we were getting into when we agreed to give this a shot. I don't want you to feel like you have to hide your relationships with us from the others." The sincere look in his eyes has the panic receding, and my heart begins to slow. "You could never and will never break us apart. If anything, you'll just make us stronger." He finishes, and his sweet words have tears welling behind my eyes.

"I'm sorry, I just-"

Javi is shaking his head before I finish my sentence, "Don't apologize. This is new for all of us, and we meant it when we said this is at your pace, and if you need us to remind you of that, too, we will. " He rests a comforting hand on my stomach.

Milo leans in and his lips are just inches from mine, if I were to move my lips to move my lips with the smallest whisper, they would touch. As if reading my thoughts, he starts talking, "Besides," he starts, looking down at my lips when he lightly brushes mine, then looks back to my eyes with such desire I start to squirm again, "you will be coming between us, Little Fox, just not in the way that you think." I hold back a gasp as he makes me aware that I am literally between them, and oh lord, there's that phantom tingling again.

Javi is snickering next to me, and before I can even imagine coming between them, Milo quickly kisses me on the cheek and jumps off my bed with the speed I can only describe as that of a child sticking a fork in an electrical socket. "Now, you two get dressed so we're not late for school." He orders before walking out, keeping his back to us.

"Come on, Red, we need to get moving," Javi says,

pecking me on my other cheek much like Milo just did, and hops out of bed.

Now that they're both no longer crowding my space, it sinks in that Milo is in my house. Did he let himself in? Why is he even here? My last question is answered when Javi goes for the bag Milo left sitting by the doorway, and he pulls out a change of clothes.

I figure Mom must have left the door unlocked when she got in from work this morning, and he just let himself in. The idea of him letting himself in doesn't bother me as much as it should. The chances of him running into my mom are pretty slim since she would actually have to be around for that to happen, and now that I know Ashley is spending more time at Sylus's, it means she's spending less time here. I chalk up my nonchalance to the situation to the fact that I'm used to Zeke coming and going as he pleases, so what's a few more people? What's the worst that's going to happen? Hell, they could probably walk around naked and my mom would be none the wiser.

That's the thought that prompts me to get out of bed because if I sit and think about any of them naked for too long, I won't be leaving this bed any time soon.

I'm instantly regretting my decision not to stay home and think about hot naked men as we pull into the school parking lot next to Kyler's car, which is hot by itself, but with the tattooed stud leaning against it, he looks like he should be in some kind of calendar with hot shirtless men. The only thing that would make it better is if he were holding a puppy. I can't help but snicker at the thought. Thank god no one heard me, I don't know how I would explain that without bursting into flames.

I climb out of Milo's car and fling my backpack over my shoulder, but I stumble as it's pulled back off, and I turn to see Javi holding it by the strap. "I can carry it for you. I know you're still sore." He says, catching my shoulder to steady me.

"Thank you," I smile, remembering how upset he got last night and decide not to argue with him.

Turning back around, I walk the few steps to a beaming Kyler. "Good morning, Gingersnap," he greets, wrapping me in a hug.

"Good morning," I sigh, nuzzling my face into his chest and breathing in the smell of his woodsy cologne.

"Hey, Josie!" I hear Liam hollering and waving wildly. I hadn't realized he was standing so close.

"Hey, Lia- I mean lord." I correct myself when he cocks his eyebrow at me at the mention of his given name.

"Do you want to walk with me to class?" He asks with a bashful grin on his face.

"I would love to," I tell him, and he links his arm through mine. Kyler is on my other side and intertwines his fingers with mine. I feel students staring as we make our way through the busy parking lot and down the hall, but for the first time in my life, I can't bring myself to care what they think.

Milo and Javi are having a heated argument behind us, but I can't make out what they're saying because Liam is talking a mile a minute about his Lord of the Rings LEGO collection. A sliver of doubt pokes at my brain, and I wonder if they're fighting about this morning.

Then I remind myself of what they told me and decide I need to trust what they said and not let my insecurities get in the way. I focus on what Liam is saying and let them work it out amongst themselves and trust that they will tell me if something is wrong.

"Alright," Kyler says, getting Liam's attention as we stop in front of his classroom door "Don't forget I have some stuff to take care of after school, so you're riding the bus today," I want to question him on what he's doing after school, but our relationship is still new so I don't feel confident in asking him.

"Liam," his teacher addresses him, walking over to greet him at the door. She's wearing a black pencil skirt and a blouse that's cut inappropriately low for a high school special education teacher. She flicks her long black hair over her shoulder, and when she stops in front of us, all the while her eyes are glued to Kyler.

My defenses go up, my spine straightens, and I want to scratch her eyes out for even looking at him. If she looks at him with any more heat, she's going to set the whole school on fire.

"Hey, Ky, how's our guy doing today?" she asks as if Liam isn't standing here next to her and can't answer for himself. The fact that she called him Ky and is blatantly ignoring Liam has my hackles rising.

"Good," is all he says to her, brushing off her obvious flirting, and I relax a little at his disinterest in her. "I was just reminding him I won't be around after school, so he'll need to take the bus."

A pout begins to form on her lips, but she catches herself and says, "Don't worry, I'll make sure he gets on the bus." She then turns to acknowledge her actual student and frowns when she sees me standing between them. Her eyes glance at my hand connected with Kyler's so quickly that I would have missed it if I wasn't paying attention.

"Ms. Knudson, this is my friend Josie," Liam says excitedly, completely unaware of the disturbing interest his teacher is showing his brother.

"Hello, Ms. Knudson," I snark, emphasizing the Ms. to remind her that she's a teacher, and the way she was staring at my boyfriend didn't go unnoticed. Milo and Javi's arguing comes to an abrupt halt when they hear the irritation in my voice, and they step closer.

"Hello, Josie," her greeting sounds as fake as her overfilled lips look. "I didn't realize Ky had a girlfriend."

"Do you make it a habit of taking note of all students' relationship status, or is it just Ky?" I say with a little more anger than I intended. Someone's hand settles on my shoulder, and the tension lessens somewhat.

"I just meant, I've never seen him with a girl before," she answers, and I don't miss the annoyance in her voice. Her gaze roams up and down my body in an assessing manner. "Liam, why don't you go get your backpack put away, and we'll get the day started." She spins and walks away, apparently having nothing else to say.

Liam hugs me and tells me he'll see me later, and Kyler tells him he'll stop in to say bye before he leaves for the day. Kyler's hand never leaves mine, and we go back to walking side by side, while Milo and Javi go back to arguing a few steps behind us.

I don't miss the stares and whispering as we make our way down the hall and to my locker. The angry huffing from Sophie and dirty looks from her bitch brigade as we pass them has dread coiling in my gut.

"What are you smiling at?" I ask Kyler as we reach my locker. After taking my backpack from Javi and stuffing it in, only taking the binders for my first two classes.

"You're really cute when you get mad." I roll my eyes as he repeats the exact words Javi said yesterday. Even though Kyler brushed off Ms. Knudson's obvious attempt at flirting, a hint of jealousy still prods at me. I don't want to be that girlfriend who is constantly wary of who her boyfriend is talking to or texting, and none of them have given me a reason not to trust them. It's my insecurities, and it's not fair for me to project them onto them.

Kyler must take my silence to mean that I'm upset with him. He gently grabs my elbow and turns me to face him. "You know you have nothing to worry about, right?"

The gentle look on his face is in total contrast to his muscular build, and his tattoos enhance those muscles to only look angrier, giving him the bad boy look that every woman dreams about. The sincerity in his eyes shows his softer side and makes my insecurities evaporate completely. "I know," I say, closing my locker and stepping closer to him, and resting my forehead on his chest. "Just ignore me. I'm acting like a petty, jealous girlfriend."

His chest rumbles with laughter at my mumbling. "Hey," he says, prompting me to look up at him. "There's going to be times when I act like a petty jealous boyfriend," he pauses, "now times that by four. Can you imagine all the testosterone you're going to have to put up with?" he chuckles, shaking his head.

"I guess I never thought about you guys being jealous. Though I don't think you have anything to worry about." I say, letting out a chuckle of my own.

His face falls to an expression I can't read, so I reach up on my tiptoes and place a soft kiss on his lips. I turn to scan the hall for Kiera, but come up short. I do catch Chance and Cody conversing at the far end of the hall, reminding me I need to talk to Zeke about what I overheard them saying yesterday.

As if they could feel my eyes on them, they both look up and lock eyes with me. Drilling them with a stare like it will convey everything I heard them talking about yesterday, I refuse to look away first. I stand my ground, then see Chance's eyes flick to the person behind me.

Focusing back on Cody, I almost startle when I see the carnal look on his face. It's so intense I find myself taking a step back, and a possessive arm wraps around my waist, making Cody's face contort with anger. His hands clench at his sides, and his lips draw back in a snarl. Any moment, I think he's going to charge at me like an angry bull, but Chance finally breaks his stare and drags him away.

"What the fuck was that about?" Milo grumbles, staring down, obviously putting a stop to what they were arguing about. The urge to tell them what I heard them talking about yesterday is on the tip of my tongue, but the bell rings, signaling for us to start making our way to class.

All three guys give me a peck on the lips with promises of seeing me at lunch, and I head to my photography class. After the display of affection, there seemed to be more stares and glares from my classmates. Feeling a little less confident without my guys behind me, I rush to class thinking this is only the beginning.

W alking out of first period, I pull out my phone and shoot off a text to Zeke to see if he'll be around for lunch. Mrs. Whipple gave us homework to do over the weekend, and while some people still use film for photography, most of it's digital now. Unfortunately for me, I don't have a computer, but luckily, my best friend does.

> Josie: You gonna be around for lunch today?

> Zeke: I have to drop by coach's office. Why? What's up?

He seems to be meeting his coach a lot, and their practices seem to go on longer than I ever remember them. It is his senior year, though, so I just write off my suspicion that he's just practicing more so he's in tip-top shape for scouts.

> Josie: I need to talk to you. Meet me in the cafeteria when you're done?

A few minutes go by, and I don't get a response. I start to worry that he's going to tell me no and blow me off for this mystery person he's seeing. I know he said he wouldn't forget about me, but it already feels like I'm being pushed to the back burner.

By the time I make it to my second-period class, he hasn't responded. I shove my phone back into my pocket and make my way over to my desk next to my other best friend, who is practically bouncing in her seat with excitement.

I plop down in my seat and quirk an eyebrow at her. "What are you so excited about?" I ask curiously.

"Is it true?" she asks and squeals before she continues, "Are you dating all three of them?"

"Well, you would know if you would quit blowing me off," I tell her with a little more annoyance than I intended.

She stops bouncing and starts twirling a strand of her long brown hair around her finger. A nervous habit she's had for as long as I've known her, "I'm sorry," she quickly states, "I've had a lot going on. I was exhausted after having a late dinner with Chance's parents, and last night my mom wanted me home to watch my little brother while they went out on a date."

She continues twirling her hair and gives me puppy dog eyes that make my annoyance crumble away. "Are you mad at me?" She asks, and when I don't say anything, she pouts out her bottom lip like a child looking for their parents' forgiveness.

"If you stick that lip out any farther, someone's going to trip on it," I say through a smirk, knowing I can't stay mad at her for very long. "No, I'm not mad at you."

The bell rings for class to start, and Mr. Lambert makes his way to the front of the room to call roll. After taking roll, he hands out a math worksheet that needs to be completed and handed in before the end of class. As I begin working on my worksheet, my leg starts to bounce anxiously when I decide I need to tell Kiera what I saw at that party. With the rate she keeps blowing me off, I need to do it now while I have the chance.

I lean toward her, "I need to tell you something," I tell her quietly out of the corner of my mouth.

"What is it?" she says, keeping her eyes focused on the assignment.

"I saw something at Chance's party I need to tell you about," which gets her attention. Lifting her head, she's looking at me expectantly, and for a split second, I don't want to tell her. I don't want to be the one to give her the bad news, I don't want to see her heartbroken, but she deserves to know. I huff out an anxious breath. "I caught Ashley in bed with Jake and Chance," I whisper quickly in one long run-on sentence before I lose my nerve.

Her chest starts to rise and fall as her breathing grows heavy. I don't miss the way her jaw twitches, and her eyes have narrowed to slits. I know she's holding back her emotions because she doesn't want to make a scene in math class. After a few moments, I see tears shining in her eyes that she refuses to let fall.

"I'm so sorry, Kiera. I've been wanting to tell you, that's why I've been trying to get you to hang out after school, but I couldn't hold it in any longer. You deserve to know."

"It's not your fault, Jo," She says, and a tear leaks out of her eye. The moment the wetness touches her cheek, anger clouds her eyes. Whether she's mad that she's crying or because Chance cheated on her, or both, I'm not sure. "I'm going to cut his fucking balls off." She says through clenched teeth.

Seeing her upset makes me upset, and I want to castrate the man I once considered my friend. "Do you want me to get one of the guys to kick his ass?" I ask, trying to make her feel better, but also wanting to kick his ass myself. "I bet they would if I asked them, no questions asked."

The tiniest smirk crosses her mouth, but then "Oh my god!" she whisper yells, earning a glare from the boy next to her. I mouth sorry to him, and that seems to have his glare fading and his attention quickly back on the worksheet. "You said Jake, too? I'm so sorry, Jo." She looks at me with sympathy, and I shrug my shoulders. I have better things to worry about. In fact, I can name five of them.

"It's okay. I've got five boyfriends now, so I can't complain," I wink at her, and her face lights up like she stuck a lightbulb in her mouth, forgetting about the conversation we just had. I can tell she wants to ask me a million questions. "I know you have questions," I tell her, "but we don't have enough time. We can talk at the game tonight?"

She dips her head in agreement, and we get back to the assignment. I feel my phone vibrate in my pocket, slipping it out just enough to see the text from Zeke saying he'll meet me in the cafeteria. Pressure feels like it's been lifted from my chest, that I didn't realize I was holding there, knowing that he's not blowing me off.

Class goes by quickly after I drop the bomb on Kiera, and after the bell rings, I tell her my offer still stands to have one of the guys kick Chance's ass. She pulls me into a hug and squeezes me so hard it feels like my eyes are going to pop out of my head. She finally lets go of me, and I tell her I'll see her at lunch.

History class is uneventful but drags on much slower than

the first and second periods. The gossip mill has started, and my so-called peers have graduated from whispering and glaring to openly talking about me and pointing. Being the center of attention makes my skin prickle, and I wonder if the guys are getting the same treatment. I knew there would be people who would have an issue with our relationship, but I didn't think they would be so obviously disgusted with it. I guess that's my fault for overestimating them.

"Slut," someone says, trying to cover it with a cough, as I walk into fourth period and sit down at my desk at the back of the class.

I keep my head down, hearing the snickering from other students. Of course, the teacher doesn't say anything; he's too wrapped up with whatever he's looking at on his computer.

Weirdly, the one person I expected to say something is the only one who doesn't. Watching Sophie sit at the front of the class quietly talking to her friends puts me on edge. The way they were glaring at me this morning, I was sure she would have something to say, but she said nothing. I stare at her back all period, waiting for her to turn around and shoot her bitch venom at me, but it doesn't happen. She doesn't look at me, she doesn't giggle at me under her breath, she doesn't even breathe in my direction.

I hate it.

Her giving me the cold shoulder has me practically tearing through the skin down to the bone on my poor thumbs. She reminds me of a jungle cat when she's this silent, she sneaks up and pounces on you when you least expect it, and by the time you see her coming, it's too late. She's already on top of you, digging her claws into you.

I know what to expect from a loud Sophie, but a quiet one is much more dangerous.

I stop by my locker after fourth period to drop off my books and go straight to the cafeteria to meet Zeke. Knowing he was meeting his coach before lunch, I don't see any of my other guys either, so I make my way over to wait in line for food.

"Are you going to share your taco?" Someone says in my ear as the lunch lady sets a taco on my tray. The sour look on her face gives away that she heard him loud and clear. I feel my cheeks heat from embarrassment.

Ignoring the wannabe Sylus behind me, I continue through the line, loading my tray with rice and beans. Right as I pay and step towards my usual table, Cody cuts me off. "Come on, Josie, I know you like to share," he sneers, thinking he's clever.

"Get fucked, Cody. I wouldn't share my taco with you if your life depended on it," I retort, very aware of the double entendre.

Something over my shoulder catches his attention. "Pretty soon, you won't have a choice," he grunts. Looking back at me, he notices the goosebumps that break out over my skin at his ominous statement. Before he walks away, he flashes me a smile so sinister it would scare even the devil.

"Sweet pork tacos!" I shout, startled when a hand lands on my shoulder, causing me to almost drop my food.

"Sorry, I didn't mean to scare you," Jake says, holding his hands up to show he doesn't mean any harm.

My heart rate comes back down to a normal speed, allowing me to think clearly, "What do you want, Jake?" I ask exasperated. He may have had three months to come to terms with what he did, but it's still fresh for me, and I'm not sure when I'm going to be ready to talk to him.

Stuffing his hands in his pockets, " I just wanted to make sure you were okay," he answers. I don't know if he's asking because of the whispering and name-calling, or if he heard what Cody had said to me. Either way, the pity in his eyes makes me want to poke them right out of his head. Shrugging his shoulders, he continues, "And you know, I wanted to see if we could talk. I still want to be friends; besides, I owe you an apology."

My grip on my lunch tray tightens at the word friends, reminding me that that's all he ever wanted to be. Before I say anything hasty, Carter walks in, scanning the lunchroom, and when his eyes land on me, I can see them sparkling behind his thick-framed glasses. An infectious smile tilts his lips, and I find myself smiling back.

Five more figures, including Zeke, step in behind him, and I feel my smile grow so wide you would see my wisdom teeth if I had any. My annoyance toward Jake is long forgotten. "We'll talk later, Jake," I tell him, never taking my eyes off my guys. My feet start moving me toward them of their own accord.

"Hey, baby," Carter says when I reach him. He rests his hand on my neck and bends down to plant the gentlest of kisses on my lips. Time stands still as his minty breath wafts over my lips when he places his silky smooth ones against mine.

"Hi," I answer breathlessly when his mouth leaves mine. Smiling at the guys behind him, each of them with a different level of adoration showing on their faces. I turn to find a table for all of us, but am met with a sea of judgmental stares.

Attempting to avoid eye contact is difficult, especially when I notice the jealous and hateful stares I'm getting. Those are nothing compared to the longing and lustful stares my guys are getting from both guys and girls. Fighting the need to rub up against them like a raver on ecstasy to show everyone they're mine is proving to be difficult.

I know Zeke is my friend and I have no right to claim him, but it still feels like I'm being replaced with a person I haven't even met, which is all the more tempting to rub against him.

Sitting at an empty table in the far corner, Zeke sits next to me, and my eyes immediately go to the small purple spot behind his ear, mocking me that someone has already claimed him. My stomach twists, and I can feel another inch of space being put between us, pushing us just the littlest bit further apart.

Chapter Nineteen

JOSIE

"So, Jake's throwing a party tonight," Milo says, and it's the distraction I need that pulls me from the dark spot that's mocking me on Zekes' neck. "After the game." He finishes, and I realize he's talking to me; his eyes are pinned to me, assessing my reaction.

My nerves begin to buzz at the idea of going to a party, because, well, the last party I attended didn't exactly turn out great. I've vowed to never touch alcohol again, and being the only sober person around a bunch of drunk people doesn't sound very appealing. "I think it would be best if I don't go," I say nervously, not wanting to disappoint him.

"Go where?" Kyler asks, returning from getting his food. Sitting down, he dips some French fries in ketchup and shoves them in his mouth, a growing teenage boys who hasn't eaten in minutes. He moans out when the saltiness touches his tongue, and I can't help but snicker at the sexual sound coming from his mouth at the taste of his food.

"If you like them with ketchup, you should try them with fry sauce," I mention, and he looks at me like I'm speaking a different language.

"Ketchup is sauce for fries," he says slowly, eyeing me as if I have brain damage. To be fair, I kind of do.

"No," I say, giggling at his confusion. "Fry sauce. It's ketchup and mayo mixed together. It's so much better than plain old ketchup." He abruptly gets up from the table and marches over to the condiments station to grab some ketchup and mayo packets.

"Red, I know some crazy shit went down at the last party you went to, but we'll be with you this time," Javi explains, refocusing my attention.

The thought of them being with me this time does mollify my nerves. Even though they were at the last party, they weren't with me, *with me*, then. This time I'll be with all of them, and the fact that it's at one of their houses is even better. Because Milo can let whoever he wants in or kick whoever he wants out.

But that won't stop anyone from bringing in a gun, my anxious mind unhelpfully offers.

Like Milo can read my mind, he adds, "There will be security there. It's the only way my dad will let Jake have a party, given what happened at the last one."

Having security there is a bonus, and people will be less likely to cause problems. Hopefully. As I'm mulling this over, Adrian leans over from Zeke's other side. "We all just want to spend time with you," he states, surprising me with his directness, " you don't have to drink if you don't want to. We just want you to feel safe and let loose and have a good time." My heart flutters at his words and the way he seems to come out of his shell the more I'm around him.

I flash him an appreciative smile and feel a warm hand press against the small of my back. I turn to look at Carter, "If you aren't having a good time, we can always hang out in the theater room and watch movies or something." He suggests, and I notice the slightest of speech impediments as he talks. I don't know how I haven't noticed it before, he usually traces on my hand or gives short answers. It just makes my cute, reserved quarterback all the more adorable, and I just want to smother him with hugs like he's a puppy.

I give him a peck on the tip of his nose and turn to the rest of the table, including Kyler, who is now mixing his condiments to make fry sauce, "Okay, I'll go," I decide, feeling a rush of excitement I haven't felt in a long time. They all nod their heads in acknowledgment.

Just as Javi, Adrian, and Milo get up to get food, Zeke bumps my shoulder with his. He's been uncharacteristically quiet; I almost forgot he was sitting next to me. "What did you need to talk to me about?" he asks with a timidness I rarely see from him. I instantly feel bad, hoping he doesn't feel left out or like I've forgotten about him. "Is it that you have five boyfriends?" he barely contains a playful smirk, and the slight guilt I felt dissipates.

I roll my eyes at his teasing, and his infectious smirk forces one of my own. "Oh, I just wanted to know if I could come over and use your computer sometime this weekend for some of my photography homework?"

Relief washes over him. "Is that all?" he asks, and his tension visibly washes away.

"Yeah?" I say as more of a question, confused at his reaction. "Should there be more?"

"No, I just thought you were mad at me," he sighs out like the world has been lifted from his shoulders.

"I don't have a reason to be mad at you," I reply, taking a bite of my delicious taco, "but the day is still young," I mumble around a mouthful of food.

"So ladylike," He smarts, and I flip him the bird. "I do need to talk to you, too," he leans in to whisper, eyeing the rest of the table as if he doesn't want them to hear. "Come over Sunday, and we can chat while you do your homework."

I bob my head as my stomach drops with an unease that comes when you get called to the principal's office.

"Sweet baby gingersnap!" Kyler shouts, slapping his hand on the table.

People had just stopped staring, but Kyler had quickly captured their attention again with his outburst. My first reaction is to be embarrassed by the attention he's drawing, but it's quickly quelled by the gleeful look on his face that reminds me of Liam, and it melts my heart.

"God bless you, sweet girl, for bringing this creamy, delicious concoction into my life." No sooner does he get the words out than he is stuffing fry sauce-covered fries in his mouth. Which are more fry sauce than fries, and I'm surprised to see he isn't drinking it and forgoing the fries altogether.

I shake my head and chuckle. "If you think that's good, wait until you add barbecue sauce to the mix." I grin, and his eyes go wide like I just handed him a map to hidden treasure.

Milo's warm hand engulfs mine as they all walk me to my locker after lunch. The warning bell rings, signaling students to get to our next class, as we reach my locker and gather my folder for English. Milo's furrowed eyebrows greet me as I turn to say goodbye to them, and I don't miss that he's chewing on the inside of his cheek like he wants to say something but is holding back for some reason.

"Is everything okay?" his worrying behavior rips the question from my mouth.

"We won't be around after school. Text us when you make it home so we know you got there safe," The order is firm but gentle, and i would argue about him bossing me around if it weren't for the way he frustratedly shoves his hand through his inky black hair "Just be safe, okay?" he rushes out, quickly kissing me on the lips before I have the chance to answer and scurries off.

"Don't worry about him," Javi says from next to me, obviously noticing my concern at Milo's strange departure. "He doesn't like leaving you after what happened at Sylus', none of us do." he bends to kiss me, though not as quickly as Milos, it's still over sooner than I would like. "Don't forget to text us," he finishes and follows after Milo.

I can feel my eyebrows furrow much like Milos just were, and my gut is telling me that his worry has more to do with the incident that happened at Sylus'. Was that the first time Kyler had met Sylus the other day at my house? It sure seemed like it, but the way they came bursting through his front door once I told them where I was made it seem like they knew exactly who he is and what he does.

Javi did tell me his uncle is the leader of *Los Caminantes Nocturnos*, who so happens to be the number one enemy of the Northside Sovereign. I don't think it's a coincidence that they were at a party that also turned into a shoot-out. Javi said he didn't want to join his gang, but is he already ingrained in it? Are they all a part of it?

My gut churns as theories run through my head, and for the first time, I feel like I'm seeing things with open eyes. Kicking myself for being so fucking desperate for their attention, I couldn't see what was right in front of me.

Calm down, Josie, you're just making assumptions. I chastise myself as Kyler, Adrian, Carter, and Zeke all say their goodbyes and leave me contemplating what is actually going on and what they're always running off to do, oblivious to my spiraling thoughts.

I shove it all down when I step through the door to my English class; it's just as well because the first thing I notice when I step toward my desk is Kiera with her red, puffy eyes. My steps quicken, and I plop down next to her, pulling her into a hug. "Do you want to talk about it?" I ask, already knowing the cause of her tears and feeling partly responsible for them.

"Not right now," she sniffles, squeezing me tighter.

"Do you still want to cut his balls off? I'm more than happy to help." I offer to try to lighten the mood, but also one hundred percent serious, after I heard him and Cody talking about me in the hall yesterday.

She snorts a laugh and pulls away to look at me with a watery smile. "Babe, please, you couldn't hurt a carebear," she teases, " but I love you for offering."

The rest of the day goes by in a flash, but without the guys here, everyone seems to be more blatant with their name-calling. They've even come up with a clever new nickname, calling me ho-sie, along with the obvious slut, whore, and tramp.

Even though Sophie was still abnormally silent in gym class, I couldn't get out quick enough. When the teacher tells us we can head to the locker rooms to change, I grab my regular clothes and head for a bathroom stall. She may be silent, but that doesn't mean everyone else is, including her bitch brigade. I change into my clothes and wait in the stall to avoid any confrontation. Once I'm sure everyone is gone, I head to my gym locker to grab my phone and run a brush through my hair.

Exiting the locker room, I'm still on alert like she's going to pounce on me out of nowhere, and am pleasantly surprised when that doesn't happen. Unfortunately for me, the feeling doesn't last long.

Walking toward my locker, through the throng of students after the last class of the day, uncertainty trickles in when I come to stand in front of it, only to see a note taped to it.

*Thought you could put these to good use...*are the words that ridicule me, on the white piece of paper.

Trepidation snakes up my spine. I look around as if I'll see who put this note here, but everyone goes about their day as if I'm invisible. Chewing on my bottom lip, I anxiously reach out to spin the combination lock. A nagging feeling urges me not to, but I need to get my homework.

The moment my locker opens, hot dogs and condoms spring out like snakes from a faux jelly bean can. I squeak in surprise and startle back a step, bumping into someone. "Watch where you're going, hot dog." The male voice scolds, shoving me, and I almost slip on hot dog water.

If the contents toppling out of my locker didn't get their attention, then the loud, angry person I bumped into did. Time all but stands still when everyone's eyes land on me, and the Costco-sized pile of hot dogs and trojans lies scattered around me.

I get a few pitiful looks, but mostly the hall booms with laughter. Keeping my head down, I feel my cheeks ignite with embarrassment, and tears sting the backs of my eyes. A hot dog hits me in the head, and people start to chant "hot dog, hot dog, hot dog." Another hits me as the chanting and laughter continue.

Somewhere in the melee, Sophie decides to finally make her presence known as she shouts ho-sie, and the chanting switches to ho-sie hotdog. I knew she was up to something, and yet I still let myself walk right into her little trap. I grit my teeth and force my eyes to stay on the floor, and away from the deranged cackling that only grows louder and louder from Sophie and her deranged posse.

Without my guys at my back, or hell, even Kiera and Zeke, my confidence is nonexistent. Instead of speaking up and putting these assholes in their place, I lecture myself. For not having the guts to stand up to them, for making it so easy for them to walk all over me, for looking so pathetic, I'll probably be single by the end of the day, because who wants to be with someone as embarrassing as me?

The first tear tracks down my cheek, and I spin to grab my photography homework, soggy with hot dog juices, and shove it in my backpack. I don't miss the phones that are now pointing at me to document my humiliation, but before I shut my locker, I notice another note taped to the inside of the door ...*In case five isn't enough.*

Tears flood out of my eyes like an angry river, and I quickly slam my locker, shoving through the crowd of students and beeline for the nearest bathroom, closing and locking the door behind me so no one follows. I slide down the wall and hug my knees to my chest and sob until my legs go numb.

The halls seem to have finally quieted down when I lift my head from my knees. I don't know how long I've been sitting here, but I figure enough time has gone by that the school has cleared out and everyone has gone home.

I stretch my legs out, and they prickle and tingle, waking back up. Once I'm able to stand, I make my way over to the mirror and grimace when I see black mascara tracking down my face. I wet a paper towel and wipe it away as best as I can. There's nothing I can do about my red, puffy eyes or frizzy strands of hair that have taken on a life of their own. Attempting to tame them, I pull my hand away when a whiff of hot dog stench fills my nostrils, forcing an abrupt gag escape me.

Deciding my first order of business is getting home and taking a boiling hot shower to scrub away the smell and shame, I shrug on my backpack. Flipping the lock, I unlock the door, peeking my head out to make sure the coast is clear. When I don't see anyone, I step out and swiftly head for the front doors. I instantly relax when I notice the buses are gone and there are only a few cars lingering in the parking lot.

My heart thumps against my chest when I hear shouting, and I brace myself for whatever is going to be thrown at me next. When nothing happens, I start my descent down the stairs, but freeze when I hear more shouting coming from a familiar voice.

My eyes skim over the parking lot looking for him, but I don't see him anywhere. Another shout, I snap my head to the left to the area where buses usually pick up and drop off students.

Rage fills me when I see him surrounded by a group of guys, caging him in like lions teasing their prey. Before I can think twice, my feet begin carrying me toward them, unable to stop even if I wanted to.

"Come on. We just want to know if your brother is working for him." One of them taunts Liam, and my hands clench at my sides, my nails dig into my palms so hard I'm surprised I haven't hit any bones.

Liam is stuck in the middle of them as they pester him with questions. I can see his red eyes the closer I get, and his hair is disheveled like he was tugging on it out of frustration. "I don't know what you're talking about. Leave me alone," he shouts, in a stern voice that would make his brother proud, but it's laced with a panic that pisses me off.

His nervousness causes me to pick up my pace as red invades my vision. I can feel the adrenaline coursing through my veins as the emotions I keep locked away threaten to surface when I see this innocent soul being tormented.

"Come on, just tell us." Another teases, stepping closer to him.

"No," he shouts shakily, clinging onto the straps of his backpack for dear life.

Shouldering past two of them, I force my way into the

middle and grab Liam and pull him into a hug, narrowing my eyes as one of them tries to step forward. With his head down, he cries louder and tries to push away from me. "It's okay, Liam, it's me, it's Josie," I whisper.

Without looking up, he throws his arms around me and clings tight, "I missed the bus. Kyler's going to be so mad at me." He sniffles against my shoulder. My chest cracks at the thought of him being concerned about his brother, and these idiots probably made his worry ten times worse by interrogating him.

I'm once again baffled at how someone could pick on someone so sweet and innocent. Someone so pure and loving, who, for some reason, is not reciprocated with the same care he puts out into the world.

My anger ratchets up tenfold at the thought when I spin on my heel, tucking Liam behind me. He grips the strap of my backpack as if he's scared I'm going to leave him here.

I get a good look at the pieces of trash in front of me. They all have moved to form a half-circle around us, with two in front of us and one on either side. It's then that I realize these dirtbags are four of Cody's minions, and I feel my lip curling with disgust. Though I'm not surprised they're messing with him, I am surprised Cody's not with them. Usually, they're attached at the dick.

"Looks like you were able to remove your lips from Cody's dick. With the way you guys follow him around, I thought they were permanently attached," I snarl out the words before I can stop them. Shocking myself with my blunt words, I almost don't recognize the sound of my voice.

"The fuck did you just say?" Trevor, the one in front of me, says, taking a threatening step forward.

My back stiffens, and I feel my confidence beginning to fade when he towers over both of us as he steps forward. Forcing the anger to stay on my face, hoping he doesn't notice the effect he has on me, "Did you not hear me? Or does giving too much head cause hearing loss?" I retort, folding my arms over my chest.

"Shouldn't you know the answer to that, seeing as you have five boyfriends, *hot dog*?" Derek from my left sneers, and the others chuckle.

I hear Liam sniffling behind me; he's practically pressed against my back, holding onto my backpack for dear life. I reach back to rest a hand on his back to try and comfort him, but it's difficult from this position. "I want to go home," he rasps, and I nod my head.

Letting out a heavy sigh. "I don't want any problems, okay. We're going to go." I tell them that deciding Liam is more important than goading them.

"What's the matter, princess, don't you want to add four more men to your roster?" Trevor says, holding his arms out, gesturing to his friends around him, before he closes the gap between us. He steps so close to me that I can smell the stale scent of weed clinging to his clothes.

The anger falls from my face and is replaced with what I can only assume looks like alarm. My throat bobs as I gulp down my nervousness, trying to keep some composure. Rubbing soothing patterns on Liam's back, not sure if it's more for him or me at this point.

"She must have a golden pussy if she can lock down five guys," Kyle from the right interjects with a hungry smile on his face, making my hands tremble.

"Dibs," Chris says with a chuckle, as they all groan their annoyance at not saying it first.

"I'm not adding any of you to my roster, and I'd rather stay a virgin for the rest of my life than fuck any of you." I grit as they talk about me like I'm not even here.

I immediately regret my words when four sets of eyes snap to me, and the feral looks they're giving me have my blood turning to ice, and my flight instinct is telling me to run. I take a slow step back, so as not to spook them, and Liam steps with me.

I no longer hear him sniffling, but I can feel him trembling. Or is that me?

"I don't want any problems." I repeat with a shaky voice, keeping my eyes locked on Trevor since he is the closest to me, "We're leaving."

When no one says anything, I take another tentative step back, but before my foot hits the ground, Trevor snaps out and pulls me back by the straps of my backpack. I cry out as his nails dig into my skin when his hands curl around the straps, pulling me back so his body is flush with mine. "You didn't think you could get away from us that easily, did you, princess?" he says, running his nose along mine.

Fear licks up my spine, and I press my palms on his chest to attempt to separate us, but it just causes his grip to tighten on my backpack. "Let go of me," I cry, turning my head, uncomfortable with how close his face is to mine, shoving at his chest.

"Mmm," he grumbles in my ear, "I like a fighter." His breath on my skin causes a shiver of dread to shimmy across my shoulders, and my breathing turns rapid.

"If you don't let go of her, you'll be fighting for your next breath." A deep, unrecognizable voice says from behind me, and the menacing tone makes the hair on the back of my neck stand on end.

Everyone freezes in their spot, and when I see Trevor's eyes go to whoever is behind me, widening to the size of a planet, he instantly lets go of me like he's been burned. When his eyes flick back to mine, all I see is terror... and apology?

In fact, that's how they all look.

"I'm s-sorry we didn't mean any harm," Trevor says

quickly before he turns and sprints away with the others, a look of pure terror blanketing their faces.

I hesitantly turn to see who has these men running away like the Grim Reaper is chasing them. Liam keeps his head down but stands next to me rather than behind me. He laces his fingers through mine as if I'm going to run away, too.

I swallow down a gasp as I take in the person in front of me. His buzzed hair reminds me of Javi's, and his eyes are so dark they scream danger. His height is just about the same as my 5'5, maybe an inch or two taller. He's wearing a white button-up shirt with the sleeves rolled to his elbows and black slacks, with a silver chain hanging from his neck. Tattoos peek over the collar of his shirt, down his exposed arms to his hands. There's an intricate tattoo tracing along his hairline, and one little tattoo under his eye that I can't quite make out from here.

"Do I know you?" I ask with a trembling voice, scared that I may already know the answer.

A sly smirk covers his mouth. "No, *Preciosa*, I don't think you do," he takes a step closer, "but allow me to introduce myself," another step closer, "I'm Matteo."

Chapter Twenty

JOSIE

Matteo.

His name turns over in my head, and trepidation turns me into a statue, unable to move or say anything at his very unexpected appearance. Now that I'm putting a face to the name of the infamous leader of the *Los Caminentos Nocturnos*, I understand why Trevor and the others didn't waste a second getting away from him. I take a deep breath to force myself to remain calm for my sake and Liam's. Anxiety claws just below my skin, and if it breaks the surface, we're fucked.

His appearance alone is intimidating, and the way his eyes bore into me causes sweat to bead on the back of my neck. The way he stands, with his feet shoulder-width apart and his head cocked to the side in amusement, is reminiscent of a cat trapping a helpless mouse and watching as it struggles futilely to get away.

I suck in another deep breath to calm my nerves, but it has the opposite effect when his eyes track the movement of my chest moving up and down, and an indecipherable look crosses his face. Before I can examine that too closely, Liam squeezes my hand, pulling my attention to him. My heart splits when I see his red eyes and tear tracks on his cheeks. "I want to go home," he whispers, and the sound forces me to find my voice.

"Javi isn't here," I force out, turning back to Matteo. Assuming that's the only reason he would have to be here. I can't imagine he would come to his enemy's side of town for nothing.

"No…he isn't," he replies with a smirk returning to his face, and his tone implies he knows exactly where his nephew is, "he's busy at the moment."

My skin prickles with unease at him knowing his nephew's whereabouts, pushing my earlier theories to the forefront of my mind, waving around like a giant red flag.

He takes another step closer, "I was just passing through town checking on a couple of jobs," he says, emphasizing the word job like it's supposed to mean something. "Lucky me, as I was heading back out, I came across a damsel in distress who just so happens to be the *la belleza* who has been distracting my nephew." Running his tongue across his top teeth, irritation flashes in his dark eyes.

"I don't know what you're talking about." The lie is weak, and my earlier suspicions of all of them already being a part of his gang ratchet up, but I push it aside and focus on a way to get Liam out of here.

He takes another step toward us, and he's standing so close now that the tips of our shoes are almost touching. "Oh, *Preciosa*, I think you know exactly what I'm talking about," he whispers ominously, and the beading sweat on my neck trickles down my back. This close, I can see the tattoo under his eye is a Roman numeral for the number five.

"Josie?" I hear from the other side of Liam. For the first time in three months, I'm thankful to hear that voice, "Are you okay?"

My shoulders relax, somewhat, at Jake's perfect timing. I

look at him over Liam's head with pleading eyes to get us the hell away from this man. His chocolate-brown eyes examine Liam, who is now squeezing my hand so tightly that his knuckles are turning white, and my bones are starting to ache; Liam's eyes are glued to his feet.

I see his jaw flex, and when he sees the desperate look on my face, he marches over with an angry look in his eye. He stands in front of Liam, shielding him from view and standing so close to me I can smell his cologne. His eyes are locked on Matteo, challenging him to say something.

I would be worried for Jake if he weren't so much larger than Matteo. He towers over him, and he obviously has more muscle than him. I'm honestly surprised he's not on the football team. He could easily beat Matteo if this turned into a physical altercation. However, Matteo is dangerous, and Jake is smart enough to realize that no matter how much bigger he is, Matteo is just as powerful. If not more.

"Relax, pretty boy," Matteo scoffs at Jake and pins his eyes on me. "I'll be seeing you around, *Preciosa*," he winks at me and turns to walk away, leaving me to squirm with his parting words.

A heavy silence weighs the air as we watch Matteo retreat. Once he's no longer visible, I take in a long, deep breath to calm my shaking nerves. I turn to Liam, who is still clutching onto my hand like he's going to be ripped away from me at any moment. "Liam, are you okay? Did those guys hurt you?" I ask gently.

He shakes his head as his eyes meet mine, and the sadness I see staring back at me has me choking back tears, but they are quickly replaced with anger at the people who put that look on his face in the first place. "I want to go home," he pleads again, never letting go of my hand.

"How about we go to my house, and I can call Kyler from

there to come pick you up?" I offer, not knowing where he and Kyler live.

He nods his head and gives me a watery smile. "Can we watch a movie while we wait for him?" he asks, and my shoulders relax somewhat, seeing his mood improving. Even if it's just slightly.

"I can give you a ride," Jake says, and the anger that was in his eyes is quickly replaced with uncertainty. We're still not on the best of terms, and I'm still not ready to forgive him. "Please, I would feel a lot better knowing you got home safe. Besides, Milo would kick my ass if he knew I let you walk home while Matteo was around." The mention of Milo makes my heart skip a beat, and he's not wrong; he would kick his ass.

"Fine," I say through the small smile, tipping my lips from the image of him getting his ass kicked. "Come on, Liam, Jake's going to give us a ride to my house."

We start making our way to the parking lot. My hand is numb at this point from Liam's strangling grip. Jake doesn't question what happened with Liam or why I'm with him, but I see the curious way he keeps glancing at the way Liam clings to me.

"Whoa, cool car," Liam says as we approach Jake's car. Finally letting go of my hand to run the rest of the distance, stopping in front of it, gaping at it like he's never seen a car before. "It's so shiny."

I open and close my hand to get some feeling back into it, as Liam climbs into the backseat of Jake's Audi RS 7. Rolling my eyes at the typical rich kid car that I used to be impressed by until I saw Kyler's sexy red muscle car.

"Thanks, man," Jake says to Liam, flashing him a friendly smile.

He pushes the start button and it purrs to life, making

Liam bounce in the back seat with giddiness, "How fast can it go?"

"It can go up to 190 miles per hour, but I've never taken it over 120," Jake answers him.

My chest suddenly feels heavy, and I feel like the car is shrinking in on me. Their small talk about how fast the car can go has made me very aware that I am sitting in a car. A fast one.

Jake presses on the gas, and my hand flies to the handle on the door to hold on, the same way Liam was holding onto me moments ago. I squeeze my eyes shut, inhaling deep breaths, attempting to calm myself. "You okay?" Jake asks.

Nodding my head, "Yes, cars just make me a little anxious now," I tell him, keeping my eyes shut, not wanting to see the pitying look on his face. Though I've found I don't get nearly as anxious when one of my guys is driving, I'm still terrified to drive myself, and equally as terrified when it's not one of them driving.

"I promise I'll drive carefully," Jake tells me with understanding in his voice.

Pulling out of the school parking lot, keeping my eyes closed, I try to focus on taking deep breaths. With each breath, my grip on the door handle lessens, and before I know it, we're pulling to a stop in front of my house.

I peel my eyes open and let out a sigh of relief. "Thank you for giving us a ride," I say, turning to Jake, "I appreciate it."

"You don't need to thank me, Josie," he answers. The questioning look on his face shows that he wants to say more, but he's holding himself back.

"Look, I know we need to talk. I'm coming to your party after the game tonight. Maybe we can talk then?" I offer. I can see that he still wants to be my friend, and though my feelings are still fresh after what happened, he is trying. Wish I could say the same for Chance.

"I would like that," he says sincerely.

Liam and I climb out of the car and make our way into the house. "Can I pick the movie?" Liam asks, bouncing on the balls of his feet, excitedly.

For someone who was being tormented less than an hour ago, he's in much higher spirits, and I can't help but grin at his excitement, "Only if you pick a good one," I say teasingly.

"Yes," he pumps his fist in the air and runs over to rifle through my movies stashed in the entertainment center.

Chuckling at him under my breath, I pull my phone out of my pocket to text the guys and see a few texts from them already.

Shit. It took me longer than usual to get home because of everything that happened, and they obviously noticed. Sure enough, when I open our group chat, there's a text from each of them, each sounding more worried than the next.

> Milo: Did you make it home okay?
>
> Kyler: Gingersnap, are you still at school?
>
> Carter: Babe, please let us know if you've made it home.
>
> Javi: You're starting to worry us. Milo's going to turn into a pile of ash with all the stress smoking he's doing.

I can't help but laugh at that one, and Liam lifts his head to see what has me laughing, but then quickly gets back to his task of picking a movie.

> Adrian: Don't make us come over there.
>
> Zeke: Jo, Mom said she hasn't seen you come home. Where are you?

> Me: Sorry, I got caught up with a few things after school. I'm home now, and I have Liam with me.

Almost instantly after I sent the message, my phone floods with messages from all of them.

> Milo: What happened? Are you okay? Whose face needs rearranging?

> Kyler: What?!?! I told his teacher to make sure he got on the bus. Is he okay to stay with you until I can come to get him? We should only be a half-hour longer.

> Carter: Thank god! You had us all worried, babe. I'm glad you're safe.

> Javi: Red, I'm going to spank that ass until it matches your hair.

My cheeks heat, and a warm, fluttery feeling settles in my lower abdomen. I'm not sure if it's from embarrassment at Javi's crass words that everyone can read, or the thought of him spanking me while they all watch. The next text that comes intensifies the butterflies in my stomach, and I don't need a mirror to tell me that I'm as red as a fire truck.

> Adrian: She needs to be spanked until she can't sit down.

Cheese and rice! What are these men doing to me? How am I supposed to respond to that without sounding like a blushing virgin?

> Me: Of course, he's okay to stay here. I like the company. We're going to watch a movie and hang out. Really, it's no problem at all. I'm sorry, I didn't mean to make you all worry.

There, simple enough. Hopefully, they won't notice that I ignored the whole spanking thing. To my surprise, the only response I get is from Milo telling me that they will see me tonight when they pick me up for the football game.

Before I shove my phone back in my pocket, I notice that Zeke sent me a message separate from the group chat.

> Zeke: I felt like I was intruding on your conversation with the guys. I just wanted to let you know I'm glad you made it home safe. I know you have them looking after you now, but I'm still here for you, Jo. I always will be.

A knot forms in my throat, feeling like there is more distance between us than there ever has been. My feelings toward Zeke lately have been confusing, but I don't want him to ever feel like he's intruding or unwanted. I'll always want him.

And if those four words aren't a hard slap to the face, I don't know what is.

My heart starts to beat harder against my ribcage as those four little words sink in, and I realize how deep my feelings are for my best friend. I don't know what changed or why, all I know is how right it feels.

> Me: Please don't ever feel like you're intruding, Zeke. I know you'll always be there for me. It's one of the reasons why you're my best friend.

Nibbling on my lip, I decided I'll tell him how I feel on Sunday when I go over to do my photography homework. He said he needed to talk to me, too. Maybe he feels the same way? No, that can't be it, can it?

Thankfully, another message from Zeke comes through, preventing me from spiraling. After I read his message that says he'll see me after the game tonight, I set my phone on the counter and make some popcorn for Liam and me.

"This is not the movie I was expecting you to pick," I say, plopping down on the couch next to Liam.

Shrugging his shoulders, "I'm in the mood to watch something funny."

When the credits start to roll, Liam whispers, "Josie?"

"What's up?" I answer before shoving delicious salty popcorn into my mouth. When I look up to see the sadness lingering in his eyes, I rest my hand on his forearm to try to comfort him.

He hesitates with what he's going to say, and just when I think he's not going to say anything, he simply says, "I'm glad we're friends."

Those simple words fracture my chest, and it hurts to swallow the popcorn I was chewing. I give him a sympathetic smile. "Me too, Liam. We're friends, and friends stick up for each other."

A smile spreads across his face, not quite reaching his eyes, obviously not wanting to talk about what happened after school, I attempt to lighten the mood. "Next time I'll just have to introduce them to Chuck," I say, holding up my right fist, and Norris," I finish, holding up my left fist.

My ridiculous attempt at making him laugh works. He starts giggling and shaking his head, "I'm so glad you're with my brother."

Wiping tears from my eyes from his infectious laughter, " Me too Lia-"

He narrows his eyes at me before I can get his full name out. "Lord," I say, correcting myself, "me too, Lord."

Nodding his head in approval, I toss a piece of popcorn in my mouth and hold the bowl out, offering him some of the salty snack. "Good, now let's watch Hot Rod and laugh until our faces hurt."

And that's exactly what we did.

"I'm going to fucking kill them!" Kyler growls after I finish telling them what happened after school. Well, just the part about Liam, I skipped over the part about what happened at my locker, and that I met Matteo. Judging by the murderous look on his face, I'm not sure I want to tell him, or the others, for that matter.

All of the guys showed up about halfway through the movie, but Carter, Zeke, and Adrian were only here long enough for me to tell them they're going to kick ass at the game tonight. I kissed them on the cheek for good luck, and they were out the door.

I'm debating if I should tell them about Matteo now, or if I should wait until I'm with all my guys. I subconsciously start picking at my thumb, and I want to smack myself. If picking at my thumbs isn't a sign that something is bothering me, then I don't know what is. Of course, they immediately pick up on it. "Little Fox," Milo says, softly placing his hand over mine to stop the fidgeting, "did something else happen?"

I swallow nervously. "Well, Trevor asked if I wanted to add more men to my roster, and I basically told him I'd rather die than touch any of them." Taking in a breath, I continue, "Apparently, he didn't like my answer because he grabbed onto my backpack strap and got in my face." I pause, hesitating to say the next part, unsure of how they're going to react.

Sitting at the kitchen table with Milo on one side, Kyler on the other, and Javi leaning against the wall behind Kyler. I meet all of their concerned, angry gazes. "Trevor wasn't able to take it any further because, um, Matteo showed up."

I see Javi's shoulders stiffen, and his jade eyes now have the same murderous look that Kylers had moments ago. Milo's grip on my hand tightens, almost painfully, and the table creaks with how hard Kyler is gripping it.

The tension in the air is thick enough to choke on, and I start to fidget with my other hand sitting in my lap. I can hear Liam laughing in the living room, thankful he's feeling better, but also envious that I'm not in there laughing with him.

The silence grows unbearable, and my mouth takes that as a sign to say more words that will only make them angrier. "He told me he was passing through town checking on some jobs." More silence, "he was on his way out of town when he saw Trevor harassing us," still nothing, "before he left, he said he would be seeing me around."

That statement was the one that pushed them too far.

"FUCK!" Javi yells unexpectedly, causing me to flinch. Rubbing his hand over his buzzed hair, he starts pacing back and forth behind Kyler.

"What's going on?" I ask nervously, knowing something else is going on, based on their reactions, I'm not sure I want to know the answer.

"We can't leave you alone for five fucking minutes, that's what's going on," Javi snaps, and his outburst makes me speechless, seeing this side of Javi.

"Javi," Kyler grinds out in warning.

Javi rushes over to my chair, lifts me, sets me across his lap, and buries his nose in my copper tresses before I can blink. "I'm sorry, Red. I'm not mad at you, I'm mad at the situation."

"What's going on?" I repeat, desperate to know what they're not telling me.

"Matteo's not a good guy," Milos answers.

"He's dangerous," Kyler adds.

They try to placate me with vague answers. I know something is going on since Matteo confirmed my suspicions earlier when he all but admitted to knowing where Javi and his *guys* were, but them purposely holding back information is what irritates me.

Javi's arms tighten around my waist when I attempt to stand from his lap, and an exasperated sigh slips past my lips. "Matteo will use whatever he can to manipulate me, and that includes you," Javi says shakily into my hair.

"Gingersnap," Kyler says, getting my attention, "he's unpredictable and reckless. We just want you to be safe."

"I understand that," I tell them truthfully. Especially after what happened with Sylus. I mean, Sylus and Matteo are pretty much the same people, just on opposing sides. I wouldn't put anything past either of them at this point. What I don't understand is what they aren't telling me. Are they keeping secrets from me to protect me? Because they don't trust me? Are they trying to protect themselves? "But-"

"Trust us, Little Fox," Milo says, cutting me off, "we would never purposefully hurt you, or put you in harm's way. I promise we will always protect you."

My heart flutters, and my irritation cools as I reach over to place my hand over the top of his. "I do trust you, but you have to trust me, too. Remember, this will only work if there are no secrets," I reiterate my words from the other day, looking each of them in the eye to see my sincerity.

They all dip their heads in understanding, and at this moment, I'm choosing to trust them. They have always been there for me when I've needed them the most, and they always seem to have my best interests at heart.

A fit of giggles sounds from the living room, breaking up the seriousness of our conversation, and I can't help but let out a giggle at the happy sound. Kyler chuckles and shakes his head, "I swear that kid could make an orc smile."

Pressing my hand to my chest, gasping, "Did you just make a Lord of the Rings joke?"

Milo and Javi let out annoyed groans, and a beaming smile spread across Kyler's mouth. "Do you like it when I talk nerdy, my little Gingersnap?"

"I don't hate it," I say, shrugging my shoulders, "I'm just surprised, is all."

"I have seen those movies more times than I can count, thanks to Liam." He tries sounding annoyed, but I see the warmth behind his eyes at the mention of his brother.

"Well, now that Josie and I are best friends, you are relieved of all things Lord of the Rings," Liam chimes in, walking into the kitchen to stand behind his brother.

"I thought I was your best friend?" Kyler questions, sounding offended.

"I can have more than one best friend," Liam tells him in a tone as if to say Duh! A cell phone, I've never noticed him with before, vibrates in his hand, and a mischievous gleam twinkles in his eyes. "Kenny and I want to know if you can really lose your hearing from sucking too many wieners?"

Just as the last word leaves his mouth, Milo spits the soda he was drinking across the table. He and Javi roar with laughter, and my eyes grow wide, stunned that he heard what I said to Trevor. I cup a hand over my mouth, trying not to laugh, not sure how Kylers going to react. He can't be too mad. I would bet anything Liam has heard them say worse.

"Where the hell did you hear that from?" Kyler asks, sounding like he's trying to hold back a laugh himself.

Javi is shaking with laughter from behind me. "Josie," Liam throws me under the bus, "when Trevor was being mean to her, she asked him if sucking Cody's dick too many times is causing him to go deaf."

Sinking back into Javi, covering my face with my hands out of mortification. Javi's arms wrap around my waist. "Does our little Red have a filthy mouth?" he teases.

I spread my fingers, peeking through to see Kyler looking at me with a cocked eyebrow, "I'm sorry, I didn't think he was listening." I defend weakly.

"Also, what's a golden pussy?" Liam adds.

My face feels like it's on fire with embarrassment, and with my pasty skin, I'm sure it looks like it too. "Okay, that's my cue to leave," I say and quickly jump to my feet, "I'm going to go get ready for the game."

Before I get too far, Kyler gently grabs my wrist, "You're not getting out of this that easily," he says sardonically, then places a kiss on my lips. "I'm going to run him home, and I'll be back."

Javi and Milo are doubled over, still laughing as I say goodbye to Liam. Once they're out the door, I rush to my room, slamming the door behind me. With my back to the door, I begin fanning my face to cool the shame. I don't know how I'm going to make it through a football game, let alone a party with them, but the fluttering that grows in my stomach at the idea of just being around them for that long has me fanning my face for a whole different reason.

Chapter Twenty-One

CARTER

I always thought the worst person I knew was my sorry excuse of a father. He's been an alcoholic for as long as I can remember, and an abusive prick even longer. When I was a toddler, I remember lying in my dingy little bed, curled up with the only blanket I had, which was barely a scrap of fabric, listening to my mom and dad fighting.

Most of the time, it was my dad yelling at my mom for some bullshit reason that his drunk and belligerent mind conjured up. Oftentimes, I would hear him stomping around like a toddler throwing a tantrum because his mommy wouldn't let him have any candy before bed. He would shout, slamming doors and cupboards, slurring indecipherably.

Then there were the other nights. The nights when he wouldn't shout at all. The nights when the tension felt so heavy, you could hear the house groaning from the weight of it. Those were the nights that scared me the most because, in my experience, a silent alcoholic is more dangerous than an angry alcoholic. I would lie, waiting in silence for the inevitable moment when the smallest inconvenience would make him snap quicker than a tree branch in a hurricane.

When he did snap, the sounds that would come from the other side of my door were nothing short of a horror movie. Scuffling feet, shattering glass, a body being banged against walls and floors, are nothing compared to the terrified screams and cries coming from my mother.

Fear and panic would claw at my chest, forcing me to burrow further into my mattress and cover my head with my small blanket as if the worn fabric would block everything out. Snuggling my little stuffed dog, Bosley, as tightly as I could while humming my favorite lullabies, my mom would sing to me.

His anger was never directed at me…until one night.

One night, when I could hear the house groaning almost the second he walked in the door. One night, I made sure to drink some apple juice before bed so I wouldn't wake up thirsty and risk his attention by leaving my room. One night, all I was trying to do was get to the bathroom, because my five-year-old bladder can only hold said apple juice for so long.

I waited as long as I could until the pressure on my bladder became so painful I thought I was going to wet the bed. So, I got out of bed and opened my door enough to peek my head out, the quiet volume on the TV was the only thing I heard. As I tiptoed passed the couch, I kept my eyes on my passed-out father, never wanting to take my eyes off of him in case he woke up.

Just as I was about to take another step toward the bathroom, I bumped into the side table next to the couch, causing the glass on top of it to topple over and spill golden liquid over his head.

At that moment, time seemed to have stood still as I watched my dad's eyes snap open with instant rage. He stood up so fast that my little feet couldn't move fast enough. He snatched me by the arm and squeezed painfully, causing me to cry out.

"What the fuck!" he roared in my face.

I started to tremble, too scared to move or say anything.

I saw his free hand clenching, and fear engulfed me, knowing what was about to happen. A trickle of something warm traveled down my leg, but I was too frightened to bring any attention to it.

"Do you know how much that whiskey cost?" he spat through his teeth.

I shook my head frantically. I knew we didn't have a lot of money, so it couldn't have cost that much, but when you're poor, spilling a drink or throwing out leftovers is like throwing money down the drain.

"Well, you're going to fucking pay for it." He raised his hand, and I squeezed my eyes shut, bracing myself for the hit, but it never came.

Just as I peeled my eyes open, I saw my mom shoving my father sideways before his giant hand made contact with my face. In his drunken state, he stumbled over and caught himself on the couch.

He staggered to his full height, towering over my mother. I saw the moment her whole body stiffened and she braced herself as his fist connected with her jaw, sending her down. "Mama!" I cried out, as hot tears ran down my cheeks.

I rushed over to her, but my father fisted the back of my pajama shirt, tossing me back onto my butt. "You need to be taught that we don't waste anything around here, especially my whiskey," he ground out, leaning over me, the smell of alcohol on his breath.

"I-I'm sorry. It was an accident," I plead.

"We can't afford to have accidents in this house," is his only answer before I feel the hot sting of his palm against my cheek.

A sob burst from my mouth, which only seemed to anger him more. My eyes widened in fear when he winds up for another slap, but before his hand connects with my face, something smacks into the back of his head.

He whirls around, and for just a second, it's so quiet I hear a groan that sounds like the house is trying to send out a warning.

He stares at my mother with deadly rage, and if I didn't know my mama so well, I would think she wasn't afraid, but I saw the tremble in her hands. In a flash, he lunged toward her, wrapping his hand around her neck and throwing her across the room. She slammed into a wall, but he was on her again before she could even blink.

"Stop!" I screamed, my heart beating so hard it felt like it was going to burst free of my chest. "Stop."

I hugged my knees to my chest, squeezing my eyes shut, rocking back and forth, humming to myself. The screaming became louder, and I could no longer hear myself humming, so I started to sing quietly to myself.

"You are my sunshine,"

Glass shatters.

"My only sunshine."

Loud thumping on the wall.

"You make me happy when skies are gray."

The floor rumbles as furniture is tipped over.

"You'll never know, dear."

The sound of skin hitting skin.

"How much I love you."

My mama's cries.

"Please don't take my sunshine away."

Just as the last sentence leaves my mouth, a heavy object connects with my head, causing everything to go dark.

I woke up in the hospital a few days later, deaf in my left ear and with enough stitches in my head to leave an ugly scar. Turns out getting hit in the head with a solid glass ashtray will do that to you.

Unfortunately, my asshole of a father didn't get arrested. When the cops showed up, my father just told them that two men had broken into our trailer while we were sleeping, and he woke up to one of them attacking his wife. I was knocked in the head when I ran out to see what the commotion was, at least that's what he told them. When the cops questioned my mom and me, we both confirmed his story, too scared to tell them what happened.

Of course, I don't think they believed the story. They know who my father is, and it's not the first time they have been to our house because an anonymous person called to complain about the noise.

About a month after the incident, my father was fired from his job. Unsurprisingly, he also drank at work, and one day, he had a little too much and someone got injured because he was drunk and could barely walk a straight line, let alone operate heavy machinery.

We were forced to move because word spread around our small town, and nobody wanted to hire an abusive alcoholic. Can't say that I blame them.

We moved to a town an hour away into another trailer in another run-down trailer park, where Dad eventually found a job at a local production plant. Dad stayed the same. Always drinking, and his moods were unpredictable. I guess the only thing that changed was that Dad started to beat me just as much as Mom. It was like the incident broke the seal, and once he started, he couldn't stop.

I eventually started school, and that's when I met my best friends. We gravitated toward each other on the playground as if we were being forced together by destiny, and we've been inseparable ever since. Some of us have grown up in similar homes, and some of us grew up well...normal.

Javi and I grew up in homes that are nothing short of toxic, and the others have been nothing but accepting. They have never judged us or made us feel less than, and during particularly tough times, they've even welcomed us into their homes. Once their parents found out about our home situation, they would try to get us to stay over more often. Always shoving food at us and making sure we had everything we needed.

Most of their parents feel like my parents more than my own parents do.

When we hit junior high, I discovered football, and I was actually good at it. After years of growing up in an abusive household, I learned to observe and anticipate my father's movements and moods. In turn, it taught me to read people, and having heightened senses from losing my hearing in my left ear has helped as well.

By eleventh grade, I was the first-string quarterback on our high school team, and one of the best in the state. Luckily, I've had Adrian's grumpy ass as one of my wide receivers since I started. Now that we have Zeke back in the mix, we're like a well-oiled machine, both on and off the field.

That thought brings my focus back to this asinine job Mattoe sent us on. "We need to wrap this up. We have a game to get to. Coach wants us there early to warm up." I whisper to Milo on my right side.

When Matteo sends us on stake-out missions, the guys all know to stay on my right so I can hear them better. Such as now, I'm on the far end with Milo next to me, then Javi, Kyler, Zeke, and Adrian on the other end.

For some reason, Matteo has suddenly taken an interest in the Irish and has sent us to spy on them without even a word about what we're supposed to be looking for. So here we sit at one of their many warehouses. Watching them like a bunch of dumbasses doing whatever Matteo tells them to.

"What the fuck are we supposed to be looking for?" Adrian asks exactly what I'm thinking.

"Just watch for anything out of the ordinary," Milo answers.

"Why is Matteo suddenly interested in the Irish anyway? They have more power than anyone in this city, hell, the state, even. The only reason *Los Caminantes Nocturnos* are a gang is because the Irish *allow* it," Zeke says, as his eyes scan the boxes being unloaded.

There are so many people unloading boxes that it's impossible to keep tabs on all of them. If we had more than two hours fucking notice, we could have planned better, but when Matteo calls with a bug up his ass and he demands that we check out their shipments we do as we're told.

The warehouse we're watching in the industrial park, the industrial park they own by the way, is only one of many. We just happened to see people working at this one and decided to check it out, since Matteo didn't give us any direction other than "check it out". Unfortunately, there's not much going on. It mostly looks like they keep liquor in this one, which makes sense since they own quite a few pubs around town.

"This is a waste of time," Milo says, sounding just as annoyed as I feel. Crouching behind this cement barrier to hide ourselves isn't helping much either.

"Has anyone heard from Josie?" Javi voices, and we all stop to check our phones.

Just hearing her name sends a flutter through my chest, but it is quickly replaced with a bit of panic as I look at my phone and see nothing from her. The guys are obviously worried too, because the next second, the group chat lights up with a text from each of us. I can't say I blame them. School let out a half hour ago, and she was supposed to let us know when she made it home.

Worry starts to gnaw at me, and the urge to run to her has me shooting to my feet. The thought of not being there for her makes me feel as helpless as I did when my parents would fight when I was younger. When she told us she was at Sylus' fear coursed through me like a raging river, and I sprinted from class, leaving my bag and all my books behind. Luckily, I ran into the guys in the hallway.

Sensing my worry, Milo places a hand on my shoulder and pushes me back down before I get too far. He pulls a cigarette from behind his ear, quickly lights it, and takes a puff before offering it to me. I don't smoke much anymore, but when I'm stressed, a small puff helps to calm me.

"She might have just forgotten to text us. Give her a minute. If she doesn't text back, we'll leave." Milo tells me. I can see him struggling to take his advice as he sucks down his cigarette in record time and is lighting another one in the blink of an eye.

"I swear your ear is like a Pez dispenser for cigarettes," I say, trying to lighten the mood, but really, I'm just trying to distract myself.

Milo smirks at me, and I turn back to watch the shipment that's being unloaded. He's never told us how he magically pulls the nicotine sticks from behind his ear, and every time we ask, he gives us the same smirk and ignores us.

Finally, our phones all ding with a text from Josie telling us she made it home, and the small space behind the cement barrier suddenly feels more spacious as the tension drains from all of us. My heart rate finally slows to a normal speed, and I feel like I can take a deep breath.

When I picture her gorgeous face and her sweet peach smell, anticipation flutters in my chest for the moment I get to wrap her in my arms. The moment I saw her at that park, I knew I was done for, knew we were done for. Her bright smile was a beacon to my darkened heart, and for the first time in a long time, it beat with purpose.

"What are those?" Kyler questions curiously.

Large wooden crates are being unloaded from the trailer of the semi-truck and loaded into a smaller box truck, rather than being taken into the warehouse with the rest of the shipment. The crates are so large that it takes two men to carry them, one on each end, making it obvious that whatever is hiding inside them is definitely not liquor bottles.

A large black clover with a knife stabbed in the center of it bleeds green gems instead of red and is stamped on the side of each wooden crate, making it clear exactly who owns them. Rumor has it that the gems symbolize their love of money. To me, the image feels too personal for it to represent something so minor; the Irish have more power than god in this state, and money is no object to them. I get the feeling that it represents something more valuable than money, something precious.

"I don't know, but I don't think it's alcohol," Javi answers.

"Whatever is in them isn't for business, at least not any of their legitimate businesses," Adrian adds as we watch them load the last of them into the truck.

"Where do you think they're taking them?" Zeke asks.

"They own this whole industrial park; they could be taking them to one of the other warehouses," Milo answers.

We watch in silence as they load the last one. Pulling the door closed, the men climb into the truck and pull out of the industrial park. Unease coils in my stomach, and my instincts are telling me to run, but I can't quite figure out why. "I don't have a good feeling about this," I voice my concern, hoping one of them will tell me I'm being paranoid.

No one says anything, and their deafening silence takes me back to those nights when the house would groan and creak in warning that something bad was going to happen.

My leg bounces with excitement as we pull onto Josie's street, and I can't keep the smile off my face when her house comes into view.

"If you bounce that leg any harder, you're going to put a hole in the floor," Milo says, looking at me through the rearview mirror. He can talk all the shit he wants, but I don't miss the gleam in his eyes when we pull up to her house.

We all pile out of Milos' Range Rover and walk to the door. Just as Kyler raises his hand to twist the doorknob, the sweetest giggle comes from the other side. We all freeze like that, giggling was a bullet straight to the heart and killing us with her happiness. A bullet I would gladly take if it meant I could hear that noise again and again.

Looking around at the others' dazed expressions, I have no doubt they're thinking something similar.

Another giggle erupts, only this time it's accompanied by Liam's, and we all let out chuckles under a breath, not wanting to disturb the joy on the other side of the door. "She's good for him," Milo says, squeezing Kyler's shoulder.

Shaking his head, laughing, "Why do I have a feeling they're going to be nothing but trouble?" Kyler says with a giant smile on his face, showing the love he has for his brother, and his eyes twinkle with affection for our girl.

My heart swells with something that feels a lot like love, but I push it down quickly because it's too soon for those kinds of feelings, right? Right.

Clearing my throat, "Are we going to stand here all day like a bunch of creeps, or are you going to open the door so we can go see our girl?"

He finally pushes the door open, and Josie's head snaps in our direction when she hears our footsteps. An infectious smile curves her lips as she rounds the couch and throws her arms around Kyler.

My hands twitch with the urge to pull her from Kyler and

feel her in my arms. I'm saved from doing so when a moment later she's throwing her arms around my neck, and I wrap my arms around her, hugging her close to my body. I nuzzle into her hair, inhaling that sweet peach scent as my heart swells with that feeling again.

"Quit hogging her Car, we have a game to get to and I need my good luck kiss," Zeke whines, and I reluctantly let her go.

Before she steps away, I grab her hand and trace a heart on her palm and kiss it to show her how much she means to me. She smiles at me, reaching for my hand as she traces a heart on my hand and places a kiss on my palm, mimicking me. I wink at her as she steps away while internally kicking myself. I know I need to tell her I'm partially deaf, but I'm a little insecure from past experiences.

Girls have always just assumed I'm a quiet person, introverted. When I finally tell them why I'm so quiet, they either baby me like I can't fend for myself or they treat me like I'm some kind of pariah. I know Josie won't treat me like that, but there's always that kernel of doubt. Besides, I like communicating with little tracings on her palms. It's like we get our own little private moments throughout the day; it's our thing.

She moves to Zeke and gives him his good luck kiss, which just turns out to be a kiss on the cheek, but I can't help but be envious of the bastard. He's spent more time with her than any of us and has a stronger relationship. I can't wait for the day when all of this becomes second nature.

She makes her way down to Adrian, and I don't miss the hesitance from both of them before she stands on her tiptoes and plants a kiss on his cheek as well. His hands rest on her waist, and he leans down to whisper something in her ear that causes her cheeks to tinge pink. He winks at her and kisses her on the temple.

She steps away and stares at the three of us. "Good luck, I don't think you need it though. I know you're all going to kick ass out there."

Her belief in us has my damn heart swelling again. At this rate, it's going to fucking explode, but at least I would die knowing what it's like to love her than never have experienced it at all.

Chapter Twenty-Two

JOSIE

I feel his warm presence at my back just as I lower my black V-neck over my head. His warm arms wrap around my middle, and I snuggle back into his chest as he buries his nose in my neck. "You know Milo's going to flip his shit when he sees what you're wearing, right?"

Normally, I would feel self-conscious about the outfit I chose, but the more comfortable I get around them, the better I feel about myself. Catching their lingering stares, they think I don't notice, doesn't hurt either.

"It's not that bad," I tell Javi, stepping away from him to stand in front of my floor-length mirror to give my outfit a once over "Is it?"

I mean the shorts might be a little short, but it's a simple outfit, so I don't see any problem. My denim shorts go to just above mid thigh, and maybe they're a bit form fitting but at least my giant ass is being contained. The V-neck shirt shows off a little cleavage, but not enough to be indecent, but it also hugs me, making it obvious that my stomach is far from flat.

Doubt starts to filter in the longer I stare at myself in the mirror, and I get the urge to cover up. I tug on my shirt a little to stretch it out of habit, so it doesn't cling to me so tightly. I tug a little harder when it doesn't stretch like I want it to. Okay, so maybe I'm still a little self-conscious, I'm a work in progress. When I go to do it a third time, Javi places his hands on my shoulders and spins me to look at him.

Placing a finger under my chin, he tips my head up to meet his icy green eyes. Seeing the frustration on my face, "Hey, what's wrong?" he asks, brows pinched in concern.

I start to fidget with my hands, embarrassed that he caught me in an insecure moment. "I–I–I should probably just change," I answer, hoping he won't pick up on my internal freak out, but of course, he does.

He cups my face with both hands. " Red, you look hot. When I said Milo's going to flip his shit, I just meant because any man with working eyes is going to be staring at you," he rubs his thumbs over the pink I can feel flooding my cheeks, and the playful smile tilting his lips calms me.

Resting my forehead against his chest, I take a deep breath. "I get a little self-conscious sometimes," I admit softly, though he already knows.

"I know Red, but trust me when I say you're gorgeous and I will kill anyone who makes you feel any less," I let out a small chuckle at his dramatic words as he runs his hands up and down my back soothingly "Now, if we don't get moving I'm going to throw you down on this bed and we're going to repeat last night."

I let out a surprised squeak when his hands travel further down to squeeze my ass before he places a kiss on my forehead and walks out, leaving me flustered.

I pull on my long white tube socks high enough that the red stripe at the top circles above my calf, then slip on my Converse, and fasten my favorite black velvet choker to complete my outfit. Just before I walk out, I remember to put on my favorite silver shamrock earrings to bring good luck.

As I approach the kitchen, I hear "...don't go all caveman asshole on her." Javi warns in a hushed tone, and I have to stifle a smile when I step into the kitchen. Kyler, Javi, and Milo's heads all turn in my direction from their huddled position.

Where Javi and Kyler's looks are heated, Milo's is hungry with just a bit of frustration beneath, and based on the vein popping in his neck, he's doing everything he can not to go *all caveman asshole*.

Kyler whistles as he walks toward me, "If I didn't know any better, I would say you're trying to give me blue balls." I laugh and slap him lightly on the chest. He leans down, "I think you broke Milo," he whispers against my lips before kissing them.

Javi steps up to my side and gently tugs on one of the braided pigtails that hang low on my head. "Maybe we should have repeated last night," he says, winking at me. When Kyler steps away, Javi places a kiss on my lips, and they both head out the front door, leaving me with Milo.

He rubs his thumb over his bottom lip as he continues to stare at me with hunger in his arctic blue eyes. His stare drifts up and down my body before he finally takes a slow step toward me. "You know," he starts, taking another slow step. "If you leave the house dressed like that, I won't be responsible for what happens to the sorry souls who stare at what's mine."

I let his words hang in the air because I don't know if I should be scared or excited. Judging by the warm feeling gathering in my lower stomach, it seems my body has made up its mind for me.

Jesus Christ, I'm such a virgin! If his words do this to me, his actions are going to put me six feet under. If the way his eyes are eating me up is any consolation, that's exactly what he's intending to do.

He slowly steps into me, forcing me to step back into the kitchen counter. Reaching out, he tugs my bottom lip from between my teeth that I hadn't even noticed I was chewing on. His tall frame towers over me. Placing his hands on the counter, he cages me in. "I don't know whether to rip you out of your clothes now so you have to change, or wait to rip you out of them later when I can put my hands all over your delectable body."

I'm pretty sure his body is putting off more heat than the sun, and I feel like I'm going to melt the second he touches me. He twirls a finger in my wavy red hair that hangs from my pigtail, and I swallow nervously. "Well, I'll be happy with either," I lamely say.

Before I can think, he grabs me by the back of the thighs and lifts me onto the counter, slamming his lips on mine. His kiss is hungry, much like the look he had in his eyes, as he dominates my mouth, taking whatever he can get. He pries his tongue between my lips as my own submits to his, letting him have control and giving him what he needs.

His hands travel down my sides, settling at my hips. He pushes my shorts down just enough to trace small patterns on my skin. The sensation causes a shiver to roll over me, and just as a small whimper escapes me, a car horn blares.

"Fuck," Milo curses, sounding pained as he pulls away. Taking a second to catch our breath, he adjusts my shorts to cover my hips back up and helps me off the counter. "I meant what I said, Little Fox," I blink up at him, confused. "If anyone makes you uncomfortable or looks at you wrong, I won't be responsible for what happens to them."

A fuzzy feeling invades my chest like an avalanche. I haven't known my guys for very long, but already I can see and feel how much they care for me, and I for them. Cupping his cheek in my hand, I look into his light blue eyes and say, "Thank you," hoping he can see how much I mean it.

I stand on my tiptoes and place a small kiss on his lips. "Now let's go caveman." I spin on my heel and walk out. I climb into the front seat of the Range Rover, and Milo climbs into the driver's seat with a pinched look on his face. "I need to stop and get more cigarettes," he grumbles.

Kyler and Javi laugh from the backseat. "Damn, Red. What did you do to him?" Kyler laughs, slapping Milo on the shoulder.

I turn to look out the window to hide my smile. When we pull out of the driveway, a small prickle of awareness traces down my spine when I notice the sleek black car that's parked in front of the house across the street. This isn't the first time I've noticed it, but it's not parked there very often. I assumed the person who drives it knows the occupants of the house it's parked in front of, but judging by the overgrown grass and weeds, it doesn't look like anyone lives there. Not to mention the car looks like it costs more than any house in this neighborhood.

You're just being paranoid, Josie. Not everyone is out to get you. I tell myself but the persistent little voice in the back of my mind tells me that everything is not as it seems is practically screaming at me.

"You guys freaking killed it!" I shout, throwing myself at Zeke. I lock my hands around his neck and plant a big, sloppy kiss on his cheek. He drops his sports bag off his shoulder and wraps his arms around me, spinning me in a circle.

I giggle as he twirls us around, and when he sets me back on my feet, he says, "Thanks, Jo," returning a lingering kiss to my cheek that feels more than friendly.

I don't think I've ever had so much fun watching a

football game before. Carter is a better quarterback than I ever imagined he could be. He always knew who to throw the ball to and when. Like he could see into the future and just knew how it would all play out. When Zeke and Adrian got on the field, they couldn't be stopped; the three of them were like a well-oiled machine.

Walking into the game with Kyler, Javi, and Milo, we got all the attention I knew we would and then some. Most of it from students and parents staring out of curiosity, others simply stared like they didn't know what to think. Then there were the people like Cody and his friends, and the bitch brigade who sneered at us the whole time

I tried not to let it bother me, but every so often, my eyes would drift over the crowd, and I would catch Cody glaring at me or Sophie pointing and whispering. All the extra attention didn't seem to bother the guys; if it did, they didn't show it.

At one point, I started to pick at my thumbs out of habit. Kyler would grab hold of my hand, or Javi would squeeze my leg reassuringly. I swear to god I heard Milo growl at someone like he was an actual caveman.

The only person who didn't seem to have a problem with it was Kiera. I knew she wouldn't. She's always been more open-minded and free with her body. It's one of the things I envy most about her. "Fuck 'em. They're just jealous," She had said, shrugging her shoulders in a 'so what' gesture.

Her nonchalant attitude helped to relax me a bit, and for the rest of the game after that, I found myself not giving a shit. With her support and my guys', I soaked in their quiet confidence and ignored all the attention for the rest of the game.

Now waiting in the parking lot for the rest of the guys, everyone's attention seems to be on us now that there isn't a game to distract them, so I just focus on Zeke in front of me.

"You played good tonight, I'm so proud of you," I tell him, bouncing from foot to foot with excitement.

"It's all because of that good luck kiss, you know," Zeke answers, staring down at me with a twinkle in his eyes. My stomach dips when he tucks a strand of hair behind my ear, and I freeze to the spot when he starts to lower his head.

Before he gets too close, though, loud footsteps sound behind me, and I'm suddenly being lifted in the air and spun around once more. I almost panic, not knowing who it is, but when the person sets me down and turns me to face them, I'm a little surprised to see Adrian.

I'm not used to this side of him, but I like it. The bright smile on his face is contagious, and I only hesitate for a split second before I throw my arms around his neck and kiss him on the cheek the same way I did to Zeke. "You guys did so awesome!"

"Thanks, Sweetheart," he says, his eyes gleaming with an emotion I can't quite pin down as something pokes at my brain when he calls me that. A sense of familiarity I can't put my finger on.

Raised voices have me peeking around Adrian, and I see Carter standing by the locker room door, arguing with a man who has his back to us. "Who is that?" I ask curiously.

The angry expression on Carter's face has me taking a step toward him, but a hand gently wraps around my wrist, stopping me. "It's Carter's dad," Adrian answers, annoyance in his tone. I spin to look at him and find a thunderous expression on his face as he watches the exchange, but when he looks at me, his face softens a bit. "Trust me, Sweetheart, you don't want to go over there, and Carter wouldn't want you over there."

Confusion furrows my brow at his words, not sure if I should be offended or concerned by that statement. If Adrian had said that to me a couple of days ago, I would have been offended, but his hard exterior has been softening toward me lately, and I don't think he meant any harm by it.

"He's not a good guy, Gingersnap," Kyler says, and I notice all my guys are now standing near me, forming a half circle around me, almost as if to shield me from his father. They all have the same thunderous expressions on their faces and are intently watching, poised, ready to be at Carter's side if the need arises.

I turn back and watch, ready to do the same. From here, I can see the tightness in Carter's jaw, his fists are clenched by his sides, and his posture is stiff like he's holding himself back from punching his dad in the face. I can't hear what his dad is saying, but his yelling raises my hackles. I fight the urge to march over and pull Carter away from this man, who is making him put his defenses up.

I flex my hands to give an outlet to the growing anxiety that's slowly building beneath my skin. His father's reprimanding tone and aggressive stance look like it's second nature for him. If making a scene like this out in public is so easy for him, I fear what he's like behind closed doors.

That's it, that's the thought that makes my feet move, but I only get a few steps before someone wraps their arms around my shoulders and pulls me back against a solid chest. "I can't let you go over there, Little Fox," Milo says softly in my ear.

"I don't like this," I tell him just as softly, a sense of helplessness filling me as we just watch.

Milo places a soft kiss on my temple in agreement and rests his chin on top of my head as he squeezes me tighter against him. I hear the rest of the guys step closer to us, and some of my anxiety eases a bit, knowing they're all so willing to jump in if they need to.

The movement catches Carter's attention, and he flicks his eyes toward us, his eyes land on me. I flash him what hopefully comes across as a supportive smile, and some of the tension drains from his shoulders. The distraction causes his dad to turn to see what caught Carter's attention. I see his eyes travel over the guys, but when they land on me, my shoulders stiffen, and I latch my hands on Milos' forearms.

His dad's eyes turn appraising, eyes I've seen before, as they travel up and down my body. A sadistic gleam flashes through them, and my mind goes back to when I saw him stumbling out of Sylus' house with two other men. His skin is still the same gray color, and his eyes are glassy, like he's been on a bender and hasn't come up for air in days.

I curl myself back into Milo's chest as if I can hide myself from his perusal. Absorbing the comfort of his protective arms, banded around me. "What the fuck!" Milo snarls out when his dad doesn't look away. "If he doesn't stop looking at you like that, he's going to be eating all his meals through a straw," he grinds out.

"I saw him at Sylus's the other day," I confess, as if that will excuse why he's staring at me. Though I'm not sure if the explanation is more for them or if I'm just trying to ease the curdling feeling in my gut.

My grip on Milo's arms tightens the more uncomfortable I become, and I subconsciously start to pick at his arm. Carter's eyes track the movement, and for the first time, I see nothing but rage behind my shy guy's eyes as they flick back and forth between his dad and me.

He fists his dad's collar and yanks him around, forcing his eyes to leave me. He snarls something I can't quite hear, but his dad just laughs, laughs, in his son's face. Pure hate leaks out of Carter, and my heart breaks for him as I can only imagine what made him hate his father so much.

My anxiety ratchets up, and I watch in slow motion as Carter cocks his fist back and connects with his dad's face. Blood sprays from his mouth as his head snaps to the side, and when Carter pulls his fist back for another hit, everyone snaps into motion.

Milo releases me, and he races toward Carter with the others hot on his heels. Panic freezes me to the spot as I watch everything happen. Kyler's large build easily overpowers Carter's dad as he yanks him back and pins his arms behind him to restrain his thrashing. My eyes swing to Carter as anger I've never seen before consumes him. Fury vibrates through him so hard that I can see the strain it's taking on Javi, Milo, and Adrian to hold him back.

The cut I notice on his face has a gasp escaping my lips, and propels me forward, "Stop!" I shout, standing between the two groups with my hands out like I have some sort of super power that freezes everyone to the spot.

"Wow," Carter's dad taunts, "now that I get a closer look at her, maybe she is worth all the hype." A low chuckle leaves his throat that makes my skin crawl.

"Don't you fucking look at her, you piece of shit," Carter spits, attempting to break free of his friend's grip.

"Oh, come on, son. Word is you guys like to share, why not share with your old man too?" He grins when that gets another reaction from Carter. "What do you say, gorgeous?"

Fear rakes down my spine at his vile words, and my skin prickles when his attention is directed back on me. Not wanting to acknowledge him, I turn toward Carter; he's the one who deserves my focus right now.

He's still blinded with rage, and he doesn't seem to notice me standing in front of him, his eyes glued to his father. "Carter," I say softly, but he doesn't hear me. "Cater," I repeat a little louder. His eyes flick to mine, he instantly softens, and I hear sighs of relief from my guys that have been holding him back.

The rage he was feeling earlier is replaced with what looks like guilt, and he ducks his head. Whether it's guilt for what his father said or guilt that he let his temper get the better of him, I don't know. Either way, he has nothing to feel guilty for, and I need him to know that I don't blame him for anything that just happened.

When I step closer to him, he tilts his head back, and I cup his cheek to comfort him. His jaw ticks with anger, but his eyes are soft, pleading almost, as he fights to get a handle on his emotions. "I'm here, Carter, we're here." He nuzzles my hand, and when his jaw relaxes, I step into him.

He bends to press his forehead to mine, but tenses slightly when his father starts mumbling. "Ignore him, just focus on me." His warm, minty breath fans over my face, and his hands go to my sides, and he fists my t-shirt in his hand like he's in pain.

I lift on my tiptoes to press a light kiss to his lips, his arms band around me, and I let out a surprised squeak as he lifts me off my feet. I wrap my legs around his waist as he nuzzles his nose to the crook of my neck. "We'll meet you at the car," he mutters as he stalks off.

He yanks the door open to the Range Rover, and I climb in, but don't get very far when he pulls me back to straddle his lap. Burying his nose in my hair, "I'm so sorry. I didn't want you to see that side of me, at least not so soon," he pulls me closer, my chest pressed to his.

Concern washes over me when I feel him start to tremble beneath me. "You have nothing to be sorry for," I gently tell him, threading my fingers through his hair at the base of his neck. "I never want you to feel like you have to hide yourself from me."

A shiver dances over him as I lightly run my nails over his scalp, his breathing seems to turn back to a normal rhythm, and his trembling, most likely from the burst of adrenaline, slowly ebbs. We sit in silence for a few minutes, but he becomes so still, I'm beginning to think he has fallen asleep.

"I'm partially deaf," he whispers so low I don't know if I would've heard him if his nose wasn't still buried in my hair.

Suddenly, everything makes sense. The moments I tried talking to him, but I thought he was ignoring me, the smallest of speech impediments I've picked up, the way he traces on my hand. A smile stretches my face at that one. I love that he's chosen that way to communicate with me at certain times; the way his fingers tickle my palm makes it feel intimate. It's become our thing, and I wouldn't want it any other way.

A frown pulls my face down as I begin to wonder why he felt like he couldn't share this with me. Did he think I would feel differently about him because of it? Is he embarrassed by it? Does he think I'll be embarrassed by it?

When he pulls back to look at me and takes in the frown on my face, hurt flashes over his, and he begins to lift me off his lap. "No," I state, when I realize he thinks I'm frowning over the fact that he's partially deaf, "I'm not upset. I just don't want you to feel like you can't be yourself around me."

Halting his movement, he sets me back down on his lap and sighs in relief. "It's just...from past experiences whenever I tell someone they either baby me or treat me like some disease," he explains, and my heart hurts for my adorable, shy guy.

People can be cruel towards those who are different because they are just that, different. It throws people off, and they don't know how to take it, like their uniqueness is something they should be ashamed of, when really, they're just insecure because they're as plain as a white crayon.

He grabs onto my fingers and lifts my hands to rub them behind his ear. I scrunch my brows in confusion but gasp when my fingers feel the hardened scar tissue running in a long line behind his ear and up into his scalp "This is my fathers doing and the reason I lost the hearing in my left ear," he swallows, vulnerability shining in his eyes and my heart clenches for the little boy who had to live with such a cruel man. Carter is such a sweet person, I can't fathom how he came from someone as disgusting and mean as the man I saw arguing with him moments ago.

I will never let him feel like he has to hide who he is and tell him as such, "I never want you to be afraid to tell me anything. I hope you know I would never judge you." his golden brown eyes light up with fondness behind his thick-framed glasses. "As far as I'm concerned, you're just a regular teenage boy in high school, and I will treat you the same as I treat anybody else," I rub my palms up his hard, muscled chest. "Well, maybe not the same as *everybody* else," winking at him, I kiss his soft lips, but we're interrupted by the door swinging open before I can deepen it.

The car erupts with a cacophony of voices, and I can't help but giggle when Carter groans his annoyance at being interrupted. Once again, burying his nose in my hair, he whispers, "You are my sunshine."

Chapter Twenty-Three

JOSIE

If I didn't know any better, I'd think we were pulling up to the hottest nightclub Boston has to offer instead of Milo and Jake's house. Curtains are pulled across all the giant glass windows, attempting to hide the partying teenagers inside. Unfortunately, if all the cars that line the street weren't a dead giveaway, then the loud music is.

My nerves make themselves known when the memory of what happened at the last party I went to filters through my mind. After parking in the garage, we all pile out of Milo's car and head through the door that leads into the kitchen, where the party is well underway. Liquor bottles and mixers litter the counter, while two kegs take up residence next to it. Just about every person is holding the ever-present red plastic cup that you see at every party while mingling with their friends.

My eyes devour the room, taking in the crowd of people watching for any suspicious activity. "You okay?" Zeke asks, obviously noticing my unease.

I nod my head and flash him a small smile as we make our way over to the counter to get a drink. Well, the guys get drinks while I just grab a bottle of water. I don't judge them or anyone for that matter for wanting to let loose and have a good time, but what happened to me after the last party, I find myself having a hard time relaxing at the moment. While I'm sure this isn't the first party my classmates have been to since that terrible night, it's the first one for me since I woke from my coma, and I'm starting to second-guess being here.

I start picking at the label on my water as I wait for the guys to get their drinks. I scan the room, making note of the faces and what everyone is wearing, looking for anyone or anything that looks out of place. A group of people occupies the table, playing what looks like a drinking game, while most of the other people in the kitchen are getting drinks and socializing with their friends. My eyes flick through the open doors that lead to the backyard, where people are swimming, playing beer pong, or dancing in the open space in front of the DJ booth.

Movement from the corner of my eye snaps my attention to a burly guy standing against the wall in the kitchen. He folds his big arms across his chest, making his rigid posture all the more intimidating, which, judging by the stoic expression on his face, I'm assuming that's what he's going for. His black t-shirt and black pants are what get my anxiety spiking. It's not exactly what the shooters were wearing at Chance's party, but it's not far off either. I notice another man standing on the opposite wall with the same outfit and the same expression. My eyes wander back through the open doors that lead to the backyard and notice a couple of guys in black out there, too.

My shoulders tense when I notice one of them has a gun strapped to a holster on his belt, and I squeeze my eyes shut hoping that when I open them, I'll just be a crazy person imagining things because there is no fucking way this is happening again.

Only when I open my eyes, I startle when I see concerned,

icy blue ones staring back at me. "Are you okay?" Milo asks, repeating Zeke's earlier question. Clearly, I'm terrible at hiding my unease, and I want to smack myself for making such a big deal of a stupid party.

The big guy against the wall catches my attention again, and my water bottle crinkles as I continue to nervously pick at the label. Milo pries the water bottle from my hands before I pick a hole through it. His warm palm settles on my cheek and gently turns my head to meet his eyes again. "It's just security, Little Fox."

His words settle the tension in my body as relief washes over me, and I suddenly feel ridiculous for getting so worked up. "Sorry, I just –"

"I know. It's okay," he tells me, knowing exactly where my train of thought was. His thumb rubs gently across my cheek. "If you decide it's too much, let us know. I told security not to let anyone upstairs, so it's nice and quiet if you decide you need a break."

His thoughtfulness makes my heart flutter, and I stand on my tiptoes. "Thank you," I whisper against his lips, pressing a small appreciative kiss there.

His stare turns heated, and when he goes to open his mouth to say something, someone yells, "Get a room, you dirty hot dog!" When I turn to see the heckler, I'm not surprised when I see the scornful look on Sophie's face, but is that a hint of jealousy hiding underneath? No, that can't be right.

"Hot dog?" I hear Javi behind me quietly asking one of the guys if that's supposed to mean something.

Humiliation burns through me at the reminder of what happened at my locker, and I get the urge to run as far away from this party as possible. I knew coming here was a mistake; there's a reason I rarely show up to these stupid parties.

Just as I take a step forward to dart away, Jake steps up, "Leave her alone, Sophie." He says, and surprise roots me to my spot.

She rolls her eyes like a spoiled brat who was scolded by her parents, but then her eyes land on Milo, and my spine straightens at the devious look in her eyes. She steps forward to stand in front of him and runs a pointy manicured nail down his chest, and I want to rip it off her finger and stab it in her eye.

"Come on, Milo, what do you say we go out back and go skinny dipping like we talked about?" she says in a sultry voice. I know she's trying to get under my skin, and god damn it, it's working.

My hands curl into fists, and my nails dig into my palms as anger and insecurity war within me. I've never seen him talk to her before, so when could they have had a conversation? Unless...he's talking to her behind my back. Milo doesn't seem like the kind of person to go behind someone's back, though. None of them do, but then again, I haven't known them for very long. They just showed up out of nowhere and into my life like they already knew who I was, yet I hardly know anything about them.

If he is into Sophie, who am I to hold him back? I'm dating four of his friends for crying out loud. It's not fair of me to ask them not to date anyone, yet I'm seeing all of them. Not to mention the meteor-sized crush I have on my best friend. Does it bother them how close I am to Zeke? They're not stupid, I'm sure they've noticed our close friendship.

"Breathe," Kyler whispers, halting my spiral and placing his palms on my shoulders in support. I take a deep breath and relax into his chest, just as Javi and Carter intertwine their hands with mine. Their comfort is reassuring and causes the tension to leak from my body.

Milo snatches Sophie's wrist from his body just as it

reaches his belt. "You're as transparent as the silicone that fills your oversized tits." A scowl mars her face, and I hear a few snickers coming from partiers who stopped to watch the interaction. One of them being the bulky security guy who's failing to hold back a smirk. "If you haven't noticed, I already have a girl and she's the only one I want."

My body tingles at his words, and I don't miss the stares that turn to me. Much like at the game, most are out of curiosity, while the rest are more judgmental, and it's easy not to let it bother me when I have the guys around me. Now that they're surrounding me, it hasn't slipped my attention that no one has dared to call me any names to my face, either. Well, except for Sophie, of course.

"You're not the only one she wants, though, right?" Sophie says, flicking her eyes at me and eyeing me up and down with disgust, then looking at the guys surrounding me. "Seems like you are a whore after all, just like your sister," she flicks her hair and walks away with her sniggering bitch brigade following dutifully on her heels.

Anger like I've never felt before courses through me. Not because she called me a whore, but because I am NOTHING like my sister. If she wanted to get a rise out of me, she fucking got it. "That's pretty hypocritical of you, isn't it?" I ask before she gets too far, stopping her in her tracks.

She spins on her heel, looking at me with confusion. "What the hell are you talking about?" she sasses, folding her arms in front of her.

"Calling me a whore," I state as if it should be obvious. I take a step toward her and away from my guys as my anger builds. " I mean, you're the one foaming at the mouth over someone else's boyfriend like you have slut rabies, but then again, I guess like mother, like daughter," I finish. Everyone knows her mom is a homewrecker and has wrecked more than one home, specifically the homes of rich men.

Oh's are murmured throughout the gathered crowd, and her eyes blaze with fire, and I know I've gotten under her skin. Just as she prepares to launch herself at me, a strong arm bands around my waist, and Kyler's large body steps between us. I try to push away from whoever is holding me back, and hear all my guys chuckle when Kyler says, "Who knew our little Gingersnap had a mouth on her?"

Wait, how is Kyler in front of and behind me? I turn to see his smiling face, but then, if he's behind me, who's in front of me? When I turn to look at the hulking figure I mistook for Kyler, I realize it's the big security guy. He's built similarly to Kyler. Broad and muscular, he even has a hoop pierced through his nose. That's where the similarities end, though. His hair is blonde with a red tint to it, while it's short on the sides, it's longer on top. When our eyes meet, I notice they're an emerald green, much like my own, and I feel a sense of affinity towards him.

"You good?" he grumbles. I nod my head. "You need to leave," he says, turning towards Sophie, and I can't help the smirk from lifting my mouth.

"What?!" she screeches. "She started it! If the party had been at my house like it was supposed to be, this wouldn't have happened," she shouts, glaring at Jake.

"You started this, and this wouldn't have happened if you had just kept your mouth shut," Jake tells her, exasperated by her tantrum. "And, since you didn't want to have security at your party, nobody felt safe going to your house." That seems to shut her up.

She huffs out an exasperated breath and turns to leave. "Will you please follow her to make sure she leaves?" Jake asks the security guy, still standing between us. He dips his head and walks off in the same direction as Sophie.

"I guess what they say about redheads is true, huh, Red?" Javi says with a grin on his face. "They have fiery tempers," laughing, he steps forward and pecks me on the lips before he steps back over to the counter and makes himself another drink.

Chuckling at Javi, I turn to my other guys to see them laughing and shaking their heads at their friend. His attempt at lightening the mood worked, and I couldn't love him more for it.

All their eyes land on me, and suddenly I feel embarrassed for letting my pent-up anger get the best of me. That seems to be happening more and more lately, and I hate that I let my emotions build to that point instead of just talking about what's bothering me. One of these times, I'm going to take it out on the wrong person, and I don't think I could forgive myself if I let that happen.

"Save it, Jo," Zeke says as I open my mouth to apologize. Stepping in front of me, he pecks a kiss on my forehead. "She deserved it. Now, if you'll excuse me, that beer pong table is calling my name," he winks. "Adrian, be my partner?"

Adrian's been so quiet, I almost hadn't noticed he was here. He flashes me a smile, but I don't miss the guilt in his eyes, but guilt for what? For staying quiet? For going to play beer pong with Zeke? Ditching me to hang with my best friend? All of which seem so small compared to the remorse lingering in his deep brown eyes.

"You don't mind, do you, Sweetheart?" he inquires, and I force myself to keep my jaw from hanging open at his show of consideration. The Adrian I'm used to doesn't ask for permission, and I take that as a good sign.

"I don't mind," I assure him. He places a soft kiss on the corner of my mouth as he and Zeke head for the beer pong tables.

Most of my guys are congregated back at the drink counter, refilling their cups. I notice Milo and Jake huddled together in a conversation off to the side, and I think it's the first time I've seen them together where one doesn't want to bite the other's head off.

"You okay?" Carter asks as I grab a soda from the counter.

"Yeah, I'm good. Just a little embarrassed." He tilts his head in question, "I don't often go off on people like that, but it seems to be a pattern this week." Remembering the way I snapped at Jake and my snarky attitude towards Cody and Ashley.

I don't feel bad for doing it, and it's not like they didn't deserve it; it's just so unlike me.

"Don't be embarrassed. It's okay to stand up for yourself, but if you ever need to talk, you know you can talk to us, right?" I nod, and he wraps an arm around me, pulling me closer. "Besides, it's sexy when you get all fiery like that." He whispers, and a small shiver runs down my back. He presses his soft lips to mine and kisses me like he's desperate to finish what we started in the car.

A loud whistle pierces my ears. "Get it, babe!" I hear Kiera call from the other side of the counter. I see her standing with Kyler and Javi with an approving look while my two guys look like they're ready to pounce. "Now that you guys have come up for air, come dance with me."

I bury my face in Carter's neck to hide the red creeping into my cheeks. "We'll continue this later, Sunshine," he says, placing a kiss on my temple, as Kiera rounds the counter and snatches me by the elbow to drag me outside.

Pulling me through the crowd of sweaty bodies, she stops in the middle and stares at me expectantly. "Seriously," I groan, "You know I can't dance."

"Oh, hush. I've seen you dance plenty of times," She huffs.

"Yeah, well, usually I have a little liquid courage helping me out." She looks at me with a pitying look, no doubt remembering the last time we did this was that night.

I sigh and give in so she'll stop looking at me like a wounded puppy. "Fine, but you're going to have to show me again."

Her face lights up, and she places her hands on my hips and guides me to mimic each move she makes. "See, I knew you could do it." She grins, letting her hands drop, and I follow her moves as she continues to roll and rotate her body.

I know I complain a lot about dancing, but once I get my body moving and feel the music moving through me, I find it easy to let go. In the moment, it's freeing, and I forget about all my troubles and just let the music hum through me and wash away all the negativity.

Kiera steps behind me and starts to roll her body with mine, and I can't keep the smile from my face as she says, "We have an audience."

I scan the crowd for said audience, and goosebumps sprout on my skin when I see the devilish stare of four sets of eyes. Carter, Javi, Milo, and Kyler are all standing just on the outskirts of the dancing crowd, with their eyes locked on me. Their intense stares heat me from the inside, causing sweat to trickle down my back and chest. Although that could just be from dancing in the tight crowd. I notice the side glances I get from Adrian and Zeke as they try their hardest to focus on the beer pong game.

My Cheshire smile gets wider when I turn to face Kiera, and she wraps her arms around my neck. "You lucky bitch. They haven't taken their eyes off you," she tells me with proud jealousy. "Should we give them a show?"

Before I can answer, she drops down and glides her fingers in a seductive motion up my calf, and when she reaches my thigh, she stands back to her full height and runs the tip of her finger under the hem of my shorts. Pressing her forehead to mine, she trails her fingers over my ribs and gently grazes the side of my breast, stopping at my neck.

"Are they still looking?" I whisper without trying to be obvious.

"Oh yeah," she giggles. "Remember that one time we did this, when I wanted to get with Tyson Vanderbilt, and he almost came in his pants?"

I throw my head back laughing at the memory, "How could I forget? Didn't you lose your virginity to him that night?"

"Pfft, hell no. We made out and dry humped for five seconds before he came in his pants." She pouts as she begins to run her finger down my sweaty chest and into my cleavage. "Anyway, your guys look like they're about five seconds from pulling a Vanderbilt," she finishes, chuckling.

I get newfound confidence as I exaggeratedly roll my body into Kiera's, practically gluing us together. My hands travel along her sides and down her tight dress, leaning in close to her lips, I whisper, "I don't know if I can do this, Kier. I've never had one boyfriend, let alone five." Keeping up our little show, her hand drops down my back and lightly grazes my ass, "and I can't help but feel like there's something else going on. Like they're keeping something from me."

"You got this, babe. Don't be so down on yourself. You're smart and gorgeous and have one hell of an ass," she tells me as she squeezes my ass, causing me to yelp in surprise making us both laugh.

"Ladies," Our laughter is interrupted by a deep voice. "That was quite a little performance you put on, but do you mind if we dance with Josie?" Javi asks, Milo standing next to him.

"Knock yourselves out. I'm going to get a drink," Kiera tells me before she winks and walks away.

My heart begins to pound as I look between the two sexy men in front of me, suddenly unsure of myself now that Kiera has walked away. "Relax, Red, we can take it slow," Javis says, stepping behind me.

"Here, drink this." Milo hands me a bottle of water. "You look a little parched," he says with an amused expression.

After gulping down the water, I hand him the empty bottle, "Thank you."

"You're welcome," leaning in, he places a soft but firm kiss on my lips, but pulls away before it turns indecent, "have fun dancing with Javi."

"You're not staying?" I ask before he walks away.

"No, Little Fox, I just came over to make sure you stay hydrated." My chest flutters at his attentiveness as I try to duck my head to hide the permanent blush I seem to have around my guys. "Besides, if I put my hands on you right now, I'm going to want to do more than dance," and with those parting words, he gives me one last small peck on the lips and walks away.

Javi's chuckle vibrates my back as I stand speechless, staring at Milo's retreating form. "Does my little Red like that idea?" he whispers in my ear, giving my hips a slight squeeze as a small shiver works its way up my back. "I'll take that as a yes."

Javi begins to sway his hips and moves mine along with his, guiding my body to follow. The more our bodies move to the rhythm of the music, the more I relax back into him until my back is firmly against his chest.

"That's it, Red," Javi says against my neck, "just lean back and follow my lead." his hot breath skates over me as I remember how his body felt on mine when he stayed the night with me.

The tantalizing tune of Slow Motion by Juvenile comes over the speakers, and I rest my head against Javi's shoulder and close my eyes, letting the music take over, pushing away all thoughts of doubt and uncertainty.

Our bodies writhe and roll together with longing as sweat trickles down my chest as if my body is crying out in relief of finally feeling the gentle touch it has craved. I lift my arm behind me to cup the side of Javi's neck, rubbing slow circles he lets out a soft "hmmm," at the soothing action.

Both of his hands lay flat over my stomach, stroking his hands over the small, heated strip of skin that peeks out between my shirt and the hem of my shorts. One song bleeds into another, and then another, and then another.

I have no idea how much time has passed as I grind my ass into Javi's and feel something hard poking into the small of my back. "Red, gorgeous, I think we should take a break. If I feel you grinding into my dick like that, this will end very embarrassingly for me."

"You're going to pull a Vanderbilt," I chuckle.

"A what?" he asks, confused, as he peels himself away from me.

Shaking my head, "Nothing. Let's go see what everyone is up to."

Grabbing my hand, he leads me through the dancing crowd. A prickling sensation pokes at my spine, and not the good kind, as we make our way out. Looking around at the dancing bodies, I spot the reason for the intruding feeling when I lock eyes with Cody. The unfortunate soul he's dancing with is oblivious to his wandering eyes, and apprehension rakes over me as I somehow keep showing up on his radar. The sinister look in his eyes makes the hair on my neck stand and stalls my breath.

I feel a tug on my hand, and the slime ball winks at me before I turn and follow Javi back inside the house.

"You okay?" Javi asks, stepping into the kitchen.

Internally smacking myself for making my guys worry so much, I paste on a smile, "Yeah, I'm good. Just need a break."

Placated with my answer, we make our way over to the

drink counter and I suck down a bottle of water, while Javi makes himself a drink. I spot Milo, Kyler, and Carter sitting at the table, talking to a few guys I've never seen before.

Kyler catches me staring and waves me over. Feeling awkward that I don't know the strangers sitting with them, I nervously saunter over to the table.

"Hey, Gingersnap," he grins, pulling me into his lap.

"I'm all sweaty," I protest, trying to get away from him.

Burying his nose in my neck, he takes a deep inhale, and I giggle, trying to push away from him. "You can sweat all over me for all I care," he replies, keeping planted against my neck. It's no use trying to get away from him when his arms wrap around my waist and he holds me against him. All the dancing has made me tired, and I don't have the energy to get away from him right now. Not that I could even if I wanted to. The man is as big as an ox and as strong as one, too.

I rest against him, and he kisses me on the temple when I notice my other guys at the table are looking at me with adoration. "Hey, Sunshine," Carter says, sitting next to Kyler, getting my attention. He plants a soft kiss on my lips when I turn to him.

"Hey," I say shyly, remembering there are strangers at the table who have seen Kyler and now Carter kiss me.

"These are some of our friends from Southview High," Milo tells me from his seat at the end of the table, on Kyler's other side.

I look at the three strangers and can't help but wonder what the hell they're pumping into the water at Southview High because these men are attractive. Not as attractive as my guys, but I don't doubt their ability to pull any girl they want.

"Hello," I say, giving a bashful wave, "It's nice to meet you."

The one sitting across from me flashes a smile so perfect it should be in a toothpaste commercial. "It's nice to meet you as well, beautiful," I wiggle in Kyler's lap, unsure how to answer. "It's nice to meet the girl who was able to wrangle these heathens," he says, and his playful manner makes me smile. "I'm Legend, and these two are Abel and Royce," he gestures to the two men sitting next to him.

Once the introductions are out of the way and my awkwardness has dissipated, they go back to talking, gossiping about the goings on at their old school. Feeling drained from all the dancing, tiredness starts to seep in the longer I sit in Kyler's lap. Javi takes up one of the empty chairs, and I notice his slumped posture when he sits down, looking just as tired as I feel.

My eyes catch the two vacant chairs at the table, and I poke my head around Kyler to see if Adrian and Zeke are still outside playing beer pong, but there are too many people blocking my view.

"Are Adrian and Zeke still playing beer pong?" I voice my thoughts, not asking anyone specifically, but surprisingly, it's Legend who speaks up.

"I'm pretty sure I saw those two heading for the quieter part of the house," he laughs. I can feel my brows pinch with confusion as every conversation at the table comes to a screeching halt.

I can feel Kyler's body tense, and Legend's eyes flick behind me, and his playful manner quickly disappears. He sits up straighter in his chair, and all emotion is wiped from his face. There's a quiet conversation going on that I seem to be on the outskirts of, and I confirm just as much when none of them will look me in the eye.

Humiliation crawls over me at being the odd man out, and for the first time since meeting my guys, I feel unwelcome.

When it becomes apparent no one is going to explain, I turn to Milo and ask, "Where's the bathroom?" Annoyance tinges my voice because they're not holding up their end of the agreement when we all decided this would only work if we're honest and there are no secrets.

"Josie-" Milo starts.

"Where is the bathroom?" I repeat, interrupting him, just needing to get out of here before my annoyance turns into something else.

"You can use mine. It's at the top of the stairs, last door on the left." No sooner does he get the last word out than I'm off of Kyler's lap and carrying my sleepy body up the stairs.

Stomping a little harder than I intend to, I walk toward the end of the hall while grumbling my annoyance under my breath. I try to convince myself that maybe they just didn't want to say anything in front of their friends. No, that can't be it. When I brought up Zeke and Adrian, Legend knew who I was talking about, like he knows who Zeke is. Maybe he met him while Javi and I were dancing?

My internal tangent is cut off when I walk into a hard body "oof," I grunt, the stranger grabs me by the shoulders to keep me steady, "Sorry, I wasn't watch-Zeke!" I shout, cutting off my apology when I glance up to see the person I bumped into.

He quickly yanks the door shut to the room he was just walking out of, when his eyes widen in shock. His hair is mussed, and his lips are puffy as if he's been making out with someone.

Suddenly, all my irritation is gone when it dawns on me, "Oh my god! Were you hooking up with someone?" I say half excited, half jealous, and a lot curious. I knew he's been seeing someone, but I can't figure out who.

A look of shame takes over his face as he smooths his hand down the front of his shirt to try and get rid of the wrinkles. "What are you doing up here Josie?" he asks, sounding peeved. I'm not sure if he's embarrassed that he got caught, or if he doesn't want me finding out who is on the other side of that door.

Either way, his tone has me taking a step back as my irritation bubbles to the surface once again. "I could ask you the same thing, Zeke."

He blows out a breath. "I'm sorry, Jo," he says, running a hand through his hair. "I...I...I just," he stutters and pauses as he contemplates what he's going to say next, as he studies the carpet.

"Zeke," I whisper, and when his shame-filled eyes meet mine, I want to throw my arms around him and squeeze him tight. "You know you can talk to me, right?"

His eyes snap to mine at my question, and he plasters a fake smile on his face, but it does nothing to hide the shame. "Yeah. Sorry, Jo, I'm just not ready to talk about it," he shrugged his shoulders. "I'm going to go get a drink," he changes the subject quickly.

When I don't follow him up the stairs, he turns back. "You coming?" He asks, sounding nervous.

"No, I'm going to use the restroom real quick," I answer, and his eyes flick to the door and back to me. He shrugs his shoulders again as if to say "suit yourself" and makes his way downstairs. His standoffish demeanor is a large contrast to how happy he was after the game. When I threw myself into his arms after the game and we both laughed as he kissed me on the cheek, that's how our friendship is supposed to be.

My heart hurts as I spin on my heel before I'm tempted to see who's on the other side of the door. Zeke and I have never kept secrets from each other, and with every second that I don't go after him to convince him to tell me what's going on, it feels like a mile is being put between us. He's never had an issue with opening up to me, and I can't help but think that maybe he's threatened by my relationship with the guys. I have been spending a lot of time with them. I need to learn to balance my time with them and him, because I can't lose him. He's the one who's been the one constant in my life since we met, the most loyal, and the most trustworthy.

God, but I can't lose my guys either. They're quickly worming their way into my heart. Always making sure I'm never alone and that I'm taken care of. If I have to choose between them, then I choose none. The outcome would be the same no matter who I chose, and whoever I didn't choose would always have a piece of my heart, and I would never be able to fully give myself to anyone.

Wiping a stray tear from my eye, I push the door open to Milo's room, forcing away my melancholic thoughts.

Taking in Milos' room, my eyes are first drawn to the giant bed that occupies the middle. The frame is made up of black wood, and the charcoal grey comforter matches the equally grey walls. Bare grey walls, with not even a shelf, or poster, or picture hanging on them. Nothing to show that the room is lived in.

There are no picture frames on the nightstands that sit on either side of the bed. There are no dirty clothes or shoes that teenage boys leave strewn about their rooms. I start to second-guess if I walked into the wrong room, but then I notice a pack of cigarettes sitting on top of the dresser and know that I'm in the right place.

To the right, there's a midnight blue loveseat and chair that faces a fireplace I'm envious of as I picture myself snuggling in front of it with a book or watching a movie on the flat screen that hangs above it.

To the left, there are two doors that I'm assuming are the bathroom and closet. Opening one door, I find a massive closet that could fit my entire room in it, but there's hardly anything inside. A few pairs of shoes fill the large shelf they're sitting on, and the clothes that are hanging barely fill half of the closet.

When I step into the bathroom, I find it's decorated with the same dark colors as the room. Black tiles and a stone floor make up the shower. The sink itself is white marble, but the drawers and cupboards it sits atop are black. Everything else is black with white accents, making the bathroom look sleek yet relaxing.

When I look in the mirror, the numbers I painted on my face are smudged from sweat from all the dancing. My body feels heavier as I take in the exhaustion that stares back at me while I unwind my braided pigtails. Wetting one of the washcloths I find on the sink, I wipe off the smudged numbers and wipe the dried sweat off my chest, and splash cold water on my face.

Walking back into the room, I kick my shoes off before I plop down into the cushy chair. I fold my legs underneath me as I snuggle in and get comfy. After the awkwardness with guys and the weird run-in with Zeke, I'm not really in the partying mood.

Forcing my mind from another downward spiral, I close my eyes and quietly think of the movie night I have planned with Liam. If my intuition is right and everything takes a turn for the worse, at least the one good thing that came out of all this is my friendship with Liam.

Chapter Twenty-Four
JOSIE

Pressure on my waist rouses me from sleep, and I snuggle in deeper to the cool feel of silk underneath me, not yet ready to get up from what can only be described as a cloud. An involuntary "mmm" is forced from my mouth as I rub my cheek into the smooth pillow.

A chuckle sounds behind me as warm breath fans my neck. The arm draped over my waist pulls me closer, and I'm pressed against someone's chest. "Did you sleep good, Little Fox?"

Realizing that it's Milo who's behind me because, duh, this is his room. "I think this is the most comfortable bed I've ever slept in," I answer, refusing to open my eyes, soaking in the comfort of this paradise. "I'm never leaving. You're going to have to drag me out."

"Only an idiot would drag you out of his bed," Milo says, nuzzling his nose into my hair. His hand on my waist goes to my hip, tucking his fingers under the waistband.

I feel the mattress shift when someone's finger tickles my cheek as they tuck a stray strand of hair behind my ear. A large hand finds its way under my shirt and rests on my embarrassingly untoned stomach, but a soft set of lips pressing against mine has my eyes flipping open. Carter's affectionate brown eyes stare back at me, making my heart rate pick up as I take in the fact that I'm in bed with two very attractive men.

"Good morning," Carter says, voice sounding sexily husky, having just woken up.

"Good morning," I duck my head out of shyness, never having been in this situation before, and not quite sure what to do. I'm sure my pasty ginger skin resembles a hot tamale when I feel his thumb stroke back and forth on my stomach. Milo's grip on my hip tightens, and my shirt is dragged up slightly when Carter's hand travels up my torso.

I roll onto my back, hoping this flat position will make my stomach look a little less thick, but the movement just causes Milos' hand to rest under the hem of my panties just above my, wait...what the? Lifting the blanket, I notice I'm no longer wearing my shorts, and I'm in a large black t-shirt that nearly drowns me.

"Um, who undressed me?" I ask, becoming incredibly nervous. Though I'm not sure if I'm more nervous that they saw my flawed body or more nervous that someone was able to take my clothes off without waking me up.

Swiveling my head side to side, both guys look unashamed, and my nerves settle somewhat. "When you didn't come back from the bathroom, Zeke came up here to check on you and found you sleeping in the chair. So he put one of my shirts on you, and took your shorts off before he put you in bed," Milo answers.

A weight I hadn't realized I was carrying feels like it's been lifted from my shoulders at the mention of Zeke being the one to look after me. I have never felt further from him after the encounter we had last night, but his putting me to bed just shows how much he cares.

A loud snore startles me and forces the two men on either side of me to groan in annoyance. Propping myself up on my elbows to see where the snoring is coming from, I see Adrian is sleeping on the couch. Though I don't know how he's sleeping so soundly. His tall frame barely fits on it. His feet dangle off one end while his head is propped on the other at an odd angle, and his arm hangs to the ground like he's preparing to catch himself if he happens to roll off.

"How does he sleep like that?" I ask on a quiet chuckle, just as another loud snore erupts. If he snores any louder, this whole house will shatter.

"I have no idea," Carter answers as I lay snuggly back down between them. Carter runs his fingers up and down my stomach as Milos still rests under the hem of my panties. "He's one of those people who can go to sleep the second their eyes close, and he can seriously fall asleep just about anywhere. I swear to god, one time he fell asleep standing up."

"He can sleep through just about anything, too," Milo whispers, his frosty blue eyes fixed on my lips.

"Anything?" I whisper back, my lips tingling with anticipation, the longer he stares at them.

"Anything," Carter whispers from my other side. His soft lips trail kisses down my neck to my collarbone, causing goosebumps to pebble my skin.

"Do you like his lips on your body, Little Fox?" Milo asks, noticing the goosebumps.

"Yes," I answer breathily when his fingers begin to move teasingly along the hem of my panties. My body begins to thrum, and the virgin inside me isn't sure how to ask for more without sounding like, well…a virgin, but the tramp inside me wants to beg until my voice grows hoarse.

"Do you need more Little Fox?" Milo asks, and I can't decide if he's some sort of sex wizard who can read my mind, or if he's just far more experienced than I. It's the latter, but I'm choosing to believe it's the former. Besides, wizards are kind of hot.

A pathetic whimper escapes me when his hand inches closer to my mound. "I think that's a yes," Carter chuckles, assaulting my neck and shoulder with his delicious kisses.

"Words, I need your words, Josie." Hearing my name, instead of Little Fox, on Milo's lips makes my body flutter, and I blurt out a quick "Yes," hoping the quicker I say it, the quicker he'll move his fingers to the bundle of nerves sitting just below them.

At the same time, he leans in to capture my lips, and his fingers descend, a loud snore tears through the room, startling all three of us, and both of my men curse at the interruption, ruining the moment.

"*Maldito idiota*! You fucking ruined it!" I hear someone shout, and a pillow goes flying through the air and hits Adrian right in the face, but of course, it doesn't wake him up. He rouses a bit and turns to his side, snuggling into the cushions, oblivious to what is happening.

Javi's head pops up on the other side of Carter with a scowl on his face, pointed in Adrian's direction. "Fucker. If he snores any louder, the foundation of this house will crumble and kill us all," he growls.

Carter grunts his agreement into my neck. "At the rate we keep getting interrupted, I'm going to die with blue balls."

I laugh at his dramatics, reaching up to run my hand through his hair. "We'll get our time," I tell him, kissing him on the cheek, "I promise." Tracing a little heart on my stomach, he sits up and returns a kiss to my cheek before climbing over bodies and blankets to get out of bed.

"To be continued," Milo whispers in my ear, giving my hip a light squeeze and a kiss to the temple, grabbing his cigarettes before he follows Carter out the door.

"Were you spying on us?" I tease Javi.

"Forgive me, but when I woke up to the sound of you being pleasured, I had to see how it played out. Besides, I wasn't about to cockblock." He smirks.

Javi pulls me to him, and I settle my hand on his warm, shirtless chest, reminding me of the night he stayed at my house. The ache that had mostly faded was brought back to life thinking about his hard body draped over mine.

"What are you thinking about that's putting that look in your eye, my gorgeous little Red?"

Lightly dragging my nails down his chest, his body gives a slight shiver. "The other night," I answer. Seeing how his body reacts to my touch makes me feel a little braver as my hand travels lower down his chest to his hard abs.

"What about the other night?" he asks, tracing his thumb over my bottom lip, staring at it, willing it to spill the delicious memory so he can lick it up.

"Breakfast is ready," Kyler says from the doorway with a knowing grin on his face, "better come get it while it's hot." He winks and walks away.

I don't know whether I'm more annoyed or amused, but I'm starting to agree with Carter that I'm going to die with blue balls, or whatever the female equivalent is.

"*Ay dios mio,*" Javi groans out, flopping to his back, pinching the bridge of his nose. "If cockblocking were an Olympic sport, these assholes would take all three medals."

"If you were an actor, you would get an Oscar for how dramatic you are," I poke fun at him, but also feel his pain as I try to distract him and lighten the mood.

He turns his head to glare at me, and I can't help but giggle at the childlike pout on his face. "Make that two Oscars."

He launches at me, and I squeal when he starts to tickle

my sides. "No, please, stop," I say between giggles, trying to get out from under Javi.

"Take it back and I'll stop Red," he demands, laughing with a huge smile on his face. I push on his shoulders, trying to get away. He gathers both of my hands and pins them above my head with one hand while he continues his assault with the other.

"Please," I wriggle, giggling.

He grinds the hard bulge in his boxers into my center, and the giggling and tickling immediately stop when an involuntary whisper like moan leaves my mouth. "Fuck Red," he lowers himself over me and peppers kisses along my jaw. As if right on cue, a loud snore rips through the room, making me wonder if Adrian is doing it on purpose because the timing is freaking impeccable.

"Right on queue," Javi whispers against my lips defeatedly, "come on, Red, let's get some breakfast before it's gone." Kissing my lips with a silent promise that we will pick up on this later, we climb out of bed, and already I'm anticipating the moment.

"Morning, Gingersnap," Kyler greets me when I walk into the kitchen, handing me a cup of coffee.

"Good morning," standing on my tiptoes, I place a thankful kiss on his lips. On a normal day, I would've woken up alone, my mom works graveyard shifts, and I don't ever know what's going on with Ashley these days, fending for myself. Which I don't have a problem with, but constantly waking up alone makes me feel forgotten.

So waking up to a house full of people who care enough to make me breakfast and have a cup of coffee ready for me makes my heart flutter, and I can't keep the smile off my face as I sip my coffee, "Thank you."

I wander over to the counter and stove to get some breakfast and realize the place is spotless, other than what was used to make breakfast. "How did you guys clean up so fast?" I asked, surprised they cared to get up early enough to clean up.

Kyler chuckles behind me, while Javi and Carter do the same from their seats at the table, as if their cleaning up after a party is so absurd.

"Jake hired a cleaning crew, they were here early this morning," Milo answers, walking through the open back door that leads to the backyard.

"Oh," I nod my head, looking around, wondering what a pain in the ass it would be to clean all this glass, while simultaneously imagining how nice it would be to be able to afford to have someone clean up after you. Hearing Jake's name reminds me, "Is Jake here?" I ask no one in particular, but when no one answers, I clarify, "I was supposed to talk to him at the party last night." The small amount of pressure his name caused seems to leave the room when I explain why I would possibly even want to talk to that sister screwing asshole.

"He's still sleeping," Milo says when he stands next to me at the counter. "Go sit down, I'll make you a plate," he says, effectively changing the subject, giving me a little nudge toward the table. Picking up a plate, "Is there anything you don't like?"

I sat at the end of the table with Javi and Carter on either side. "Just bacon," I take a sip of my coffee, "well, pork in general is gross." Lowering my coffee cup, I notice they're all looking at me with varying degrees of confusion and disbelief.

I smooth a hand over my hair to make sure it's not sticking out, and look down at my shirt to see if I spilled any coffee, trying to figure out what the heck has them looking at me like that. I know there's nothing in my teeth because I haven't eaten anything. "What?" I ask when I can't figure it out.

"Who doesn't like bacon?" Javi is the one to speak, sounding offended by my dislike of the horrendous food.

Shrugging my shoulders, "It's disgusting."

"Who even are you?" he gasps dramatically, like he can't possibly fathom the idea of someone hating bacon.

"Maybe we should just change your name to Oscar. I'm beginning to think the award was named after you." I taunt jokingly.

The guys all laugh, and Javi clutches his invisible pearls. "How dare you?" he gasps out, feigning offense, and now it's my turn to laugh at my goofy guy.

A plate of eggs, fruit, and toast is placed in front of me. "Don't listen to him, he doesn't even like chocolate," Milo whispers in my ear and kisses the top of my head before he sits down with his own plate.

My eyes bug out of my head because what kind of psycho doesn't love chocolate? He puts his hands up in a surrendering gesture. "Just American chocolate, it's too waxy," He defends.

"Fair enough," I tell him, remembering a time when my mom brought us European chocolate that her boss had given her. It was richer and smoother and didn't have the waxy texture that he's referring to. "I've never tried Mexican chocolate."

"Stick with me, Red, you can try all kinds of things," he winks at me, and I dip my head, using my breakfast to distract me from his flirting.

"So what's everyone's plan for today?" Carter pipes up, changing the subject.

The guys all say they need to check in at home and take care of a few things. "I'm supposed to have a movie night with Liam," I remind them.

"He's pretty excited about it," Kyler says, taking a seat at the table. "He asked my mom if she would take him to buy candy and snacks for you guys," I smile at his brother's kindness. "She's actually really excited, too. She can't wait to meet you," he finishes.

My fork slips from my fingers and clatters against my plate, growing instantly nervous at the thought of meeting his parents. "You're mom wants to meet me?" I ask, beginning to fidget. "I've never met a boyfriend's parents before," I begin, chewing on my bottom lip. "What if they don't like me? Do they know I'm dating all of you? Will they think it's weird I'm dating all of you? Oh god, they're going to think I'm some kind of hussy." I begin my bad habit of rambling and start to wonder how all of their parents will feel about our relationship, and how my mom will react to it.

I've been so focused on them and figuring out what the crap is going on around here that I didn't stop to think about how our relationship will be perceived by our families, and how it will affect them.

"Gingersnap, it will be okay, I promise. My parents are going to love you," Kyler says from his seat next to Carter.

I blow out a breath and force myself to relax. "Okay," I say, nodding, while still freaking out a little inside.

They carry on with the conversation as I attempt to finish my breakfast. Once everyone is done eating, I help to clean up the kitchen to get rid of some of my anxious energy. I leave a plate of food for Adrian since he still hasn't woken up, and help Milo load the dishwasher and wipe down the counters.

Just as we finish, I ask Milo if he can give me a lift home, and give my guys all goodbye kisses with promises to text them later. It's not until I'm climbing into Milo's car that I realize I'm still wearing his clothes. "Oh shoot. I forgot my clothes."

"It's okay, you can get them next time," I raise my brow at his assuredness that there will be a next time. "My clothes look better on you anyway," he grins at me, putting his car into drive. I turn my head and smile at the window. If he keeps saying things like that, there will most definitely be a next time, and a next time, and a next time.

I'm going to throw up. I'm actually going to throw up, and then I'm going to meet Kyler's parents with puke breath and smell terrible. They probably won't let Liam be friends with me, because who wants their son hanging out with a smelly, mental person who fidgets more than a crackhead. Not to mention my DUI and community service. Then Kyler will break up with me because it would never work if his parents hate me, then all the guys would follow suit, and I'd be alone once again.

Shit! Now I'm starting to sweat.

"Gingersnap," Kyler says gently, placing his hand over my fidgety ones. I hadn't even noticed we pulled into the driveway of his gigantic house, and my anxiety ratchets up about twenty notches when I look down at my plain old black skinny jeans and A Day To Remember band t-shirt. Thankfully, my hair looks decent. I decided to cooperate today when I curled in the loose waves. "Take a breath."

I take a deep inhale, feeling my lungs inflate, and some of the tension leaves my chest. "What if they don't like me?"

He pulls a napkin out of the glove compartment and starts to wipe off the small smearing of blood from my picking. "I promise they will. Just be your adorable self. If you get too anxious, just tug on your ear, and I'll jump in. Deal?"

His offer makes my heart melt. Who would've thought this intimidating mountain of a man covered in tattoos, who looks like he could win a fist fight with a bear, could be so sweet and considerate? He's my gentle giant. "You're so good to me," I tell him and lean over to kiss him. His soft, warm lips are as gentle as his words, but strong like his body. "Thank you."

"You're welcome," he says fondly. "Now, quit stalling and let's go," he boops me on the nose and climbs out of the car.

I huff out a laugh and climb out to follow. As we're walking to the front door, I take in the beautiful, luxurious house. It's mostly made up of white shiplap siding, while the columns and porch are grey stone. Black metal frames the windows, and a large wooden door makes the front of the house pop. Neatly trimmed hedges and flowers line the yard, making it feel homey.

Kyler tugs me through the door, and the inside is just as luxurious. Grey walls are complemented by the wooden floors, while the grey stone and black metal accents make it feel like I just stepped into an interior design magazine. It's so immaculate, I'm afraid to move, fearing I'll break something or dirty it up.

"Josie!" Liam shouts excitedly, forcing my attention from the glamorous house. He runs up to me and throws his arms around me in a hug that's not quite as tight as the ones he usually gives. I can't help but wonder if Kyler told him to be more gentle.

"Careful, Liam," Kyler chastises, proving me right, but Liam ignores him. I dip my head to Kyler to let him know I'm okay. I feel a small tinge of pain in my ribs, but not nearly as bad as it was the first time he hugged me.

"I'm so excited. I got us candy and popcorn and soda, and a bunch of other snacks too," Liam reels off as he bounces in place. His excitement is infectious, and I can't help the grin taking over my face.

"I can't wait," I say, smiling at his excitement, "I brought my camera too, so we can take pictures." Patting my camera bag, I don't know how, but he grows even more excited.

"Liam, why don't you go make sure everything is set up in the theater room?" A tall, gorgeous blonde woman says, entering from the other side of the kitchen. Liam gives a quick okay and leaves to do what he was told.

"Mom, this is Josie," Kyler introduces me. "Josie, this is my mom, Annabelle." She flashes me a kind smile, making me feel more relaxed. I instantly notice her familiar blue eyes that match both of her sons, and her similarly blonde hair hangs to her waist in waves.

"It's so nice to finally meet you, Josie." Her voice is soft and motherly. "It seems you have stolen the hearts of both my boys. They have talked about you non-stop."

I can feel my face flaming, and I hear Kyler groan behind me, muttering something about having an embarrassing family, which just causes his mother's smile to widen.

"It's nice to meet you as well," I say, too embarrassed to address the rest of her statement, "you have a very beautiful home."

"My sons were right, you are a sweet girl." Kyler groans again, which forces his mother to laugh, "You have my permission to put those heathens in check if they ever step out of line." Her casual mention of the others made any lingering anxiety I had dissipate.

"I don't think that will ever be a problem," I chuckle, "but you have my word."

"I'm glad my boys found you, especially Liam. Lord knows he could use a good friend," her mouth morphs into a sad smile. I can see her throat work as she holds back emotion, "he's had a rough go of it."

"He told me about his last school," I say quietly, knowing this is a sensitive topic. "No one should ever be made to feel like they're less than just because they're different," though I don't necessarily know what it's like to be bullied for who you are, I do know what it feels like to not fit in, "besides some people are just miserable assholes." I finish attempting to lift the heaviness in the room.

Annabelle throws her head back and laughs, "I knew there had to be a fiery temper in there with all that red hair," she says, pulling me into a comforting hug. "I'm glad he has you as a friend, both of them."

"We'd better get going or we're going to be late," a tall man says, walking into the kitchen, adjusting a cuff link. As I take in his expensive suit, I notice his mom is also wearing a gorgeous, deep blue silk dress that will no doubt have her husband scaring men away all night.

"Dad, this is Josie," Kyler introduces. I can see where Kyler gets his good looks from. They have the same dirty blonde hair, but where Kyler's goes past his shoulders, his dad's sits just on top of his, and his dad's beard is just a bit longer but still well-kept. Tattoos peek out from the collar of his suit, and both his hands are covered. "You have a little drool there," Kyler whispers teasingly into my ear.

My shoulders tense, and I want to smack myself for being such a perv. I didn't mean to check out his dad so blatantly; they just look so much alike, it took me by surprise. I go to turn to apologize, but before I do, he says, "I'm just teasing," and kisses me on the cheek.

"Nice to meet you, Josie. I'm Shay." Thankfully, he chooses to ignore my embarrassment.

"Nice to meet you," I greet back.

"We'll be back around midnight," Annabelle tells Kyler before his dad rushes her out the door.

"Come on, I'll show you where the theater room is," Kyler says, holding out his hand for me to take. "I can give you a tour later if you'd like," he offers.

I nod my head, "I would love that," I answer, swiveling

my head around to take in the alluring house as he shows me to the theater room.

"What movies are we watching?" I ask stupidly, already knowing the answer, but I can't help but be mesmerized when we step into the large movie room.

"It's just you and Liam. He's excited to have a new friend from school, but I don't want him to feel like I'm intruding on his friendship with you."

"That's understandable," I sympathize, knowing far too well how that feels. "What are you going to do then?" I ask with a slight frown, not wanting him to feel left out either.

"Are you worried about me, Gingersnap?" he razzes, wrapping his arms around my waist and pulling me to his chest. "Don't worry, the guys are coming over. We'll probably hang out in the game room."

My mouth drops open. This place has a game room, too?" I ask in amazement. I was so anxious when he pulled into the driveway, I didn't notice how big the place is. When we got out of the car, I only saw the front of the house, and suddenly, I'm anticipating a tour of the place so I could see what other types of rooms they have.

Kyler's phone buzzes before he can answer me. "The guys are here," he pulls me over to a panel on the wall, "this is an intercom system that's connected to every room in the house. If you need anything, just choose the room you want to connect to."

I nod my head, figuring I can figure it out myself if I need to use it, or I can just call him from my cell. He kisses me and leaves to meet up with the guys.

I turn to find Liam's happy face, "Let's get this party started."

He pulls me over to a large bar area where there is popcorn popping in a machine that you would see at a movie theater, with a little butter spout next to it. The candy is set up neatly just below the counter on little shelves, along with other snacks. There's a mini freezer on the counter that holds ice cream and popsicles, and next to that is a fridge holding soda.

"I didn't know what candy you like, but Kyler said all chicks love chocolate, so I got a bunch of different kinds," he says enthusiastically, grabbing as much candy as he can possibly hold.

"Kyler is right," I snort a laugh at him so innocently, throwing his brother under the bus. "I love chocolate, but I have a sweet tooth, so I love any candy," I grin, grabbing my own and filling a bowl with some freshly popped popcorn.

"Where are we sitting?" I ask, scanning the three rows of black leather couches.

"Let's sit in the middle. It's my favorite." Liam answers, leading the way. We each plop down on either end and set our snacks in the middle. "I have a surprise for you," he tells me with a sly grin on his face, "but you have to close your eyes."

"Okayyy," I say suspiciously and close my eyes. I hear his laugh behind me, and a cupboard closes. Figuring he went back to the snack bar, I assume it will be another snack of some kind.

"Open them," I startle when I hear his voice in front of me, having not heard him walk back. When I open my eyes, I'm confused when I see no snacks; he just has both of his arms hiding behind his back. Before I ask him what's going on, he brings his arms around and shows me two crowns, one in each hand. "I picked them out for us to wear while we watch the movie," he's almost bursting at the seams with excitement.

Warmth spreads through me at his thoughtful gift. "Oh my gosh, Liam, I love it," I gush when he hands me the one with purple velvet fabric encased in plastic silver accents, while his is red velvet encased in gold. I place mine on my head and jump up, "We have to take pictures with them on." I say eagerly, reaching for my camera that I haven't used in three months.

"Oh hell yes," He agrees, but then pauses and gets a look on his face, and I can practically see the light bulb going off over his head. "I'll be right back." He dashes out of the room, leaving me to chuckle while I get my camera ready.

He's back in a flash, wielding a plastic sword. "Awesome. It goes perfectly with your crown, Liam," he gives me a faux frown, adjusting his crown, "ah, sorry, I mean Lord."

"Let's take a picture over there," I suggest, pointing at the curtain that hides the movie screen. I set my camera on one of the couches in the front row and set a timer for 10 seconds. "Quick, do a pose." We both turn in the same direction, with the same idea. Liam is behind me with his sword raised above his head and a wicked grin on his face. I have one of my legs raised to look as if I'm running from him.

We hear the click of the camera, and I go back to set another timer for ten seconds. "Let's do a funny face," he suggests. He sticks his tongue out, and I cross my eyes. For the next thirty minutes, we do every pose we can think of. From Charlie's Angels, to him getting on his knees and me knighting him, and vice versa. We even got our snacks and snapped pictures trying to throw popcorn in each other's mouths. My favorite one is Liam with two Kit Kats tucked into his upper lip, acting like a walrus, while I'm off to the side, bent over laughing.

In the moments we spent just goofing around and having fun, capturing our antics, I remember why I love doing this so much. For just a little while, all the craziness fell to the background, allowing us this precious time to create memories of silliness and build a friendship. Reality became fantasy, and fantasy became reality. Giving us time to pretend that in this world, I'm just a teenage girl who is overwhelmed with joy, and Liam is just a teenage boy who is just like everyone else, and when reality gets to be too much, we can look back on the memory through photographs.

Once we're able to contain our laughter and take a full breath, we start the movie. "I'm glad you're here, Josie," Liam tells me with a fond smile just as the opening credits roll.

My chest pangs with the sincerity in his words. Returning his smile, "Me too, Lord Liam, me too."

"Good. Now let's watch these little dudes kick some ass," I can't stop the laugh that bursts out of me. Shaking my head in amusement, wondering where he hears half the shit he says.

As the movie begins to play, Liam leans forward in his seat, resting his elbows on his folded knees. He still has his crown on his head, and his face is glowing from the light on the screen, but it's his smile that has me reaching for my camera. It's a smile of wonder and awe. It's a smile of hope and happiness. It's a smile that should be remembered. My camera clicks as I take the picture, but not even that can distract him from this fantasy.

Shuffling and whispering cause me to stir, but the smallest of pinches on my cheek forces my eyes open. I'm met with those honey-colored eyes behind thick frames, then I notice the M&M in his hand and the happy, constipated look as he tries to hold back laughter. "Please tell me you did not just pull that off my face?" I groan, sitting up.

About twenty minutes into The Two Towers, my head started to loll, so I lay my head down on the arm of the couch, and I must have fallen asleep. The M&Ms I was eating are clutched in my hand. Now would be the ideal time for the couch to open up and swallow me, and I live out my days as a couch monster. I must look like a child with candy stuck to my face, and it's my, yep, my crown is still on my head.

Covering my face with my hands, "I completely understand if you dump me right now," I moan into my hands to hide my embarrassment.

"Now, why would I do that?" Carter chuckles, reaching out, he gently pulls my hands from my face. "You are quite possibly the most adorable girl I've ever met."

"I look ridiculous," I point out as I fiddle with the M&M wrapper still in my hand. Figuring if I can point it out first, it won't sting as bad as when he, or someone else, does.

He tilts my chin, and the tender look on his face makes my chest flutter, and I feel a little less ridiculous. "The only thing that's ridiculous is how cute you are," his eyes darken slightly, "and anyone who makes you feel any less will feel the wrath of six very pissed off men," he finishes, and I don't point out that he accidentally said six instead of five, I knew what he meant. "Besides," he pops the M&M into his mouth, "that crown looks good on you." I give his shoulder a playful shove when he starts to suggestively wiggle his eyebrows.

I stretch my arms above my head to awaken my tired muscles. "I hope Liam's not upset I fell asleep. I hadn't realized I was so tired." I say as Carter helps me clean up our candy wrappers and popcorn bowls.

"I wouldn't worry about it. We came in to check on you guys since we hadn't heard from you, and you were both sound asleep," he holds up the abundance of candy wrappers that were scattered on the couch. "Maybe it was all the sugar you guys ate," he says sardonically.

"Hey, don't judge, if someone offers me free candy you better believe I'm going to eat as much as I can," I say, poking his chest as I pass him to throw away the offensive candy wrappers.

"Didn't your mother ever tell you not to take candy from strangers?"

"She did, but I only take it if it's the good stuff," I grin at him sarcastically. I could have sworn I heard him mumble something like "I'll give you the good stuff."

When I step into the hall, I quickly realize I don't know my way around Kyler's house. Carter wraps his arm around my shoulder and guides me down the hall. We pass the kitchen and step into the foyer, and it's so quiet it's like no one is even home. "Where is everyone?"

"Sorry, I was putting Liam to bed," Kyler says, coming down the stairs I hadn't even noticed were there when I first got here. "He has a bad habit of not brushing his teeth, and after all the candy you guys ate, I had to make sure he did it before he got into bed." he winks at me as he thumbs the spot where Carter pulled the M&M off my face.

I tilt my head back and let out a mortified groan, "Is this going to be a thing now?" I can feel my cheeks burning. "If it is, I don't think I can ever see you guys ever again."

"Relax, Gingersnap, I'm only kidding," Kyler says, pulling me into his arms, and I bury my face in his chest. His hard chest. How can something so hard feel so comfortable? I ponder as I snuggle in deeper. His warmth forces my eyes closed, and the urge to fall back asleep is tempting. His laugh vibrates my cheek, "How about that tour sleeping beauty?" he teases.

"I'll meet you back in the game room," Carter says, kissing me on the head and making his way up the stairs.

"Okay, so, you've mostly seen this part of the house. This is my dad's study," he points to the giant double doors just inside the foyer. Stepping out of the foyer, we immediately step into the connected living room, and just beyond that is the kitchen.

"There's the kitchen. The stairway at the back of the

kitchen leads up to the master bed and bathroom. I would show you, but gross, my parents sleep in there." He shivers, and I laugh at his over-dramatics. The theater room is located at the end of the hall that's next to the kitchen, along with a closet for storage.

We pass back through the foyer and head up the stairs. The door to the left is Kyler's bedroom. We stayed in his room long enough for me to notice how similar his room is to Milos's. His large bed sits in the center of the room. He also has a sitting area to the right of his bed, but instead of a fireplace, it's pointed at a large TV mounted to the wall. On the other side is an en suite and a closet. Unlike Milo's room, Kyler's room looks lived in. He has posters on his wall and pictures on shelves that I'll get a closer look at next time.

The door to the left is Liam's, but I don't want to disturb him, so I decide I'll see it another time. The hallway directly in front of the stairs leads to a guest bathroom and two guest bedrooms that are embarrassingly larger than mine. In fact, this whole house could probably fit five of my matchbox-sized houses easily. I have yet to see what the backyard holds, but I can only imagine it's nothing short of amazing.

"And this," Kyler says, pushing open the door at the very end of the hall, "is the game room."

I stand in the doorway, gaping at the sheer size of this room. A Large U-shaped Sectional that looks like it could seat at least twenty people sits facing a screen that's almost the same size as the one in the theater room. A shelf next to the screen houses just about every gaming console you can think of. The space behind the couch has table games like air hockey, a foosball table, and even a pool table. Arcade games line the back wall, and a snack bar similar to the one in the theater room sits on the wall opposite the door. LED lights line the ceiling and fade to different colors, and the neon Pac-Man sign makes it feel like a game room.

"Pretty impressive, huh?" a voice says, drawing my attention back to the present. My eyes take in the three figures sitting on the couch. "Come, sit," Milo says, motioning me over to the couch.

He pulls me into his lap as I go to sit next to him on the spacious couch. "How was your movie night with Liam?" he asks after kissing me on the lips.

"It was fun, though I fell asleep during the second movie," resting my head on his shoulder, I attempt to stifle a yawn.

"Well, I hope you're not too tired to hang out with us," Carter says, pulling my feet onto his lap where he sits next to Milo.

"Of course not," I snuggle deeper into Milos's lap to get comfortable, noticing the cigarette that sits permanently tucked behind his ear. "What are you guys playing?" I ask, turning my body slightly to get a better view of the large screen.

"Mario Kart. Wanna play?" Javi asks from the other side of Carter.

A little thrill shoots through me, and I perk up a little. This is the only game I've played with Zeke growing up, but we haven't played it in a while because I usually win and, well, he's not a very gracious loser. The last time we played, he got mad and threw his controller and put a hole in his bedroom wall. He wouldn't talk to me for the rest of the day. He apologized later that night when he climbed through my window, and all was right again.

My thoughts drifting to Zeke make me realize there are two absences in the room. "Where's Adrian?" I ignore Javi's question. I don't think he's in the bathroom because he would've been back by now, but I'm also bummed to think he would just leave without saying goodbye.

I feel Milo's muscles tense beneath me and watch as Carter, Javi, and Kyler's shoulders stiffen just enough for me to notice. "Is he okay?" I blurt, feeling worried by their weird reaction. I thought I was making progress with him, maybe only an inch at a time, but I'd take it. However, with their lack of a response and the obvious effort not to make eye contact with me, I can't help but say, "He doesn't like me, does he?"

Four sets of hard eyes snap in my direction, but the heat in them doesn't seem to be directed at me. Javi curses under his breath and storms out of the room, slamming the door, which hopefully doesn't wake Liam.

"It's not that he doesn't like you, Little Fox. He has some things he's dealing with right now, just give him time." The juxtaposition of the reassuring squeeze he gives my thigh and the disheartened look on his face, all of their faces, makes me believe it's not just me who's disappointed at Adrian's distance. "I promise he'll come to you when he's ready."

Resolving to take Milo's word for it and trusting Adrian will come to me when he's ready, I nod my head in agreement, for now. I had a feeling something was going on, but having confirmation from the others settles some of my worry that it's not me, or this thing we're trying, that he's unhappy with.

I let out a sigh, "Okay," I slump back against Milo. "Now, who's ready for me to kick their ass in Mario Kart?"

Chapter Twenty-Five

JOSIE

Nothing is more infuriating than being told to calm down during an argument, at least that's what I thought until I decided to play a video game with the most obnoxious players in the universe. I now understand the urge to throw the damn controller since it's obviously working with them and forcing me in last place the last six rounds. I clench the plastic, causing it to creak as I refrain from launching it across the room. I always thought Zeke was overreacting when he would get upset and throw his controller; now I fully understand the appropriate reaction as my knuckles turn white.

"Oh shit! I got first place, again," Javi taunts, dancing around in his seat. "Where's all this ass kicking you were supposed to dole out, Red?" he smirks, and I grit my teeth.

During the first two rounds, I chalked it up to Milo's warm body against my back, distracting me. Feeling his hard muscles flex and jump as he worked his controller was enough to make me squirm when I realized he was exaggerating his movements on purpose to throw me off. I slipped between him and Carter on the couch so I could buckle down.

"Come on, Little Fox, I was only teasing," he whined after I vacated his lap.

I stuck my tongue out at him playfully, slipped off my shoes, and pulled my t-shirt over my head, leaving me in the white camisole underneath, so I was comfortable and could concentrate. Luckily, the camisole showed just enough cleavage to be distracting, and I could use that to my advantage, unluckily it only worked for one round.

They started playing their own game to see how they could distract me, and fuck was it working. Kyler made himself comfortable between my legs on the floor in front of the couch, and every so often, he would trace circles around my ankle and slowly trail his fingertips up my calf, but then would abruptly stop so he could focus on his game. Leaving me wanting more.

During the short time between breaks, Milo plants his hand on my thigh, placing it higher each time, making my heart beat erratically. Each time I hold my breath in anticipation, hoping he'll touch the spot that so desperately wants to feel his warm hands. Each time he moves away, just as swiftly as Kyler, leaving me more desperate for the next touch.

At the end of the fourth round, the sexual tension grew thicker when Carter started to pepper soft kisses along my neck. His silky lips felt so light on my skin, I questioned whether they were even there in the first place, but then I would feel his hot breath on my neck, causing little sparks to dance over my body.

By the sixth round, they started coordinating their torture, touching me and kissing me when I would get too focused. All of them touching me at the same time was a heady kind of torment, making my body thrum with need. I tried snapping my legs together to quell some of the throbbing, but with Kyler still sitting between my legs, he blocked the movement. He let out a sardonic chuckle at my pathetic attempt and just said, "Easy, Gingersnap."

Yeah, they knew exactly what they were doing.

That brings us to now. Though now that I think about it, my white-knuckle grip on the controller probably has more to do with sexual frustration than the constant losing.

"Trust me, if these guys would let me focus, I would be kicking your ass," I hiss out as Milo's hand sits painfully close to my core. If he were to extend his pinky, he would relieve some of the ache.

"Baby, if you hold on to that controller any tighter, you're going to shatter it," Carter whispers, placing a soft kiss on the sensitive skin below my ear.

"I'll make a deal with you," Javi offers. The shit eating grin on his face is a far cry from the quiet rage he was in when he returned to the room after storming out.

"What kind of deal?" I ask cautiously.

"If you can get any place other than last, we have to take an article of clothing off, but if you come in dead last, you have to take something off." He says that same grin never leaves his face.

"You want to play strip Mario Kart?" I ask, raising a brow. I've never been naked in front of other people before. Well, except for Javi the other night, but to be naked in front of all of them at the same time is a little daunting. On second thought, it would be nice to take Javi down a peg or two.

"Deal."

The first round starts, and I'm hot out of the gates, passing up Carter and Milo. Gaining on Kyler, excitement fills me when it begins to look like I might win this. I'm not able to get around Kyler, but the round is over in the blink of an eye, and I let out a happy squeal when I notice I didn't come in last place.

"Alright, boys," I grin, "remove a piece of clothing."

They glance around at each other, nodding subtly, and begin to remove their shirts as if it were choreographed. I have to force myself to keep my jaw from hanging open as their toned abs are undressed and on display.

I feel the urge to remove my shirt, because it suddenly feels like an inferno in here. Not because, you know, I'm a sex crazed teen who's only just gotten a taste of what it's like to be worshiped, and now apparently I'm a nympho.

"Ugh," I groan and throw my head back when I notice the devilish grins on their faces and realize they did this on purpose. If I come in last place, I remove a piece of clothing. If they come in last, they remove a piece of clothing and distract me. So, basically, they win either way. "Shit," I repeat. They knew what they were doing this whole time.

I'll just have to beat them at their own game.

"Everything okay, Gingersnap?" Kyler asks from between my legs in a sarcastic tone.

"Just peachy," I answer. With a plan of my own in mind, I say, "Let's do this."

The race starts, and my plan of hanging back to purposely take last place is working, until I try to pass Milo's player in front of me, so it's not so obvious that I'm losing on purpose. However, when I try to maneuver around him, he moves to block me so I can't pass him. Then Carter's player falls in line next to Milo's, and they team up, holding my player back, and it's nearly impossible to get past them.

Feigning frustration, I grit my teeth and grasp my controller a little tighter, while holding back a smile as I let them win.

"Yesssss," Carter says high high-fiving Milo over my head when the game ends and I come in dead last.

"Well, I guess you guys won that one," shrugging my shoulders in a mocking gesture, I can't help it when the smile breaks free.

Looking around at them, they're all wearing varying degrees of confusion. "Why do I feel like we just got played?" Carter asks with a raised eyebrow.

"I don't know what you're talking about. I lost fair and square," I answer tauntingly, feeling victorious.

Understanding lights their faces, but before they have a chance to say anything, I reach back and unhook my black lace bra. Pulling the straps down my arms and yanking it from the front of my tank top, I toss it on the floor in front of Kyler.

The room goes so silent that I'm pretty sure I can hear Liam snoring in his room down the hall. I can hear Carter's breathing pick up as they all continue to stare at me, or is that mine?

When none of them says anything, I start to feel self-conscious. I have to refrain from lifting my arms to cover myself, causing me to squirm in my seat. A small gasp leaves my lips when I feel my nipples brush against the fabric of my tank top.

Milo groans next to me, running a hand through his hair, he blows out a breath. On his other side, I catch Javi running a hand over his buzzed head, mimicking Milo's actions.

"What," I ask, batting my lashes at them. "I lost. I'm just trying to keep up my end of the deal."

"Baby," Carter whispers in my ear, his hot breath causing chill bumps to sprout on my skin, "You're playing a dangerous game." His eyes flick down to my chest. My nipples hardened even more at his attention. If I'm not careful, they're going to cut a hole in my shirt, but the way he's looking at me makes me want to strip down and offer myself to him like some sort of sacrifice.

I swallow, forcing down the urges. "I don't know what you're talking about. I'm just playing the game. Besides, I could say the same," I all but whisper, and a sly smirk tilts his lips.

We start another game in complete silence, the sexual tension so thick I can feel it lying over me like a blanket. My skin is in a permanent state of goosebumps, and my nipples keep rubbing against my shirt like they're trying to rip free. I should have thought this plan through a little harder. I'm so distracted from the feeling of my shirt rubbing against my sensitive skin, I don't even realize that I've come in last place until Kyler says, "Well, Gingersnap?"

They're all looking at me expectantly, and I'm debating if I should be *that* person and take off my socks, but I'm feeling a little bold with all this tension and their wolfish stares.

I hand my controller to Milo and pop the button on my jeans, hook my thumbs in the sides, and lift my hips to shimmy them down. My heart pounds in my chest waiting for the look of disgust on their faces, but it never comes. Instead, Kyler turns and helps to pull them down my thighs and off my legs.

He tosses them over his shoulder and lays his warm, tattoo-covered hands on top of my thick thighs. "There is no way I'm going to be able to focus now knowing these mouthwatering thighs are sitting behind me," he says, squeezing gently, licking his lips, and turning abruptly to stare at the TV.

Milo sets my controller on my lap slowly, brushing his fingers over my bare thighs as he does so. The next game starts up before I can pick up my controller. Between my thundering heart and the need that is now coursing through my body, I can barely hang on to it.

Warm lips ghost over my neck. "Keep your eyes on the game," Carter says as he continues kissing down my neck and over my shoulder. He rests his hand on my knee and begins kissing his way back up to my neck, as he trails light fingertips slowly up the inside of my thigh.

The feel of his lips and fingers exploring my body is paralyzing, and my ability to focus on anything else is quickly waning. Just as he reaches my center, he stops, and a small whimper escapes my lips. He chuckles against my neck. "Patience, baby," he says, nipping my earlobe.

I squeeze my eyes shut as I grip the controller that's still somehow in my hands. He scoots his body closer to mine. Feeling his heated skin pressed against mine feels comforting and has me relaxing back against the couch. Pulling my right leg to drape over his lap, his hand goes to rest on the purple lace covering my center.

"Fuck," he hisses, "I've only just begun to touch you and your panties are already wet."

My hips move of their own accord, hoping his hand will move just the slightest bit, trying to get more pressure when someone tries to pull the controller from my death grip. My eyes fly open when I remember where I am and that there are three other people in this room. "Sorry," I say, immediately letting go of the controller like it burned me.

I dip my head down to hide my embarrassment of getting lost in Carter's touches, when a finger tilts my chin back up, and I'm met with heated navy blue eyes. "Don't apologize for letting yourself let go. It was hot as hell. I can't speak for the others, but I can't wait to see more of it." Kyler's calm voice forces my embarrassment to recede somewhat.

I glance around as everyone grunts in agreement. Nibbling on my bottom lip, I feel a blush creep over me as I try to figure out how to put words to what I'm thinking. Luckily, they know what I'm thinking before I begin my nervous ramble.

Milo turns my head to look at him, "I can see your wheels

spinning, Little Fox, and you don't need to worry. At your pace, remember?"

A grateful smile spreads across my face at how easily they can read me and know what's on my mind before I even have a chance at attempting to get my words out. My heart flutters with that feeling. I shouldn't be feeling this soon. "Thank you," I say, making sure to look at all of them, "I just um…I don't know how…to um…navigate this…" I fling my hands between the five of us, "situation." I finish.

"You leave that to us," Kyler says, winking from his position between my legs, now facing me. He begins rubbing his hands up and down my thighs in a comforting gesture.

"However," I hear from behind me. Tilting my head back, I see Javi standing above me with a devilish smirk, "You did lose that last round." Bending down, he plants his lips on mine, and his fingers go to the hem of my tank top, and my heart thrashes in my chest. Both out of excitement and nervousness that they're about to see me naked. Javi stops and stands back slightly with a questioning look in his eye, and when I give him a nod, he lifts the shirt from my body.

Once my breasts are exposed, it's like all of their brains unanimously switch from gentlemen to cavemen, and they descend on me like I'm the last woman on earth.

Javi's lips meld back to mine, and two hot mouths envelope my nipples, as another trails along my thighs. There are hands all over my body, and I'm not entirely sure which ones belong to whom. All I know is I never want this to stop. Javi's tongue rolls against mine as Kyler nips, kisses, and licks his way up my thighs.

Milo's and Carter's actions mimic Kyler's. Nipping, licking, and kissing on my peaked nipples, causing me to arch into their mouths, and I moan into Javi's. Digging my nails into Milo's hair, I run my nails gently but firmly along his scalp, eliciting a groan that vibrates on my nipple and spreads throughout my body, forcing my hips to thrust slightly upward, hoping Kyler will pick up on the hint.

Between the feel of his soft lips and the way his beard tickles my thighs, my hips squirm, anticipating the moment when his hot breath reaches my core. When it doesn't happen, I want to scream in frustration and yank his head to the throbbing spot and bury it there until I'm too numb to feel anything.

An impatient whine slips from my mouth, and Javi pulls back with an amused look on his face. "Is someone feeling a little needy?" He teases at my pout, "It's okay, Red, we'll take care of you."

No sooner do the words leave his mouth do I feel a hot tongue licking up the damp, lacy fabric covering my pussy. I suck in a gasp as intense tingles thrum through my clit, and I lift my hips, begging Kyler for more.

"Holy shit," I breathe into Javi's mouth when he does it again, failing to hide my inexperience by his very experienced tongue.

"Mmmm," Kyler moans as if he's eating the most decadent dessert. He hooks a finger under my panties, causing my heart to pound, and pulls them down my legs, discarding them over his shoulder. Cool air greets my pussy, and I can't help but shiver at the chilling feeling. "Jesus Christ, you're perfect," Kyler says under his breath.

I stare at him bashfully, once again fighting the urge to cover myself, while simultaneously being turned on by the raw hunger in his eyes. He runs a thumb over his bottom lip, staring at me, ready to pounce, but for some reason, he seems to be hesitating. For just a split second, I wonder if I'm not what he expected, but that thought is wiped away quickly when he leans forward.

Right as he reaches my center, he stops again and searches my eyes. I dip my head, giving him my consent to put his mouth on me, and apparently, that was all the confirmation he needed. He dove toward my pussy like an Olympic swimmer and only came up when he needed air.

The heat from his mouth and the sensations streaming through my body, caused by my other three guys, were creating a tornado of tingles in my lower belly. The more they lapped, kissed, and caressed me built me higher and higher but my orgasm was just out of reach. As if I were on a treadmill running in place toward an unreachable destination.

"More," I whined breathily, not sure what I was asking for, just that I needed it.

"You need more baby?" Carter teases, trailing his fingers over my trembling stomach and running his hot tongue up my neck.

Nodding my head frantically, I grip their thighs to keep me from launching off the couch when I feel Carter's fingers meet my clit as Kyler licks up and down my slit.

"Fuck, your sweet pussy is so wet," Carter hisses, running his finger along my slit alongside Kyler's tongue, gathering wetness and circling my sensitive clit, "It's practically crying to cum."

"Oh god," I moan, lifting my hips, attempting to get more pressure from both Carter and Kyler.

"Does my Little Fox need to cum?" Milo asks, laying an arm across my waist to hold me in place, nipping at my nipple.

"Yes," I whimper, attempting to lift my head to meet their eyes, but a hand pulls my head back by my hair, causing a bite of pain that I find questioningly arousing.

I'm met with jade green eyes and a salacious grin, "Keep your eyes on me, Red," Javi demands while softly running a finger along my cheek, "I want to see your face when you cum."

His husky words must be laced with magic because the second he says them, sparks ignite all over my body, and I elicit a moan that I hope doesn't wake Liam. The tiny flames are intensified by Milo's nipping, and I can feel my wetness soaking Carter's fingers and Kyler's beard at the onslaught of my orgasm.

Javi's eyes never leave mine, and all the emotions coursing through me are staring back at me: desire, lust, need, longing. The longer I stare at him, the more intense his stare becomes, causing the air in the room to turn blazing. He lifts his hand and wipes a bead of sweat from my brow with such care, I see the moment his stare turns from intense to thoughtful. My heart flutters with that damn feeling again, and I squeeze my eyes shut.

My chest is heaving as I come down from one of the most fervent orgasms I think I've ever had. "I think you guys broke me," I say, feeling like a blob of Jell-O as I try to catch my breath.

"That was nothing," Milo chuckles. I open my eyes and sweep them over Carter, who is now gently rubbing his thumb along the inside of my thigh, and Kyler is sitting back on his heels, wiping his beard with triumph. A finger hooks under my jaw, a gentle gesture that seems to be becoming a habit, turning my head to face Milo, "We're not done yet."

His words come out husky, bringing light back into my dimming arousal, and my pinky mindlessly pops out to run along the bulge in his pants. When I'm met with denim, I quickly realize how overdressed they all are, and I feel a little selfish for not realizing sooner. "You're wearing too many clothes," I state, looking around at all of them.

Carter raises his hand to smooth the wrinkles between my furrowed brows. "It's okay," he says, "we wanted to take care of you first."

I give him a small thankful smile at their thoughtfulness

and lean over to press a light kiss to his lips. "Well now it's my turn to take care of you," I say quietly against his soft lips, "but you may have to help me, I don't have a lot of experience with men of your," my eyes flick down to his intimidatingly large bulge, "caliber." I finish as my cheeks heat up out of embarrassment.

"Are you sure, Gingersnap?" Kyler asks, leaning in closer from between my legs.

The moment I nod my head, Carter and Milo shimmy out of their pants and boxers, never standing from the couch. Kyler quickly stands and flings his off, and when I look back at Javi, he's already naked. They undressed so quickly that it would put a NASCAR pit crew to shame. I can't help but let out a little giggle at the thought.

"You know it's not nice to laugh at a man's nakedness," Javi voices, and it registers that they couldn't hear my internal joke, and they think I'm laughing at them.

"Oh god, no," I quickly say, hoping I didn't just ruin the moment. "I was just thinking you guys work faster than a NASCAR pit crew. I'm sorry, I didn't mean-"

"Red," Javi interrupts, and steps closer to lay a hand on my cheek, "I'm just giving you a hard time."

"Okay," I murmur, as I run my eyes down his hard body, remembering the night we had. How good his body felt against mine, and how skilled he is with his tongue. My body heats up when I think about returning the favor, and I dig my teeth into my bottom lip.

"Have you ever sucked a dick before?" Javi asks, catching onto my train of thought.

"No," I answer, resting my head against the back of the couch as Javi steps to the side, closer to my head. Nervousness fights with the butterflies in my stomach when I notice the size of his cock. My other guys must notice my growing nerves and begin touching me to help calm me.

"Trust me?" he asks softly, with an all too worried look in his eyes for someone with a hard-on, about to get a blow job. Is he more worried that he won't get a blow job? Or that I don't trust him? Once again, I get the feeling that there's something else going on, but it's shoved away by the caresses on my thighs and the hands roaming over my breasts.

"I trust you," I tell him breathily.

I see his shoulders drop with relief, and a wicked gleam quickly fills his eyes. He bends and places a tender kiss on my lips, and he whispers, "Good," standing back to his full height, "now open your mouth." He demands.

Opening my mouth, he steps closer and slowly slides the smooth tip into my mouth. "Wider," he says, and I open my mouth as wide as I can. When the tip hits the back of my throat, I gag, causing him to pull out and rest the head against my lips. "Are you okay?"

My tongue darts out in answer, licking a drop of precum. All the guys groan at the action, and a different kind of spark comes to life in my chest. One that's confident and daring, knowing that I have the power to make these men feel the same way that they make me feel. Except there are four of them in this room, making me feel powerful and giving me confidence I have never felt.

I close my lips around his tip and flick my tongue along the bottom, hoping to hear that noise again. I'm rewarded with the sound the further I slide my lips down. Wanting to hear the noise from the others as well, I reach my hands out and begin to stroke Milo and Carter's cocks.

Just when I try to think of a way to include Kyler, he leans forward and slides his dick up my slit. I tense when he slides it back down, waiting for the moment when he slides into me.

"Relax, Gingersnap," he says, sliding back up, rubbing the tip against my clit, "not today." I feel a mix of relief and disappointment at his words, but I know already this is a big step for me, for us, and more might be a little overwhelming.

I take Javi in deeper, and his tip hits the back of my throat, causing me to gag again. This time, he doesn't pull out, but he pulls back slightly and says, "Relax your throat and breathe through your nose."

Trying to relax, I focus on Milo and Carter's large cocks in my hands, working them up and down. I hear Carter hiss when I tighten my hold, "That's it, baby," wrapping his hand around mine. Milos sucks my nipple into his mouth as I thumb the precum leaking from his tip.

"Fuck," Javi groans when he pushes himself further down my throat. When I get the urge to gag again, I swallow, and the way my throat undulates around his cock forces a moan out of him that makes my belly tingle.

"Jesus, her pussy is so slick, I don't think I'm going to last much longer," Kyler says, sliding his cock up through my slit. My hips lift, seeking more friction when the ridge of his head causes lightning to shoot through me.

Just then, I feel Milo's hand wrap around mine, guiding me to pump him faster, "Christ, I'm not either," he moans. In a coordinated action, Carter and Milo both latch onto my breasts, flicking and licking my nipples firmly but gently. My clit begins to throb, and I let out a pathetic mewl.

"You're doing so good," Javi praises, looking into my eyes fondly. I begin to bob my head faster, taking him as deep as I can. My nose presses against his lower stomach, and I suction my lips around him as tightly as I can.

Tears stream out of my eyes as I continue the motion, and when I feel Javis' dick twitch against my tongue, I know he's close. He shoves his fingers into my hair and grips, "I'm going to cum," he warns, looking down at me. I give him a nod to let him know it's okay, and in three more pumps, I feel his hot cum coat the back of my throat. I swallow it down, and he pulls out, wiping the tears from my eyes and slumping against the couch with his chest heaving.

The minute my mouth is free, it's taken over by Milo's fervent kisses. The fact that his friend just came in my mouth and now he's devouring it like he's trying to get a taste is one of the hottest things I've ever experienced.

Milo's mouth leaves mine, and my chin is pulled toward Carter. His tongue pushes eagerly past my lips, consuming me like he's the last man on earth and I'm his nourishment.

I moan into his mouth when Kyler picks up speed and begins to frantically slide through my folds, nudging my clit with each pass. My orgasm is right on the precipice, and I grind harder against Kyler as my brain turns fuzzy.

An exhilarating current of electricity shoots down my spine when Milo runs his tongue across my sensitive nipple and explodes when Kyler rubs harder through my slit and against my clit. He rubs tight circles around it, helping me ride out my orgasm, and a second later, his hot cum paints my stomach.

"I'm going to cum, Sunshine," Carter grunts. My grip is firm, and I begin to pump him harder, his dick pulses, and his release covers my hand. I tighten my grip just slightly on Milo, and it's like I've hit a magic button, because without warning, he's next to erupt.

The room is quiet as we all try to catch our breath, and for once in my life, I'm not in a hurry to cover myself up. These men have made me feel so cherished and safe that I don't care if they see my flaws. Because these men have made me feel like I'm more than my imperfections, and that makes me feel even more vulnerable than lying here naked with them on display.

Chapter Twenty-Six
JOSIE

A soap opera, that's the only thing I can think about as I sit in the passenger seat of Kyler's gorgeous old school muscle car as he drives me home. In just three months, my life has changed from being a typical high school student to that of the female lead in a cheesy daytime soap opera, where the story lines are more dramatic than the acting.

I mean, what's next? The guys are going to tell me they're secret spies and have known me my entire life? Or am I going to find out I've been adopted and my real parents are royalty from another country, but wanted me to have a "normal life" away from constant control and danger?

I can't help but chuckle at that, because who wouldn't want a life of royalty? Money wouldn't ever be an issue, I would get to live in a castle, and I could eat all the gourmet food I want. That sounds like freaking paradise to me.

"What's got you giggling over there?" Kyler inquires, cocking his brow.

"Oh, nothing," I shrug, "Just thinking about how much my life has changed."

Pulling into my driveway, he puts the car in park and

turns to me with a contemplative look on his face, "For the better, I hope?"

I undo my seat belt and scoot across the bench seat and link my fingers with his, "Much better," I answer, placing a kiss on his mouth. I let out a "hmm" against his lips when his beard tickles my chin, reminding me of the way it tickled my thighs.

"Gingersnap, I don't think your mom would appreciate it if I bent you over my seat in her driveway," I pull back, feeling gross that he's bringing up my mom in this moment. He chuckles, caressing the back of my hand with his thumb, "Because that's what's going to happen if you keep making those noises with your lips on me," he threatens, and after last night, I'm not completely opposed to that.

I bite my lip, looking over his muscular body covered in tantalizing ink, imagining the weight of it draped over me as he thrusts into me from behind. His towering form holds me against him as he grinds his hips into me, trying to fuse my body to his.

Don't get me wrong, last night was amazing, and I can't wait for more group activities, but I also can't wait to have one-on-one time with them. To grow my relationship with each of them, and get to know them the way they seem to effortlessly know me.

"Josie," he grunts, snapping me from my lustful thoughts.

"Sorry," I say, shaking my head, "I'll see you at Zeke's later?" I scoot back to my side of the car and open the door to put some distance between us; otherwise, I'll never get out. When I told them I would be at Zeke's tonight doing homework, they decided we would just make it a group thing since they also have homework they need to catch up on. I figured Zeke wouldn't mind since he seems to be getting closer to them.

"Yes. I'm just having Sunday lunch with my family, and

I'll be over after." A sliver of jealousy flickers in my chest at how close his family is, and for just a split second, resentment towards my mom slips in. But then I remember how hard she works to keep us fed and to keep a roof over our heads, and it washes away quicker than it came on. "You're more than welcome to join. I just figured you would be overwhelmed since you just met them last night."

I smile at his thoughtfulness. "Thank you for the invite, but I need to check in with my mom and take care of a few things here," I say.

"Well, the invite stands if you change your mind." Warmth fills my chest, and tears prick my eyes at his considerate offer. I nod my head and quickly climb out before they fall, waving as he pulls away.

I dab the moisture from my eyes and walk the steps up to my house, feeling like I'm taking the dreaded walk of shame in a t-shirt that isn't mine and my hair a tousled mess. However, instead of feeling shameful about my appearance and last night's game, I find myself feeling giddy.

Last night was unexpected in the best way possible. I had wondered before then how it would work with so many people, and worried someone would end up feeling left out, as always, I worried for nothing. They were patient and took enough control that they didn't feel too demanding or pushy. Though the idea of being controlled in the bedroom makes my knees a little weak.

The heat building in my belly is instantly cooled when I remember a piece was missing last night, two pieces if I'm being honest. Adrian has been stand-offish since we met, and I thought we were making progress, but his absence feels like we took ten steps back. This is a unique situation; I don't want him to feel like he is obligated to be in a relationship with me because his friends are. Not that I wouldn't like to be with him as well, but I want him to want me. If he doesn't, it will hurt like a bitch, but I don't want him to feel forced to want me.

Stepping through the front door and down the hall to my room, I kick my shoes off and decide I'll pull him aside at Zeke's later and talk to him, assuming he'll be there with the rest of my guys.

The thought of Zeke spurs my feet toward my window, and I look across to his. Usually, the sight of his window brings me comfort, but when I see that his curtains are closed, I scrunch my brows in concern. His curtains are *always* open. I do the same for him, ever since he moved next door. He has never closed his curtains, no matter what, so the fact that they're closed feels like he's purposely pushing me away or trying to keep me out.

I grab a fresh change of clothes and head to the shower, deciding I'll head over to Zeke's early so I can talk to him and figure out what's going on with him.

Stepping out of the shower, I pull on some panties and black leggings with a bra and plain white t-shirt. I grab my camera bag and meander into the kitchen, and startle when I see Mom up and racing about the kitchen like a chicken with their head cut off. "Mom!" I shout to get her attention when she doesn't notice me.

"Shit!" She yells, "Sorry, baby, I didn't see you there." Flinging the cupboard open, she grabs a travel coffee mug and quickly pours coffee into it. "I'm running late for work."

She normally has Sundays off, as I am about to say, just that she speaks before I can open my mouth, "I picked up an extra shift to get some overtime." She says, tossing a questionably brown banana into her lunchbox before zipping it shut. "I left some money on the counter for groceries," flinging her lunch box strap on her shoulder, she grabs her coffee mug off the counter. "Oh," snapping her fingers like she forgot something, she walks to the fridge and yanks on a paper that was stuck under an old magnet for a local pizza restaurant, "don't forget you need to pick a place to do your community service. Here's the approved list of acceptable organizations the judge gave you to choose from." She sets the paper in front of me and, with a quick I love you and peck on the cheek, the front door slams closed before I can get a word out.

Feeling a little discombobulated with how fast Mom just rushed out of here at tornado speed, I set my camera bag on the counter and walked to the fridge, grabbing the last Coke.

I bend the tab, snapping it open, and I hear the satisfying sound of hissing bubbles. I take a drink, and the fizzing soda slides down my throat as I absorb all the information Mom just threw at me.

Forcing down remorse, knowing she's only working overtime because of my medical bills, I pocket the grocery money, hoping Zeke will give me a ride to the store when my homework is done.

The list of options for community service feels heavy in my hand as I skim over it, feeling remorseful for a whole different reason. The reason for having to do community service in the first place is unfortunate, but when I see an animal shelter on the list, the little girl inside of me jumps for joy because who doesn't love animals?

But as I scan the list further, a name sticks out to me, a name I've seen before. A name I've seen every two weeks for as long as I can remember. A name that makes a cautious tingle zip up my spine. A name that causes nervousness and curiosity to swim in my veins.

The words Callaghan Enterprises might as well be flashing like a giant neon sign, because I can't tear my eyes away from them. The longer I stare at them, the more I think I'm just imagining them. I read them over and over in my head until they lose meaning, and the words turn blurry.

The reaction I have to them should scare me, but it's not the reaction I'm concerned about. It's the sense of familiarity and relief that replaces the nervousness. They feel right, and it's then that I realize this is no coincidence, and I intend to find out what, or should I say who, is behind Callaghan Enterprises.

Snatching my camera bag off the counter, sliding it over my shoulder, and stepping out the door, I walk over to Zeke's with a little extra pep in my step. An excited sort of anticipation whirs just under my skin, and maybe just a smidge of anxiety that seems to be becoming a permanent part of me.

Lifting my Coke to take another sip, my hand freezes mid-air when I notice that fancy black car sitting across the street again. The more I see it, the more I realize it's not parked there by chance. It looks far too expensive to belong to anyone in this neighborhood. The black paint is so shiny I could probably see my pores in my reflection if I stood close enough, and the windows are tinted so dark that someone could be sitting in it naked and no one would know.

As the thought enters my mind, the car rocks, and I choke on the soda as I take a sip. My throat burns from the fizzy drink when a laugh-cough combo bursts out of me. "Sweet mother of cola," I splutter-chuckle, wiping my mouth.

I pick up my pace, giggling under my breath like a child, hoping the randy occupants of the now swaying car don't notice me. I quickly step over the small flower patch in front of Zeke's house and climb the few stairs up to his front door. I hurry and fling the door open and lean my back against it after I shut it, trying to get my giggling under control.

It has to be someone from the opposite, wealthy side of town coming to get some from his side piece, while his plastic wife sits at home in her designer dress, planning the next charity event while ogling her hot pool boy. That's the only explanation.

Thankfully, loud music distracts me and halts my imagination before it can make up any more crazy scenarios. I scrunch my brows when I walk further into Zeke's house and notice the empty beer bottles on the coffee table. The empty beer bottles aren't what confuses me. It's the number of bottles, because it looks like he had a party and didn't tell me.

Is he mad at me? Did I do something to upset him? Why wouldn't he tell me he was having a party? My brain begins to search for an answer when I walk into the kitchen and see an open bottle of liquor and sticky shot glasses scattered across the counter.

My happy mood has completely disappeared and is replaced with worry when I follow the loud music that is evidently coming from his room. The hallway seems to stretch on with each step I take, like the house itself is trying to keep me from him. My feet grow heavy, and uneasiness tightens my chest when I hear muffled voices over the loud music through the crack in the door.

My heart begins to beat against my chest, and the soda can in my hand is starting to feel like a lead weight. I lift my free hand to push the door open, but something in me hesitates. Zeke's words flit through my head that he's not ready for me to meet his latest fling, and suddenly I feel like I'm intruding as I assume that's who is in his room.

I drop my hand out of guilt and am ready to turn around when I hear a muffled voice. I can't make out what the voice is saying over the music, but the voice sounds familiar. So familiar that it can't possibly be who I think it is, because there is *no way* Zeke would ever do that to me.

A prickly sensation skates up my spine, and I brace myself as I push open the door. All the bracing in the world couldn't have prepared me for what I saw on the other side of the door.

My shattering heart is silenced by music, and the lump building in my throat is threatening to choke me, yet somehow the sight in front of me is what makes me feel like I'm dying.

Everything I've ever known or felt for my best friend has all been a lie, and what makes it worse is the man I thought hated me, and was just dating me out of obligation, is loving him in a way I have been hoping, wishing for. The two pieces I've been missing have found each other and fit together without me.

A sloshing sound snaps me out of my staring when I realize I dropped my soda can and it has spilled all over the carpet, creating an ugly brown puddle. The motion causes Zeke and Adrian's attention to snap to the doorway, and both look at me with wide eyes like they've been caught with their hands in the cookie jar.

Well, in this instance, the cookie jar is Adrian's pants, and the hand is, well, Zeke's hand. Adrian freezes his attempt to pull Zeke's shirt over his head, while Zeke quickly yanks his hand from Adrian's pants as if I didn't just see what was happening. Both of them have tousled hair and puffy lips, making it obvious this isn't their first go-around today. Seeing how comfortable they are with each other, I'm going to go out on a limb and say this has been going on for a while.

I turn and run before the tears welling in my eyes have a chance to fall. Unfortunately, I'm not as strong as I like to think because when I hear a panicked "Josie" and "Sweetheart," the dam breaks and the tears fall.

I fling open his front door, not bothering to close it. Sprinting home, I burst through the front door, slamming it behind me, and running to my room. Tossing my camera bag on my bed and digging my hands into my hair, pulling, hoping to feel anything other than this sorrow.

Another sob is ripped out of me as I feel the cold iron fist of betrayal clenching my heart, which is now associated with Zeke's voice. "Josie," He croaks as if he's the one in pain.

Ignoring him, I continue my pacing, pulling on my hair, hoping this pain will go away, then another voice speaks. "Sweetheart," Adrian murmurs.

"Save it," I snap, glaring at them standing in my doorway. Zeke's eyes are wide with worry, and Adrian's face is pinched in concern. "You don't get to call me that," I get out on a sob.

"Josie, please," Zeke begs, taking a step toward me, and I take a step back, needing to be as far away from him as I can. A sorrowful look falls over his face, and his eyes turn shiny.

"How could you?" My teeth clench together, attempting to hold back another sob, "You're supposed to be my best friend." My chest heaves, and tears stream down my face as I take in the one person in front of me who was supposed to have my back. The one person who knows me almost better than I know myself, the person who knows my insecurities and where they stem from, and helps me to overcome them.

Only now the person standing in front of me isn't my best friend, because a best friend would never do that. The man standing behind him is just as much to blame, only Zeke's actions feel worse. But why would he agree to date me with his friends if he was hooking up with Zeke? I study him, trying to figure out why, "Please, let us explain," Adrian begs.

Shaking my head, I turn toward the window, wiping the tears from my eyes only to have more wet my face. My eyes go to his closed window, and I chastise myself for not realizing sooner. How fast they became friends, the hickey I saw on Zeke's neck, and his weird demeanor when I ran into him in the hall at Jake's party.

I'm so fucking stupid, how do I fall for this every god damn time?

"No, you're not Josie." A hand gently rests on my shoulder, and I don't have the energy to care that I said those words out loud.

"Leave me the hell alone," I grit as the hand feels like it's burning through my shirt and searing my skin. I sniffle, wiping my face again as I feel numbness soaking in.

"Come on-"

"I said, leave me alone," I all but shout, cutting Zeke off. Just as I turn to tell him to get the hell out of my house, I see movement in my doorway and see the rest of my guys standing there, taking in the scene in front of them.

None of them even looks slightly surprised, and I tilt my head observing them, and it dawns on me that they knew this whole time. "He'll come to you when he's ready," or "he's just dealing with a lot right now." Are only some of the reasons they gave to placate me, and a fresh wave of sadness washes over me.

"You knew, didn't you?" I question no one in particular. Looking at all of them, their postures stiffen like it was choreographed, but no one denies it.

Turning back to the window, I shake my head at my naivete and obvious desperation of just wanting someone to see me for me.

"Get out," I sniffle, "all of you." Maybe if I don't watch them leave, it won't hurt as badly, but I can't stand the sight of any of them right now.

"Red," Javi steps into the room. The nickname he so easily gave me now sounds loaded with anguish. When I don't turn to acknowledge him, he tries again, "*Roja.*"

My blood runs cold, and the hair on my arms stands on end. My entire being freezes as I'm thrust back into a memory from three months ago.

A large, warm palm gently comes to rest on my cheek. That's so comforting, I would nuzzle into it if I weren't in so much pain. " Fuck!" I hear a panicked voice shout in the distance.

" You weren't supposed to be in the car, my sweet Roja. I'm so sorry." I hear him sniffle. He rubs his thumb across my cheek, wiping away a tear or blood, which one, I'm not sure. Most likely a little of both.

I attempt to lift my heavy lids to try and get a look at him, but everything is so blurred that I can only see the outline of him. I hear footsteps again as another outline appears from over his shoulder, and I only have a few seconds to take in before I have to close my eyes again. I hear the other man crouch down beside me, and feel as another hand comes to rest on my head.

I want to savor their warmth and bathe in their affection. Affection I've never felt before, I think, as I move to lift my hand, but a whimper of pain comes out instead.

"Shhh, it's ok. Try to hold still, sweetheart." One of them murmurs.

"We have to get out of here." The same voice says.

"We can't just leave her." The other snaps

"I called 9-1-1. The cops are on their way. There is nothing else we can do."

Before they can argue further, a shrill siren blares out, causing the pain in my head to intensify.

A soft kiss is placed on the top of my head, followed by retreating footsteps.

Another kiss is placed on my forehead. If I weren't crying from pain, then I would cry at how tender their warm lips feel against my skin and the affection that they pour into it.

The sirens sound like they're getting closer, and I feel his palm lift from my cheek. "Don't go." I yelp. Suddenly, the warmth is gone, and I feel a coldness settle into my bones.

"Lo siento, hermosa, por favor, perdóname." He says, and I have *no idea what any of it means. All I can focus on is his retreating footsteps and the start of an engine.*

"Don't go", I cry out. "Please don't go," tears stream down my face as I beg them not to go, even after I've heard them drive off. At this point, I don't know who I'm begging more. Them or me.

Quiet rage fills my veins, and I turn to look at Javi. "It was you," I grit out. Angry tears are leaking from my eyes, staring into Javi's confused jade ones. My eyes snap to Adrian, but he knows. The look of concern he was wearing is replaced with realization and fear, "and you."

"You, you ran me off the road." I accuse, looking between Javi and Adrian. Once again neither one of them are denying it, *none* of them are denying it, and my chest begins to heave.

"You fucking left me there to die!" I shout, as my quiet rage bubbles over. My breaths are coming faster as emotions of betrayal, deceit, and treachery collide with the sorrow, disloyalty, and misery. The feelings all collide together and create a wild vortex drilling into my sternum, as my mind races and my heart beats wildly.

My eyes frantically scan the room, trying to look at their lying faces, but I can't see past the tears blurring my vision. Everything hits me at once, knocking me off balance, forcing me to fling a hand out to lean against my dresser. The very men who brought me back to life are the very men who tried to take it.

I press my hand to my chest, trying to suck in a breath, but my throat is too tight making my anxiety spike. "Sit down, Little Fox," Milo says in a whisper, and I cringe at the cute nickname that now feels fake.

"You don't get to call me that," I glare at him, and notice they're all staring at me with different levels of shame and guilt. When my eyes land on Zeke, I notice he's not as horrified as I am, and his reaction to my outburst is the same as theirs.

"You knew," I whimper, not knowing how much more I can take.

"Josie, please let them explain," he begs, reaching for me, but pulls back when I flinch.

"Get out," I repeat, attempting to take a breath.

They all begin to talk at once, but I can't hear what any of them is saying as the effort to breathe becomes harder. I look up to see the frantic look on Carter's face, the terror on Kyler's, the guilt on Adrian's, the desperation on Zeke's, and the anguish on Javi's, but when my eyes connect with Milo's, I see the moment it registers.

He sees the moment I reach my breaking point. His eyes glaze over with apology and regret when he sees the moment everything I've been holding in is about to erupt. Everything from resenting my mother for leaving me alone, to the anger I feel toward my sister, and the hate I feel for myself for letting this happen *again*. For opening myself up and letting five strangers in, only for them to prove to me that they are just like everybody else.

"Get out! Get out!" I yell, but none of them hear me over their pleading "Get out, get out, get out! GET THE FUCK OUT!" I scream when everything finally boils over.

The room instantly grows quiet, and the only thing that can be heard is my uncontrollable sobbing as I let it all out. My throat is raw, and my hands and lips start to tingle when I can't get enough air. Panic overtakes me, and I start eagerly digging at my thumbs as anxiety overwhelms me.

After what seems like hours, but is only minutes, resignation settles in, and they can't take my tormented state any longer. One by one, they reluctantly file out of my room, each of them slamming the front door on the way out, until I'm left with Milo and Zeke.

"I'm not leaving you like this," Zeke croaks, and I can't

help the maniacal laugh that bubbles out of my throat at the irony.

I don't even have the energy to answer him, so I just shake my head, attempting to take another breath. Milo steps forward and kisses me on the forehead, muttering some bullshit apology.

"The last thing I would ever want is to hurt you, Jo," Zeke says before walking to my door.

"You're just like *her*," I huff out on a voice that sounds like gravel in a garbage disposal. He stiffens momentarily, and I try to ignore the way I *know* how deep that accusation cuts him. I close my eyes and dig my teeth into my tongue when I feel another sob building in the back of my throat. I focus on my breathing, and it isn't until I hear Milo and Zeke's muffled voices make it out my front door that I'm finally able to take a breath. I slide my back down the side of my dresser and pull my knees to my chest, and rest my forehead against them, as precious air filters into my lungs.

When I finally lift my head, the sun has gone down and my but is numb from sitting in the same spot for so long. Darkness floods my room, and the only light is coming from my night light. I stand up with a hollow feeling in my chest and walk to my window.

Looking across the way, I see Zeke sitting in a chair in between the now-open curtains. His shoulders are hunched, and he's wearing the same clothes from earlier, but they look crinkled and askew. The moment he sees me, he jolts up and reaches to open his window as if to climb out and run to mine, like we so often did when we were friends.

But we're not friends, because friends wouldn't do what he did. He's just one of the boys who broke my heart in the worst way. Before any mounting has the chance to fall, I yank my curtains closed, closing the metaphorical curtain on our friendship.

I curl up on my bed and let the tears loose, purging all these emotions out of me because once my tears dry up and the pain in my chest lessens, I will get up. I will show them they haven't broken me, and I will make them regret it.

EPILOGUE
Adrian

Pain radiates through my jaw as Carter lands another blow, yet it's not enough to overshadow the turmoil of emotions swirling in my chest. I can't say I don't deserve it, which is why I don't stop him when he cocks his arm back to deliver another hit. Zeke grabs onto his wrist to stop him, except he doesn't anticipate the hit from his other fist and lands a hard hit to his cheek.

Carter is never violent towards the people he loves and cares about most because of the way he grew up. Most of his fights with his father are verbal, and I know he tries to avoid physical fights with him, but you can only push someone so far before they snap. In this moment, when I notice his wild, anger-filled eyes, I realize we pushed Carter too far.

Technically, I pushed Carter too far. Zeke has been pushing me to talk to Josie about our relationship, and I've been the one putting it off out of fear. Fear that she would hate me and Javi for the accident that we caused three months ago. I wouldn't blame her. I've hated myself every day since. Everyone assumes I'm the strong, silent type, and I am in a way, but mostly I just keep my mouth shut because the hate I feel for myself will spill out and hurt the people closest to me.

When we left school to drag Josie from the shit hole that is Sylus' I stayed in the car, because I knew if I walked in there I would unleash my hate on that prick and end up in a prison cell for murder. When I saw how frightened she was walking out of the house with Carter, I couldn't stop the worried words disguised as irritation from leaving my mouth when they got in the car. Which just piled on to my self-loathing.

So, I understand why she thinks I hate her, but it couldn't be further from the truth. Ever since we saw her in that park, I haven't stopped imagining how soft her lips are, or how well her soft, curvy body fits against mine. When I saw how her smile alone lit up everyone around her, I knew we had to protect her.

The only other person who has ever made me feel that way is Zeke. I had been living under a dark cloud ever since he moved away.

We had always been closer than the others, living as close to each other as we did, and we were hardly ever apart. Growing up, we all lived close together, but where the guys were a few blocks away, Zeke only lived a few houses down from me. When he told me he was moving, I felt like my world was ending, and to an eight-year-old, it basically was. We agreed to talk on the phone as often as we could, and we even played video games online together.

The older we got, the less we kept in touch. We were both busy with football and school, and Zeke spent a lot of time with Josie. At the time, I resented her a little bit for taking all of his attention, but after being around her warmth, I see how addictive her presence is.

When we came to Zeke eight months ago and told him what was going on, he didn't hesitate to offer his help. He knew what we were doing for Matteo and why. He always offered to help on certain occasions because no matter how long we went without talking or seeing each other, his loyalty never wavered.

After rekindling our close friendship after so long, I also realized it's one of the reasons I love him. He and Josie are similar in so many ways, they're practically the same person. The only difference is that he's outgoing and she's more introverted, but when they're around each other, you can see how comfortable she is with him.

Well, she *was* comfortable with him because we just fucked it all up.

"You guys fucked it all up!" Carter yells, reading my mind. Milo grabs onto his elbows and holds his arms behind his back, preventing him from punching Zeke again.

"What the hell happened?" Kyler asks through barely restrained anger, clenching his fists at his sides.

Zeke and I had planned on talking to her today. When I came over last night, we had every intention of sitting down and writing out what we were going to say to her so we didn't sound like babbling idiots, and we did. Then it got late, and when he told me his mom wouldn't be home, we decided to have some of our own fun.

We passed out and woke up sometime in the afternoon, and took a shot with our lunch to help calm our nerves, plus hair of the dog and all that. One shot leading to two, and two leading to three, which leads to a small buzz. When I'm buzzed, I can't keep my hands off the man who I've had more than enough distance from.

We got a little carried away until we both noticed Josie standing in the doorway. My heart cracked, and panic invaded my lungs at the devastated look on her face. I froze, and everything I had written down to say to her flew out the window as her wide, glassy eyes volleyed between us. It wasn't until she ran that I snapped out of it

"She was early," I grit out, barely containing my self-loathing, as if that's any excuse. I instantly want to ask Carter to punch me in the face again because I know they don't deserve my anger.

"She was early," Zeke repeats, "We were going to talk to her. We had it all planned out, it wasn't supposed to happen like this," he finishes, and the sorrow in his voice is enough to calm Carter.

Milo slowly lets go of his arms, and Carter walks over to the window and stands next to an abnormally quiet Javi.

I felt so helpless in the moments that she broke down, knowing that I was the reason for her heartache and pain. I would tear out my heart and give it to her, but it's tainted with so much resentment it would poison her. So I did the next best thing for her and left.

We were thinking the same thing because we all ended up at Zeke's window, hoping for a glimpse of her, or any sign, really, that she's okay. Well, okay, as she can be.

A tense silence settles over Zeke's room as we all process what just happened. Milo sits on the edge of Zeke's bed and rests his elbows on his knees, hangs his head, and lets out a heavy sigh. Kyler takes a stance behind Javi and Carter at the window, watching for any sort of movement from the woman we broke.

We were supposed to be protecting her, yet somehow we're the ones who ended up hurting her. We're no better than everyone else around her. "She's never going to forgive us," I voice my concern, standing in the middle of Zeke's room, attempting to keep my emotions in check.

A cold washcloth wipes at my face before I have a chance to spiral out. "Are you okay?" Zeke asks, wiping the bit of blood trickling out of my lip from Carter's hits. His hazel eyes are so flooded with guilt I feel it spilling over to me, and now I feel like an even bigger asshole. Here he is worried about me when I should be asking him if he's okay. I feel like my heart has been beaten with a meat tenderizer, and I've only known her for a short time. Zeke has known her for a whole decade longer, and I can't even imagine what he's feeling.

"I should be asking you that," I say softly, lifting my hand to run my thumb over the bruising on his cheek from Carter's unexpected hit.

He shrugs his shoulders and ducks his head, hiding his glassy eyes. I dig my fingers in his hair and pull him towards me to rest his head on my chest, placing a kiss on the top of his head.

"Yeah, well, maybe if you guys weren't fucking behind her back, she wouldn't be over there with her heart in pieces," Carter says snidely, never taking his eyes from the window.

"We'll get her back," Zeke croaks out dejectedly, wiping the few stray tears from his face, sounding like even he doesn't believe his words, "We just need to give her time."

"That's easy for you to say. You've had ten years with her," Kyler says, crossing one arm over his chest and stroking a hand over his beard with the other, deep in thought.

"We had her, we fucking had her," Carter grits out, spinning and pinning his resentful eyes to Zeke and me. "She actually thinks you hate her, Adrian, she said so last night. We had to tell her you don't and that you're just trying to figure some shit out." His eyes are drilling into me so hard I gulp and look away, as it dawns on me that Josie isn't the only one we hurt. "Other than Kiera, Zeke, you're her only other friend, and she trusted you. How do you think she felt walking in on the two of you?" He says, flicking his intense eyes to Zeke. "Do you think we deserve to get her back? We're just like everybody else, and that's how she's going to see it." With that parting shot, he turns back to stare at her window with such longing, and remorse begins to settle in my bones.

"I thought the worst thing that could ever happen to me was working for Matteo," Javi finally speaks with an empty voice, "Then we accidentally ran the woman that we all love off the road and left her there, and I thought that was the worst thing that could ever happen," he turns to look at us with a devastatingly defeated look on his face. I choke back the lump in my throat to keep the tears back. "Then I saw the moment when she reached her limit and the light in her eyes went out."

Javi stops and is silent for a moment, gearing up for what he's going to say next. Kyler gives his shoulder a supportive squeeze, and it's the encouragement he needed to go on. "Now working for Matteo doesn't look so bad." My stomach bottoms out, and a new wave of panic hits me, knowing what he's about to say. "We don't deserve her," he gulps so loud I wouldn't be surprised if Josie heard it, "and I don't deserve you guys. It's my fault she almost die-"

"Javi, we were all at fault for that. Not just you," I grit out, needing him to understand we're all to blame.

"But we wouldn't be in this situation if it weren't for me. Matteo is my family, and you all stepped up to help so I wouldn't be stuck with him. You guys are my brothers and I would do anything to protect you, and the woman we love," he stares at each of us and I notice Milo has stood from his spot on the bed and is clenching his hands at his sides bracing himself for what we all know is coming, "Which is why I'll be the only one working for Matteo from here on out. We can all work together to figure out what's going on with Josie, but after that, we're done. I can't have more people I care about getting hurt because of me." With those last words, he walks out of Zeke's room without looking back.

For the second time today, I feel like my world has gone

up in flames, and for the second time today, I can't help but think maybe I deserve to burn.

"Fuck!" Milo shouts, tugging on his hair, his frustration breaking through. His fingers go to his ear, searching for a cigarette to puff on. "Fuck!" he repeats when he doesn't find one of his trusty stress-reducing sticks. I would be shocked that for once he doesn't have one, but given the situation we're in, my mind is elsewhere.

After Javi slams the front door, the only thing that can be heard is Milo's rapid breaths. Without a cigarette to pacify him, he doesn't have anything else to focus on, and the fact that this afternoon was a total shit show is beginning to sink in.

"I think we all just need to take a breath and re-group," Kyler suggests when he notices the beginnings of Milo spiraling.

"Yeah," Milo answers on an exhale, trying to calm his breathing. "Yeah, that's a good idea," he places his hands on his hips as his eyes flick over all of us, taking in our sad state and stopping on Carter, whose eyes are glued to the window. He's entirely too calm for someone who was throwing fists a moment ago. "We'll figure it out, Carter," Milo tells him gently.

A humorless chuckle falls from his mouth, and I watch his jaw clench so hard his jaw muscles might just pop through his skin, but he doesn't say anything. He just continues to stare out the window, making it clear he's not leaving any time soon.

The sympathy I feel for Carter cuts me just as deeply as my betrayal toward Josie. If any of us are deserving of love, it's Carter, and I just royally fucked that up for him. "I'm sorry," the words burst from me before I have a chance to stop them as my emotions press heavily on me.

Everyone turns toward me, except for Carter, of course.

"This is my fault," I say to them, then look to Zeke, who is looking at me with a mix of anger and sadness. Panic swirls in my chest, "I'm sorry," I repeat, stepping closer to him. "If I had just listened to you, we wouldn't be in this situation."

My heart is pounding as I brace myself to lose another person tonight because of my stubbornness. "This is both of our fault," Zeke answers, "I'm to blame just as much as you are, Adrian." His voice cracks, and I know he's holding back tears.

"But I was the one who didn't want to tell her," I argue, attempting to take away some of his guilt. "You kept trying to get me to tell her, but I just kept pushing it off," he shakes his head in disagreement, but I keep going, "I hate myself so much for the accident that I distanced myself from her so I didn't taint her with my poison. I convinced myself that if I kept my distance, then she would grow to despise me as much as I despise myself, but it only made me fall for her harder because she doesn't have a hateful bone in her body." I finish, taking a heaving breath to calm myself.

"Adrian," Milo says my name with concern, and when I meet his eyes, that's all I see. All of them look at me with concern, even Carter. "This isn't all on your shoulders."

"He's right, man," Kyler chimes in, "We're all responsible for the accident. We all came up with the plan, and if those shooters didn't show up at the party, we all would have been in that truck."

Carter nods his head in agreement and then turns back toward the window. Zeke steps closer, placing a comforting hand on my arm, "They're right," he says, looking at me with watery eyes, "It's all of our fault, but you can't carry all that guilt on your own. Let us help you; otherwise, it will just fester and turn dark. Besides, I think we all know you well enough to know that you're being so hard on yourself because of your family."

I choke back the golf ball-sized lump in my throat when the last words leave his mouth, because he is absolutely right. My family would be disappointed in my actions, but they would know I was acting out of love, much like we all do.

Some of the tension leaves my shoulders at that thought, making me realize these fools I grew up with are my family, and everything we have done is not only for Josie but for each other as well.

I nod my head at Zeke, placing my hand over his and returning his comforting squeeze. Looking around at the others, I dip my head in understanding, "So, what the hell do we do now?" I ask, not knowing where to go from here.

Milo lets out an annoyed huff when he reaches up to grab a cigarette and still doesn't find one. "Let's all just take a breather for tonight," he answers, running his hand through his hair. "We can meet up tomorrow before school and figure out how we're going to get Josie back."

"And what are we going to tell her about the accident? Surely she's going to have questions about it." Kyler voices what we're all dreading.

"I think it's best if we're up front with her," Zeke states.

"I agree. I think it's best if we put all of our cards on the table." I add.

"We can discuss it tomorrow, and come up with a plan TOGETHER," Milo puts emphasis on the last word, pointing out we won't be making any decision without Javi. "Fuck!" he shouts again when he reaches for a missing cigarette, "Let's go track down Javi," Milo tells Kyler, shoving his hand through his hair, "and a cigarette before I murder someone."

I follow Kyler and Milo to Zeke's front door, but just before they step out, Milo turns to open his mouth, "I'll keep an eye on him and make sure he gets home." I tell him, already knowing he was going to tell me to keep an eye on Carter.

He claps me on the shoulder, and he and Kyler head to his car. When I walk back to Zeke's room, I find him planted in the window, standing right next to Carter, not going anywhere until they see any sign of Josie.

I walk back out to his kitchen and clean up our mess of shot glasses and beer bottles, needing to rid myself of this lingering nervous energy. By the time I wipe down the counters and coffee table, throw away our garbage, wash the shot glasses, and even sweep the kitchen, I begin to calm down a bit.

Neither of them has moved an inch, standing at the window keeping guard like a couple of gargoyles, so I decide to order some pizza. Getting them to leave the window just so they can grab a piece of pizza is what I can only imagine moving a solid gargoyle statue is like.

Around eight o'clock, Carter gets a frantic call from his mother asking him to come home. We all know the only reason, or should I say who, would have his mother in such a panic. Tearing himself away from the window, he's out the door quicker than he came in with his fists swinging, making him promise to call if he needs anything.

I scoot one of Zeke's lounge chairs closer to the window so he can sit down. He's been standing so long I can see the tension in his shoulders, and he's balancing his weight from foot to foot. I urge him to sit down and drag over the other chair to sit next to him.

Without breaking his stare from the window, he rests his arm over the armrest of my chair, silently asking for comfort. Tangling my fingers through his, I settle my eyes across the way to Josie's room. The darkness bathing her room makes it look like a black void, forcing a foreboding feeling to worm underneath my skin.

"Why do I feel like this isn't the worst of it?" Zeke questions with furrowed brows as he continues to stare at her black room, obviously feeling the same sense of apprehension.

"I don't know, but whatever happens, we won't go down without a fight," I squeeze his hand, meaning every single word. We will get her back, even if I have to get down on my knees every day for the rest of my life and kiss her feet, I will do it.

She may not know how much I care for her, but she will. If she thought I hated her, she's about to be disappointed. All my spare time will be hers, and I'll be by her side until she wishes I hated her. Never will I go another day without her knowing she is nothing less than my, *our*, everything.

Vibrating from my pocket startles me, and I realize how late it is as I pull my phone out, signifying the text is most likely from my moms.

> Mom1: Just checking in. Will you be home tonight?

I haven't been home for most of the weekend, and I should probably make an appearance at home, so they don't worry. I stand and stretch my muscles, grabbing a blanket off Zeke's bed. I drape it over his stretched-out form on the chair, hoping the blanket will entice him to at least get some sleep.

"I need to go home so my parents won't worry. Will you be okay?" Kneeling at his eye level, my chest pangs when I see the sadness in his eyes is still there.

He nods his head wordlessly. Cupping his cheek, I gently rub my thumb against it. "We'll figure out a plan," I tell him, knowing right now he won't believe a word I say. Vowing to be strong enough for both of us, I kiss his lips and stand to leave with one last look at Josie's dark window.

> Me: I'm on my way home now.

Twenty minutes later, I walk through the front door and close it softly, so I don't wake the rest of the house, but my efforts are pointless when I find my mom's sitting at the kitchen island spooning ice cream from the container and giggling like two gossiping teenagers.

They haven't noticed me yet, and I stand in silence and can't help but appreciate how amazing my moms are. My mother, Sundae, yes, like the dessert, has her own pastry shop in the city and has worked her ass off running it, and my mother, Millie, is an accountant at one of the top enterprises in town and is as smart as a whip. I have seen the struggles they go through as not only successful women but also as successful women who are lesbians.

The harassment and misogyny that I have seen and heard them deal with would break even the strongest person. Yet somehow, they still have smiles on their faces and are two of the happiest people I know. They have always taught me and my baby sister to treat everyone with kindness because you never know what they could be going through.

On days when they would come home with tears in their eyes or in a gloomy mood, I'd throw my little arms around them and try to squeeze their bad mood away. As I got older and better understood what was going on, I would throw my arms around them and offer to kick someone's ass. In those moments, I always vowed to myself that I would never treat a woman with anything but love and respect.

"Besides, I think we all know you well enough to know that you're being so hard on yourself because of your family."

Zeke's words ring through my head, making me feel like a fraud and failure. If my mom's knew what happened with Josie and the way I treated her, they would be so disappointed in me. My baby sister is still too young to understand, but if anyone treated her the same way I treated Josie, I would be cracking skulls.

"Holy shit!" Mama Millie shouts, clutching a hand to her chest, "You scared me. How long have you been standing there?" She asks.

Placing a kiss on her cheek and Mama Sunny's cheek, "Sorry. Didn't mean to startle you," I say on a chuckle when Mama Millie shoves another spoonful of ice cream in her mouth, "You seemed to be enjoying yourselves, and I didn't want to interrupt."

My mom's met in college, got married almost immediately after graduating, and didn't want to waste any time starting a family. Mama Sunny carried me with the help of a sperm donor, and I have been their pride and joy for eighteen long years.

About a year ago, they sat me down to talk about college and my future. I told them I wanted to go to college with my friends out of state. Thus began the empty-nest syndrome and the urge to have another baby, this time carried by Mama Millie. My baby sister Amelia came into this world, and I fell in love with her the second I held her little form in my arms. I wanted to be mad at my mom's for waiting so long to give me a sibling, but when she squeezed her tiny fist around my finger, I knew we would be thicker than thieves.

"You know I have to have my nightly sweets before I go to bed," Mama Sundae says. My grandma and grandpa, who also love sweets, named her after their favorite dessert and created the sugar monster that she is today. It's a miracle that her teeth haven't all decayed with how much sugar she eats.

Laughing, I shake my head at her craziness. "How are you and Zeke doing?" This is coming from my mom, Millie, who grew close with Zeke's mom when they lived down the street from us.

I've never hidden who I was from my mom's, and they've never made me feel like I've had to hide who I was from them. The second I knew I was Bi, I told them, and they have been nothing but supportive. "We're good," I say, hoping they don't catch onto the uncertainty I feel.

"I know he can't get pregnant, but you guys are still being safe, right?" Mama Sunny asks around a mouthful of ice cream.

"Mom," I groan with embarrassment.

"What?" she says, like what she asked is a perfectly normal thing to ask. At least for her, it is. Sometimes I think they may be a little too open. "You still need to protect yourself from-"

"Please, for the love of god, do not finish that sentence."

"Sundae, you're embarrassing him," Mama Millie elbows her in the ribs, failing to hide her smirk. "We trust you, baby. We just want to know that you're being safe."

"I may not like penises, but I still want you to keep yours safe." Mama Sunny adds, ignoring her wife.

"You made special brownies again, didn't you?" I ask, eyeing them. "You don't usually voice your hate for penises unless you're high or drunk, and I don't see any empty wine bottles."

They both erupt into a fit of giggles, and a small bit of longing pokes at my chest, seeing how happy they are with each other, hoping I can get there one day with Zeke and Josie.

"Yes, we're being safe," I quickly peck them both on the cheek before they can ask me any more embarrassing questions, "I love you, good night."

"Love you too, baby," they holler at the same time and immediately shush each other so they don't wake Amelia. I shake my head at their craziness and stop at Amelia's room to make sure they didn't wake her.

Her baby gurgling noises are coming from her crib when I step inside. She's staring up at her spinning mobile, chewing on her fist with drool hanging from her mouth.

She makes a happy squeal when I pick her up and begin to rock her in the rocking chair next to her crib. I cradle her in my arms, and she looks up at me with such happiness, I feel it flowing into me. A smile spreads across my face at her infectious glee, and tears of joy spring to my eyes.

The days of feeling this much happiness with my friends seem out of reach, but I will get there no matter what.

No. Matter. What.

ABOUT THE AUTHOR

Sydney Lee lives in Northern Utah with her husband and two fur babies. She loves reading paranormal and contemporary, second-chance, why-choose romance. She enjoys creating stories that will have you reaching for the tissues for sad or happy reasons ;)

When she's not reading or writing, she's binge-watching her favorite shows with a big bowl of popcorn and annoying her husband by blurting random quotes.

Keep up to date on WIPs and future books by following her on Instagram and TikTok @SydneyLeeAuthor.